book one

Shattered pieces

JO MCCALL

COPYRIGHT

Jo McCall

Shattered Pieces: Shattered World Bk. 1

Copyright Jo McCall 2021
All Rights Reserved
First Published 2021
No part of this book may be reproduced, stores in a retrieval system or transmitted in any form by any means, without prior authorization in writing of the publisher *Wicked Romance Publication*, nor can it be otherwise circulated in any form of binding or cover other than that which it is published and without a similar condition, including this condition, being imposed on the subsequent purchaser. All characters and places in this publication other than those clearly in the public domain are fictitious, and any resemblance of actual persons, living or dead, is purely coincidental.

Edition: 3456789

Cover design: Kate Farlow @ Ya'll That Graphic
Editing: Beth @VBProofreads
Formatted by: WickedGypsyDesigns

For those of us with darkness within.

Revel in it.

PLAYLIST

Warparth:
Tim Halperin

Cruel World:
Tommee Profitt

Man or a Monster:
Sam Tinnesz

STALK ME

Jomccallauthor.com

BookBub
Amazon Profile
Goodreads
Wicked Romance Book Box

WARNING

The content within this book is DARK and may be triggering to some.
For a full list of triggers for this particular book go to jomccallauthor.com

PROLOGUE

Ava

My thoughts stalled as the hinges on the warped wooden door creaked ominously, filling the dark silence that had been stifling me. My breath caught in my throat, heart hammering away in my chest as the soft light from the other room bathed his lean frame in an almost angelic glow, while his face remained entrenched in the lurking shadows.

I could almost sense his stormy gray eyes roaming my nearly naked body with such intensity it made my skin crawl. His hands rested lazily in his trouser pockets, his head tilted slightly, as if I was a mystery he needed to unravel.

This was not my avenging angel. Nor was he my white knight. The man standing before me was nothing more than a demon with a devilish smile wrapped in an expensive suit. A snake in the garden, ready to strike.

Instinctively, I brought my arms up to shield myself as he

stepped froward, ignoring the chafing of the manacles against my already raw wrists. The soles of his shoes echoed loudly against the concrete floor, signaling his approach. The sound echoed like thunder in my ears.

There was nowhere to run. I was trapped, like a caged animal. Even if I could escape, if these manacles didn't chain me to the wall, there was nowhere for me to go. The approaching demon had taken everything from me. As he always promised he would do. Now there was only him.

Just like he wanted all along.

CHAPTER ONE

Matthias

The boy was begging again. His useless cries echoed off the steel walls of the warehouse I used for the seedier side of my business. My gaze roamed lazily over the pathetic boy as Dima, one of my top brigadiers, sank his fist into the forger's gut. The boy heaved, the contents of his stomach violating the cement floors at Dima's feet.

"Christ," Dima muttered darkly, barely slipping out of the way of the sudden upheaval. "*Otvratitel'naya svin'ya.*"

Next to me, my *Sovietnik* Vasily snorted his amusement. Disgusting pig was right. Leaning my massive frame against the glossy black Navigator, I watched my man in action as he delivered blow after blow to the boy's weak, bony body. I was often surprised at the soldiers' unwavering loyalty. Dima had taken up the role of brigadier after executing his predecessor for attempting to betray me. That kind of loyalty deserved to be rewarded.

Smoke flooded my lungs as I inhaled the cigarette in my hand. A nasty habit I'd picked up since moving to this godforsaken city.

The sound of the forger getting the shit beaten out of him didn't faze me in the slightest as I let the sweet taste of nicotine invade my system. Over the years, I'd become numb to the violence of this world. My world. You didn't become *Pakhan* without shedding a decent amount of blood, and I'd shed my fair share.

My skeletons had skeletons.

Throwing down the half-smoked cigarette, I sighed as the boy's screams tapered off into pathetic whimpers. He'd break soon. Or die. I wasn't quite ready for the latter just yet. Questions needed answering. And if he wanted to remain silent, it wouldn't be too hard to make an example of his corpse.

You didn't mess with the *Bratva*.

Dima took a step back as I approached the bloody and beaten forger. My Tom Fords barely made a sound on the dirt-covered floor despite my stature. Power and wealth were key in my world, but so was stealth. Being able to go unheard and unnoticed was the difference between life and death.

I grew up an orphan on the streets of St. Petersburg from the tender age of eleven. Most people saw me as an uneducated, tattooed gangster who'd go nowhere in life. Once a sewer rat, always a sewer rat. Then one day, I'd donned my first expensive suit. Armani. Crisp and black with a blood red tie. Suddenly, I was worth knowing, easily catching others' attention with my attire that was worth more than most people's yearly income. Now I was worth something in their eyes.

Today, however, I was playing the gangster, despite my outward mien. A wolf in sheep's clothing amongst a world of lambs.

With my head tilted to the side, I studied the boy on his knees before me, taking him all in. He was in his early twenties, skinny, with greasy black hair and pale skin. If I hadn't seen it a thousand times before on the cold streets of Russia, I might've been appalled at his current state. The scrawny boy was on his knees before me, broken and bloody, skin painted in shades of black and blue. Just the way I wanted him.

"I'm not a patient man, Mark. Are you ready to tell me what I want to know?" The forger spat out the blood in his mouth before giving a weak answer.

"I don't know anything. I swear."

Lie.

Humans reflect certain tells. Small expressions or tics that give us away when we've lied or shifted the truth. Some may be subtle. A twitch of an eye or a flutter of lashes. Others, less so. A hand on the back of the neck. A rise of redness in the face. Those small micro-expressions, those tells, have saved my life on more than one occasion throughout the years. This boy had obviously never played poker. His tell was written all over his face like the front page of the *New York Times*.

My eyes darted to Dima, who nodded as he whipped his handgun from its shoulder holster before pressing the barrel against the boy's temple. Mark tensed as the cold metal collided with his heated skin. I was done pulling punches. I wanted answers.

"This is your last chance," I threatened him, voice calm, eyes hard. I rarely let myself lose control. The one thing my father taught me in his miserable life before throwing me to the wolves was that you couldn't ever let your anger get the best of you. Anger led to mistakes. Mistakes were something I couldn't afford. Not anymore. I had more than just myself to think of now. My brothers were depending on me to maintain control and I wouldn't let them down.

It fell on my shoulders as *Pakhan* to ensure their safety when I could.

"Where is she, Mark? I know you helped her create a new identity. You didn't wipe your hard drive as well as you thought you did. So, tell me, what do you know?"

I was still irked that the girl in question had managed to slip her gilded cage without so much as a breadcrumb trail to her whereabouts. It was bad enough her father had once again cost me a fortune in lost shipments, but now, the girl had up and disappeared without a trace. I'd given him ample time to find her and bring her back. The old man had come up short—again. Sometimes, you just needed to do shit yourself to get it done.

I could wait it out. Let the ticking clock I gave him expire and take from Elias what I had originally planned on. The life of his pathetic excuse of a son. But I wouldn't. Not yet anyway. The beast inside me laid claim to the girl the moment he laid eyes on her. Now, she was mine to play with. My toy. My pawn to move around the chessboard at will. Whether she wanted it or not.

"Tell me where she is and I'll make it worth your while," I continued casually, sinking my hands into my trouser pockets as I stared down at him. "I'd think quickly, though. This deal expires in five seconds, and Dima here has an itchy trigger finger."

The forger's skin paled dramatically, his breath growing ragged with fear as Dima began his countdown. In Russian. What a dick. The poor bastard wouldn't have any idea how far away he was from Zero. The smirk on my brigadier's face told me that was exactly what he planned. Mark's one good eye darted between Dima and me. I could almost see the gears shifting in his head, assessing if my threat was legitimate or not.

It was.

At least he had a chance with me. If Elias Ward ever found out the boy was involved with helping the girl disappear, he'd be a dead man. But me? Fuck, I couldn't allow talent like his to go to waste. His forgeries were the best I'd seen in a long time. Plus, I had no qualms about paying him handsomely for his betrayal.

"Fine! Okay!" The boy weakly threw up his hands in defeat as Dima's countdown came to an end. "I honestly don't know where she is. I never knew her last destination." He started sobbing, his tears mixing with the blood and dirt on his face. I almost felt sorry for him. Almost. "But I know who does."

Now we were getting somewhere. I waited patiently for him to collect himself and elaborate. After a few moments, he was still quiet, his swollen eyes cast down at the ground stained with his blood and tears. He wanted to still try to remain silent. I could tell.

But I couldn't allow that.

Honestly, I was impressed. Seeing how Elias had treated Ava the first time I met her, I doubted she had ever been shown as much loyalty as this greasy-haired forger was showing now.

There was just one problem with his loyalty. Ava Ward now belonged to me, and I always collected what I was owed. I'd been doing business with Elias Ward since I'd arrived in this dismal city nearly six years ago. His legit importing and exporting business made the perfect front for my more illicit dealings.

Although I mostly dealt in money laundering and property takeovers, the local gangs under my control took care of the darker side of my business, like gun running and drugs.

Ward Enterprises was a sinking ship until I all but

dredged it from the depths of bankruptcy. And how did Elias repay me? By losing 5.5 million dollars' worth of premium products.

Or so he thought I believed. The product loss was just one of his many indiscretions over the past few years. The man's arrogance knew no bounds, and the fool truly thought I bought the bullshit story he and his pathetic son had laid out for me. He'd tried to hide his underground dealings from me. The man thought he had fooled me, but my source inside the family was deep, something Elias would never fathom possible. He thought himself untouchable. Like Midas. Word had gotten around that he'd begun forging new deals, expanding his empire.

He fancied himself a corporate gangster. The man didn't even know what that meant. Elias was nothing more than a little fish in a big pond trying to play with the sharks without getting eaten. It didn't surprise me that he was trying to increase his revenue. The wealthy and powerful would do anything to stay that way. But the man had crossed a line when he took my merchandise and sold it to the highest bidder. My product. Like a fucking snake.

I didn't take betrayal lightly.

The problem was that I couldn't make an example of Elias. Without his company, none of my shipments would get through the Seattle Port. I'd have to grease another palm, find leverage, and that could take years. I didn't have that kind of time. Elias had been a lucky find; he'd been drowning in debt after the scandal with the FBI. Not to mention that if I killed Elias, I would inherit his son as the new owner. Not ideal. The frat boy would be just as bad, if not worse, than his father. So, I went after the son.

In a twist of events, with a gun to his son's head, the

bastard had offered up his eldest daughter in his stead. A daughter no one knew he had.

That caught my attention damn quick. Christian Ward was Elias's only son and heir, the one to inherit everything once his father passed. He had significant value, which was why I'd gone after him. The girl was nothing more than a mere commodity to be bartered and passed around at his convenience. Like the women he sold. Her death would mean nothing to him. A mere inconvenience.

It made no sense for me to want her. She'd be useless. But as I'd stared down at her that night, her emerald eyes wide with fear, I'd formulated a new plan. One that would bring Elias to his knees.

"Mark." The snot-nosed forger's time was up. The more I thought about Elias Ward and his sniveling son, the angrier I became, and I couldn't afford to lose control. Not now. "Tell me where she is."

Dima clocked him in the face with the butt of his gun, a sob wrenching itself from his bloodied lips. The pain would keep him compliant. If he didn't want the pain, he would answer the question. Otherwise, he would be in for far worse, and he knew it.

Mark coughed uncomfortably, his chest rattling, blood dribbled down his chin, and his eyelids sagged beneath the weight of near unconsciousness.

"Maleah Ford," he murmured the name so low I almost missed it. "Maleah knows where she is."

Maleah Ford. I'd heard that name once or twice. A young blonde socialite. Not only was she Ava's best friend, but she was also the mayor's only daughter. That explained how the redhead managed financially. Maleah would have a large amount of money at her disposal to get Ava started. I could see why the forger was so reticent to give up her name. She wasn't a girl who belonged in this world.

"You did well," I assured the trembling boy as I patted his head with gentle reassurance. I'd only planned on killing him if he hadn't given up the name or told me where Ava was. Most men in my position would have killed him for the perceived betrayal, but I hated wasted talent, and this boy had it in spades. Despite his flaws, with a little training, he would make an excellent asset to our brotherhood. Even if he wasn't Russian.

His sobs became nearly hysterical at his betrayal as I turned to Dima.

"Make sure you get him settled in at the compound and that Dr. Grant takes a look at his injuries." Dima nodded at my orders as he helped the beaten boy to his feet with a gentleness few would expect from a man his size. He was a fighter, large and fierce, and after seeing the damage he had just caused, many would be afraid.

At six-three, with over two hundred pounds of raw muscle, the man was built like a deadly giant. Like he was trained to be a killer. For his family, he could be so much more. Mark Marzano was now family, and he'd paid his dues in blood.

"What do you need, boss?" Vasily stepped up behind me, a toothpick hanging loosely from his mouth as his eyes watched Dima lead the forger away.

"Send word to Elias that we know who helped Ava fly the coop." Vasily nodded, turning to leave without another word. I couldn't have asked for a better second-in-command. The loyalty he had always shown me was beyond anything I'd ever witnessed in the *Bratva*, save my loyalty to his father. Most men in the *Bratva* only looked out for themselves, like my father. As the eldest son of the Boston *Bratva Pakhan*, my mentor Tomas, Vas was meant to inherit his father's seat. Instead, he'd relinquished said seat to become my *Sovietnik*. My right-hand man. My lead spy and my brother. There was a time I worried that the kindness and opportunities his father had given me would breed animosity between us. Competition. It had never happened.

Something I was more than grateful for.

Sighing, I cracked the tension growing in the back of my neck from staring down at the forger for so long, groaning low at the release. It would be a few days at least until Elias would have the girl's exact location, and I didn't envy her friend in the slightest.

Ava had no idea the dominos she had set into motion when she fled the city, but I was fine with that. The little redhead would soon find out just what I liked to do with those who refused to follow through on a deal. She might not have agreed to it, she might not have liked it, but that didn't matter in our world. She knew this.

I slid in next to Vas in the back seat of the Navigator, a small smirk playing on my lips as I signaled the driver to move out. My gaze shifted to the phone in my hand where a picture of Ava was stored. It had been taken just before she pulled a Houdini. Her long red hair fell around her face like a curtain, head tucked in a book as she lounged on the back patio of the Ward house. She looked like Little Red Riding Hood, her loose vibrant curls acting like a hood of a cape, ensconcing her in her own little world.

What she wasn't aware of was that I was the Big Bad Wolf, and I would have her—Even if I had to break her.

CHAPTER TWO

Ava

He was there again. In my nightmares filled with violence and sex. He was always there with his broad muscled form and stormy gray eyes constantly watching, wearing his fitted black suit, lips slightly parted as he took me in with his hungry gaze. Large hands ghosted over my body, kneading the flesh at my hips, fingers digging into my thighs, ghosting over the curls between my legs—it never got much further than that.

Not before the darkness began to appear, barraging my sleep like a sledgehammer through a concrete wall. There was no stopping the screams, the cries, the crack of a whip on soft flesh. No reprieve from the stench of blood and vomit. The only way out was with my good friend Jose and his not-so-distant cousins, Jack and Jim.

Cracking an eye open, I tried to orient myself.

My head was pounding, mouth drier than a cotton mill,

but at least I hadn't woken up in the darkness of that dank room again. There was no mistaking the outdated shaggy orange carpet of my living room that had somehow managed to survive past the sixties. Stifling a groan, I attempted and failed to sit up straight on my couch. The world seemed to be spinning a little faster this morning. Like a tilt-a-whirl at the county fair.

Gravity was a real bitch, and her stripper name was Karma.

The dozen or so beer bottles that littered my coffee table told me all I needed to know about last night and my non-existent coping skills. Who needed therapy when you were over twenty-one and had access to an all-night liquor store downstairs?

Not me. That was who.

"Ms. Moore, are you there?"

Apparently, the pounding in my head wasn't just taking place within the confines of my head. Seriously, who knocked unannounced on someone's door at...all right, so it was noon on a Friday, but that was hardly the point. Bartenders kept odd hours.

"Hold on to your knickers," I grumbled as I attempted to stand without tipping over like a little teapot. Jesus, I needed some Tylenol. Maybe the mystery man at the door was the Tylenol Fairy. Ignoring the nausea in my stomach, I shuffled gracelessly to the door and peered through the peephole I'd had installed when I first moved into this crappy apartment.

The man on the other side was definitely not the Tylenol Fairy.

Which was kind of disappointing.

He was also wearing khakis and a collared polo. Nothing like the crisp white shirts and tailored suit pants that the men in my life normally sported, but my hackles were still raised regardless. I doubted this man was someone my father had sent. They weren't the knocking type. Plus, Christian would want to come for me himself. He wouldn't send his goons.

Still paid to be safe.

I grabbed my gun from the side table next to the door and held it loosely in my right hand as I slowly turned the fake-crystal doorknob. Instinct told me this guy was about as violent as a Girl Scout, especially dressed like Jake from State Farm, but my instincts had been a bit rusty. Plus, those girls were vicious during peak cookie-selling season.

I cracked the door open just enough to level my gaze at him. "Can I help you?"

"Ava Moore?"

He seemed utterly unperturbed by my disheveled appearance. I tried pretty hard to find some dignity standing in front of him wearing nothing but a pair of spandex running shorts and a faded New York Mets T-shirt while he sported the dad bod look, complete with coiffed silver hair. He looked like he was ready for a luncheon at the country club, and I hadn't even bothered to put on a bra. I was fairly sure I'd left my dignity in the middle of the coffee table with the dozen or so beer bottles, but I liked to look at the glass as half full.

"And you are?" Maybe if we kept answering questions with questions, we could set some sort of record.

"Jonathan Archer, FBI." Explained the polo getup. The way he said his name sent a chill up my spine. Not the good kind, either. There was a smugness in his tone that I didn't appreciate. Like he was a hunter who'd finally caught himself a fox.

That wasn't the only thing that bothered me. If the FBI had found me, it wouldn't be long before my father and brother did, too.

"Good for you." Vaguely, in the dark recesses of my mind,

I knew it wasn't good to bait this man. He might have looked like the 40-year-old virgin in that getup, but he held himself like he was the richest man in the world. Like his posture could somehow convey his power. My father did the same thing. Elias Ward never needed an introduction. The way he held himself said it all.

If only I could get some damn Tylenol so the little drummer boy in my head would quiet down. Then maybe I could think more clearly. At that moment, the little shit was too busy pounding out Metallica's greatest hits for me to listen to the warning bells going off in my mind. Anyone like my father deserved to be treated with a high dose of suspicion. And a lethal dose of poison.

"Listen, Agent Archer, I'm sure we could keep this little dance going, and while I enjoy a little verbal sparring from time to time—I am tired, hungry, and hungover, so cut the shit. Why are you here?"

The man had the nerve to tilt his head back and laugh like I was some kind of stand-up comedian at the Apollo.

"I have no doubt you know why I am here, Ms. Moore." The man smirked. "Or should I say—Ms. Ward?"

My face paled, eyes widening as his smirk deepened. "I don't know who that is." I swallowed hard as I tried to deny the truth. Problem was, I was a shit liar. "You have the wrong person."

"I don't think I do." He blocked my attempt to shut the door in his face by wedging his foot inside the frame and throwing his weight forward. He might have been on the verge of becoming a senior citizen, but he sure as hell wasn't a desk jockey like most men his age. Surprised, I stumbled back, my grip on my gun loosened, sending it skittering across the hallway floor. His gaze darted to the fallen weapon, eyes darkening. A sharp cry of pain wrenched itself from my lips as the agent's hand wrapped itself in my mass of loose red curls, pulling harshly as I attempted to lunge for the gun.

"Now, that wasn't very nice, Ava," the agent hissed, once again tugging harshly on my hair, causing me to elicit another pained cry as he tossed me to the floor. "Not that I was expecting much hospitality from Elias Ward's daughter."

He ran a large hand through his disheveled hair. Straightening it before he calmly closed my front door. The dull click of the deadbolt felt like a sudden weight bearing down on my chest. Stooping down, he scooped up the gun, disassembling it with practiced ease before setting it on the entry table. Not that I had planned to use it on him. It was more of a deterrent than anything else.

The man looked down at me, head tilted to the side as he surveyed me. "Are you going to play nice? Or do you need more incentive? I could always handcuff you to a chair, or we can have a civil conversation. It's up to you." The edge of my lips turned up in a sneer as I shook my head. "Good."

"Don't pretend as if you know me, agent. You know nothing about me," I snarled at him, brushing myself off as I stood. My eyes met his in a stubborn glare, jaw clenching, but he seemed unfazed. Funny, that move normally had grown men in the bar crying. I was off my game. Or it didn't work on muscled senior citizens. "I am nothing like my father." Archer's eyes lit up at hearing the obvious disdain and bitterness in my voice at the mention of my father.

"Avaleigh Ward, formerly Moore, born March 26, 1996, to Katherine Moore in Portland, Oregon." The man doled out my information like Wikipedia. Here I thought men his age had dementia. "Witnessed your mother's murder during a home invasion when you were ten. State located your father shortly after, and he took you in. Valedictorian of your class. Went missing from home nearly a year ago..."

"I ran away." As if he cared about that little tidbit of information, but I felt like I needed to set the record straight after his little information dump.

"Excuse me?" His forehead creased like he was puzzled, but I could see the triumph behind the mask.

"I didn't go missing." I took a long breath as I stepped into the kitchen to rummage around through one of the drawers for some damn Tylenol. Grabbing a bottle of water from the too small fridge, I downed the tablets as I watched Mr. FBI Agent out of my peripheral. Now that he'd had a good chance to look around, he was standing somewhat awkwardly in my small, dirty living room, looking about as comfortable as a priest in a whorehouse. His hulking frame stood out in the tiny space, and now that I had a good look at him, I realized just how powerful he was.

This wasn't some rookie fresh out of Quantico. He was a seasoned agent. My gaze roamed over him, and I could see that my dad bod snipe was off. The man towered over my five-foot-five frame by several inches. He had to be at least six-one. I could see the sharp definition of his muscles beneath the too-big polo, and his khakis wrapped too provocatively around his muscular legs. He had the kind of muscle that gave women my age a whole new set of "daddy" issues.

If I was right, and I usually was, this silver-haired fox had never sat behind a desk in his life. Everything about him screamed predator even if he was ready to receive Medicare.

"Can I get you anything? Water or…water?" I needed to go shopping.

"No, thank you." The pleasantry surprised me, seeing as he had just been holding my hair in a death grip, but I shook it off as I watched him awkwardly angle himself into the chair opposite the couch. He looked uncomfortable now that he wasn't directly confronting me. I didn't care much. Barging into someone's apartment at an ungodly hour was rude. "We have a few things we need to discuss, Ms. Moore."

At least he was smart enough not to use my father's last name. That wouldn't have earned him any brownie points. I had never wanted to change it, but tradition was tradition. Or so he beat into me.

"Ava."

"Right, Ava."

I moved into the living room and flopped down on the sofa. "You can relax, Jonathan. I know it looks bad, but I promise I didn't drag it off the street corner," I said, pointing at the chair he was sitting on.

This time anyway.

He smiled, leaning back slightly more comfortably. "I know you didn't run away, Ava," he started. "That is simply what your father is telling his men to save face."

That didn't surprise me.

"Well, congratulations," I sniped, leaning back on the sofa. It was lumpy and uncomfortable, but beggars can't be choosers. I hadn't always lived a cushy life. "You found me. Now, what do you want?"

"You."

CHAPTER THREE

Ava

I gave a rather unladylike snort. "Sorry, I don't have a daddy kink."

The man chuckled, shaking his head as if my antics amused him. They probably did. I was hilarious, especially under stress.

"We both know your father will find you, Ava." He leaned forward, bracing his elbows on his knees, his face growing hard as he took me in. Who did he see? The eldest daughter of Elias Ward, who had been trapped in a gilded cage most of her life, who had every right in the world to be meek and submissive? Docile, like younger twin sisters, Kenzi and Libby?

Or did he see a survivor? A fighter whose past still came back to haunt her on a nightly basis in the form of shadows and sobs.

I could play the victim. My mother, however, didn't raise no daisy.

"I'm offering you a chance," he pressed earnestly. "Help me, and I'll make sure you get away from your father for good. Be my inside man."

Well, that sounded about as appealing as a trapdoor on a canoe.

As nice as the notion was, I was no snitch. Snitches got stitches, or in my father's case, they got dead. Really dead. Really fast. Elias Ward may not have invented cement shoes, but he sure as hell liked to use them. I would be no exception. Hell, being fish food at the bottom of Lake Union would be a vacation compared to what my father would do to me if I were to betray him.

"Woman," I muttered, rolling my eyes. So not the time for feminism, brain. "Thanks for the offer, but I like my tongue attached to my mouth." The man simply smirked, not moving from his spot on the chair. He wasn't going to leave this alone.

"I doubt you'll lose your tongue, Ava." He shrugged casually, like him putting my life in danger was no big deal. "Elias still owes the Dashkov *Bratva*, you know." He saw me tense, and his eyes glowed like a fucking Christmas tree in Times Square. I should've known this wasn't just about my father.

"That's what I thought." He relaxed back into the chair, one arm slung lazily over the back, ankle on his knee like he owned the place. I was desperately rethinking shooting him. "Matthias Dashkov is still holding your father to his deal. Even after all this time. You, in exchange for an extension on the money he owes him. A little archaic if you ask me, but who am I to judge?"

Archer had me right where he wanted me, and the Cheshire grin that stretched across his smug face told me he was well aware of it, too. My father wouldn't kill me if I was still required for his deal with the Russian *Bratva*. It was the reason I had run as far as I could. Thousands of miles out of my father's reach. Or so I'd thought.

Nearly a year had passed since my escape from the gilded walls of my prison. Months of surviving on my own, always looking over my shoulder, jumping at every shadow, worrying that one day he would come out of the darkness like Dracula. It was lonely, but at least I wasn't someone's property to be bought and sold like chattel.

No harsh words or harsher blows to put me in my place. Wondering if I'd be allowed food or freedom. My life before was nothing more than surviving, and I couldn't—I wouldn't—go back to that.

"No."

Jonathan scowled, his jaw tightening beneath his stubble, the relaxed demeanor from before fading by the second. The more I fought him, the more I could see the predator beneath the homey exterior. Like a Venus flytrap right before it ensnared its victim. He certainly was no Girl Scout.

"No?" He chuckled darkly as he stood from the chair and stalked toward me, eyes lit with fire. Instinctively, my body curled in on itself. My arms came up to protect my head as he approached, knees curling toward my stomach. There was no stopping my reaction. It was instinctual. Years of muscle memory taking over, and I was once again hiding like the victim I used to be instead of the woman I'd become.

"Jesus," Archer whispered, but from beneath my weak protection, it sounded more like a growl. When the expected blow didn't fall, I cautiously peeked at him from beneath my useless shield. His hazel eyes were wide, lips parted in shock as he ran an anxious hand through his perfectly quaffed silver hair, effectively mussing it.

After a moment, the shock faded from his face and his

body relaxed, muscles uncoiling. Slowly, he crouched so we were at eye level, his hands up in a sign of peace. He wanted me to understand that he wouldn't hurt me. Not like that. What he didn't realize was that going back to that place was far worse than any physical blow he could ever deal me.

"You're the only chance I have, Ava." His tone was pleading, eyes begging me to understand, but I could still see the darkness, the hardness, beneath those hazel eyes. He may have had some sliver of sympathy for my plight, but not enough to derail whatever plan he had set in place. "And I am yours. Your father's men are already on their way. Someone gave you up.

"The way I see it, you have two choices. Take my offer to spy on him and the Dashkov *Bratva*, and I will guarantee you I will get you out from under his thumb." He paused for a moment, holding my gaze to no doubt try to intimidate me. "Or I will haul you away right now with enough charges to bring you in as an accomplice. Spread the word that you are willing to testify against your father."

Wait. What?

"An accomplice?" My voice pitched slightly as I sat forward, my fear taking a back seat to something much stronger. Anger and disbelief. "To what exactly? I'm not involved with anything my father does. Not in his day-to-day business and certainly not in his underground ones."

Crickets.

Fuck. Me and my big mouth. If he didn't have me before, he sure as hell did now.

"His underground ones," he nearly whispered, a devilish glint to his eyes. "That right there tells me you know something about his illicit dealings, Ava. Dealings that you haven't bothered to report. That, my dear girl, makes you complicit."

"That's bullshit and you know it," I hissed at him, lips

curling in a sneer as I snagged a half-empty bottle of beer from my coffee table and chugged it. "No judge is going to convict me of being complicit in his acts. They can't force me to testify against my family, either. I'm his daughter and a victim." The Cheshire grin returned, making him look like the cat that ate the canary.

I'm the fucking canary.

"Maybe not," he admitted with a casual shrug. God, he really couldn't care less if I ended up dead. "But that won't stop me from arresting you and spreading the word that you're willing to testify against him. Tell me, Ava, how long do you think you'd last in GenPop before he sends someone after you? Two? Three hours tops?" Tears gathered in my eyes. Blinking rapidly, I took a deep breath to center myself. There was no way this fucker was going to see me cry.

"No matter what I choose, I'll be dead by the end."

The agent scoffed. "Don't be so dramatic. Ava." He rolled his eyes as he stood. "I won't let that happen." It was my turn to scoff.

"I bet you say that to all your informants before they end up dead in a ditch somewhere." Archer shrugged, ignoring my jab. "What's in this for you?"

"Nah, just the ones I like." He winked at me as he turned to leave, completely ignoring my question. "Last I heard, your father gained your location a few hours ago. It won't be long before they find you. Make sure you're here, Ava, or you won't enjoy the consequences."

My teeth dug into my cheek so hard I could taste blood as I bit back a scathing reply. Just when I thought I was free and out from under their thumb, something pulled me back in.

"How do I get in touch with you?"

Archer smirked as he pulled open my front door.

"Don't worry, Ava, you'll see me around."

Then he was gone, and I was left to let the tears that had been brimming fall loosely down my cheeks as I screamed my frustration into one of the couch pillows. When I finally pulled myself together, I realized something was missing.

The bastard took my gun.

CHAPTER FOUR

Ava

It was nearly four in the morning by the time I trudged up the wrought iron stairs that scaled the outside of the bar to my apartment above. I glanced nervously down the empty alley as I unlocked my door and swiftly entered. The knot in my stomach warned me that something felt off. There had been no sign of Christian all week, and it made me wonder if maybe Archer had his information wrong. One could only hope.

I still remember that night. The night everything changed. Libby had come rushing into my room in the dead of night, spinning a tale so wild, I thought it was something she had dreamt. The muffled screams and slamming doors that filtered up the stairs told me that, for once, Libby wasn't being dramatic.

Still, despite her past histrionics, her recollection of three men busting down our front door and dragging our father into his office by the scruff had me leaving her in the safety of my room to sneak down the servant's stairs with an overabundance of curiosity to find myself having landed at my father's study door, listening in on the hushed conversation.

"I WANT MY MONEY, ELIAS." *The dark tone of the man's voice from the other side of the wooden door sent a shiver down my spine. I couldn't name it, but it wasn't fear that caused such a reaction. His voice was smooth, like aged cognac, deep and gravelly, causing an unfamiliar warmth to slide over me.*

"I promise you, Mr. Dashkov, I will get your money. I'm just a little..." I'd never heard my father sound so submissive before. It was almost like he had been trying not to cry. I snickered quietly at the thought of my father begging to any man.

"You've been promising me that for weeks now," the man, Mr. Dashkov, interrupted with a snarl. "My patience is wearing thin, and I believe a little incentive is in order, hmm?" Curiosity clawed at me, taking over the rational part of my brain that told me I should retreat to the safety of my room. Instead, I ignored that gut feeling and pressed my ear to the door, straining to hear what was happening.

"Please! We can work something out." I heard another voice rise above the arguing. The sharp sob of a wounded animal. Holy shit. It was Christian. My asshole of a brother was openly crying like a wee little baby. It was hard, but I managed to stifle the laughter bubbling up in my throat as I continued to spy, my curious nature magnified by the simple fact that someone had managed to bring my father and brother down a notch.

Or two.

"I have given you enough time, Elias," Dashkov hissed.

"Either give me the money now or say goodbye to your only son."

The familiar click of the hammer of a gun caused me to elicit a sudden gasp. Loudly. Too loudly.

There was no time for me to react as the office door was yanked open, revealing two burly men scowling down at me with narrowed eyes. I screamed when they grabbed me, yanking my arms viciously as they threw me down onto the ugly ornate Persian rug that decorated my father's floor.

"What do we have here?" The deep, gravelly voice was now above me, and I could feel my heart hammering away in my chest as I slowly drug my eyes up to meet his. He was tall. Nearly a good foot taller than me, with broad shoulders, dark hair, and a square chiseled jaw that sharpened his already deadly looks. Even beneath the well-fitted suit, I could see the definition of his hard-earned muscles. He was all hard lines and jagged edges, a true Adonis if there ever was one.

Tattoos decorated his hands, a colorful swirl of ink snaking up his arms to disappear beneath the starched sleeves of his jacket. I recognized some of the lettering. Russian. This man was Bratva. His stormy gaze held mine hostage as he tilted his head, taking me in.

"Her," my father spouted off urgently, his face beet red. "Take my daughter."

SHAKING myself from the memory of that night, I let myself in, blindly switching on the main light as I yawned and tossed my keys onto the entry table that had once held my gun.

I looked up. Then froze.

He was sitting on one of my bar stools in the kitchen, a beer in his hand, looking like he belonged there. My eyes simply stared at him, a sense of dread washing over me like a tidal wave as I took in his crisp black suit. This was different from his casual attire of jeans and T-shirts full of holes. If he were to remove his suit jacket and roll up the sleeves of his white dress shirt, I would bet good money there would be new ink running up his left arm.

He was now a made man.

The unease in the air thickened at this sudden revelation as we took a beat to study one another. I'd never felt like this with him before. Uneasy, like I was on a hill of sand that could suddenly shift. He had always been somewhere safe to land, but now, looking at his cleanly shaven face and stony gaze, my stomach clenched in terror.

He wasn't here to save me but to condemn me.

"Step away from the door, Avaleigh," my cousin Neil ordered sharply, his tone leaving no room for disobeying. I was aware of what would happen if I did.

Avaleigh. He'd never called me by my full name before. Said it didn't fit me. Too formal or something like that. The only one who called me by my full name was my father and—

Panic grabbed at me as I frantically looked around, eyes wide, my chest constricting in fear, waiting for him to pop from the shadows like Ramsay Bolton in Game of Thrones.

"He's not here right now." Right now. That didn't mean he wasn't here at all, he just wasn't in my apartment. Christian always was one to make others do his dirty work.

"Please," I whispered pleadingly, vision blurring from the tears that were on the cusp of falling. "Don't take me back there."

I'd lied to Archer. There was no way in hell I could go back. I thought I could, but now, with my past sitting in my kitchen staring me in the face, I knew I couldn't do it. I wouldn't survive. Not again.

"You shouldn't have left home." He withdrew a phone

from his pocket, his fingers nimbly running across the screen. "You've made quite the mess."

My bottom lip trembled as I contemplated my options, my heart hammering away in my chest like a jackhammer. Running seemed like the best option, but how far would I get before he caught up to me? Probably wouldn't even make it to the door. I knew it was pointless, but I still took a small step backward toward my exit.

"Don't even think about it." The threat in his voice was unmistakable, causing my body to freeze on instinct. Didn't even make it to the damn door. Neil didn't give idle threats. I knew this. He would be loyal to my father and brother now. Unflinchingly so. Like our cousins before him. No amount of begging would get me out of this.

"Neil..." Didn't mean I was above trying. His face, however, was as hard as granite and unreadable as he pulled his focus back to his phone. He knew just as well as I did that I was too afraid to run. My inner bitch, the one I'd been honing for nearly a year, was busy throwing a nuclear-sized temper tantrum in my head. Fuming at the fact that I wasn't fighting back.

"Uncle," Neil reported, and my blood turned to ice. So did my inner bitch. She was just as afraid of my father as I was. "We've got her." We've—not I've. Damn. Neil turned the phone toward me. It took everything I had not to reach out and smash the fucking thing to pieces. Consequences be damned.

The man on the video screen hadn't changed much in the year I'd been away. Maybe a few more frown lines and a streak or two of gray hair. Hopefully, all named after me. Otherwise, my father still looked like the same surly, dangerous man I had always known him to be.

"Avaleigh."

The deep timbre of his voice caused my lower lip to tremble as unwanted terror surged through me like a jolt of electricity. This was the man who was meant to keep me safe, to love me like all fathers should love their daughters. Mine apparently had a code flaw because all I had ever received from this man was pain and heartbreak. All he had ever done was use me and throw me away like yesterday's trash.

"What a disappointment." There was no mistaking the harsh disdain dripping from his words like acid. I resisted the urge to roll my eyes. Of course, I was the disappointment. Forget the fact that he had allowed me to be sold like a cow at auction for his mistakes. Sounded legit to me. Grade A parenting.

"You've been telling me that for years, Father." Pushing his buttons probably wasn't in my best interest, but the distance between us made me bold. Neil may have been a made man now, but he would never strike, even at my father's orders. I hoped. "If that's all you called to tell me, you wasted your time. I'll be sure to send Neil on his way. I'm a little busy right now."

"Such an impetuous tongue." His dark chuckle baffled me just as much as it terrified me. He was hiding something up his sleeve. "Just like Katherine." My heart stuttered at the mention of my mother's name. My father rarely spoke of her, and when he did, he never called her my mother, simply Katherine. It was like he didn't believe she deserved the title.

She deserved it more than he deserved to be called my father.

"Go to hell," I snarled, lips curling up in a sneer. "I'm not coming back so you can sell me off."

He chuckled again, dark and low, and I knew instinctively that whatever he was about to say wasn't going to be good. "You might want to reconsider that." His dark eyes glittered dangerously before he disappeared from the screen. Neil pressed the phone closer, giving me an unobstructed view of what my father was about to show me.

It took my mind a moment to process what my eyes were seeing. The room was dark. My stomach churned at the sight; bilious and sour. The tiny figure on the screen was naked, curled in on itself in the fetal position, body trembling. Quiet feminine sobs reached through the speakers, assaulting my ears, the sounds steadily growing as my father approached.

The girl screamed as my father wrenched her head back by her long tawny hair, and my world came crashing down around me.

The past had a way of coming back to bite you in the ass. An endless cycle of rinse and repeat. The same stains reappearing again and again.

This was my father's trump card. The ace up his sleeve. I knew at that moment there would be no escape. No running. No fighting. There was no other choice but for me to submit.

"Maleah."

"Did you honestly think I wouldn't find out the little whore helped you?" My father sneered as he shifted the phone back to his face for a moment before centering it back on my best friend. "Do it."

My world tilted on its axis as I watched with wide eyes as one of my father's men pulled a gun from his waistband, pressing the barrel to my best friend's temple. Maleah screamed through her gag as she struggled uselessly against her bonds and the man's iron grip, fat tears making streaks down her bruised face.

"Don't," I cried and snatched the phone from Neil, who let it go without a fight. My body was trembling, causing the phone to shake like a maraca in my hands as my chest stuttered and tears simmered just beneath the surface. Where was my badass bitch side when I needed her? Probably hiding. The fucking coward.

"You have two choices, Avaleigh." The old bastard's voice drifted through the phone's speaker above Maleah's whimpers. "You come back willingly, and Anatoly here doesn't shoot her like the dog she is. Or Neil and Christian can drag you back kicking and screaming, and your friend here dies. Your choice."

The finality of his words hit me like a bag of bricks, and I choked back a sob. There were no options here. Not really.

"Please—" And she was back. The pitiful girl who could never stand up to her tyrant father. The girl who simply took the abuse without question. Apparently, I hadn't dug her grave deep enough because here she was, alive and well and cowering like the little bitch she was.

"You know the consequences of crossing me," my father stated simply, uncaring of the fact that he was willing to end a young girl's life just to get what he wanted. "This is where your actions have led you. Now, what are you willing to do to ensure your friend's life?'

A cold sweat broke out over my body, and tears were pushing at the corners of my eyes, trying to overtake the floodgates, but I refused to let him see me cry. Never again. He'd had enough of my tears. "I'll come home." It was barely a whisper on my lips as the knowledge that I'd lost sunk in.

"Neil and Christian will escort you," he says.

"Father, wait—"

"You will not fight them, Avaleigh, or Maleah will pay for your actions."

I couldn't speak without crying, so I simply nodded. The screen went blank, and I crumpled to the floor in a dramatic heap, hyperventilating as my legs gave out beneath me. I wanted nothing more than to hurl the phone at the nearest wall and scream until there was nothing left. A year's worth of independence, building myself up, and all it took was one phone call from him to break down everything I had worked so hard to build.

"Get up," Neil growled impatiently as he hauled me to my feet. "Go pack your stuff. You have ten minutes. Christian is waiting in the car."

"The car?" Why hadn't my brother come up? Humiliation and fear were right up his alley, he fed off them like a vampire fed off blood. Especially if it was mine. I'm surprised he hadn't wanted a front row seat to watch our father tear me down bit by bit.

"Now you have eight minutes." I narrowed my eyes at my cousin as I all but stomped to my bedroom and slammed the door shut behind me, locking it.

How could I have been so careless? My best friend had helped me escape, and now she was the one paying for it. Seeing her like that, naked and shaking in my father's *stables* —it made me sick. I was not naïve to what my father did and the business he had gotten himself into. After my mother left him, his business had gone nearly bankrupt when the FBI investigated him for fraud. Along with a whole host of illegal activities that were miraculously ruled as trumped up charges.

You'd think he would have learned, but money was a powerful drug that grabbed at your soul, twisting until there was nothing recognizable left. The wealthy wanted nothing more than to stay wealthy. No matter the cost.

Neil pounded on the bedroom door. "Let's go, Avaleigh."

Biting back a slew of curses rolling around in the back of my mind, I quickly stuffed my meager belongings into a duffel bag. The caring cousin I had once followed around like a lost little duck had been replaced by a puppet whose strings were held tightly in my father's hands.

I learned at a young age that my Uncle Dante was the head of one of the Italian mob families that ran the city unhindered before Matthias Dashkov's arrival six years ago. My father had never involved himself in the family business, he didn't even carry the same last name. He and my other Uncle, Jerry, were the products of a mistress my late grandfather had taken to when my grandmother was no longer able to bear children.

A recurring theme with the men in my family. Although my Uncle Jerry seemed to be a faithful husband, it wasn't a secret that my Uncle Dante slept around. In fact, I'm pretty sure the one woman he slept with the most was my stepmother. Not that I could blame her since my father stuck his corndog in any woman he could find at the *stables*, willing or not.

"Open the damn door, or I'll break it down."

Fucking prick. I had always liked Neil. It would be a shame to have to break his pretty nose. Fuck the consequences. Whatever was going on with my cousin was a bit bothersome. He'd always sworn he would never join the family business. Neil had wanted to go to college and major in architecture, not spend his life working for our uncle.

Unlocking the door, I barely managed to avoid being hit when it slammed open and Neil charged in with a sneer as he grabbed up my meager bag.

"Come on. Christian is getting impatient." I winced as he ensnared my wrist in a bruising grip and towed me toward the front door. Hearing my brother's name, knowing what was waiting for me just down the stairs, had me dragging my feet to buy time. I was too terrified to leave the safety of my apartment and the life I'd built up for myself. No matter how meager it might seem.

"How could you let him do that to Maleah?"

Neil snorted. "You should ask yourself that question."

"What does that mean?" I wrenched my sore wrist out of his grasp, stopping to stare at him, completely bewildered. "You saw what he did to her. How is that my fault?" My father was the monster. He was the one who decided to kidnap and beat a young woman like it was just another day. The man didn't have a conscience, and apparently my cousin had lost his along the way. The question was why? What had happened while I was away that had him so changed?

Neil's dark eyes surveyed me with cold indifference. "What did you think was going to happen to her, Ava?" He slipped back into my nickname, sounding almost exasperated, but his face still remained a hard mask. "Did you honestly think he wouldn't go after her when she helped you? Come on, you're smarter than that."

"Who told him about her?" There were only three people who knew Maleah had helped me flee that hell hole. "It's been almost a year, Neil. How did he even know she was the one, and that it wasn't Libby or one of his men?"

Libby. Jesus, I was throwing my little sister under the bus, but the one thing I knew above all else was that my father treasured my younger sisters. Not as much as my asshole brother, though. No one compared to him. I knew for a fact, however, that he would never harm them.

"You'll have to ask your soon-to-be jailer that." He opened the apartment door. "He's the one who gave Uncle the information. Now, let's go."

My eyes were brimming with tears as I looked around the small, dingy apartment that had been my home. My haven. For the last year of my life, I had allowed myself to believe I was truly free. That no one would ever find me. That maybe they had forgotten me. Truth was, I'd never be free. Not really. And the only way to keep Maleah untouched was to go back to the prison I had fought so desperately to escape.

Swallowing back the lump that had formed in my throat, I followed Neil out of the apartment to the large sedan near the back of the alley. I hadn't seen it on my first inspection earlier. Time seemed to slow as I pushed my body forward. One painful step at a time. Fear splintered my heart, sweat trickled down my spine, and my palms felt clammy as panic washed over me.

I was rooted to my spot just a few feet away from the sedan. My lower jaw trembled, and my breath caught in my chest as Neil opened the door to the back seat. I tried to swallow back the panic rising to the surface as I prepared myself to come face to face with the one man I feared even more than my father.

Christian.

The breath I hadn't realized I'd been holding released in a large whoosh. The car was empty. My brother wasn't there. But then—where was he?

"Hello, Little Lamb."

The scream rising in my throat was stifled by a large, smooth hand from behind me. My eyes widened in shock, and I whimpered as I felt the prick of a needle at the side of my neck.

His low, gruff voice was the last thing I heard before the inky blackness of unconsciousness took hold.

"Let's go home."

CHAPTER FIVE

Ava

The first thing I registered was the pounding in my head. My body trembled, wracked with shivers as the cold of the cement seeped into my bones. Groaning, I clutched at it, the ache in my gut all too familiar. It was the same ache I used to have when my father would starve me for days as punishment. How many days had Christian kept me drugged? The scent of urine, sweat, and the musky tinge of sex did nothing to assuage my revolting stomach, and I tried my best to keep the bile from rising in my throat.

I didn't have to open my eyes to know exactly where I was.

The stables. The place my father kept his women before he sold them to the highest bidder like chattel. It was also the place where his enemies met their last.

Maybe I would finally meet mine.

I opened my eyes to darkness. The only light came from

the small window on the opposite wall that barely allowed the small tendrils of the sun's rays to trickle through the iron bars. It was hauntingly quiet in the small room, putting me even further on edge. The only sounds were soft sobs coming from farther in the cell.

"Hello?" My voice was hoarse from disuse as it echoed throughout the cell. I pushed myself up, freezing when the distinct sound of clinking chains reached my ears. I wiggled my left wrist, then my right. Christian had chained me to the damn wall.

"Who's there?" I called out a bit stronger this time, but the sobs didn't stutter or stop. Blinking a few times, I shook my head to clear out the cobwebs Christian's drug had caused. The thin strips of light from the window cast an eerie glow over a naked form huddled on a dirty mattress in the far corner.

Maleah.

I whispered her name in an attempt to garner her attention. It didn't work. She either couldn't hear me or wouldn't. I tried again. The only response I received was her soft sobs. My teeth clenched, jaw tightening as I leaned back and wrapped my arms around myself. The shorts and tank top I had been wearing when they took me did little to ward off the chill. These cells were specifically designed to make people uncomfortable. And scared.

Fear and panic sneaked up my spine unbidden as the reality of the situation sank in, and old memories were dredged from the depths of my mind. I closed my eyes and took a calming breath, anchoring myself. There was no way in hell I was going to allow them to make me the weak, scared little girl I was before. Never again.

I wouldn't be broken.

Sighing, I rested back against the stone wall with a tired

sigh. My gaze drifted lazily around the room, lingering on the cameras fixed to the ceiling in each corner. The red blinking lights gave them away even under the cover of darkness, but I had long ago memorized their positions.

I wasn't sure how much time had passed as I sat in the darkness alone with only Maleah's soft sobs as company. From the way the shadows moved across the floor, it had to have been at least an hour, if not more. Neither my father nor brother had made their presence known. I should be grateful they hadn't bothered with me, but I knew them all too well. Knew how they thought. How they planned. Their sudden rage was easily dealt with. A scream here, a kick there, and then it was usually over. The silence, however, was telling. It meant they were plotting their next move.

That never ended well for me.

Once again, I reached out to Maleah, the manacles on my wrists preventing me from going to her. Comforting her. She was scared, vulnerable, and in shock. Her entire world had been spun on its axis, and no amount of comfort could amend that. I knew. I'd been there. When she didn't respond to yet another call of her name, I let it rest. Instead, I closed my eyes and let the darkness take me.

Hell, maybe I'd wake up in Oz and realize that this had all been nothing but a terrible dream.

THE SLAMMING of the heavy wooden door jolted me from my uneasy slumber. My teeth chattered as a rush of cool air gusted in from the outside, and I glanced toward the disturbance.

My breath was shaky as he stepped into the room. The little light permeating the room with him was blocked out again. He stepped toward me, head tilted slightly to the side, eyes hard as he took me in with his cold, emotionless glare.

He was dressed in one of his tailored suits. Leather shoes that cost more than most people's entire wardrobe accompanied pressed black slacks and a black-button down with gold cufflinks that could feed a third-world country for years. There was no tie, however, and his shirt was unbuttoned.

That was never a good sign.

"Comfortable, Little Lamb?" He broke the tense silence surrounding us. I hadn't seen him in nearly a year, and yet the fear and panic still clawed at me like a rabid animal. He wasn't expecting an answer, not if his smirk was anything to go by. My guess was that he was still expecting me to be exactly what he called me. What I was before I ran. A meek, quiet little lamb. I relished the thought of disappointing him.

"Fuck you, Christian."

The smirk on my brother's face faded into a snarl as he stepped forward. The dim overhead light of the room flicked on to reveal him fully. His coiffed blond hair sat perfectly in place, slicked with gel, giving that almost greasy look. There wasn't any stubble along his jawline, and a hint of spice filled the air between us.

Women thought him handsome. The ultimate catch. A mix of old money and perfect genes. Charming. Well-mannered. Well-dressed. Every debutant's wet dream. What they didn't see was the darkness that simmered beneath the surface of his cognac eyes. The embers of sadism that lit up like fire at the pained screams of his victims. He liked to hear them beg as he cut into their flesh.

He was a demon with a charming smile, housed in a suit. A snake in the Garden of Eden.

"Careful, Ava," he snarled, crouching so we were at eye level. He cupped my cheek, running his thumb gently back and forth before taking my chin in a bruising grip. "Do you know what you almost cost us with your little stunt? What you almost cost me?"

I would have smirked if his grip on my chin hadn't been so tight. Instead, I settled for glaring in what I hoped to be a threatening manner. "Your life?" I guessed with a nonchalant shrug of a shoulder. "Too bad. I would pay good money to see you blubbering like a baby at Dashkov's feet—again. Do your men know what a weak, pathetic crybaby you..."

The pain registered before the act. My cheek stung, and stars danced across my vision as my brain processed the backhand. The fucker had hit me. I turned my head, leveling a glare at him, and spat in his face. A mix of blood and saliva landed in his right eye.

"Fucking monster."

Christian's face darkened, eyes glittering with the promise of pain as he wiped my spit from his eye. He looked like he wanted to beat me, but something was holding him back. His face contorted angrily, muscles coiled as he clenched and unclenched his fists. But he didn't make a move to hit me again. My brother wasn't known for his restraint.

Then it clicked.

Our father still owed Matthias Dashkov.

Agent Daddy Kink's words rang in my ears. That was why the old son of a bitch didn't have any qualms about sending me straight into the hornet's nest. They couldn't touch me.

"Be very careful, Avaleigh," Christian whispered darkly. I snorted.

"What are you gonna do?"

The insidious grin on his face was out of place for someone with no leverage against me. He couldn't touch me. My brain realized my mistake too late, and Christian saw the horror that painted itself across my face the moment it dawned on me what I'd done.

"No!" I attempted to lunge for his pant leg as he turned and walked away from me, but he was already out of reach. "Don't."

"Neil," he looked up at the camera and tipped his head. A moment later, my cousin appeared in the doorway, looking a little worse for wear. "Make sure she watches." Neil nodded, but I could see the corner of his mouth turn up in a sneer as my brother turned his back.

Still, he was a dutiful soldier and did exactly what he was ordered to do. In an instant, he was kneeling behind me, clutching my face in a harsh grip and forcing me to watch as my brother approached Maleah.

She let out a high-pitched scream as Christian grabbed a handful of her tawny hair and dragged her to the middle of the room. She was on her hands and knees in front of him, sobbing as he unzipped his pants.

"Christian, stop," I pleaded as he splayed open my best friend and spit on her back hole. "Don't do this. I'll be good. I promise. Please. She didn't do anything. God..."

What had I done? Neil tightened his grip on my face when I tried to look away as my brother gripped his pathetic dick. I'd seen my brother naked plenty of times throughout the years. He'd never been a modest man and constantly had girls coming and going through the house at all times of the day. There were more than a few times that I'd accidentally interrupted him. It wasn't pleasant, and the memories still made me want to wash my eyes out with bleach.

"I warned you, Little Lamb." Maleah cried out as he thrust into her without restraint. "Damn, she's tight. Doubt she's going to enjoy this much. Good practice for what Father has planned for her."

"Christian!" My voice was shrill, my chest heaving as Maleah's guttural scream of pain filled the room. He thrust into her over and over, harsh and demanding. I didn't want to watch but couldn't look away. This was my fault, and Neil further cemented it in my brain as he whispered the same phrase in my ear repeatedly.

God. Poor ignorant Maleah. I never should have involved her.

I'd never confided in my best friend the extent of the abuse I'd truly suffered at my father and brother's hands. How could I? Sure, she knew they hit me occasionally, and that had been enough for her. But I'd left her blind to who they really were. What they were truly capable of.

Maleah's world, like my sisters', differed from mine. Their lives were filled with money and shopping. Trips to the movies and coffee house chats with friends. As the mayor's only daughter, Maleah's world had always been safe and protected. She'd always been cherished.

I was the one responsible for tearing that down.

Christian took his time, the sound of his grunts burning like acid in my ears. By the time he was done, Maleah had stopped crying, her eyes vacant and glassy, blood running down her bottom and thighs.

"I swear to god, Christian, I am going to kill you one day." Neil pulled away from me as my brother zipped himself back into his pants, a dark smile on his lips.

"You can try, Little Lamb." He smirked as he strode over and crouched in front of me. "But we both know you don't have it in you."

"You'd be surprised," I hissed at him. "Push someone far enough and they're capable of a lot of things."

"We'll see." Christian stood, nodding to my cousin, who

began undoing my chains. "Take her back to the house and get her cleaned up. My father wants a family dinner."

Neil nodded as he helped me stand. I shifted to try and go to Maleah, who was still laying in the middle of the room, covered in blood and cum, but my cousin simply tightened his grip and led me toward the door.

"And make sure she covers up that bruise on her face," Christian added as Neil and I passed him on the way out. "My father won't be happy if he sees it."

"What about the Russians?"

"Hell if I know," he admitted with a shrug. "I'm trying to convince him to make alternate arrangements. He hasn't said anything about turning her over but hasn't said he won't, either."

What? The wheels in my head were working overtime as I processed what this could mean. Was my father not planning on holding up his end of the bargain? Would my deal with Archer still stand if I couldn't spy on Dashkov?

Neil just nodded his head silently, his expression blank, eyes emotionless. What had happened to him while I was gone?

"Neil," I whispered sadly as he all but dragged me from the *stables*.

"Shut your fucking mouth, Ava." The venom in my cousin's tone kept me silent, but the tears continued to flow. "This is all your fucking fault."

I didn't disagree with him.

CHAPTER SIX

Ava

I wasn't stupid enough to test Neil's patience as he shoved me in the back of a SUV parked out front for us. I recognized the driver, Giano. One of my many other cousins. Last I'd heard, he was at college trying for a business degree. What was he doing back in Seattle as one of my father's drivers? He'd barely even glanced at me as he shut the door to the back seat before settling himself behind the wheel.

He was different. Just like Neil. It was depressing, really. Giano had always been a warm and welcoming soul. Never judged. He was a jokester. A prankster. Now—now he looked distant. Lost. There was a hardness to his eyes I'd never seen before, and his body was tense, muscles coiled like he was waiting for trouble.

What had happened while I was gone?

The silence in the car was stifling as we made our way up the gravel access road and into traffic. Neil was typing away furiously on his phone in the passenger seat, pointedly ignoring me. Not that I minded. I wasn't even sure what I would say. Sorry you're stuck in this? Welcome to my life?

Who were they to pass judgement on my actions? They were not the ones who were constantly beaten, starved, and in fear for their lives since childhood. They weren't the ones who had to watch what they said so as not to anger their father. They wouldn't ever suffer the degradation and humiliation I had at my own brother's hand.

Fuck them.

Fuck me. I let out a soft sigh as I turned my gaze to the passing scenery. Maleah. There was a jagged hole in my heart as my thoughts turned to my friend. The image of what Christian had done to her was seared into my mind like a white, fiery brand. What had I ever done to them to deserve such treatment? Such hate? I wasn't sure I'd ever know, but what I did know was that it was my fault the rage they held for me was turned on her.

The drive to West Seattle hadn't changed much in the past year. I'd never been allowed off the grounds of the estate except to travel to the *stables*, so I had pretty much memorized the scenery to and from. I watched the sky fade into a burnt orange as the sun made its slow descent behind the steel trapping of skyscrapers and mountains in the distance. The car's dash said it was only five in the evening, but it was March, which meant early nights.

The air reeked of sewage and diesel fumes as we rolled along I-90 toward West Seattle. A glance at Christian's phone screen told me it was Saturday. Fucking Saturday. Neil held me drugged for nearly four days. No wonder I was starving.

Traffic was light, but the cacophony of honking horns, passing cars, and descending planes was enough to make me miss the simplicity of the small Texas town. Twenty minutes into the drive, Neil still hadn't spoken a word to me. The silence gave me time to weigh my options, though. Part of me wanted to run again, but I knew that once I reached my father's house, there wouldn't be another chance. Plus, I wasn't too keen on finding out if Agent Archer's threat was real or not.

I would not do well in jail. Seriously. I'd be the female equivalent of the bottom. Whatever that was.

By the time we turned down my father's street, the sky had shifted, and the streetlamps illuminated the darkened road of Mulberry Lane. The ominous creaking of the iron gate swinging open sent a jolt of anxiety through my heart.

I was not ready to face him.

The driveway was short, but it felt like a death march. Giano pulled the SUV up to the large Tudor house, parking it directly in front of the entrance. Guess they weren't taking any chances. Neil exited the passenger side, and I quickly realized why he hadn't bothered sitting in the back seat with me. The damn child locks were engaged.

There was compliment in there somewhere.

"Let's go."

My feet dragged across the cobblestone drive as I attempted to stall the inevitable. The lurid red door loomed ominously before me, beckoning me to it like the Dark Side to Anakin. I wanted to beg, to plead, but I knew that nothing I did or said would alter my fate.

Neil gripped my upper arm in a tight hold as he pulled me toward the door. It opened before we had even made it up the steps. My stepmother held the door open, her chin tilted up as her narrowed eyes took me in. Kendra Ward had an icy beauty to her that was the result of one too many trips under the knife. The timeless look she once held had been stripped away time and time again until there was nothing left but a woman who looked twenty years younger but somehow out of place.

Her bottled blonde hair was held in a low bun at the back of her neck, pushed back so you could see the angular cuts of her face that was caked in too much makeup. Her too slim figure was emphasized by the too tight black dress she wore with a pair of too high stilettos. These were things she wore to appease my father. To make her look younger. What Kendra would never fully understand was that my father's taste ran younger than she would ever be able to cut back to.

Kendra stepped back from the door as I was hauled inside, her dark eyes narrowing beneath her false lashes as she took me in.

The familiar smell of fresh-baked cookies and vanilla immediately overwhelmed my senses as the front door clicked shut behind me, locking me back inside my gilded cage. The woman spent way too much money on wax melts to make the house smell like a bakery when she didn't even allow sweets in the house unless it was for one of my father's events. Kendra and the word carb weren't on friendly terms.

"Who gave her that bruise?" Her gaze swept over my bruised and dirtied face. *No, it's fine, talk about me like I'm not here.* Neil muttered my brother's name, refusing to look at me. Maybe the asshole finally felt bad. My stepmother let out a huff as she brushed her thumb over my sore cheek. "She isn't his to punish anymore. Dashkov won't take kindly to this." Neil merely shrugged his indifference.

Kendra had never been directly cruel to me. Never raised a hand to me or shouted at me in anger. Instead, I was met with a cold indifference. Like now. She wasn't worried that I was hurt, more like concerned about what the consequences would be if my new owner found out that he'd received damaged goods.

"Anderson," Kendra called to someone stationed just down the hall. "Make sure Avaleigh gets settled in her room." I heard someone mumble *yes ma'am*, but I didn't bother to look up at the goon she assigned to me as I made my way toward the stairs. They were all the same anyway.

The house was quiet. The only sound was our footsteps trudging up the pine stairs toward the second floor. My escort walked a few steps behind me, probably not trusting that I wouldn't bolt if he took his eyes off me.

My gaze wandered to take everything in. This place hadn't changed one bit. It was still cold and impersonal.

Nothing was out of order. The art along the walls were hung exactly a foot apart, perfectly level. None of it really matched, though. They were all from different eras with separate styles that didn't flow from one to the next. No chi, as my younger sister Kenzi put it. Not that it mattered to Kendra, who only cared about the price tag of the art instead of the aesthetic. They were only meant to impress.

There wasn't a speck of dust or misplaced item to be seen. The furniture was pristine and looked as if it had never been used. Because it hadn't. This wasn't a home; it was a museum filled with meaningless exhibits. The only character this house had was the bedrooms. As long as the personalities were contained within those four walls, Kendra couldn't care less.

Wetting my lips, I stopped in front of the large white door that led to my room, which was at the back of the hall away from everyone else's. The first thing I noticed was that the doorknob had been modified. It was still the gaudy gold color, but I could see a deadbolt was added just above it.

Another way to keep me in my cage.

I bet they had put locks on the window as well. Kendra wouldn't ever allow them to put ugly iron bars on the outside of her pristine mansion. God forbid. What would the neighbors think? My mouth had gone cotton-dry as I continued to simply stare at the door like touching it might burn me. Maybe I'd get struck by lightning. However, I doubted I was that lucky.

"Ava." A familiar voice whispered my name from behind me.

No way. This couldn't be happening. Slowly, I turned to face my guard for the first time, blinking stupidly a few times as I took him in. Gone was the soccer mom look, replaced by a snug-fitting black suit and crisp white linen shirt. He was clean shaven, and his silver hair was styled loosely, swept back to one side. This couldn't be happening.

"What are you doing here?" I hissed at him through my teeth. The agent just laughed.

"I told you I would be seeing you around."

"I thought you meant in a more—clandestine kind of way." Archer chuckled like I amused him. "Not that you meant you worked for my father."

"Couldn't give too much away, could I?" He shrugged a muscled shoulder nonchalantly. Fucking senior citizen liked the cloak and dagger shit. "Then there would be no mystery." A growl erupted from low in my chest.

"I don't need mystery." God, this guy had no idea the situation he had put me in. "What I need is to get the hell out of here."

Archer's smile dropped as his eyes narrowed at me in an obvious threat. He pushed into my space, backing me up against the solid bedroom door as his dark gaze held mine. That man was so fucking bipolar it was giving me whiplash. Like Jekyll and Hyde. I wondered what would happen if I dosed him with one of Kendra's mood stabilizers.

Couldn't be any worse than it was now.

"There isn't anywhere for you to go, Ava," he reminded me. Like I needed one. I was very aware that I was on my own. "It's this or we can see how long you last in county lockup before your throat is slit." Sounded like a challenge to me.

"Fuck you." I was tired of his threats. I got enough of them from my father and Christian. "Do you know what I've been through in the last four days? Do you even care, or is this all some sort of sick game to you?"

Archer ran a gentle finger down my bruised cheek, and I couldn't help but flinch when he made contact with the battered skin. He frowned, but it was gone quickly, replaced with a dark determination I'd never seen before.

"Don't tell me you haven't had worse." Was he fucking kidding me right now? I clenched my fists at my sides to keep from smacking him silly. "I'm surprised you were even touched at all. I'm assuming your brother lost his temper, hm?"

I didn't bother to answer him. The question was rhetorical. Both of them.

"Back off." My hands shoved at his chest, trying to create some sort of distance between us. I didn't like being crowded, particularly by assholes. "I'm here, okay? You're fucking welcome. Now get the hell out of my face."

He must have seen something in my expression because his eyes softened, and he took a large step back. Thank god for small mercies. My eyes were stinging, and I let out a small sniffle as I swallowed back the lump in my throat.

So much for not crying anymore. Could I get any more pathetic? Probably.

Archer looked like he was about to say something, but I didn't give him the chance. My hand closed on the doorknob, and I turned it in my grasp before fleeing to the relative safety of my room, slamming the door as I went.

Solitude had never felt so good.

THE CLICK of the lock told me that Archer had sealed me in. At least he had taken the hint and left me alone. Not like he could step foot in my room. Only family was allowed in here unaccompanied, my father made sure of that. The last guard who had tried was now buried with the roses.

I waited until his steps retreated down the hallway before I tried the door, just in case. It was locked, but it was worth a shot.

My gaze drifted around the room, and I was not ashamed to admit that I was afraid it would swallow me whole if I stepped farther in. The girl who had once resided in this house, in this room, was scared and meek. She let her fear rule her. She never fought back.

I was not that girl, not anymore.

Sighing, I slipped into the enormous bathroom to wash away the stench and fear of the *stables*. It wouldn't be long before someone came to collect me for dinner, and as strong as I was trying to be, I didn't want to anger my father by not being ready. I would need to learn to choose my battles from here on out.

I switched on the water to take a shower and stripped myself of my soiled clothes. I caught a glimpse of myself in the mirror when I turned to grab my body wash and winced at the sight of the bruising along one side of my face in the shape of a handprint. Christian's handprint. It wasn't dark enough that concealer wouldn't cover it, but part of me didn't want to hide it, knowing my father wouldn't be happy with him if he saw it.

Stepping into the shower, I quickly got to work on rinsing the filth from my body, trying my best to keep my thoughts light by remembering the small amount of freedom I had managed to achieve. I missed the hot southern air filled with the scent of fresh hay and the warm salt breeze. The laughter from the bar. The friendly hellos and gentle smiles.

I let the memories fade to the back of my mind as I stepped out of the shower and locked them away where not even Christian could get to them. There they would remain, forever untainted by my family's dirtied hands. Pulling on a simple black dress with red flats, I clipped my wild mane of damp red curls into a large black clip before heading back into my room.

"Ava!" My younger sister Libby practically threw herself into my embrace the moment I exited the bathroom. A breath of relief rushed from me as I hugged her hard, smiling for the first time in what felt like months.

"Libby." I held her tight to me, my hands rubbing soothing circles on her back as she sobbed into my neck. "I've missed you so much." And that was the truth. Libby and Kenzi were the only two I truly loved and cared for in this family. They were mostly naïve to our father's way of life, and despite how cold Kendra could be, her love for them showed greatly.

"I've missed you, too." She sniffled as her sobs began to quiet, and we drew apart. Her face was red and puffy. The delicate skin beneath her crystalline blue gaze was swollen. Sometimes it was hard to believe she was related to our father. She looked nothing like him.

"I'm so sorry," she whispered, silent tears still streaming down her pale cheeks. "I'm a mess. I don't know how they found out where you were. And Maleah is missing, and I don't..."

"It's okay, Bug," I murmured her childhood nickname as I pulled her in for another hug. "It's not your fault, sweety. None of this is. I shouldn't have left." This was mostly the truth. I shouldn't have left the way I did. I should have made sure Maleah was more protected.

Libby was damn near untouchable. Our father would never raise a hand to her. Like Maleah, my sister didn't know the full extent of our father and brother's true nature. She'd only seen what they allowed her to, but her big heart wouldn't allow me to remain under their thumb. Libby might not have known everything, but the unjust behavior she did see was enough to make her take action. The entire escape plan had been her genius idea, and no one was the wiser.

It would stay that way.

We separated again, and I gently ran a hand through her long brown hair. She'd grown so much in the last year. It killed me that I'd missed that. The only other person I had ever loved as much as I loved the twins was my mother, but my memories of her had begun to fade with time. Soon, they would be nothing more than a haze in the back of my mind, unable to resurface.

"Are you okay?" I questioned as I gave her a once-over. My father and brother would never physically touch her, but that didn't mean she was immune to the verbal abuse they often threw out. I wanted to be sure they hadn't been blaming her for my Houdini act.

"It's gotten worse around here," she whispered, drawing me over to sit on the seat below the large bay window. My one true luxury. It overlooked the backyard. From my room, I could see everything that went on. I thought my father had meant it to be a punishment growing up. To show me all that I was missing from my ivory tower. It hadn't worked. If anything, it had given me an even stronger resolve to break free.

"What do you mean?" Libby, although somewhat theatrical, noticed everything. She may not be privy to what my father did for business, but she wasn't stupid.

"You remember how we used to joke about being a mob family?"

I nodded my head, remembering our late-night conversation under the sheets with flashlights. We used to make jokes that our family was really part of the Italian mob because of our Uncle Dante. He was a tall, suave Italian man, like my father, with a more youthful face and jovial disposition. He used to sneak me treats on holidays. As I grew, I learned that our jokes were true, but Libby had never been privy to that.

"Well—" She twisted her hands nervously on her lap. "I may have overheard Uncle Dante and Father talking one night with Christian about moving a shipment of guns and gir—" Libby stumbled over her words as she choked back a ragged sob.

"Girls." Libby hiccupped, her blue eyes coming to meet mine as it dawned on her that I already knew.

"You know?" Disbelief crossed her porcelain face, twisting something in my heart. I was about to shake the foundation of her reality. Ruin the childhood naivety that surrounded her. She was only eighteen and shouldn't have to worry about these things, but I couldn't hold the truth back now that she was uncovering something. If I told her, it would keep her safer than if she were to start snooping on her own.

"Yes, bug, I know." I had to keep this simple and in terms she would understand so that she wouldn't go digging deeper. I couldn't protect her if our father found out she knew about his sordid affairs. "But you need to listen to me. You can't go—"

"Libby!"

My jaw clenched tightly as Kendra breezed into my room without so much as a knock. No one had ever given me that courtesy besides the twins. Even when we were younger, the two of them had often afforded me simple acts of kindness that went beyond childhood manners. I think on some level, especially as they grew, they had understood how wrong my situation was. Even if it was never spoken out loud.

"Hello, Mother." Libby wiped at her eyes as she stood and smiled at her mother as if nothing was wrong.

"The two of you need to get downstairs for dinner," Kendra snapped as she led Libby from the room by her hand. "Your father is already in a fit, and I don't need either of you making it worse." Libby frowned and nodded as she followed Kendra like a duckling. I pulled my hair out of the clip and gave it a quick shake before I followed after them.

My mind was whirling with thoughts about what to do with Libby. I couldn't bury my head in the sand and pretend she didn't know anything. I also didn't want to encourage her, but she deserved to know the truth. The problem was, did I want to be the one to tear down everything she had grown to know?

Archer-Anderson—whatever the fuck his name was now, followed quietly after me as I made my way down to the formal dining room. His brow furrowed, and there was a concerned look in his eye that had me on edge. Or maybe I was the one putting him on edge.

Angry voices floated from the dining room, and I could already tell how the night was going to go. It wouldn't be in my favor, that was for sure.

CHAPTER SEVEN

Matthias

I sneered up at the painted double doors. The rash red color stood out against the crisp white surroundings. A bold statement in a neighborhood full of beiges and tans. The yard was well-manicured, with neatly trimmed hedges and strategically placed flower beds. It paid well to be the CEO of one of the top importing and exporting companies in the city, but that wasn't what kept Elias Ward and his family cozy in their multi-million-dollar home settled nicely in West Seattle.

No. It was the under-the-table handshakes. The dirty contracts. And sordid dealings of the underground that kept the man comfy in his bed at night.

It had been nearly a year since several men and I burst through those doors in the dead of night, intent on sending a message by killing Ward's son and heir as payment for my lost shipments and refusal to pay. There had been a time when the man was a suitable business partner. He'd been eager to earn money and build back the reputation of his company that had been destroyed.

Greed always had a way of twisting people.

Now, drunk on the power I'd given him, Elias thought himself untouchable. Invincible. Soon, he would learn how false that statement was. I wouldn't say I'm an unfair man by any standards, but the ignored phone calls and out of office emails had led me to put a gun to his son's head and demand my missing 5.5 million dollars.

I hadn't expected.

"PLEASE! WE CAN WORK SOMETHING OUT." *The man was sweating, his beady eyes darting between me and his sobbing, pathetic excuse for a son. I loved it when they begged. The rush of having a man like Elias at my mercy sent spikes of adrenaline through my body. I was revved up and looking for retribution. The man had thought himself untouchable by my hand for far too long, and it was time to pay the piper.*

"I have given you enough time, Elias," I snarled, my eyes narrowing at him. If he thought he was getting out of this without paying, he was wrong. "Either give me the money or say goodbye to your son. It's that simple."

Vas's eyes darkened as he pulled back the hammer of the gun, the metallic click echoing throughout the room. It was more for dramatic effect than anything else —

A soft feminine gasp filtered through the wooden door of Elias's office, drawing my attention away from the man. This meeting wasn't private. I nodded my head at Dima and Roman, who stood sentry by the door.

Dima forcefully threw open the door. Both he and Roman wasted no time in leaning down to yank a slim figure inside.

They tossed the girl roughly down onto the disgusting

Persian rug that decorated the floor. She landed in a heap of limbs and red hair at my feet like a sweet offering, and I was the king. With a click of the door, we were once again secluded in Elias's office.

"What do we have here?"

I'd met Elias's twin daughters, Kenzi and Libby, and this was not one of them. Interesting. She could be his mistress, but she looked too old for Elias's taste. He liked them barely legal. She certainly wasn't one of the girls he sold, otherwise, she wouldn't be spying so freely. Or be so well cared for.

The woman was striking. Her lithe frame was sprawled across the floor, wearing a pair of tight-fitting black yoga pants and a nearly see-through white tank top. Her body was supple and filled out, her belly slightly curved. But when she looked up, it was her wide, innocent eyes that caught my notice.

They were a vivid emerald green, almost ethereal looking, with a hint of golden flecks that sparkled beneath the harsh lights above. Jesus, I sounded like some man in a romance novel, not the leader of one of the largest Bratva Brotherhoods in the Pacific Northwest.

She did, however, seem familiar. Like I had seen her somewhere before.

The beast inside me clawed at my chest to be free. He wanted to claim her, here and now, for everyone to see. I clenched my jaw as I stared down at the small woman, trying my best to rein in control of my urges. I was not, by any means, a chaste man, but none of the women I had ever lain with made my cock jump to attention so quickly. And without even trying.

Her long red hair cascaded down either side of her face, framing it, creating a cape-like effect that reminded me of Little Red Riding Hood.

And I was the Big Bad Wolf.

"Her," Elias sputtered, his face beet-red as he rambled on. "Take my daughter as collateral."

Daughter? Vas's brow rose when he caught my eye. He was just as intrigued as I was. I pulled my attention from my Sovietnik and focused on the man at hand. My teeth clenched at his sudden declaration. The careless offer caused me to see red for some irritating reason, flaring up my protective instincts, and I didn't like it. Not one bit. Quickly, I silenced the man's rambling with a simple look before I turned back to the woman on the floor, smirking when I caught her gaze roaming my body freely.

Her cheeks tinted an adorable pink that caused my cock to twitch in my pants. Slowly, she pushed back her hair and got to her feet. In this position, I could see even more of her voluptuous frame. The gentle curve of her stomach and flare of her hips that begged to be gripped had images of me pounding her from behind floating through my mind. This woman was like a fucking drug. One I wanted to taste repeatedly.

"What's your name?" The woman visibly swallowed, her slender neck working against the lump in her throat. What that throat would look like beneath my hand. I could see her hands trembling slightly as she struggled to hold my gaze. Not out of fear. She didn't look afraid of me. No. There was strength behind her posture and a flare of defiance in her eyes. She was trying not to look at her father. Interesting.

"Ava." She whispered it so low I barely caught it. "Ava Ward."

Ava. Such a simple name for such a beautiful and complex looking woman. She was like a flame drawing on the unsuspecting moth. The vixen had no idea what I wanted to do to her. What the beast inside me wanted to do to her. Dark, depraved things that would have her screaming my name into *the early morning until she was hoarse and we were both fully sated.*

"Elias," I shifted my gaze back to her father. "I have a new proposition for you.

"NO ANSWER," Dima growled, drawing my attention away from the house and that night's memory. He shoved the phone in his trouser pocket. "Just kept ringing through. Not even a voicemail."

I should have expected this. My spy had made me aware the second Ava Ward had set foot off Elias's private jet and the moment she'd arrived back under the care of Elias. The man had taken his sweet time acting on the information I gave him. It had taken his son nearly a week to collect her, and now he was refusing me what was rightfully mine.

He thought he could keep her from me, at least for a while. No doubt plotting. The man was trying to prove that I didn't hold all the cards. It was a power move. One he was about to lose.

"Let's go." Dima and Vas nodded, falling in step behind me as I rapped roughly on the untarnished red door. I was not relishing the thought of having to take the girl by force, but I would if I had to. It had been four days since she had returned to Seattle. Elias had his chance to grow some balls and face me like a man.

Now, I was no longer playing any games.

"Can I—" The smile on the woman's face who answered the door faltered slightly when she saw me. She knew who I was. My reputation. How I had essentially kicked that very door down last time I showed up without warning.

"I'm here to see Mr. Ward," I growled at the elderly woman who was no doubt their housekeeper. "Now."

The woman paled beneath her caramel skin, her eyes roaming over our forms, no doubt noticing the distinct bulges in our suits where we kept our guns. "Mr. Ward is currently indisposed. If you could—"

"Does it look like I give a shit?" My lips curled into a snarl as I pushed past the trembling woman into the empty foyer. "Find him and tell him I'm here to see him. Now. And if he refuses, remind him of what I almost took the last time I was here. That might make him more compliant."

The horror on her face told me she wanted to do no such thing. Couldn't blame her. Delivering news like that was likely to get someone in her position killed.

"Of course," she fumbled slightly. "Allow me to show you to his office, Mr. Dashkov."

I followed the woman, my men on my heels, their gazes wandering as they took in the house's opulence. Laughter filtered through from the side of the house, and I could hear the clinking of glasses, no doubt from the patio. It was late winter, but the spring weather had made itself at home early this year.

It hadn't been too long ago that Elias himself almost lost all of this. The house, the parties, the social standing. An investigation by the FBI had nearly cost him everything. Investors pulled out, and most of his clients had sought other deals. No one wanted to taint their name by being associated with Ward Enterprises after the scandal. He'd jumped at my offer without a second thought. It was a simple deal. I kept his business from going under and he provided me with a way to move my products into Seattle Port and shared in a small percentage of his legit profits.

Then the fucker had gotten greedy.

Within two years, Elias had spread his services to other interested parties. He'd taken to the dark side of Seattle like a fish to water. What started with guns and drugs slowly turned into trafficking women and children and running illegal auction houses. Another reason I was keen to shut him down. There were some lines you just didn't cross. I just needed to make sure I shut him down the right way so that I didn't lose his company.

My own gaze wandered, taking in my surroundings as the woman led us toward Elias's office. I hadn't had much of a chance to look around the last time I was here. The wood floors were pristine. Polished and scuff-free. The walls were a stark white, sparsely decorated with paintings by Picasso, Munch, Bosch. To name just a few. The furniture was expensive and looked untouched. This place was more like a museum than a house people lived in.

I clenched my jaw. Growing up, I'd had nothing. No one showed me kindness or presented any opportunities to an orphaned youth, not until Tomas came along. My mother was a whore my father purchased at auction, and once she was dead, he'd had no further use for me. I had fought for every scrap of food, piece of clothing, and at times, I'd fought for my life.

The cold streets of St. Petersburg had taught me to fight and kill from a young age. I wouldn't have survived otherwise. It was hell, but that was fine with me because now I was the Devil. The Alpha. If it hadn't been for Tomas, I'd still be on those streets, fighting in the underground. Drinking and fucking my nights away in a haze. He took me in and used everything he knew and everything I had learned on the streets to hone me into the man I was today.

My riches were earned with blood and sweat. Whereas the wealth around me was just the ill-gotten gains of a privileged man fed from a golden spoon since birth.

"Here you are, sirs." The woman motioned us to step into

the generously sized office that was tucked away at the far side of the house. I smirked as I stepped inside. The last time I was here, both Ward men were begging and sobbing on their knees. The smell of fear still lingered. "I'll let Mr. Ward know you're waiting."

"Bring him now." My patience was wearing thin, though it was no fault of her own that her employer was a coward and refused to face me. She swallowed hard as I glared at her. Ignoring the chairs that were obviously meant for guests, I made myself at home behind Elias's desk, resting my feet on the cherry wood top. "I'm out of patience."

"Certainly." She turned and scurried from the room, tail tucked between her legs, leaving the door wide open.

Sighing, I made myself comfortable, eyes scanning the room, taking it all in. It was anything but simplistic. Like the rest of the house, the furniture was large and garish, oozing wealth. Pictures of him and his son hung between certificates of achievement—for his son—and the bookshelves were littered with awards, also his son's.

There were a few family photos, minus Ava, but no certificate or awards for any of his daughters. If it hadn't been for the sparse family photos, it wouldn't be obvious he had any. Not from this room anyway. Then again, the man sold women to the highest bidder as sex slaves. He even had a place he housed them. That alone told me exactly what he thought about the fairer sex. I'd been wanting to get my hands on the location of his *stables* for the longest time, but not even my spy could divulge that information.

I'd been planning Elias's downfall since I had first learned of his betrayal a few months before putting a gun to his son's head. The plan deviated unexpectedly the minute I'd laid eyes on the redheaded beauty. My Little Red Riding Hood. She was a variable I hadn't expected.

My mind drifted to what I knew about Elias. Never in all the years I had known him had he ever mentioned an elder daughter. I'd seen the twins at several functions, carefree and oblivious, but never once did I remember seeing Ava. He was hiding something. The last year had given me time to ponder what to do with her. How to use her as a pawn against Elias. The more I'd thought about her. Learned about her. The more obsessed I became.

It was what ultimately led me to hunt down the forger.

Heavy footsteps sounded just outside the office, and Elias walked in, face pale, dark eyes lit with fear. He hadn't been expecting me. Good. My spy was doing his job. The man's eyes narrowed for a moment at my feet propped up on his pristine desk, but with a simple quirk of my brow, he was back to being afraid just as quickly.

Smart man.

"Made myself at home. Hope you don't mind."

I was goading him, and he knew it. Part of me hoped he'd take the bait just so I had a reason to knock him on his ass.

"No, please, help yourself." There was a slight tremble in his voice he tried to hide, but it didn't work. Not with me.

"Where is she, Elias?"

Elias froze, eyes widening before he straightened his shoulders back and collected himself.

"I'm not sure what you mean." His left eye twitched, giving away the blatant lie. It lasted less than a microsecond, but I didn't miss it.

"Don't lie to me, old man," I snarled at him, eyes hard. "I know you have her. Did you really think I wouldn't be keeping tabs on you and your shit stain of a son?"

Elias bristled at the insult. Good. He was less careful when he was angry. Less composed. More likely to slip up.

"Look, I know I offered her up to you. However—"

"I'm not interested in your excuses, Ward." I slid my feet off his desk and sat taller in the plush leather chair. "I agreed to spare your son's pathetic life in exchange for your daughter." I leveled my gaze at him. "We had an arrangement, Elias."

"I know, but—"

"I did you a favor." I pushed myself to stand, using my height to my advantage. He was a good head shorter than me, and I towered over him, pushing myself into his space. Vas watched from his post in front of the door, and Dima moved to flank him. Just in case Elias tried to make a run for it. Not that he would get far. The man may have been in impeccable shape for his age, and he might have outrun me, but I had men hiding everywhere around his property.

"You don't understand—"

"Give me the girl," I snarled. "Or you'll find your precious heir dead in a ditch down on skid row."

"You can't—"

I didn't give him a chance to finish his sentence. Instead, I lunged forward, wrapping my large hand around his neck, and shoved him harshly into the bookcase behind him. The awards wobbled but didn't fall.

His pulse was firing away rapidly beneath my fingertips at his carotid. I smirked. He was afraid. He needed to be. No more games. "Don't tell me what I can and can't do," I hissed, tightening my grip just enough to make him work for air. "I saved your pathetic ass from bankruptcy. You wouldn't have any of this anymore if it wasn't for me. Remember that."

"Matthias—"

"Mr. Dashkov." Elias swallowed hard beneath my grip.

"Mr. Dashkov," he tried again. "I'm aware of what I promised."

"Good." I dropped my hand, watching as he wheezed. He

should count himself lucky that he was still breathing. "Now get her."

He looked ready to argue again. His eyes darted to the door, but one look at my men and he was scurrying over to his desk. I watched him like a hawk as he picked up his phone, pressing the speed dial before issuing a few short orders to whoever was on the other line.

"They're bringing her down."

I didn't say anything. Instead, I simply smirked at the old man, settling myself back down in his chair. Soon she would be mine, and I'd be one step closer to completing my revenge.

Elias had just given me the key to his downfall, and he didn't even know it.

CHAPTER EIGHT

Ava

Dinner so far was a quiet affair, but I didn't let that fool me. A storm was brewing beneath the lights, camera, action of our Oscar-worthy family dinner. Complete with Kendra's finest china and the kitchen's fanciest entrees. My father's face was tight, eyes focused on the meal before him as if he was contemplating some sort of sinister plan in the depths of his depraved mind.

Christian was livid next to me, spearing his food with angry jabs of his fork like it was a knife gutting someone instead of steak. His face was an ugly hue of red and purple, eyes narrowed at our father in silent anger. They'd been arguing when I'd arrived in the dining room with Kendra and Libby. It felt weird sitting at the formal dining table without Kenzi, but my other sister was still completing her winter session of college abroad.

Both men had clammed up tighter than a nun's legs at a

Chippendale show. They'd been discussing me, which was never good.

The ornate wooden chair beneath me was uncomfortable as I sat with my back ramrod straight and needlessly pushed food around on my plate. The drug Christian had given me when he knocked me out in Texas, combined with the recent trauma of seeing my best friend—my stomach felt like it was revolting, and the thought of eating made me sick.

I tapped my leg nervously beneath the table, my anxiety at an all-time high as I waited for the other shoe to drop. Or the anvil. Maybe even a piano. Hopefully, right on top of my father.

A hand clamped down tight on my thigh, squeezing harshly, effectively stilling my bouncing leg. I looked up from my plate to see Christian's narrowed gaze focused on me, his lips curled in a sneer. He waited a moment to make sure I complied with his silent order before he gave my leg one more harsh squeeze. His grip loosened a moment later, but he didn't remove his hand from my thigh. It was almost like he was trying to assert some kind of possessiveness over me that had my already testy stomach churning like open waters during a summer storm.

This wasn't the first time he'd done this. Growing up, it was a hand on my thigh under the dinner table, or the small of my back when Uncle Dante and our cousins were visiting. A caress of his hand through my hair when he wanted to give me attention or was trying to praise me. Small gestures that were more intimate than familial.

Gestures that made me want to scrub my skin with lye or set myself on fire. Hell, I doubted even that would get rid of the slimy feeling of him touching me. My brother was several years older than me, having turned thirty this last year. I still remembered how he had tried to cop a feel a few days after my eighteenth birthday. It didn't get far. Father had interrupted him before anything could happen, but the whole situation had left me with a sense of unease and a bitter taste in my mouth.

And not just because of what Christian had attempted to do. My father's words to my brother that day weren't of disappointment or chastisement. He had simply said, "Now is not the time."

Now is not the time? Those five words haunted me constantly, causing me to live in fear that one day there wouldn't be a time my father would stop him. The very thought still made my skin crawl. Would my father truly let my brother, my own blood, do such a thing? Sure, he was technically my half-brother, but still—this wasn't some taboo romance on my kindle. Or was that just another scare tactic to keep me in line?

The sound of the doorbell interrupted the tense silence. I looked up at my father, who was wiping his mouth with a napkin as he nodded his head to our housekeeper, Louisa.

Whoever was at the door was expected.

Louisa returned a few minutes later, followed by a short, squat-looking man in a suit who immediately eyed me before nodding his greeting to my father.

"Where would you like me to set up, sir?" My father cleared his throat, setting the napkin down next to his plate before standing to greet the man.

"In her room is fine," my father told him. "Up the stairs, third door on the right. Louisa will show you."

Wait. That was my room.

"What's going on?" I looked up at my father, who was now standing a few feet to my left.

"Dr. Stern is here to handle your exam."

"My exam?" Jerking my leg from Christian's grip, I shot

up from the table. No way in hell was he doing what I thought he was.

"Did you honestly think you would get out of a physical examination after being away for so long?" My mouth fell open, but my father stood resolute. The fucker was going to have the good doctor take a peek inside my treasure box to see if I still had the goods. Like I was one of the virgin women in his *stables* being prepped for auction. "For all I know, you were out there whoring yourself away to every Tom, Dick, and Harry. Dr. Stern is here to make sure that everything is still intact. And if it isn't..."

He let the threat hang heavily in the air between us.

"I'm not doing this," I protested harshly, my heart racing like a doped-up stallion at a pick-six. My father's face hardened, his eyes turning dark. He wasn't messing around. Not that he ever did, but I could see that I was walking a fine line with my disobedience. Fuck it. "I don't need an exam."

"Avaleigh," he warned, his voice tight with anger. I didn't heed the warning. Instead, I bolted, making a beeline for the front door as fast as my legs would carry me. I felt a hand wrap around my wrist, causing the bones to grind together as I was pulled back. A shoulder landed in my stomach, then lifted. The stench of Armani cologne told me it was Christian.

"No!" I was fighting against him, fists pummeling his back, feet kicking out. It was useless. My screams of defiance echoed throughout the empty halls and were completely ignored by everyone around us.

"Shut the hell up, Avaleigh," Christian snarled as we entered my room. Once there, he sat me down on the edge of the bed, his hand going around my throat as he pulled me toward him. His long fingers were wrapped around my chin, forcing me to look up at him. "You can either do as you're told, or I'll take great pleasure in tying you spread eagle to the bed. You decide, Little Lamb."

Little Lamb. I hated that stupid name. It wasn't meant as an endearment. Christian had once told me he called me it because I reminded him of a sacrificial lamb. One meant for the slaughter. He wasn't too far off.

"Clothes off and lie down," the toad looking doctor ordered next to us. I could hear the perverse glee in his voice. Instinct took over, and I tried once again to make a mad dash away from the perverted doctor and the budding psycho. I knew I was just making things worse for myself, but the logical portion of my brain was frozen as my fight-or-flight instincts rose to the surface.

I didn't get far with Christian's hand wrapped around my throat like a vice. My brother smiled wickedly as he ripped the dress I was wearing down the center before tearing it off my body completely. He hauled me up the bed toward the headboard and linked my hands with a set of padded cuffs at the top.

"Wait, please..." Not again. I couldn't be in those cuffs again. The last time my father had me placed in those cuffs, I hadn't been allowed anything but water for nearly a week. "Please..."

"You had your chance." That was all he said as he secured my wrists before moving on to my ankles. My body was still thrashing, my legs kicking out wildly in an attempt to do any damage I could. My brother grabbed one of my kicking legs at the ankle and dragged it wide, his dark eyes on mine, pupils blown wide.

The sick bastard was getting off on this.

A few moments later, he managed to get both of my ankles in their cuffs before he turned to the doctor with a twisted smile.

"All yours."

Dr. Stern moved to stand between my legs and pulled me slightly closer until they were bent at the knee. I winced. The move stretched my arms tightly, causing a mild pain to radiate up my shoulders. Christian was standing to one side, eyes glued between my legs. How could Father be letting him do this?

"You'll feel pressure, but it won't be too painful, Avaleigh," the doctor said as he lubricated his finger. I wrapped my fingers around the leather straps attached to the restraints and gripped them as tight as I could as he inserted his finger and turned this way and that.

"She's tight. That's a good sign," Stern muttered. I bucked my hips at the intrusion, but the doctor merely leaned forward, shoving his forearm down on my pelvis to keep me still. A tear slid down my cheek as I rested my head back to stare at the ceiling, wondering what I had done in my previous life for the universe to fuck me over so much. "Almost done."

A few more tears joined the first as he continued to probe for my hymen. It was an antiquated and outdated thought process, and I wondered if this was my father's way of further punishing me, humiliating me, and degrading me, or if the deal he had with Matthias Dashkov required that I be a blushing virgin.

"Intact." The doctor pulled his finger away and wiped it on a towel. I let the breath I was holding exhale.

"Good." My brother smirked down at me triumphantly. I made the mistake of letting my gaze wander below his belt. Fucking pervert was erect and so was the damn doctor.

"Is it over?" My voice was quiet, meek. Maybe if I showed some kind of repentance, this would end.

"Not quite," the doctor said as he moved up toward the head of the bed with a needle and a few syringes in his hands.

"What are those?"

"Birth control," he stated simply as he pushed the needle of one of the syringes through my deltoid. I flinched. Why did I need birth control? I didn't ask out loud, however. No doubt, I wouldn't like the answer. "And I'll be taking some blood for testing as well." I nodded mutely as he did just that.

"All done." The doctor pulled away and went to pack up his stuff. "She's a virgin, so I won't bother with STD tests. Just a basic metabolic panel and such."

"Thanks, Doc." Christian nodded his head to the man as he undid my restraints. Once loose, I immediately grabbed the throw blanket at the end of the bed to cover myself.

"Yeah, thanks," I muttered darkly as I tried to disappear into the warmth of the blanket, hoping to make myself smaller and less of a target to Christian, who was looking at me with a hungry gaze that made my stomach churn and bile rise in my throat.

Luck was on my side. My father came strolling into the room, a dark glint in his eyes.

"Good, he's done." He dragged the chair from my desk and planted it directly in front of me before taking a seat. "Now, let's discuss expectations."

"Expectations?" I murmured. My father nodded.

"Eventually Matthias Dashkov will come for you," he told me. *Yeah, because you offered me up like a stuffed pig at a banquet full of ravenous wolves.* I didn't say that aloud, however. I was not suicidal. "When he does, you are going to be my eyes and ears inside his compound."

What in the seven circles of Dante's Inferno? Was there some kind of sign on my forehead that said, "would make an excellent spy?" Did I somehow radiate 007 vibes and I just didn't know it? True, I had escaped this prison hell hole, but that was only after months of planning with Maleah. Matthias

Dashkov's proposition to my father only shortened the timeline. I wouldn't have been able to stay off the grid if it hadn't been for the forger she had found and the money she'd given me.

"I don't understand." And I didn't. Why did he want me to spy for him? Sure, he owed the Dashkov *Bratva* a lot of money, but they also had a business contract. From what I understood, Matthias Dashkov needed my father's business to bring his illegal goods into the country. And without Matthias, my father's business would go belly-up.

"You don't need to," he snarled harshly. "What you need to do is get me whatever information you can on his security, the layout of his compound, his men—all of it."

"How do you expect me to do that?" Did he think Dashkov was just going to let me flit around his compound unsupervised? If so, maybe my father was as stupid as he looked.

He snorted his amusement. "How do you think, stupid girl?" Oh, I was the stupid one. Right. I saw Christian's hands clench into fists behind my father, his face growing redder than a tomato as he struggled to rein in his anger. "A woman's best weapon is between her legs."

What the fuck? My father wanted me to whore myself out to a man for his secrets? Had he lost his fucking mind? Helen Keller had a better chance of finding Waldo than he had getting me to sleep with someone like Matthias Dashkov.

"You can't expect me..." My legs pushed against the edge of the bed as I scrambled away from him, struggling to keep my tight grip on the blanket covering my naked body. My father was up and out of his chair with an angry roar before I could even get the rest of my sentence out.

"You will do as you are told, Avaleigh." He advanced on me, grabbing one of my exposed ankles and twisting until I screamed for him to stop. "Think of the consequences if you don't. It's already too late for Maleah, but don't think I don't know all about Libby shutting off the security system that night."

My eyes widened at his sudden confession as I held back a sob. How long had he known?

"Please..." It was weak and contrite, but there was nothing else for me to be but repentant. I was at a blackjack table where the house held all the highest cards and was willing to use every single one against me. "I'll do it."

"Good girl." He released my ankle, massaging it for a moment before standing back up and turning to my brother. "Let's go. Your mother invited some guests over for dessert and drinks on the patio and I need your help to entertain."

The anger on Christian's face hadn't disappeared, but like a good boy, he nodded at his father's order and left without a backward glance. My father soon followed, and I was left in solitude once again. This time, however, it was not welcome.

Sniffling, I wrapped myself further into the blanket as I stuffed a pillow beneath my head and closed my eyes. What I wouldn't do for a foursome with Jose and his cousins right now. The only three men in my life who could take away the nightmares bound to slither in during the dead of night when there was nothing but me and the bitter darkness.

"GET UP."

I stifled the scream threatening to bubble out of my throat as the door to my room was thrown open and Neil came charging in with Archer...Anderson...whatever his name was, tight on his heels.

"What's going on?" Sitting up, I wiped at my tear-stained

cheek, my eyes no doubt red and puffy. I'd done a lot of crying since they'd found me. Too much, if you asked me. Neil ignored me as he nodded his head at

Archer...Anderson...hell...as he rifled through my dresser. A glance at the clock next to me told me I had barely slept an hour.

"Get dressed and make sure you cover up that bruise on your face." My cousin threw a pair of maroon yoga pants at me and a cream sweater along with some undergarments. At least he still remembered that I liked to dress comfortably. "You're leaving." His words caused a sudden tightness in my chest as I stood on shaky legs, careful to keep the throw blanket wrapped tightly around my still naked form as I stepped into the bathroom and closed the door.

One look in the mirror said everything about the day I'd had. There were now darkening bruises along my throat where Christian had grabbed me and several more along both arms and along the top of my thighs where the doctor had held me down as he probed me. I looked like a walking domestic violence campaign. No wonder Neil had chosen the cream sweater. It had a turtleneck-style collar that just barely hid the evidence of Christian's assault.

Sighing, I quickly relieved myself before throwing on the clothes and opening the makeup bag on the counter. The bruise on my face was light and would be easily concealed.

"Avaleigh." Neil barked from the other side of the door. "Let's speed this up." One last glance in the mirror showed me that everything condemning was hidden beneath cosmetics. Wouldn't want the bastard to get in trouble or anything. I snorted at the idea of Matthias Dashkov defending my honor against my family. Why would he?

He was just like them. Cruel. Twisted. A monster among men.

Grabbing the makeup bag, I threw open the bathroom door to find Neil and—Agent Daddy Kink waiting for me. I quickly threw my cosmetics in the large black duffel Archer was holding open for me. I shot him a frosty look as he zipped it without a word and strolled out the door without a second glance. Damn, he was good at the whole secret agent spy thing. Me, I couldn't contain the urge to want to strangle him. Call him out. Let my father feed him to the fishes.

Neil led me from the room, and I was smart enough to remain quiet as we made our way down the carpeted hallway toward the stairs. My father's study was tucked in the back of the house, away from the main rooms. He often conducted business during parties and large affairs so that he not only had an excuse to have certain persons around but also, the noise of the event would drown out any unscrupulous conversations. Kendra had made him promise to keep from killing people in the house. Blood was apparently a bitch to get out of carpet.

"Here she is."

My father's voice was the first thing to greet me as the door to his study swung open and Neil shoved me inside. I staggered a bit, my feet catching on the rug. Large hands gripped my shoulders, and when I looked up, I was staring straight into a stormy sea of gray.

"Hello, Ava."

CHAPTER NINE

Matthias

"She can be stubborn," Elias confided as we waited for his men to grab Ava. "You'll need a firm hand with her. If you know what I mean."

"You don't need to worry about that," I assured him harshly as I stood and made my way to the other side of his desk. I wanted to be ready to leave this wax museum as soon as she arrived. Elias didn't have to worry about discipline. Although I would garner our definition of the word varied greatly.

I was well versed in how to punish a woman, and the last year had given me ample time to think about how to dole out her punishment. The very thought of stripping her bare and feeling the taut skin of her ass beneath my hand as I spanked her had my cock waking.

"It's just a friendly warning," he told me as he took the

seat I was just occupying. "Avaleigh is a lot like her mother was. Stubborn. Hard-headed. Disobedient."

I quirked an eyebrow at Vas who, like me, was analyzing every word Elias was saying. "I'm sure she'll be fine," I told him, but I could tell he was worried about something. For a man who had so willingly offered her up as collateral without hesitation, I thought he would be more relieved to be rid of her. Instead, I could see him making calculations behind the calm mask he donned.

The way he nearly spat the words *her mother* had me curious as well. What was he telling people his relationship with her was? Mistress? Whore? None of that was ultimately true. Elias didn't have many weaknesses to exploit as he once had, but this new revelation put a chink back in his armor I could easily exploit.

Why hide Ava away for so long? That was the real question that needed answering. There was a reason behind it. Elias didn't do anything without a reason. Something about the girl benefited him. I just had to figure out what it was. And I planned on doing just that.

"I'm surprised you knew she was here." There it was. I'd been waiting for a while now for him to pry into that. Elias wasn't completely stupid; he knew it was no coincidence that I showed up tonight, her first night back in the house. From the look on his face earlier, he hadn't been expecting me for at least another few days.

"Did you think I wouldn't have my men monitoring you, Elias?" I asked coldly. "You've proven you can't be trusted, repeatedly. I wasn't about to risk you taking your promised collateral and hiding her from me."

"Well—"

"I'm curious about something, though," I cut him off, not in the mood for any more of his lame, half-assed excuses. Elias was the most vulnerable when he was ambushed and unable to plan. "Why the secrecy? I mean, she could be an asset, and here you are, hiding her away like Rapunzel. Why is that, Elias?"

The man squirmed in his chair, his mask of calm fading into panic for just a second before he slipped it back in place. I saw through it. I always did.

"Her mother was..." He paused for a moment, taking the time to choose the right words. He was being careful, which meant he was afraid to give too much away. Interesting. "...a complication."

"I see." And I did. His hesitation told me more than he would think. I doubted he was uncomfortable exploiting her. No, Elias had plans for Ava. Big plans. And if he knew what I knew, those plans could spell disaster for me and mine.

Elias had been trying to build alliances among the city's wealthiest and most powerful for years now. If it came to light he was hiding away an 'illegitimate' daughter, there would be trouble. The rich prided themselves on keeping their dirty laundry where it belonged. Elias was no different.

Instead, I turned the conversation to something else. "She's educated?" Elias let out a small breath of relief at the sudden topic change and nodded enthusiastically.

"Of course," he assured me, almost gushing like he was trying to be a proud parent. Problem was, he was too enthusiastic. Overselling the fact that he cared about her education. "Valedictorian of her class. Attended an all-girls catholic school here in the city. St. Anne's. It's where she met that wretched girl."

That *wretched* girl must be Ava's friend Maleah.

"And of course, she has a college degree as well," he continued, my eyebrows raised in surprise at this. Elias didn't seem the type of man to care whether the women in his family had any sort of higher education. Then again, he had let one twin study abroad. "Secondary education. Needed something to keep her busy and out of my hair."

Ah, there it was. Elias didn't have her pursue the degree because he wanted to educate her, he wanted to keep her out of the way.

"Good." I acted as if that pleased me, but honestly, I couldn't find it in me to care about her schooling. Ava Ward had two purposes, and neither of them required an education. Although one would certainly require some training. "And the other girl? Maleah. The one who helped her escape. That's taken care of?"

"Yes. Yes." Elias took a deep breath as he leaned back in his chair. "That whore is exactly where she ought to be. If you get my meaning."

Unfortunately, I did.

I'd forced myself not to think about the girl and her fate. I hadn't relished the thought of giving her name up to Elias, knowing the sort of man he was and what he did to those who betrayed him, but personal feelings wouldn't deter me from my mission. Not this time.

For a while now, I'd known Elias was more than what he seemed. I wished I could have caught on to his past sooner. Then I might have modified my tactics when I first approached him. But it was too late now. Had I known several years ago when I dragged Ward Enterprises out of bankruptcy that Elias had familial ties to the Italian Mafia, my direct competition, I would have let him sink and bought the company out from under him.

It was already done, however, and I couldn't continue to dwell on my mistake. Instead, I'd chosen to dedicate the time to figuring out how the man had managed to suppress that information. The Romano family was notorious throughout

Seattle and the surrounding cities. They'd ruled pretty much unchallenged until my takeover six years ago.

Their notoriety would have had them on every local and national law enforcement database. Family members included. Elias was nowhere on the list of known associates and relations despite his direct relation to Jerry Romano, Italian Cap, and half-brother to the Don. I'd only put two and two together when I began digging more into the man's personal history after Ava's disappearance and realized that he shared a mother with Jerry. Which meant he shared a father with Dante Romano, the Italian Don himself.

I might have thought it was mere laziness not to take the familial connection on the part of law enforcement until my spy recently informed me that the parentage of the Don listed in the FBI database was false.

Someone had purposely altered it. The question was—why?

"You have all the paperwork handled?" Elias broke the uncomfortable silence that had fallen over the room.

"One of my men will have it in your hand by the end of day tomorrow," I assured him.

"Excellent." He smiled as he looked at one of his computer screens. "Make sure she signs it."

"Don't worry about that." The paperwork was nothing more than a formality. It was not in any way admissible in court, this exchange of goods, but it served as a contract of ownership in the underground. "I'll make sure she signs it."

Elias breathed a sigh of relief. I could have made him coerce the little redhead into signing it but had other plans for what she was going to sign, and Ward wouldn't be happy about it. Not in the least. Once the documents were signed, though, he wouldn't be able to do anything about it.

"Here she is," Elias proclaimed as the door to the study

swung open. I turned around just as a mass of red curls stumbled forward. Instinctively, I reached out to steady her, my large hands gripping her shoulders tightly before she could fall. My senses were overwhelmed with the smell of fresh honeysuckle and vanilla.

A dark smile spread across my face as her emerald gaze slowly lifted to mine. There was fear in her eyes, but I could see a spark of defiance lingering just beneath the surface. Defiance I knew wouldn't stay hidden forever, and I relished the thought of being the one to tame that spark. To bring her to heel.

"Hello, Ava."

A faint blush spread across her cheeks as she righted herself, and I frowned when I noticed how heavily her face was covered with concealer. I didn't remember her wearing any the last time I saw her, and none of the pictures I had gained access to showed that she favored heavy makeup, either.

"Well." Elias smiled broadly as he stood, but I could see the sharpness in his eyes as his gaze wandered over his daughter critically. Ava didn't meet it; she simply lowered her eyes to the floor. Normally such a show of submission would have my cock lengthening, but this wasn't the kind of submission that aroused me. The women I required it from showed me willing submission. A need and want to please me.

This submission was caked in fear.

"I'm sure you'll want to get her settled," he prattled on. "I'll have Neil show you to the door."

For a man who just half an hour ago was nearly begging me to reconsider taking her, he sure as hell was trying to speed us out the door now. "You don't want a minute with her?" I knew full well he wouldn't.

"Not necessary." He waved the question off with a swipe of his hand. "I'm sure she'll be in touch."

"Well then." My hand gently gripped the back of her neck. She stiffened at the action but didn't move. Good girl. "It was good doing business with you, Elias." Ward nodded his head curtly as I turned and led the girl out of his study and toward the front door.

She glanced back for a second once we reached the car outside, her wide eyes looked pleadingly at her cousin, who completely ignored her as he shut the front door with a click. Disappointment flickered across her face, but it was gone just as quickly as it came, schooled into an expression of calm.

There won't be any hiding from me, Lil Red.

I opened the back door of the SUV for her, and when she hesitated, I gave her a small push forward, lowering my lip to her ear.

"Get in, Red."

She sneered at the nickname but did as I requested. My palm twitched. I ignored it. A moment later I was sitting beside her, the door of the SUV closing us into the small space.

There was no escape for her now.

AVA STARED QUIETLY OUT the heavily tinted windows of the Navigator as we rolled silently through the streets toward the center of Downtown. At night, Seattle was its own organism, a self-sustaining incessant whirl of neon lights, dance clubs, drug addicts, and adventure seekers. A cavalcade of vehicles barreled through the streets with horns blaring, tires screeching, and exhaust fumes rolling at all hours. The chaotic cacophony of sounds was the music of the city, and I relished it.

It was late. Not late enough for last call, but late enough that all the sensible crowds had long tucked themselves into bed for the night. This was when my business came alive. It was Saturday, and normally I would attend the underground fights beneath one of my clubs, watching as my well-invested money was tripled throughout the night before fucking one of the overly eager club bunnies in the VIP room.

This, I had a feeling, would turn out to be more entertaining. At least for me.

"Have you ever been downtown before?" I inquired softly to Ava, who shook her head without pulling her gaze from the passing scenery. "I require a verbal answer, Avaleigh."

The use of her full name got her attention. The redhead turned to me; eyes sharp as her gaze stubbornly met mine. The docile woman I had seen earlier in her father's office was gone, replaced with a Fury, just waiting to dig her claws into me.

"Why ask a question you already know the answer to?" she snapped. I wondered where this sudden bout of anger had come from. Or maybe it had been brewing beneath the surface since our departure, and this was her first opportunity to vent it. Whatever it was.

It was an opportunity she would regret taking.

"Careful, Lil Red," I warned, my tone low and quiet. She was right. I did already know the answer, but I still wanted to hear her say it. To submit to me without firing back. "You don't want to anger the wolf; he just might bite back."

That cowed her a bit.

"No." There was still a bite to her tone, but I ignored it for now. "The only time I've been let off the grounds was for school." She hesitated for a moment before continuing. "And when I ran. But you already know that."

"I do," I agreed. "But when I ask a question, you answer. Whether you think I already know the answer or not. Is that clear?"

Her green eyes sparked with indignation, lighting up the golden flecks that shone when she was angry. I'd noticed that the first time we met in her father's office. Her arms crossed against her chest, bringing her full breasts to my attention. It didn't escape my attention that Ava didn't answer, and it took every ounce of self-control I had not to yank her from her seat and over my lap.

"Why did you do it?" She questioned out of the blue a few moments later, her voice softer, but her eyes met mine in outright defiance. "Why did you give my father Maleah's name?"

So, that was why she was suddenly angry. Someone had told her it was me who outed the girl to Elias. I should have known she would confront me about her friend, and I wondered how long she had been waiting to do just that. From what I'd been told of Ava, she was fiercely loyal to her sisters and her friend. That didn't surprise me since they were the only ones she had the chance to develop any kind of bond with.

"Elias was the one in charge of tracking you down." I tilted my head slightly to look at her. "Who else would I give her name to?"

The disbelief that tracked across her face was stunning. "Do you know what they did to her?" Ava's voice pitched slightly when she was angry or shocked. An interesting tell.

"What happened to your friend is none of my concern." Her delicate jaw clenched at my blunt response. I underestimated the weight my words would have on her, which was why I didn't see it coming.

The silence that fell over the car was deafening. Ava's mouth dropped open and her eyes widened in shock and fear as she processed just exactly what she had done. I growled, low in my chest.

"I warned you, Red." The darkness of the car was washed away in bright lights as we pulled into the parking garage of my building. My pride and joy. "Now you get to see exactly what happens when you anger the wolf."

CHAPTER TEN

Ava

Shit. Shit. Shit.

The throbbing in my fist registered before the act. My eyes widened in shock, lower lip trembling as a deathly silence took hold of the car. Fuck me, I'd just punched Matthias Dashkov, leader of the Seattle *Bratva*, in the jaw.

His stormy gray eyes were lit with fire and an all-consuming rage as he nearly melted the skin off my bones with the glare he shot me. I swore I heard an inhuman growl emit from him, but that could have just been the shock talking.

"I warned you, Red." The darkness of the car suddenly vanished, washed away by the bright fluorescent lights as the city streets faded away and we pulled into a nondescript parking garage. "Now you get to see what happens when you anger the wolf."

A cry of pain wrenched itself from my lips as he buried a

hand in my crimson curls before he leaned over, unclicking my seatbelt and dragging me from the now idle car. My screams of outrage went unanswered, echoing uselessly off the light gray concrete walls of the parking garage as he all but dragged me toward a set of elevators.

My nails clawed uselessly at the hand in my hair. I fought back angry tears as I tried to relieve some of the pressure on my scalp. Matthias wasn't having any of it. Instead, he yanked my head backward, causing my back to arch, and my gaze to meet his.

"Stop fighting, Ava." He remained calm as he hauled me into the elevator and pressed the button for his floor. I whimpered involuntarily when the doors slid shut, the small action causing my heart to hammer even faster with the fear of being in a confined space. "I'd hoped to give you the night to settle in before I punished you, but evidently you need a lesson in respect."

Punished me? Like fucking hell! I'd been a doormat and a punching bag for my brother and father for years, and there was no way in hell I was going to keep repeating that cycle. Fuck it. I'd fight him tooth and nail if he thought I was going to let him beat me.

"If you think I'm going to allow you to beat me, Matthias Dashkov," I snarled at him as I kept clawing at any part of him within reach. "You've got another thing coming, fucker."

His large hand connected with my backside with several brutal smacks that caused me to gasp, effectively stilling my flailing body. I'd expected him to get angry. To slap me across the face or punch me in the ribs like I'd experienced so many times before. I was in no way prepared for the sudden burn of his hand coming down on my ass.

What the fuck?

"I'm not going to beat you, Red. I am going to discipline

you." He let out a small, frustrated sigh as the elevator came to a stop. He inserted a code into the small keypad located to one side that he was blocking me from seeing with his body. "Now, it's up to you whether or not you take that discipline like a wild animal or with some class."

Class? Who took a fucking punishment with class?

"But know that if you keep fighting me like this," he warned as he pulled me from the elevator and swung me around to face him. "Your punishment will be even more severe than if you simply behave."

"Fuck you," I hissed, shoving at his chest. The fact that he managed to remain calm while manhandling me pissed me off, and I shoved him harder. His hand was still tangled ruthlessly in my hair, and he gripped it even harder, twisting it forcefully until I winced from the sharp pain radiating through my scalp.

"Language, Ava." He turned away, pulling me along behind him into what looked to be the living room.

"Fuck you, Matthias Dashkov, you heartless fucking asshat."

Me and my fucking mouth.

I was in shock. That had to be it. My brain was short-circuiting, still processing everything that had happened since Christian took me. My guilt for Maleah had obviously made me suicidal because the look in Matthias's eyes was nothing short of murderous.

I think.

His lips twisted into a wicked smirk like I had just made his day. Maybe he was the Big Bad Wolf because right now he was giving me a hungry stare that made me think he might devour me whole at any moment.

"I love your defiance, Red." His voice was husky as he sat on the edge of one of the sofas before yanking me across his lap. I scrambled for purchase on the floor, but I was too short to reach it. My hands were out of range, too, and the only thing I had to hang on to his pant leg.

"No!' I screamed, my fingers clawing at his calves. "Let me go, you brute."

"But in my house, you will show me respect and obedience. At all times," he demanded calmly before pushing my yoga pants down around my knees. My cheeks heated to a solid ten with embarrassment at not only the action but also the fact he was seeing my white cotton panties.

Kenzi had, at one point, attempted to buy me a set of fancy lace thongs and panties, but the minute my father saw the contents of the Victoria Secret's bag, he'd called me a dirty slut and locked me in my room without food for a week, nearly starving me.

Three sudden sharp slaps dragged me back to the present. The man was spanking me like I was some errant child, not a grown-ass adult. A lump had begun to form in my throat as he delivered several more peppered strikes to my ass in rapid succession.

"Please, stop."

"You made a choice, Ava." His voice was irritatingly calm. "You chose to run away. You chose to strike me." He started to lay into me again, not discriminating with where he placed his smacks on my ass.

I kicked out at him, attempting to squirm and free myself from his hold. The man had an iron grip.

"This is going to get much worse if you don't remain still." Matthias pressed an arm into my lower back, keeping me in position. I held back a groan of pain that move caused. His knee was pushed right into the long bruise across the top of my thighs.

Fight or flight. Stand up or cower.

To hell with it. All my life I'd done nothing but run or hide. Trying my best to remain small. There was no way in hell I was going to be a victim anymore. Fuck it. If he killed me, he killed me. At least then I wouldn't be subjected to another man whose goal was to simply break me.

"Fuck. You."

"Worse it is, then." The tearing of fabric filled the space, and I realized with utter horror that he'd ripped my cotton panties from my body. I shivered as a burst of cool air hit my exposed bottom. My stomach clenched with the realization of what I'd done, but there was something else along with the fear. Almost like butterflies were settling themselves in the pit of my stomach.

I'd officially lost the plot.

Then I heard the slide of leather and the jingle of a belt buckle. Oh, hell no. I hissed as the sting of the leather collided with my already heated skin again and again. Fuck, that hurt like hell. The explosion of pain across my ass had seeped into my entire body as my muscles began to cramp. He didn't pause or hesitate, and after only a few strikes, I was a whimpering mess on his lap, fat tears sliding down my cheeks.

"Please, Matthias." God, I was blubbering like a child. "Please stop!" I couldn't take much more. My chest was heaving, snot dripping down my nose and onto the plush gray carpet below. There was a lump in my throat so large I felt like it might block my airway.

I threw my hands back in a half-assed attempt to stop the whipping, but Matthias simply captured them in his hand and pinned them to my lower back before continuing for a few more strikes.

"I want you to learn this lesson, Ava." The belting stopped for a single moment. "Because your next lesson will be much more severe." Then he began again in earnest.

I squirmed on his lap again, wiggling to try and loosen his hold as he kept going. That was when I felt it. The obvious bulge of his manhood poking me in the stomach as he practically beat me.

"You're getting off on this," I growled at him, attempting to dislodge myself from his lap.

"I never said I wouldn't," was his only reply.

I let out a frustrated cry. My ass was on fire from the punishing leather strokes of his belt, but he didn't let up. In fact, he aimed his tool slightly lower, causing me to howl in pain as he hit directly on the spot where my buttocks and back of my thigh met. Suddenly, I was out of fight, and there wasn't enough energy left in me to care about the humiliation of being spread across his lap half-naked.

My pussy was clenching each time the belt came down, and my thighs were becoming wet with my arousal. The redness of my face was partly from my screams of frustration, but the other half was embarrassed that something so wrong and deviant could turn me on like this.

God, I should have kept my mouth shut, but I was tired of being ignored. Tired of being used. Look at where my defiance had gotten me, though. Spread over a man's lap, who I barely knew, being spanked like some errant, bratty child.

"It's over, Red." Matthias's voice seeped through my soft sobs as he eased me onto his lap. My ass was on fire, and all I could think about was how bruised and welted it had to look. All I wanted to do was crawl under a blanket or huddle in a corner and cry myself to sleep. Instead, I buried my face in his chest to avoid facing him. I felt him take a deep breath, but he remained silent, allowing me time to gather myself before he spoke.

I was still silently sobbing, but I realized something different about it. It was cathartic. Almost spiritual in its ability to release the tension and frustration I had carried since Agent Daddy Kink had shown up on my doorstep a little more than a week ago. I'd done a lot of crying since then. None of it had felt like this.

Cleansing.

Sure, my ass hurt, but now that I was not writhing or wriggling, it didn't feel any worse than a horrible sunburn. I'd be sore as hell for a few days, that was for damn sure, but I doubted he'd left any permanent marks. It was more humiliating than outright painful.

"Look at me." Matthias's voice cut through the silence. I couldn't disobey him if I wanted to. He had a hold on me, one that reduced me to a whimpering, raw mess. He had so easily stripped me of my defenses and reduced me to tears in a way no one ever had before.

A small hiccup escaped me as I drew my gaze up to his face. My body was trembling, eyes glassy and bloodshot, nose dripping. I probably looked a sight.

"There were two parts to your punishment, Ava," he told me. "Do you understand what they are?"

Swallowing hard, I nodded. He hadn't just punished me for hitting him. He'd punished me for running away as well.

"Good." His voice hardened a bit as he shifted me on his lap so he could see me more clearly. "Never raise a hand to me again. Do you understand?" I mutely nodded. It hadn't been a smart idea, I knew that, but I'd just been so angry about how cavalier he had been about Maleah. I was lucky, if anything. Had it been Christian I'd punched; my punishment would have been a lot worse than just a belting.

"I want a verbal answer, please." He smirked as my eyes flared at him.

"Yes, it's clear."

"Good. Now—" His thumb caressed my concealer-caked

cheek, smearing the makeup. From his expression, he had seen the bruise. "Who did this?" I shook my head, attempting to bury my face in his chest again, but he easily gripped my chin to keep me from moving.

"Ava." He was warning me again, the note clear as day in his tone.

"My brother," I all but whispered. So low, I hoped he hadn't heard me. He didn't say anything, he simply let out another long sigh before he moved me from his lap, righting me on my own two feet before pulling up my yoga pants. I grimaced at the rough material against my sore bottom.

"Now, whenever I punish you, I want you to thank me for it."

He had to be kidding, but I wasn't in the mood to find out. Neither was my ass.

"Thank you."

"Sir," he added with a small smirk. My jaw tightened, lips thinning as I breathed through my nose, fighting the urge to snark at him.

"Thank you, sir."

"Good," He stood. "Now, Vasily will show you to your room, and we will talk about expectations in the morning."

"Expectations?" My tone held a note of skepticism. He sounded just like my father. Always with the expectations. What about my expectations of him? Did that even matter? Or was I simply a china doll to take off the shelf to be dusted before being put away again? I wanted to argue, put in my two cents, but one look from him quieted me.

"Yes, expectations," he affirmed as he nimbly sent a text from his phone. "You are in my world now, Ava, and there are certain things that come with that. But that is for tomorrow. It is late." I wanted to protest again, but the throbbing in my ass kept me in check. Instead, I simply nodded.

A few seconds later we were joined by one of Matthias's men. I recognized him from the night my father had sold me.

"Ava, this is my *Sovietnik*, Vasily." The man smiled down at me, his crystal blue eyes shining like a fresh storm as he took me in. What the hell were they feeding these men? Vasily, as Matthias called him, was almost a foot taller than Matthias, who stood at least six-foot-one. His long dirty-blond hair was tied up in a messy bun at the back of his head, and his angular jaw was covered in a bushy, yet well-maintained beard. The man was built like a giant with bulging muscles that were covered in a myriad of dark tattoos.

"Privet, Ava." I looked over at Matthias, somewhat confused. It sounded like he'd said preev-yet. Or something like that. Suddenly, I wished I had taken Russian instead of French in college. "It means hello, and please, call me Vas." He said it like hull-oh and Vahs.

"Vasily will show you to your room." Matthias didn't say anything after that, he simply nodded his head at Vas and walked from the room, his thumbs typing away furiously on his phone. Why was I suddenly disappointed he left? I should have felt a sudden relief, but now that he was gone from the room, I felt almost...unstable.

"This way." Vas led me out of the living room and to a pair of French doors that led into a large foyer. Another apartment? Geesh.

"What's a *Sovietnik*?" I stumbled over the unfamiliar word. It sounded like sah-veet-nik, but the way he had said it earlier was much more refined. If he noticed my abuse of his language, he didn't say anything.

"I'm his right-hand man," Vas explained as he opened the door to yet another one of the rooms. "The *Bratva* has a structure similar to the Italian Mafia, just with different titles and a few tweaks." When I didn't go to interrupt him, he continued, "Matthias is the *Pakhan*. The leader."

Pakhan was a term I was familiar with. I also didn't miss the fact that he called his boss by his first name. Vas continued, "Next comes the *Sovietnik*, that's me, and then the *Obshchak*. We're considered the 'two-spies.' The highest-ranking next to the *Pakhan*. Think of the *Sovietnik* like a counselor of sorts. Nicolai, our *Obshchak* is almost like a bookkeeper, collecting money and all that.

"Then there are the *Avtorvets*, or brigadiers as we call them in English. They are the enforcers out on the streets, and they keep track of the *Boyevik*s, or soldiers. It is mine and Nicolai's job to manage the brigadiers, and Matthias's job to manage us all."

"I didn't realize there was so much structure to your organization," I told him honestly as I drew my gaze to sweep around the room. Vas shrugged.

"Most don't. Now, get some rest. I put your bag in the closet, and Mia will be here in the morning to help you get ready." I didn't have a chance to question him further before the click of the door and the turning of a key told me I'd been effectively locked up for the night.

Again.

Taking a deep breath to center myself, I rummaged through my bag in the closet and slipped into an old T-shirt of Neil's, not bothering to put on a fresh pair of underwear. I didn't want the fabric to chafe against my skin.

Sighing, I settled myself on the large king-sized bed, letting the mattress that felt like a cloud lull me into what I could hope was a nightmare-free sleep. But I doubted it. Darkness always seeped into everything sooner or later.

CHAPTER ELEVEN

Matthias

I had to walk away from her. The feeling of her laying over my lap, her heated ass beneath the palm of my hand, had been enough to make my cock stand at attention. I wanted nothing more than to dip my fingers into her aching center and feel the wetness that was no doubt pooling there from her punishment. It hadn't escaped my notice when I held her that her pupils were dilated, nearly swallowing her emerald irises whole.

It was a dangerous game to play. Women were not something I often indulged in except to sate my primal urges. The women I saw weren't the type you date. They were merely arm-candy at an event or a hole to fill. Nothing more.

Having Ava here was a distraction. I knew this, but if I wanted to take Elias down, I had to play the "long game." If it weren't for her innocence, I would have shoved my cock into that tight pussy the minute I set my belt down. The thought of feeling her tight walls convulsing around me while I hammered into her from behind as the hot skin of her freshly spanked ass rubbed against my stomach was something I had imagined plenty of times over the past year.

I hadn't planned on punishing her so soon, but her defiance and physical outburst in the car could not go unanswered. Especially when my men had been watching from the front seat. They needed to see that I would do my job and discipline her for striking me. And she needed to understand that I was the one in control. Not her. Me.

Sighing, I stepped into my office and headed straight for the bar, pouring myself a healthy dose of whiskey. I took a swig and sank into the high-backed leather chair behind my desk. If only my father could see me now. He'd once called me weak, pathetic, a waste of space, before he threw me to the curb the first chance he got.

I'd been eleven when he left me out on the cold streets of St. Petersburg to fend for myself amongst the thieves, vagabonds, and murderers without a dime to my name and only the clothes on my back.

Now I was drinking a hundred- and twenty-five-thousand-dollar bottle of whiskey in an eighty-million dollar building that I completely owned with more than a hundred loyal men and women under my employ. Weak and pathetic, my ass. I'd built my empire with blood, sacrificing things in the process no other man would. I was just as ruthless now as I was fighting in the underground MMA rings that ran through Moscow when I was a teen.

"You're going to want to see this." I didn't need to look up to tell that it was Vas who had just unceremoniously thrown down a slim manila envelope on my desk without so much as a courtesy knock. Even Roman, my cousin, wasn't bold enough to just waltz into my office, even when the door was open. It wasn't defiance or disrespect with Vas, though. It was familial. Despite Roman being my cousin, we didn't know each other well enough. Not like Vas and I did. The two of us had practically grown up together since the age of sixteen when his father took me in off the streets and offered me training and a job.

He was a few years older than me, the brother I'd never had. He'd taken me under his wing, showed me the ropes, and helped me succeed in his father's training camp. A small compound he ran for up-and-coming men who wanted to join the ranks of the Brotherhood and had nowhere else to turn. Something I continued here in Seattle.

"Please," I commented dryly with a gesture of my hand. "Come on in. Make yourself at home."

Vas smiled. "Don't mind if I do." Out of the corner of my eye, I saw the fucker pouring himself a triple of my expensive whiskey, nearly gulping it down in one shot before refilling it. Tasteless neanderthal. Didn't matter what it was or how expensive, everything Vas drank was chugged like he was a frat boy at a rager.

"What the hell is this?" The corner of my mouth turned up in a snarl as I thumbed through the folder one document at a time. Image by image.

"Our spy had this dropped off not too long ago." Vas sank into the seat across from me, an ankle on his opposite knee, the arm holding his whiskey resting lazily on his thigh. "Some of it is the official documents Elias wanted dropped off, and the rest is from him. Wanted to make sure we had the full story of what happened over the last few days."

A slew of Russian curses loosed from my lips. The motherfucker had given me a certificate with the words, "Proof of Virginity" stamped on it in great bold red letters. He'd waited to have it delivered, too, instead of handing it over to me when I had been there to collect her.

Just like he had critically looked her over to make sure the bruising on her face was covered. The fucking coward. It took a great amount of self-control for me not to push back my chair and go to her room, demanding that she show me what other bruises she had obtained while back in their care.

The photos were even worse.

"Motherfucker," I snarled as I gulped down my whiskey. They weren't just pictures of Ava; some were of Maleah as well.

"Are you sure you want to go through with this, Matt?" Vas frowned. "I get it, Elias fucked us over. He's trying to make us look weak by selling our products right under our noses but—"

He didn't have to say it. But Ava was an innocent in all this. Just like her friend. The problem was that my plan wouldn't work without her.

"Elias didn't just fuck us over, Vas." I narrowed my eyes at him as I slammed the folder closed, the images burned into my mind even when out of sight. "He set us up. The fucker is working with someone, and it is more than just the Italians."

"So what?" He questioned. "You use her as collateral and then what?" Toss her aside? We both know you should have killed that piece of shit son that night instead of taking her. I mean, fuck, brother, look at what they've done to her. We always agreed that women stay out of it."

"I'm well aware of that," I hissed at him. "But this is different, and you know it. Plus, I don't plan on hurting her."

"Maybe not physically," he pointed out. "This is reckless, and you know it."

I clenched my jaw as I leaned back in my chair, my grip

tightening on the crystal glass in my hand. Neither of us had anything to say, both of us content to just sit for a moment in our own thoughts. Vas knew he was walking a fine line by questioning me. He was right, I knew this, but sometimes new lines had to be drawn in order to come out of the battle as the victor.

The survivor.

Someone was pulling Elias's strings, and it wasn't me anymore. Not fully anyway. I wasn't sure when he had begun cutting them or who was stringing him back up, but I would find out even if I had to use an innocent woman to do it. Over the past year, more and more of my shipments had been hijacked. Safehouses had been razed to the ground. My brothers were being murdered on the streets.

None of this could be tied back to Elias directly, but I knew it was him. He was smart, but not that smart. The man was desperate to get out from under me, to be his own man, or so he thought. Whoever his new puppeteer was would have something to say about that freedom when the time came. And that someone was targeting me directly, using him against me.

Ava was a Hail Mary. Her very existence was the key to bringing Elias down, and if that meant I'd have to break her to do it, then I would. Vas was right, we didn't use women as collateral, not unless they were deserving of it. Not unless they were willing pawns, which Ava wasn't. But I had no other choice. I wouldn't allow the empire I'd built with my own two hands, that stood because of the blood my men had shed, go up in flames.

"Did she settle in all right?"

Vas smirked.

"Yes," he assured me. "She's all tucked into bed. Antonio said her light went out about half an hour ago."

"Good," I muttered absently as I drummed my fingers on the glass.

"You're going to need to give her something to do, you know."

I raised a questioning brow at him. "What do you mean?" Vas chuckled.

"You can't just keep her locked away here forever, Matt," he pointed out as he got up to pour himself another glass of my expensive whiskey. Fucker always knew when I had the good stuff out. He was like a goddamn bloodhound with that shit. Wouldn't even touch the cheap shit. "She'll get bored."

"Your point?" The fact that he had one surprised me. She'd been here less than a few hours, and already he had a job for her.

"Elias said she went to college for education, right?" I nodded in confirmation. "Why not put her to work as a teacher at the compound? Sarah went and got herself knocked up by the *Boyevik* on the south side, so we're down a history teacher. Both Roman and Nicolai are there during the school day, and if anything, it keeps her out of trouble while you do business."

He had a fair point. My cousin Roman had been covering Sarah's class since she'd gone on maternity leave, but he was barely older than the kids in his class, and having him in the classroom left me one man short for combat training.

"She doesn't have any teaching experience."

Vas shrugged. "So? This is a girl who managed to slip out of a highly guarded house and survive on her own, with no outside world experience, I might add, for nearly a year before she was caught. And if those pictures are anything to go by, she's made of some pretty tough shit."

He was right. I doubted those pictures painted the entire story. No doubt Ava had experienced worse than what was in those photos. A weaker woman would have found other means of escaping that were more permanent. The girl was stronger than she looked. It showed in the way she had taken her punishment.

She may have squirmed and cried out while I spanked her. Fought and rebelled when I belted her ass. But she had ended her punishment with a class that many other women I had belted hadn't. There was a reason I used an escort service for my more carnal needs. They were paid to come back.

"Fine," I relented, leaning back in my chair with a sigh. "Who's monitoring her now?"

"Dima."

I suppressed a low growl. "Have all of her bedroom feeds sent through my phone and laptop. I don't want anyone else monitoring her there but me." Vas nodded.

"Will do," he said as he whipped out his cell phone to relay my orders to Dima. His response dinged a few seconds later. "Dima says it's done."

"Thank you."

Vas nodded as he stood, placing his empty glass on the bar top as he headed to the door.

"Do you honestly think using her is going to work?"

I resisted the urge to snap at him, knowing his question wasn't coming from defiance but actual curiosity.

"I do."

My *Sovietnik* bobbed his head one more time before he exited my office, leaving the door open. I took a deep breath as I pulled out my phone from my trouser pocket. I was still replaying her punishment in my head. The feeling of her pert ass beneath my hand. Her whimpers as my belt landed on her soft pale skin over and over kept running through my mind on repeat.

Dammit. My cock was throbbing as I pulled up the video

feed to her room. Ava was asleep on top of the comforter, belly down, wearing nothing more than a long faded gray T-shirt that had ridden up to expose her heated bottom.

The monster inside me roared to go to her. To take her. Possess her.

But I couldn't. Not yet. Especially after seeing that fucking certificate her father had made. I'd suspected she was a virgin even before that vile paper landed on my desk. She was too sheltered not to be. Even on the run, I still doubted that she would have risked her safety for something like sex. Ava seemed smarter than that.

Then again, she had used her mother's surname on her fake ID and hadn't bothered to fully change her first name. It was almost laughable how long she had managed to stay hidden. When I looked at all the pieces, though, it had been rather smart. Elias had been working under the assumption she was still in the state. No one suspected she had outside help, and the man couldn't fathom the idea that she had managed to get too far without money or any means of identification. Plus, the only thing that was under her alias was a plane ticket to New Mexico. After that, she must have paid cash.

So, maybe not so dumb after all.

I let out a frustrated groan as I left my office, my feet carrying me to my room, my eyes still focused on my phone. Quietly, I shut the door behind me. My room was directly connected to Ava's, but I doubted she'd figured that out.

Once inside, I threw the phone down on my bed before heading into the bathroom and turning on the shower. Disrobing, I tested the stream of water before I stepped inside, allowing the hot water to pelt down on me, relieving the ache in my shoulders.

I didn't understand my attraction to the girl. Since the

moment I saw her, she had put me under some kind of spell, and I couldn't make heads or tails of how.

Ava was beautiful, without a doubt, but I'd met and fucked plenty of beautiful women who had never held my attention like Ava did. I was half tempted to call on Katerina, one of my regulars, to come help relieve the pressure building inside me, but for some reason, the idea of her sucking me off disgusted me.

Maybe it was because we were kindred souls, Ava and I. Both rejected by the men we called Father in some form. Both traumatically lost our mothers at a young age. Both abused. Fuck, thinking of the way she fought me while I punished her had my heart racing. My hand wrapped around my cock as the image of her completely naked flashed through my mind. The hot water continued to pour down on me as I braced my forearm against the shower wall. Closing my eyes, I pumped slowly at first as I imagined her crying out as my hand made contact with her heated ass again and again. Her nipples hardening as the lines between pleasure and pain were drawn closer and closer together until she was practically begging me to fuck her.

I wanted nothing more than to spread her open, smell her, taste her, sink my cock inside her virgin cunt. The thought of the brilliant flare of defiance in her emerald eyes, dotted with golden flecks, staring up at me as her hot mouth wrapped around my cock, sucking me, had me pumping harder and harder.

Blyad'. Fuck.

I stifled a groan, biting my lip as I came, ropes of cum hitting the tiled wall of the shower, my cock throbbing in my hand as I squeezed the last bit out with a groan. This wasn't enough. It would never be enough. Because from the moment

I had laid eyes on her, I knew Ava Ward would be the only one who could truly sate my desires.

IT WASN'T long after six that I was woken by a long, slender hand caressing my bare chest. I laid there for a few moments, indulging in the soft feminine fingers massaging my skin, but as soon as they dipped lower, I sat up.

"I was just getting to the good parts," a lower feminine voice pouted from the edge of the bed. I chuckled, knowing full well that the last thing she wanted to do was service me. "You're no fun. I just wanted to get a peek."

"Don't you get a peek enough at your job?" I asked her as I swung my legs over the edge of the mattress.

"Yes," Valerie fell to her knees in front of me, slightly tugging on my briefs so it looked like I was exposed. "But my girls tell me it's legendary." This was our usual position when she came to me. To anyone spying, it would look like she was on her knees servicing me when really she was providing me with information only she could get.

Valerie was one of the best spies in the business. She used her escort agency to blackmail men and women into doing exactly what she wanted them to. Military, politicians, housewives, good ole Joe Shmoe. You name it and she would create dirt on them so deep they'd never dig their way out. She'd tried it on me when I had first come to the city. At that time, she had worked for another madam, a ripe old bitch who let her clients beat and rape the girls they chose to.

I'd killed the madam when I'd found out she had tried to gain blackmail footage on me, and then put Valerie in her place with a promise that she worked for me. The girl had easily agreed, and within a week had more intel than most spies could obtain in a month.

"It is," I teased her with a small smirk before turning serious again. "Did you find her? The girl?"

Valerie sighed, which wasn't a good sign. If Elias had already sold Maleah, it would be too late for me to obtain her without being obvious. If he hadn't, there was still a chance I could have one of my men purchase her at Elias's auction.

"You're not going to like it." Valerie pinched the bridge of her nose. She didn't like the fact that women were being sold like cattle. She'd been there herself. Now, she provided them with somewhere to go, and for those who didn't know anything else but the industry, she employed them. Gave them a chance to get a little power back. Be their own bosses. "She isn't going to auction. My source says that Elias sold her, privately, but they didn't know to whom. Apparently, it has all been hush hush."

She looked like she had more to say but wasn't sure how to approach it. I went to ask her what was on her mind when a noise caught my attention. As practiced, I buried my hand in her long blonde hair and pulled her toward my crotch, forcefully bobbing her head up and down like she was sucking my cock. I threw my head back a little, painting my face like I was in the throes of ecstasy.

It was the soft gasp that made me stop and look up. It hadn't been the door to the hallway that had been opened, but the one that connected my room to Ava's. Shit. I'd forgotten to lock it last night after I'd checked on her.

Ava stood frozen in the doorway; her hand clenched around the doorknob so hard her knuckles were white as her wide eyes took the two of us in. Her throat bobbed as she swallowed hard, and I could have sworn her eyes were glassy.

"Can I help you?" I raised a brow at her, my gaze cold as I

continued to bob Valerie's head up and down. The woman gave a long, drawn-out moan like she was enjoying sucking down air. Should have been an actress instead. Then again, escorts were pretty much just that.

"Umm..." Ava shook her head frantically before retreating into her room at lightning speed, the door slamming loudly behind her.

"Well, that was new," Valerie piped up when I let go of her hair. "Since when do you have women staying here?" Rolling my eyes, I stood up, gently moving around Val to lock the damn door. That was not meant to happen. Dammit. I'd planned to be somewhat standoffish with her, but the situation forced me to be colder than I had wanted. I hadn't expected her to be up so early, and I wasn't sure why I cared if she saw Valerie.

My plans for Ava didn't involve love. Simply obedience. I knew I shouldn't have let the hurt look on her face bother me, but it did.

"That," I snarled at the woman. "Is none of your business. Understood?" Valerie bit her lip and nodded, her eyes seeking the floor in natural submission. Sighing, I crouched down so I was at eye level with her. "I didn't mean to snap. I'm sorry." My fingers found her chin and gently lifted it so she was staring me straight in the eye. Something she had been trained for years as a sex slave to avoid.

"I shouldn't have probed." Valerie shrugged nonchalantly, but I could see the old her warring with the new her. "I'll see if I can dig up a little more and find out who Maleah was sold to."

"Thank you." I kept my voice low and nonthreatening to put her more at ease. Something she had taught me to do with the escorts she sent me if they got skittish or afraid.

"Can I ask you something?" Valerie swept her finger

through her long hair. She was a gorgeous woman, to be sure. With long tan legs that went on for days, high cheekbones, and full lips that made you want to devour her. Men loved her pert tits and round ass, but there was never any attraction there for me. She was a bit skinny for my taste and was more like a sister than anything else.

"Go ahead."

"I've never seen you look for anyone specific." Her fingers twirled around an errant piece of hair. "What's so special about this girl?" I sighed, running a hand down my stubbled face. Why was she important to find? Because I felt guilty about fate?

"Because she is important to someone else." Valerie nodded her head as if she understood. But she couldn't. Because no one had ever looked for her.

"The redhead?" It was just a guess, but an accurate one. I didn't answer. Instead, I placed a hand on the small of her back and led her from the room for one of my men to escort to the door. Seeing that she had touched a nerve, she simply gave me a small smile as a parting goodbye before closing the door behind her.

Not wanting to waste the early morning, I found some clean gym clothes, donning them easily along with my sneakers, and walked out of the room toward the elevators that led to the gym. Maybe hitting something would help me focus on the task at hand instead of dwelling on the redheaded beauty just beyond the other door.

CHAPTER TWELVE

Ava

I woke up in the unfamiliar bed to wetness between my thighs, my breathing labored, a light sheen of sweat covering my body. I sat up, wincing as the comforter beneath me brushed against my still sore ass. Nothing but a hazy fog remained of my dream, my sex dream. About Matthias. My sex dream about Matthias. God, what in the hell was wrong with me?

There was no denying the spanking he had given me last night had turned something on inside me. I'd gone to bed with a sore ass and a wet pussy, and despite how much I'd wanted to, I couldn't work up the courage to slip my fingers between my legs and work out the tension he'd created.

Not when I knew there was a guard just outside my door.

I couldn't remember much about the dream, but I still felt the ghost of his fingertips across my skin and the hot breath of his mouth on my soaking center as I screamed his name in the throes of passion as he brought me to new heights.

Yep. I had officially lost it. Who the hell had sex dreams about their captor?

I got up from the bed, reluctant to leave its warmth but needing to space myself from the thoughts it brought on. I wasn't sure what time it was; the room had no clock. There wasn't much light coming through the large, curtained window of my room, so I assumed it was probably still early.

Making my way into the bathroom, I noticed a set of toiletries laid out for me on the quartz countertop and gratefully opened the brand-new toothbrush and toothpaste that had been left for me. Neil pushing me to pack last night had me forgetting my basic toiletries. I splashed some cold water on my face when I was done and tied my mess of curls into a bun at the top of my head before inspecting myself in the mirror.

There was no point in hiding the bruise on my face any longer, not when he knew about it. The bruises around my neck were still a problem, though. Matthias didn't know about those or the ones on my thighs, but they were both easy to hide. I wondered if I shouldn't even bother covering them up now. I doubted Matthias would even bother doing anything about them.

Sighing, I walked to my closet and dug around in my bag. Archer hadn't bothered to look at what he was packing apparently because hardly any of it looked coordinated. Lucky for me, most of my leggings were black and would go with just about anything. I donned a simple pair of black legging with ruching along both thighs and a light gray sweater. It wasn't anything fancy, but then again, I wasn't the fancy type.

It was when I was digging around in the bottom for a pair of socks that I noticed it. A small black flip phone. It was old.

The outside was beaten and scuffed and peeling. I'd seen enough spy movies to know this was a burner phone. But who had placed it in my bag? Neil, on behalf of my father? Or Archer, so that I could contact him?

I picked it up and turned it over. On the back was a simple yellow sticky note with the words, "Tonight at midnight." That was it. Midnight? Seemed a bit too clandestine to be my father. Sounded more like it was Agent Daddy Kink's aisle. Guess I would find out. I set the phone back at the bottom of the bag, burying it beneath some of my clothes before I stood and left the closet.

Deciding to test fate, I tried the door to my room. Of course, it was still locked. Sighing, I scanned the room, taking a good look around to see if there was anything that would provide me any entertainment when the sight of another door caught my eye. I hadn't noticed it the night before, and it wasn't the door that led to the bathroom.

Curious, I approached it, wondering where it led. Maybe I could use it to escape. Pressing my ear against the door, I listened but didn't hear anything from the other side. Before I could stop myself, my hand was on the doorknob, turning it and quietly pushing the door open.

My eyes widened at the sight before me, and my mouth opened as I took in the scene. A man sat perched on the side of his large bed, head thrown back, eyes closed, and lips slightly parted with his hand buried in a woman's long blonde hair, bobbing her up and down on his member like a funko-pop.

Recognition dawned, and a small gasp escaped me as my fingers clutched the doorknob so tight, they ached. Matthias. Of course, my room was connected to his. I swallowed hard, past the lump forming in my throat as I stood frozen, unable to remove my gaze from the picture before me.

"Can I help you?" He raised an eyebrow at me, gray eyes cold as the woman continued to suck him off, not bothered by the fact that they now had an audience. The blonde gave a sultry moan, causing Matthias to smirk.

"Umm..." I was unsure of what to say. There was a war going on inside my mind that I didn't understand, and one thought was something akin to *"what the fuck, dude?"*. While the other ones were somewhere between wanting me to cry and trying to figure out why I gave a fuck.

Not wanting to prolong this awkward interaction any longer, I bolted from the room, slamming the door behind me as I went. I couldn't understand why there were tears in my eyes. It wasn't like we were together or anything. I'd known the man for less than twenty-four hours, but something about last night and the way he made me feel had me tied up like spaghetti on the inside.

Movement outside my bedroom door caught my attention. The blonde was leaving. A small amount of accomplishment rose in my chest knowing that I had ruined their morning, or maybe that was just leftovers from last night? Throwing my head back, I let out a frustrated groan. Why the hell was I even thinking about that shit? Who cared?

I didn't. That's who.

Keep lying to yourself. The inner voice in my head had its own opinion. Looking around my room, I saw there wasn't much to do. I didn't have a phone, and even if I did, I had only Libby to text, and I didn't have her number. Without much else to do, I threw open the curtains along one wall, revealing a long line of panoramic windows, and cozied up in the chair situated in front of them to watch the city beneath me come alive as I worked on a plan to escape yet another gilded cage.

And this time, I'd be sure no one could find me.

SOMETIME LATER, a knock at the door came before it was opened, revealing an elderly woman in her mid-sixties with short graying brown hair and electric blue eyes. She was a stout woman, pleasantly plump, with a round jovial face and gnarled hands that had seen years of work.

"Good morning, Ms. Ward." The woman's voice was deep, her cheerful tone matching the smile on her face as she let herself in the room. "I'm Mia, I run the house. I see you've found the toiletries that were left for you, good. I hope everything was satisfactory."

All I could do was mutely nod my head as the woman began bustling around the room, tidying up the bed and grabbing my dirty clothes from the bathroom where I had left them. I wasn't sure what to do or what was expected of me, so I simply sat in the chair, waiting for her to give me any kind of instruction.

My stomach growled audibly, and the woman stopped what she had been doing to look up at me and smile. It was such a stark contrast to the way Kendra's hired housekeeper, Lucia, treated me. Like everyone else in the house, she constantly approached me with a look of disdain, often refusing to help me with anything.

"I'm sorry," she apologized sheepishly. "You must be hungry. You're free to wander, of course. The kitchen is out your door, down the hall, and through the family room. There is a small buffet out. Help yourself, dear."

"Oh, okay." I was a bit taken back at her kindness and the fact that I would be allowed to wander the penthouse freely. Did Matthias honestly think I wouldn't try to make a break for it? "Thanks." She nodded her head at me, offering me another smile as I slipped out the door before she could change her mind and lock me back up.

Following her directions, I made my way through the penthouse toward the kitchen. It wasn't hard to find, and the smell of coffee and freshly baked bread wafting from that area made it even easier. The place was quiet and empty. I hadn't run into a single soul on my way to the kitchen, which had enough food laid out on its countertops to feed an army. Grabbing a plate, I placed a few fruits on it, along with a crescent roll, before pouring myself a generous cup of coffee in a way too small mug.

I realized something as I looked around for a place to sit. The penthouse was set up for a large family, but as far as I knew, Matthias didn't have any family to speak of. Everything I had seen so far could accommodate at least a dozen people, and it struck me that the emptiness would feel sort of lonely with no one to fill it.

"Good, you're up."

Dropping my crescent roll back onto the plate, I stopped and stared at Matthias. He wore a pair of black joggers that were slung low on his hips and nothing else. His broad chest was muscular and well defined, with just enough chest hair to make a woman swoon, but not enough that he looked like some weird caveman. His upper body was a palette of colorful tattoos that swept from the base of his neck to the knuckles of his hands. Sweat coated his pale European skin, and his dark brown hair was slicked back lazily.

I could feel my face heating up the longer I stared at him, and I quickly shifted my gaze back to my plate because all I saw when I looked at him was his head thrown back and the look of utter pleasure on his face from this morning. Some wild, unhinged part of me wanted to be that blonde woman on her knees for him. The sexy, luring temptress inside me needed to feel my lips wrapped around his cock, moaning my pleasure as he controlled the pace with his hand wrapped up in my curls.

Libby was right. I read way too many romance books.

Those desires, that need, they weren't right. Nobody feels something like that for their captor outside of some smutty mafia novel. This was reality, and honestly, it sucked.

"I'm up." But you already knew that. I kept that part to myself, remembering too well what would happen if I decided to smart off. My ass was already sore and still striped pink, and I didn't feel like a repeat.

Matthias nodded as he helped himself to a cup of coffee and some fruit before he sat down across from me at the small breakfast nook table I had found tucked away in the kitchen. The large formal dining table had been too daunting to sit at on my own.

"Did you sleep all right?" he asked as he took a bite of fresh strawberry.

"Just fine, thanks."

"Good." He smiled, and there was a beat of silence between us as we both finished off our breakfast plates. When he was done, he leaned back in his chair as he sipped thoughtfully on his coffee. "I hope you learned something from last night. I don't enjoy teaching lessons like that."

I gave a rather unladylike snort but didn't say anything. Matthias raised his eyebrows as he took another drink of his coffee. Like hell he hadn't enjoyed it. I had felt his rock-hard erection poking my stomach through his trousers. Not that I was going to tell him that, of course.

"Despite what you may think, Ava." He leaned forward, elbows on the small table as he clasped his mug. "I don't enjoy that kind of punishment. Not fully anyway. As much as having you strewn across my lap got my blood pumping, there wasn't any release in it for either of us. Where's the fun in that?"

"Looked to me like you got plenty of release this morning," I scoffed before I could catch myself.

"Jealousy is never a good color on anyone." Matthias smirked as he leaned back again. "Especially on you."

"I'm not jealous." I resisted the urge to roll my eyes. "I'd just appreciate it if you kept the door locked next time." The man had the nerve to chuckle.

"Maybe you shouldn't go opening random doors then, hmm?" I was surprised at how Russian he sounded at that moment. I'd noticed before that he didn't have the same linguistic cadence as Vas, whose accent was much thicker and more noticeable. "Don't worry, *Krasnyy*, she is nothing. I promise."

Krahz-nee. I tilted my head to the side at the Russian word, wondering what it meant before I shook my head. I didn't care what it meant. No stupid Russian nickname was going to sway me. Even if the sound of it coming from his mouth made my body tingle.

"I don't care how many women you have parading from your room," I snapped at him, crossing my arms against my chest. "Just keep the damn door locked."

"Watch your tone." Matthias scowled, his eyes darkening. "Do not make me remind you about respect."

It was on the tip of my tongue to tell him to go fuck himself, but since I didn't want another belting, I simply lowered my gaze to the table and nodded instead.

Coward. My inner bitch mocked inside my head. Pathetic fucking coward. But it wasn't the thought of having a sore ass that cowed me into keeping silent. God, I wish it was. But no, it was the fact that I didn't want to experience my body enjoying something that it clearly shouldn't. I mean, who in their right mind gets turned on by being belted?

Not me. Nope. But everyone knows that Denial isn't just a river in Egypt, and I was well on my way to owning a shit ton of property on it.

"Now," Matthias set down his empty coffee cup and leaned forward again. "I have some papers being brought over soon, and I want to go over expectations with you before that happens."

I lifted my gaze from the table and shot him a quizzical look. "Papers?" Matthias nodded.

"Just a few things that you need to sign before I send them to Elias."

My brow furrowed. "Like, yes, I'm agreeing to be your captive kind of signature, or my father's an asshole, sign here, kind of signature?"

The corner of Matthias's mouth twitched, and his stormy gray eyes lit up at my mocking. Even that barely-there smile had my heart stuttering and my breath catching in my throat. It made me want to see what he was like when he smiled for real.

"It's a surprise," he teased with a wink, and I swear to God, I almost lost it for a second. Then his face turned serious again. "First, just as we discussed last night, you will show respect to me and my men. You will be obedient, and when I ask you to do something, I want you to do it. No arguments."

Sounded more like he wanted a dog for collateral and not a human.

"Second, you will not go anywhere unaccompanied," he continued, getting up from the table to pour himself another cup and topping mine off as well. I muttered a weak thank you as I clutched the warm mug in both of my hands in an attempt to ward off the chill of the room. I didn't like the cold, it reminded me too much of the chill of the *stables*.

"Where would I go?" I inquired curiously as I brought the mug closer to my chest to absorb the heat.

Matthias sat back down across from me. "There will be times when you can leave to explore if you want. For right now, you have free range of the penthouse and the facilities on the floors below. Although this floor has mostly everything, including a cinema room. The gym is one floor down, along with the pool."

My eyes lit up at the word pool. I'd never been allowed in the one at my father's house, but I had gone to the small recreation center in the little town in Texas a few times. I couldn't swim, but I still enjoyed dipping my feet into the water.

"The last thing I expect from you is honesty, Ava." Matthias's stare was hard as he caught my eyes, showing me exactly how serious he was. "When I ask a question, I expect an honest answer. No lies, no subterfuge, nothing. If you lie, you will be punished. If you break any of the rules, you will be punished. Understood?"

I nodded my head, then caught myself and murmured a small acknowledgement, remembering that he wanted verbal answers.

"Good." He leaned forward with hooded eyes, his mouth opening to say something more when the jingle of the doorbell sounded throughout the house, interrupting him before he could start. "Hold that thought."

When he came back, he wasn't alone. Following behind him was Vas and a thin, gangly-looking man in his fifties with thinning black hair and a wide smile. His suit was a bit too small for him and hung above his ankles, but that didn't surprise me. He was at least a good head taller than Matthias, making him close to six-five, if not taller.

His head nodded enthusiastically at whatever Matthias was saying to him in Russian, and when they finished talking, his eyes scanned the room, landing on me. His smile widened even further, and his light eyes sparkled as he stepped forward and held out his hand to me.

"You must be the bride."

CHAPTER THIRTEEN

Ava

Did he just say bride?

What the hell was in that coffee? I was hallucinating. That had to be it, because there was no way in hell that man just said what I think he said.

Or—maybe he thought I was someone else. That was it! He probably thought I was the fiancée of one of the men. Pigs would fly before I would be marrying Matthias fucking Dashkov. I'd rather get eaten by piranhas. Or sharks. Forget it.

"Nope." I shot him a wide smile. "Not the bride. Good luck finding her, though." Clutching my coffee mug to my chest, I pushed the chair back as I made to stand, but Matthias's hand clamped down on my shoulder, forcing me to stay seated.

At least he didn't spill my coffee. That was a cardinal sin. I looked up at him with narrowed eyes, struggling with the urge to punch him in the face. No matter how handsome he was.

Trust me, it was hard. Like finding good porn hard.

"Ben, meet my soon to be wife, Ava," Matthias introduced, his tone broking no room for arguments. Oh, I'd still be arguing, all right. "Ben is my lawyer, as well as an ordained priest." Good for him. That wasn't changing shit for me. He could be the Pope for all I cared, I still wasn't going to be anyone's wife.

"I'm not marrying you," I hissed at my captor, setting my coffee down as Ben approached the table, setting his briefcase on the oak top while Vas hummed a low tune of "Here Comes the Bride."

Russian bastard.

Matthias's full, pale pink lips turned up in a grin, and I swear to all the coffee gods my panties just about combusted. The simple expression made him look years younger and brightened his stormy eyes.

"Of course you are." That statement was said with finality, but the fucker was still grinning. There was no way my coffee wasn't spiked.

"No, I'm not." I crossed my arms against my chest. "I can say it in two languages if that helps. No and noh. Hell, I'll even throw in a third so you can understand me better. Nah." His grin faded, replaced by mild amusement, but I could see his hand twitching and the hard lines of his forehead puckering.

"Let me make one thing very clear, Ava." He leaned toward me, hands gripping the arms of my chair on either side of me as his gaze bored into mine. "You will sign the papers that make you my wife, and you will do it with a smile on your face, or you will find out exactly what happens to bad little girls in this house. Is that clear?"

No clearer than muddy waters, but okay, sure pal.

"Why?" I could tell the man wasn't used to being questioned, but that wouldn't stop me. No more sidelines for me.

If he wanted me to sign a piece of paper that would chain me to him, I wanted to know why. Matthias Dashkov didn't do anything without a reason, and I wanted to know how this union benefited him.

"At least tell me that. Why, after knowing me less than twenty-four hours, would you want to marry me?"

"I don't need to explain myself to you, Red." His face darkened as he leaned in even closer, our noses practically touching. His breath mingled with mine as his gray eyes captured mine. "All you need to do is what I say. That *is* it. Or does your ass need reminding of what happens when you defy me?"

"This is insane," I murmured, shrinking back in the chair to put some distance between us. "What do you have to gain? I don't mean anything to him. I won't inherit anything. This is stupid."

He ran the back of his hand across my unbruised cheek before taking my chin in his grasp. I brought my hands up to his chest to push him away, but his other hand buried itself in my hair, wrenching my neck back.

I stilled.

"Obedience, Ava." He brought his lips to my ear, his warm breath causing my skin to break out in goosebumps and a shiver to roll down my spine. "I requested your obedience, and this is what I get? Defiance?" Tears gathered at the corners of my eyes, my chin trembling as I fought back the redness seeping into my cheeks at the heat radiating from his body as he crowded my space.

My body was confused, warring between surging desire and the cold sweep of bitter resignation.

I could fight him, but to what end? He'd just redden my ass with his belt and still make me sign the papers.

"I just want to understand." I lowered my gaze, hating how small my voice sounded. Matthias let out a frustrated sigh as he pulled away.

"You don't need to understand, *Krasnyy*." There was that nickname again. "You simply need to obey. Show me that you can do that, and we will discuss this later."

My heart was thumping erratically in my chest, which felt constricted as I tried to remember to breathe. I stood on shaky legs to make my way around to the other side of the table where my new fate awaited.

What would my father do once he found out I had been married to Matthias Dashkov? Would he hurt Libby like he hurt Maleah? Ben handed me a pen as I stared down at the damning document laid out before me.

There was no pomp or circumstance, simply two men condemning me to yet another life in chains. I would be forever bound to Matthias. Part of me thought I should be happy to be out from under my father and brother. But instead of elation, I felt like there was now an anchor tied around my ankle, dragging me down into the depths of the unknown.

Our names were neatly scrawled in handcrafted calligraphy. It didn't escape my notice that Matthias's name was already signed. The expensive fountain pen trembled in my shaky hand as I lowered the tip of it toward the ornately printed paper. Vas said something that made Ben laugh in amusement, but it was all just white noise to me now.

"Please don't do this." A few tears dropped from my eyes, landing on the paper below, but it didn't mar the neat scroll that was permanently etched into the ivory cardstock. The room went quiet.

"Ava—" Heat was suddenly at my back, and his smell enveloped me. Old leather and pine. Why were those scents so intoxicating? "Sign." One of Matthias's arms banded around my waist while the other reached out to wrap around my right hand, guiding the pen to the paper.

"I can't...please..." It was useless, though. The minute the pen met the paper, I signed. My signature shaky and jilted compared to Matthias's large swooping scrawl. A small sob escaped my lips as I dropped the pen to the table, the loud thud signaling the end of one prison sentence for another.

"Wonderful." Ben's gleeful voice made me want to break out into a full-on crying session or possible mass murder, but I managed to hold on to both urges. Barely. "Well, I now pronounce you man and wife. You may—"

The rest of Ben's sentence was lost to me as Matthias claimed my lips in a possessive kiss. His tongue teased the folds of my lips, seeking entrance, which I attempted to deny. He growled low in his chest before his teeth sank into my full bottom lip hard enough to elicit a gasp. Taking the opportunity, his tongue swept into my mouth, plundering it, taking my first kiss by force. Just like he had everything else. There was nowhere I could hide in this kiss, and I couldn't help the wanton moan that escaped me as he continued to explore my mouth.

When he pulled back, I was breathless, and my face was flushed. He must have seen something in my expression when he pulled back because his face fell when he looked down at me. I darted past him, catching him off guard. He didn't have enough time to grab for me as I sprinted out of the kitchen toward the safety of my room.

Safety. That word didn't mean anything anymore. Not after years of abuse and neglect. The only place I had ever felt safe was in the arms of my mother as she read me a bedtime story or when she was teaching me to cook.

She had been a marvelous cook, my mother. I used to stand on one of the stools in the kitchen and watch in utter fascination as she created recipe after recipe like she was a witch, and the ingredients were her potions.

Avaleigh Moore had been a happy, safe child brought up in a house filled with love, until her father took her in and changed her name. Avaleigh Ward had been a scared, pitiful shadow wanting nothing more than to escape her gilded cage.

The question was: who would Ava Dashkov be?

CHAPTER FOURTEEN

Matthias

"Well, that sure was something." Vas couldn't keep from beaming as my new bride darted from the room like it was on fire. The panic in her eyes after I had taken brutal possession of her first kiss almost made me feel like an utter bastard. It was the only reason I let her slip away instead of forcing her to stay by my side. "I can't remember the last wedding I went to where the bride ran after the ceremony. Or whatever this was. Might need to work on your kissing skills, man."

I shot him a withering look as I watched Ben pack up the contents of his suitcase. "She'll get over it." Ava would have to get used to the idea of being my pawn. This wasn't about romance or love, this was about convenience. She'd be awarded certain freedoms and niceties if she remained obedient.

"Oh, I'm sure she will," Vas snickered. "I mean, how

could she not? The romantic thought you put into this must have had her in tears...nope, wait, that definitely wasn't it."

Closing my eyes, I counted backward from ten to keep from reaching out and strangling the man I called brother. Now was not the time for his sarcasm and dry wit.

"I'm sure every girl dreams of being shanghaied into marriage at the breakfast table," Vas continued happily as he bit into a crescent roll. *Choke on it, traitorous bastard.* He was having way too much fun at my expense. "Fuck, we should have taken pictures for the cover of Vogue. I can see the headline now..."

"Shut it, Vasily. Before you end up on patrol duty." Vasily quieted, but the bastard was still grinning from ear to ear while he noisily chomped down on his breakfast.

"Sir, what do you want me to do with the paperwork Ward sent over?"

My eyes darkened as I let a feral grin stretch across my lips. Elias was expecting the collateral paperwork signed by Ava to be brought back tonight, but I had other plans. At first, the plan was to send him the marriage certificate, but with the information I had gained over the past year, I didn't want to put all my cards on the table just yet. I'd use it as the ace up my sleeve later when he thought the house held all the cards.

I'd be sending him something much better. A message he wouldn't be likely to forget anytime soon.

"Nothing." I shook my head. "Keep it on hand, but I've got other plans for what to send him." Vas groaned as he poured himself a fresh cup of coffee. The bastard knew me too well. We were always on the same wavelength. Sometimes, he was even a few steps ahead. He reminded me of that little man called Radar from *MASH*. We used to watch that on our old television back in Moscow.

"Jesus, Matt," Vas huffed. "If you don't send that paperwork back, you're declaring war." I simply grunted. War didn't bother me, I'd been in plenty, and the outcome was always the same. I came out the victor.

"Give Dima the go-ahead for tomorrow," I ordered him. "Tell him that the plan is a go. Choke Elias out of the port and empty the containers. I want everything taken back to the warehouse." Vas nodded before pulling out his phone to call Dima. My attention turned to Ben.

"File the marriage certificate but make sure the clerk keeps their mouth shut. Pay them off if you have to," I instructed him. "I don't want it getting back to Elias before I'm ready." Ben gave a short nod as he grabbed up his briefcase.

"Got it, boss." He smiled as he clapped me on the back. "Congratulations." Resisting the urge to roll my eyes, I just grunted at him as he left the kitchen whistling a damn wedding tune of his own.

"What the hell has that man so gleeful today?" The question was more for myself, but Vas, who'd hung up with Dima, caught what I'd muttered, and a wicked gleam appeared in his dark eyes.

"You don't know?" My second in command inquired, more than a bit amused at the fact that I was missing something going on under my roof.

"Know what?" I was in the dark about something, and I didn't like that. A *Pakhan* should never be in the dark when it concerned his men. That was how mutinies happened without warning.

"I can't believe you don't actually know something." Vas smiled as he let out an exaggerated sigh of happiness. "Just let me take in this rare moment."

"Vasily," I warned him, but there was little heat behind it. "Patrol duty is still a thing."

"Spoilsport." The man rolled his eyes, pretending to pout. What had I done in a past life to get stuck with this fucker? "The men all took bets on whether you'd marry her first or fuck her first. Then we took bets on how long it would be before either of those things happened. Ben won the first bet and Janice down in accounting won the second. She had very little faith in you, sir."

"You've got to be fucking kidding me."

"Nope." Vas popped the *P* as he grinned smugly. "Ben was the only one crazy enough to think you'd marry her before you fucked her. Said you were a 'proper' gentleman. We all laughed at him for that, but our loss is his gain."

"Gambling addicts," I grumbled with a shake of my head to try to hide the smile that had snuck up on me at their antics. "The lot of you." Vas shrugged.

"It was too good an opportunity to pass up." Shaking my head one last time, I made my way out of the kitchen, Vas on my heels.

"Tell Mark I need that information on her brother," I told him as we made our way to the elevator. My entire operation ran out of this building. There were thirty-two floors, my penthouse at the top, with the pool and gym one floor down. The floor below that housed my security barracks and one floor beneath that held several suites for visiting guests. Everything was completely secure, using a mix of personalized access codes and fingerprint identification.

There was a gun range on the lower levels, along with a parking garage, and everything else in between was dedicated floors to different parts of my enterprise.

As much as I wanted to partake in my new wife, there was work that still needed to be done, and I wanted to give her enough time to settle down and come to terms with our new arrangement. As much as I loved the fight, I didn't want to take her by force if I didn't have to.

I wouldn't deny that I was an utter bastard for pulling the rug out from under her like that. And for ignoring her questions, but that was something she would have to come to terms with. I was the one in charge. I was the one who made the decisions needed to keep her safe. My plans required that she be my wife, but there was no need for her involvement in anything else. Not if I could help it.

Her job was to keep our home, keep me satisfied, and one day provide an heir to take my place. It was that simple. That easy. But something gnawed at the back of my mind as I discussed the next steps in the takeover with Vas. It was telling me that nothing was ever easy, and Ava would sooner or later prove to be the chink in my armor.

That was something I could not allow.

VAS WAS busy texting Mark about Christian's whereabouts tonight as I sat at my "official" office desk on the fifth floor going over accounts. The shithead was known for visiting some of the shadier gentlemen's clubs, the ones that, if you paid enough, didn't ask questions about the girls' conditions when they were returned. Given the state of Ava's face and neck, I wasn't surprised.

I'd been working with Valerie on setting up one of her girls with him, I just needed Mark to confirm where the fucker was going to be. The boy had proven to be a useful asset. Just like I'd predicted.

I could still taste my new wife on my lips. She tasted like warm vanilla and cinnamon. When I had pulled away, I could see the flicker of arousal in her eyes as her body and mind warred against each other.

My cell phone vibrated on my desk. It was Nicolai, I had left him upstairs with Ava. Hitting accept, I brought the phone to my ear.

"Sir."

His standard greeting, no matter how many times I had told him he could call me by my first name. Something reserved only for my inner circle. I'd met Nico while fighting in Moscow's underground MMA circuit. We'd been on opposing sides a few times, but the older man had taken me under his wing and had shown me the ropes. I'd gotten Tomas to take him on as a soldier, giving him the chance to earn his way up in the Brotherhood, just like me. Now, he was my *Obshchak*. He and Vas oversaw my brigadiers. Kept them honest, collected my cut, and in some cases, spied.

The one thing they didn't do was mete out punishment. I did that myself. Tomas taught me that a man who makes the law should be the one to deliver its punishment. It was a lesson that stayed with me.

Nicolai also oversaw my nightclubs and gentlemen's bar. The man had a talent for making them thrive, and I wasn't going to let that go to waste. He was a wiz when it came to laundering money through our legit businesses as well.

"We have a problem," Nico continued solemnly.

Since he was the one I'd left to monitor Ava this morning, I could guess what the problem was. Although I was unsure of how much trouble Red could get into being locked inside a penthouse.

"What happened?" Had she managed to somehow escape from right under my nose? I doubted that. This building was more secure than the White House, and unless she could fly, there was no getting out. Plus, Nico took everything he did seriously. He was a stoic soldier, having learned over time to keep most of his emotions under a carefully crafted mask of indifference so no opponent could read him like an open book.

"Mia moved over Ava's duffel bag to your room like you requested," Nico started. "When she unpacked her things, she noticed a black flip phone hidden beneath some of her clothes with a note attached with a call time. Tonight, at midnight."

"Fuck." Vas looked up from his phone when my fist slammed against the desk, hard, rattling everything on it. "Did you say anything to her about it?"

"No," he replied easily. "I don't think she realized Mia moved it, and I didn't want to approach the situation without talking to you first." I nodded my head and sighed. That was good. I didn't want her to know we had it. Not yet.

"Good," I praised him. "See if you can track down where the cell phone rings to without alerting whoever is on the other end. Get Mark involved if you have to." My fingers drummed on the top of my oak desk as I thought about what to do with my little spy.

"Also, have Mia pick out some clothes for Ava and have them delivered before dinner tonight." Nico acknowledged the order before hanging up the phone.

"Problems in paradise?" Vas's eyebrows quirked in amusement. "Honeymoon phase over already, boss?"

I ignored that. "Mia found what looks to be a burner phone in Ava's bag." Vas groaned as he slid his phone into his pocket. "I'm having Nico see if he can trace its origin, but apparently it's some rather old tech. So, I'm not holding out for much."

"We know who gave it to her."

He was right. The only person who could have given her

that phone was fucking Elias. It didn't surprise me he had forced Ava to spy for him. I doubted she was doing it willingly. Maybe I could use this to my advantage. I would just need to ensure that Ava complied with my demands. If Elias thought he could use her as a spy, he was dead wrong.

MIA WAS WAITING NERVOUSLY for me when I stepped off the elevator. She was more than just a housekeeper here. Mia ran the entire house, including the domestic side of the training compound, which was everything from hiring the chefs and other domestic staff to ensuring rooms were prepped for guests.

The woman even had her own office, not that I could ever get her to use it. I could barely get her to keep hired staff inside of the penthouse. Mia liked to handle everything that went on in my personal space herself instead of leaving it to outside help.

"What happened now?" I asked as I handed her the suit jacket I had changed into earlier in my office. I always kept a few spare suits down there in case I didn't make it back to my room after the gym.

"She hasn't come out of her room all day or eaten anything since breakfast, Matt," Mia frowned as she hung up my jacket in the closet next to the door as a reminder to send it out for dry cleaning. "I sent in a tray for lunch, but when I went to check on her, it was still untouched, and she hadn't moved from the bed."

"Is she still in her room?"

Mia nodded. "Matt, be easy with her. She is not used to all this."

"Don't worry about that, Mia," I tell her.

"She is scared," Mia offered as a gentle reminder of something I already knew. "Be gentle with her. From the looks of it, that girl has already been through hell." I ignored her comments as I made my way toward Ava's room.

"Please make sure dinner is ready on time." Mia let out a long sigh before turning back toward the kitchen without another word. I didn't need a lecture about Ava at the moment. Not when she had been keeping a secret buried in her duffel bag. Ava was nothing more than a pawn and maybe some much-needed stress relief, but that was it.

Not bothering to knock, I entered her room through the interconnecting doors.

There were no lights on, and the curtains were shut tightly against the setting sun. The light from my room scattered the blanket of shadows, illuminating her slim figure. She was lying atop her ivory comforter, a pillow clutched to her chest, eyes closed.

"Ava." I stepped into the room, leaving the door ajar. "Why are you laying in the dark?" She didn't lift her head to acknowledge me.

Instead, she simply sighed deeply before shrugging. "I didn't realize it had gotten so late."

"You didn't eat lunch." I was pointing out the obvious since there was a tray of untouched food sitting on the nightstand next to the bed, but I didn't care. My palm twitched when she merely shrugged. Again.

"Wasn't hungry."

"Ava." Her name was a warning. Not eating wasn't going to be tolerated. If she thought she could gain my sympathy or that I would change my mind if she threw some sort of Gandhi-like tantrum, then she was wrong. "I will not have you starving yourself to make some kind of point."

"For your information." She sat up, brushing back the

stray hair that had escaped her messy bun. She looked a mess. Her emerald eyes were glassy and bloodshot, nose stuffy and red from crying, no doubt. Not that she gave a fuck how I saw her. Ava didn't seem the least bit bothered that she wasn't in a state of perfection.

That act itself was refreshing. Ava was genuine and open and not hidden behind layers of subterfuge. Her clothing choice was comfortable over fashion, her makeup, now that she wasn't hiding the evidence of her abuse, was minimal. She wasn't trying to lure me in or seduce me, she was simply being her. The only thing she knew how to be.

"I wasn't trying to make a point. I didn't eat because I was upset. Some neanderthal thought it was a good idea to force me to marry him against my will. So, excuse me if the thought of being your wife made me lose my appetite."

Khristos. Christ. My feet advanced farther into the room until I was standing just inches away from her, staring down at her small form lying on the overly large bed.

"You will eat when you are given food, Ava." She glared up at me, the gold flecks in her emerald eyes lit up with her anger. God, I loved seeing that. Her defiance was like fuel to my fire. The need to tame her. Break her. It heightened the game I was playing with my control, stoking the flames of my primal desire.

"I'm not your pet, Matthias," she hissed up at me. "You can't just order me to eat. Especially when I'm not hungry. You may have forced me to marry you, but I won't submit to you like I'm some kind of dog and you're my master."

The bed dipped under the weight of my knee sinking into the plush mattress, my body leaning over hers, causing her to lean back into the pillows, effectively trapping her beneath me. Ava flinched when my hand came up to gently caress her unbruised cheek, her breath coming out in short pants. My gaze filtered over her face, taking in every expression as I ran my fingers down her neck. She swallowed hard as my featherlight touch caused her eyes to darken and her tongue to dart out to wet her lower lip.

I wondered if she knew she had these reactions to me.

"Dinner is at eight." I let my fingers slip down the exposed skin of her chest that wasn't covered by her sweater. "Mia bought you a dress for tonight. Wear it."

Standing, I cast one hard stare down at her before turning and walking back into my room before she could argue. I shut the door behind me, making sure to lock it. Not that it mattered anyway.

Soon it would be her room as well.

CHAPTER FIFTEEN

Ava

I stepped into the dining room at approximately eight. The same moment as Matthias, who was coming out of his office on the other side. He stopped when he saw me, his steel-cut eyes roaming my body in the black form-fitting dress Mia had purchased for me. I'd tried to refuse, telling her that it was much too provocative for me, but she wouldn't hear it.

He was still wearing his white button-down and his pressed black slacks, but he had lost the tie, and the first few buttons at his neck were undone, revealing the ink below.

"You look beautiful enough to eat, Red," he complimented with a wolfish smile as he stepped farther into the room. The knee-length black dress fit tight and had wide shoulder straps and a gold zipper that ran the length of the dress. My red curls were secured to one side, the excess running over my shoulder.

"Thanks." I tried for a smile, but it wavered as he pulled

out a chair for me at the table, gesturing for me to sit. His eyes were constantly surveying everything around him, picking up on small cues that I had no doubt few others saw. If he thought I didn't know he was studying me, he was a fool. I saw everything he did.

The moment Matthias had me tucked into my chair, Mia came through the kitchen carrying two steaming trays full of what looked to be some sort of small dumplings. My mouth watered at the savory smell of meat wafting through the air.

"*Vereniki*," Mia informed me. "They are filled with pork. I boil them, then fry them for a crispier taste." I smiled up at the woman, eager to dig in. As much as I wasn't hungry at lunch, I was now, and my stomach grumbled to prove it.

She dished a few on my plate, sweeping some sour cream from a dish to go along with it. Matthias had already begun digging in, so I did as well. I dipped the *vereniki* into the sour cream before taking a bite. My eyes widened as a burst of flavor erupted on my palette. The crispness of the fried dough mixed perfectly with the minced meat and various herbs, creating a savory flavor that had me digging in for more.

Mia brought out a few more dishes, none of which I recognized. My taste for cuisine was limited to whatever Kendra's chef cooked up and the BBQ the bar sold in Texas. Most of it was close to Russian, and she easily explained each dish to me as she served it.

After the *vereniki* came a red, chunky soup called borscht that was made of beets, cabbage, beef, and a few other various vegetables. It was rich and hearty and warm. The borscht was served with *draniki*, which was essentially a potato pancake. This was then followed by *medovik*, a honey cake, for dessert.

By the time the meal was done, I was stuffed and ready to go back to my room, but Matthias apparently had other plans.

"Come, *malyshka*." Great, a new nickname I couldn't

understand. Just what I needed. Matthias held out his hand for me, and I took it, too full and too tired to argue. He led me out of the dining room and into a small seating area just off the main room.

It was cozy. A small fire was going in the large, marbled fireplace, casting an eerie glow on the low light of the room. Two large high-back chairs sat opposite it with a small table between them. Next to them sat a black leather loveseat.

"Sit." Another command. It was always commands with him. He didn't ask, he ordered, and I hated it. I'd been ordered around my entire life. I didn't know what in me thought it would change now that I was out from under my father, especially with someone like him. The clanking of crystal drew my attention to where he was busy pouring something into two glasses.

Alcohol. I sat my ass down on the sofa. Matthias turned and walked toward me, handing me one of the glasses half full of the beautiful amber liquid known as whiskey. I might not have been a liquor connoisseur, but I knew the good stuff when I smelled it, and this smelled like heaven. Taking a sip, I relished the burn as it slid down my throat, filling me with warmth.

"Thank you." Another sip, another light sigh. This was heaven.

"Make it last, Ava," Matthias rumbled from his spot on the other side. "This will be your last until you can show me you won't delve back into old habits."

I froze, the crystal glass at my lips, the honeyed liquid just mere centimeters from my lips. Old habits? It wasn't possible for Matthias to know what my old habits were. No one did.

"I don't know what you mean." It was a weak denial, even to my ears. Matthias smirked.

"What do you remember of your trip back from Texas?"

He inquired curiously as he sipped on his own whiskey. "Anything?"

Of course, I didn't remember anything. My brother had me drugged the entire trip. I'd woken up in that cell with Maleah four days later. Then again— I'd been drinking at least a bottle a day since I'd wound up in Texas. Courtesy of being a bartender and having access to an all-night liquor store. After a while, it had become more and more frequent. One bottle became two, sometimes more.

Soon, I wasn't able to go a day without—well, damn.

So much for being the brightest crayon in the box. Now that I looked back on it, I hadn't once had a case of the shakes or the sweats. No trembling or withdrawals. I hadn't just been drugged; I'd been detoxed. *Well shit.*

"How do you know about that?" The only two people who were with me were Christian and Neil and maybe a few guards.

Matthias smirked. "I have my sources. But I also had one of my men follow Christian, the incompetent fool." He set his glass down on the table next to him. "After you were seized, my man had a look around your place. Quite telling."

"So, you're a stalker as well as a perv," I snarked as I gulped down the rest of the whiskey, grimacing as it slid down my throat. Too much at once.

Matthias just shrugged. "I let you have that glass as a peace offering. But it is your last, Ava," he warned darkly. "I won't have a drunk for a wife. Understood?"

I wanted to say something snarky. If he didn't want a drunk for a wife, then maybe he shouldn't have married one, but I couldn't find it in myself to do that. Instead, I opened up. Just a little, so he could see that I wasn't a drunk for no reason.

"It was the only thing that kept the nightmares at bay." That was my confession. The one thing I was offering up to him about me so he wouldn't just see me as someone who was useless or worthless. Drinking was the only thing I could find that would drown out the noise, the screams, the pain.

"No more." His eyes were hard steel, and I got the message loud and clear.

"No more," I assured him.

"Good." His hand dug into his trouser pocket, but his eyes stayed glued to mine. I wanted to see him smile again like he had this morning. The action lit up his eyes like a winter snowstorm, his full lips stretching across his handsome face, showcasing his hidden dimples. However, the look on his face now told me there wouldn't be any smiling in the immediate future.

"Now, Ava." He took a deep breath before letting it out. "Do you have something you want to tell me?"

Red flag. Red flag. Danger, Will Robinson, danger. Alarm bells were going off in my mind. People only posed that question when they knew you had something to hide. It had been my father's favorite trick when I was a child to get me to confess to something he knew nothing about.

I doubted Matthias was using it in that same manner now. Whatever he wanted me to confess to, he already knew what it was. Swallowing back the lump in my throat, I shook my head at him because I honestly didn't know what he wanted me to confess to.

That I'm a virgin? I highly suspected he already knew about that little tidbit of information. Maybe he'd found out that my father wanted me sleep with him for secrets? Or had he caught me snooping in his room earlier? Or—

"Did you honestly think I wouldn't find this?" My mouth dropped open as he pulled out the black flip phone I had been storing in my duffel bag. Dammit. I knew I should have hidden it somewhere else. "Do you know what happens to spies in my house, Ava?"

Nope. And I didn't want to find out. So, I did the only thing I could think of. I'd probably regret it later. I threw the crystal glass at him and made to flee. Because there was no way in hell I was going to find out what he did to spies.

CHAPTER SIXTEEN

Matthias

Ava made it exactly four steps before I caught her by the hair. My anger broke like a dam, the waves crashing over me like a battering ram as my fingers gripped on to her silky threads and pulled her back into my chest. She cried out in pain, but the little vixen kept fighting me.

"Enough of this, Ava," I growled into her ear as my arms banded around her to keep her still. "You and I are going to have a conversation."

"I'm not talking to you."

"Yes, *malyshka*, you are," I hissed. "And if you use that pretty mouth of yours to lie to me, I will use it for something other than talking."

"Let me go." Her words were ridiculous. She knew I wouldn't be letting her go. Not now. Not ever. She was mine. "I hate you."

"I already know this, Red," I assured her. "But that will

change nothing. Now, we can have this conversation here, in this comfortable space, or I can make this very uncomfortable for you. Which do you prefer?"

"Neither. Just let me go." Well, this was getting rather repetitive. Sighing, I unwound my arms and turned her to face me. Her small hands came up to shove at my chest, but I simply caught them in my grasp and held them at the small of her back with one hand.

I brought the other to wrap around her neck, holding her in place as I lowered my head until our lips were barely a breath apart. She struggled in my stony grip, but I simply tightened it, squeezing just enough that she could feel how easy it would be for me to cut off her oxygen. Not that I would, but I needed to scare her into settling down.

And she did. Her green eyes widened, and her pupils dilated as she stilled and stared up at me. Her lower lip trembled, and her teeth came out to nibble on the plump flesh to keep it from quivering. That was all it took for the rope to snap on my resolve.

I pressed my lips against hers. Her body remained stiff and unyielding, and she shrunk back in my hold as much as she could, but I wasn't having that. Exhaling, I pulled away by several inches before claiming her mouth again. She whimpered when my fingers came up to grip her jaw, digging into the tender flesh just enough to get her to open her mouth.

My actions were forceful as my tongue plunged inside, swirling against her own, teasing her. She tasted like warm vanilla and notes of whiskey, enticing my tastebuds. Ava moaned against me, her body melding to mine as it responded to my kiss.

Hissing, I pulled away from her, my fingers probing my now bleeding lip. She had bitten me, the little vixen. My eyes blazed with fury as I picked her up and threw her, fighting and screaming, over my shoulder and moved toward the bedroom.

She kicked out, struggling to grab at anything within reach. The sound of several priceless pieces of art being knocked about forced me to react. I brought my palm down on her ass with several brutal smacks, one after the other, chuckling as she moaned several times.

"Ouch. Don't do that," Ava complained, pummeling her small hands on my back. It was light, like a kitten batting at a new toy.

"Fight me all you want, Ava," I chuckled darkly. "I gave you a choice, and now you have to face the consequences."

"Bastard."

I had seen this conversation going an entirely different way, but something about her defiance ignited the primal and dark passion within me, and there was no denying it now. I'd planned on fucking her tonight, but I'd hoped to make it somewhat nice for her. Now, I didn't care.

Storming into the bedroom, I flipped on the lights, dimming them to a low setting so it wasn't too bright. A warm glow filled the room. Ava was still fighting tooth and nail to get away. She'd managed to kick me in the side with her now bare feet. Her shoes had been lost somewhere along the way. I slid my hand beneath her dress, cupping her bottom.

"I suggest you stop fighting me, Red," I growled at her.

Her body bounced on the bed when I dumped her there. Within seconds she attempted to scramble off the other side, but I was quicker. Like a snake, I struck. My hand clasped around her ankle, preventing her from escaping while I quickly dug through the drawer of my nightstand for what I needed. Within moments I had her on her stomach beneath me, my knee pressing down on her back while her lower half hung off the side of the bed. Grabbing the rope I had snagged from the nightstand, I methodically tied one wrist, then the other before securing them to the bed.

I stepped back. Beautiful. Ava sobbed into the comforter as she pulled at her arms. She was spread out like an eagle before me, one arm tied to the headboard and the other to the footboard. Perfect for what I had planned.

Fingers crawled up her spine before pulling at the golden zipper at her back. It fell away, revealing the creamy expanse of her bare skin. Her chest rose and fell as she narrowed her eyes at me from the side. Still so full of defiance.

I couldn't help but be drawn to her like a sailor to a siren, although I knew that nothing good could come of this. That I very well could be sending us to a watery death. She was smart, smarter than Elias ever gave her credit for. I could see the intelligence behind those wide eyes, no doubt well aware of her father's dealings in the underground.

What I couldn't put my finger on was why she would spy for a man who she so clearly detested. My instincts told me there was more going on than simple spying. Otherwise, why would Elias fight so hard to keep her when he had been so willing to give her up.

Unless it was an act. Did Elias want me to believe she meant something to him, when in fact, she meant nothing? Or was it the opposite?

No matter. Soon I would have the information I needed; the rest could wait.

"You've been naughty, Lil Red," I murmured in her ear before biting the tip harshly.

She yipped, her breath ragged. "Let me go."

There were those words again. Three words she could repeat over and over but that would never come true. I would never let her go. She was mine.

Smiling, I kissed down her turned cheek to the exposed

part of her neck, biting and nipping as I went. Ava jolted as the sound of my knife being released filled the air. She stiffened as I dragged the cold blade along the exposed skin of her back. Her breath caught as I tore the straps of her dress and yanked it from beneath her body, leaving her in nothing but her bra and panties.

I swept my knuckles back and forth across her exposed buttocks, enjoying the redness that was still present from last night's punishment. She wasn't wearing cotton panties tonight, but a black lace thong. She squeezed her eyes shut as my hand moved closer to her heated core. Her hips bucked the moment my fingers gently swiped against her folds.

"Don't—" she practically pleaded as she struggled against her bonds. The movement only served to rub her ass against my hardening cock.

"This is happening, Red," I told her as I stepped away. "Whether you like it or not."

Last night, I had used my belt in a manner befitting a punishment. Tonight, I would use a lesser instrument meant to bring her to the edge. Something that had a bit more of a bite than a sting. I wanted her to answer my questions, and I had a feeling pain was something she was used to. I would need to take a different approach.

With a smile, I removed a feather-tipped riding crop. Tame, compared to some of the other instruments I had lined up in my closet. I didn't want her too striped to enjoy tonight's later festivities. I pocketed one last toy as I made my way back to my new wife.

Her eyes followed the riding crop in my hand, no doubt taking in the feathered tip and the little strip of leather at the other end.

"What are you going to do with that?"

"This," I informed her as I swatted the leather end on my

hand. The sharp crack made her jump. "Is a riding crop meant for sensation and impact play." I let it fly. The leather struck her, making a small, faint pink patch bloom against her pale skin. Ava let out the most beautiful little cry. I lashed her again and again, each flick of the crop harder than the last.

She cursed at me, grumbling under her breath but unable to get away. Then she whimpered, her lower body squirming as the intensity of my blows increased. Once I'd painted her ass a deeper shade of pink, I stopped.

Ava was panting, her legs rubbing together as she tried to gain some kind of friction on the heat that was no doubt pooling down there. I had no doubt that if I were to stick my fingers between her legs, she'd be sopping.

"Now," I ran the feather side of the crop down her sore backside, and she gasped as the unusual sensation took over. "Who gave you the phone?" Her lips remained zipped closed. I traced the feather up and down her bottom before I flipped the crop again and gave her another sharp spank.

Another cry from her. Another strike from me.

"I can do this all night, Ava." Growling, I struck her again, a strangled sob leaving her throat when I hit the sensitive spot where her ass met her thighs. "Tell me who gave you the phone, and I will end it."

"I can't."

So be it. I continued my torturous teasing, alternating between harsh smacks and the tickle of the feather until she was moaning, her hips rising.

"Tell me."

"Please—"

"Why are you protecting him, Ava?" I grilled her as she sobbed. "He's the man who gave you away."

"Why did you buy me?" She all but screamed at me. "I wouldn't be here if you hadn't offered him that fucking deal.

JO MCCALL

Or if you hadn't tracked me down. I don't want any of this. I didn't want to—"

She stopped, realizing she had said too much already.

"Didn't want to what, Red?"

Clenching her jaw, she refused to answer.

"Fine," I snarled at her. "We'll try this another way instead." I reached into my pocket for the second toy and held it up for her to see. "Do you know what this is, Ava?"

"Yes." Her cheeks flamed as she muttered the name beneath her breath, so low I barely heard her.

"Good." I pressed my hips against her raw ass, leaning forward slightly as I snaked an arm around her stomach, my hand resting over the small patch of curls between her thighs. I pressed the vibrator between her lips, feeling as she bucked against me, protesting. "Now, are you going to tell me who gave you the cell phone?"

"I can't—" she whispered. "Please."

"Well then, Red," I sighed as I flipped on the vibrator, allowing it to just barely touch her swollen clit. Just enough to make her body react. I could see her hands fisting the bedding beneath her, her eyes closed tightly, jaw clenched.

I pressed the vibrator harder against her. She fought the urge to buck her hips against me. I could tell by the way she clenched her ass together. Chuckling at her weak attempt to not be affected, I moved the vibrator lower, teasing her entrance.

"Tell me, Red," I whispered in her ear, nipping at her earlobe. When she didn't respond, I pulled away and dropped into a crouch behind her, the vibrator still glued to her entrance. I shoved her lacy thong aside and then rolled my tongue around her clit before sucking it into my warm mouth while I pushed the vibrator into her pussy.

Ava moaned above me, her hips bucking against my

mouth as her pleasure built. I slowly fucked her with the vibrator as I continued to lick and nibble on her clit. Just when I felt her body getting ready to leap off the edge of the cliff, I stopped.

"Wait!"

"Not liking that, are you?" I laughed as her face turned sour. "If you don't want me to do that again, then tell me what I want to know."

"I can't tell you."

"Fine then," I shrugged my shoulder before returning to my assault on her clit. I pushed the vibrator deeper, my tongue flicking faster, knowing that everything was now more intense. Seconds went by, and I let her build up again to just before the damn was about to break.

Then I stopped.

"Matthias!" She sobbed loudly.

"Tell me!"

"My father, okay?" She screamed, large tears running down her cheeks. "He wanted me to spy on you. He'll hurt my sister if I don't do it. I'm sorry, all right? I'm sorry."

"Good girl," I whispered, bending over her and planting a kiss on her sweat sheened forehead. "Brave girl." Righting myself, I backed away from the woman beneath me. Her chest was heaving, eyes bright with tears, face and ass flushed a brilliant pink. I took her in for one more moment before turning and making my way toward the bathroom.

"Wait," she whined. "You aren't going to leave me here, are you?" I turned back to face her and smile wickedly.

"Don't worry, Lil Red," I assured her. "We aren't finished quite yet." Without looking back, I walked from the room and shut the door.

We were definitely not finished yet.

CHAPTER SEVENTEEN

Matthias

That was not how I had wanted to start our first night as a married couple. I might be a cruel man at times, but I knew full well that she was a virgin. Even if Elias hadn't provided that damn certificate. She was stubborn and hard-headed, and god, did she piss me off. I left her lying across the bed after the belting I gave her, and now I had the largest hard-on.

I quickly shed my clothes and stepped into the cold shower, my rock-hard cock springing free. Groaning, I took it in my hand and leaned against the heated tiles of the shower wall. Fucking Christ, she had me in this same position last night. The only difference was, I wouldn't be finishing in here, but in the slick pussy of hers that was just waiting to be fucked.

There wasn't much choice in what we had to do tonight. In part, it was a job. Tradition, as old as it was, still required for me to consummate our marriage. Not that it would be much of a chore. I was more than eager to sink into that hot virgin cunt of hers. Idly, I stroke my cock, calming myself before I got out of the shower to go back in there.

If I hadn't walked away to cool off, I wouldn't have taken her the way she needed. I was not a gentle lover, by any means. The beast inside me wanted to rut into her tight pussy without restraint, but I didn't want to hurt her. She wasn't ready for that kind of rough play. Not yet, at least. Sighing, I turned off the cold water and exited the shower, grabbing a towel to dry off with before slipping on my briefs.

I opened the bathroom door to find Ava still where I left her, belly down on the edge of the bed. Not that she could go anywhere with the ropes around her wrists keeping her in place. Still, she could have chosen to struggle against her bonds, and she hadn't.

Good girl.

"Did we learn our lesson, *Krasnyy*?" I leaned over her, nudging her wild locks aside, and whispered in her ear. Whimpering, she nodded her head fervently, her emerald eyes glassy, the gold specks in them shining brightly. "Verbal answer."

"Yes."

"Yes what, Red?"

She visibly swallowed. "Yes, sir."

I smiled. "Good girl." Her eyes widened at the praise. Now that was interesting. Does my Lil Red like being praised? Time would tell.

Reaching over her, I undid the bindings of her wrists with a quick tug to one of the ropes. Ava let out a sigh of relief as she stood up, rubbing at her wrists. It may have been uncomfortable, but the ropes wouldn't have caused any damage. She took a few steps back from me, stopping when her back hit the dresser.

She'd been all fire and rage when I'd belted her, but now her eyebrows were raised in uncertainty and her body trembled slightly as she hugged herself. The girl's bravery had fled, and now that she wasn't raging, she was scared. But I couldn't let that prolong this. I needed the evidence of our consummation.

"Come here, Ava." She shook her head at me as her breath stuttered.

"We don't have to—"

"Yes, we do," I told her, motioning for her to come forward. "You will do well to obey, or you won't like the outcome of the night. This can be good for both of us, Ava, or it can be good for just me. You decide."

She held my gaze from across the room, eyes narrowing slightly at my answer.

"Are you just going to punish me every time you don't like something I say?" She asked. "Will I never be able to have an opinion or a say in anything?"

"You can have an opinion on anything you want, Ava," I tell her honestly. If she had something on her mind, if she had an opinion, I would listen to it. I would hear her out. "What I won't tolerate is disrespect and lying. I also won't tolerate you disobeying me in front of my men. If you want to talk about something, you wait until we are in the privacy of our room to do it."

"Your room," she muttered petulantly. I could see the wheels in her head turning as she fought to find a way to delay the inevitable, but I wasn't about to let her keep talking. That, I learned, was her primary source of defiance.

"Our room," I told her. "Enough talking, Red. I said to come here."

She took a deep breath, pushing back her shoulders, and walked to me. Hesitantly. Like prey to a predator. When she was barely a foot away, she stopped and bit her lip as her uncertain gaze met mine.

I reached for her, gripping her hip and dragging her until she was standing between my legs. My hands roamed her soft skin. She was only wearing a bra and a thong, nothing else.

"I don't understand why you want me." It was so low, I wondered if I was meant to hear it.

"Because I wanted you the moment I laid eyes on you," I let my hands wander her bare skin. It was soft, my hands skimming her perfect curves as I sought to map out each dip and valley. "And I take what I want."

"But I've never—"

"I know."

"I don't—" She pushed at my hands, which were currently unhooking the front clasp of her bra. "Wait—"

"No more waiting, Red," I murmured in her ear as I slid the bra off her shoulders. "You are mine." She opened her mouth in rebuttal, but I silenced her with a kiss before she could say anything. If she kept talking, I would have to punish her again, and as much as I relished the thought, I wanted this to be somewhat nice for her.

Her eyes fluttered closed, and she let out a small moan as I explored her sweet mouth. She tasted like vanilla and warm honey, hot and rich, and the more I tasted her, the hungrier I became. When I pulled away, her emerald eyes caught mine in their thrall. They shone with excitement and fire, and I knew in that moment, I could lose myself to her, and I hadn't even fucked her yet.

CHAPTER EIGHTEEN

Ava

He was intoxicating.

His lips pulled away from mine and our gazes met. His stormy eyes were dark, pupils blown wide with hunger. I'd be lying if I said that his punishment hadn't awakened some kind of beast inside me. He'd left me tied to his bed, unable to move, warning me to keep my thighs apart. I had desperately needed the friction. My pussy was aching, but I did as he instructed. I was both afraid and aroused, two emotions that I had never thought would overlap, but they did. And it was delicious.

He took possession of my mouth again. Owning me. Possessing me. With a quick swipe of his tongue, he pushed past my lips to tangle his tongue with mine, and I had to remind myself to breathe as the taste of smoke and whiskey assaulted my senses. With every stroke of his tongue, a little more of my rational mind left, leaving nothing but Matthias Dashkov behind.

The way his large, muscled, imposing body held mine, the way he always smelled like fresh pine and old leather. The way his touch seemed to brand my skin, forever marking me as his. It was intoxicating.

Pulling away abruptly, he let me catch my breath as he buried his hand in my messy curls, wrenching my head back so he could place hot kisses along the edge of my jaw while his other hand slid tantalizingly over my bared breasts. On a particularly sensitive patch of flesh, just below my jaw, he bit down, sucking hard to keep the pleasurable sting of pain at a gasping level, pulling a forced mewl from my mouth as I arched in his grasp, gripping him tighter.

He continued his assault on my neck, leaving sizable love bites and bruises down to the juncture where my neck met my shoulder while his free hand massaged my left breast. The stubble across his jaw scraped against my now-hypersensitive flesh, making me groan as he licked across my collarbone, pulling a shudder from my spine.

What the hell was happening? I was unable to keep up with the flood of sensations nipping at my body. I was hyperaware of everything, while at the same time, it seemed to become nothing but dull noise in the background as Matthias pulled one new sensation after another out of me like it was his job. My pussy throbbed and was pulsing with a need I didn't quite understand.

Sure, I'd gotten myself off a couple of times since I'd discovered exactly what the wonderful bundle of nerves could do when stimulated, but nothing I did to myself ever felt like this—this fire in my blood. I whimpered in protest when his lips left mine. I watched in annoyance as his sinful mouth twitched at the edges, showing his amusement at my protestation. Before I could snark at him, his hands went firmly to my thighs and lifted me up in the air as he stood. Quicker than I could comprehend, I was airborne, his grip on me gone.

The bed was plush and comfortable as I landed on it, bouncing slightly. Matthias wasn't far behind, and by the look on his face, he was hungry for more. He was on me in an instant, his powerful thighs straddling my legs as he gripped my shoulders and shoved me down onto the bed. Faster than I could gain my bearings, his large hands slid down my body and ripped my panties from my body, exposing my pussy to his ravenous gaze.

"Matthias!" I cried, annoyed at the fact that he'd destroyed one of the few pair of nice underwear that Mia had bought for me. Still, my stomach clenched with excitement.

"Up on the pillows, Red." His voice was husky and low with need.

Swallowing hard, I shifted to crawl out from under him and farther up the bed, settling against the pillows nervously. Laying comfortably on my back, I watched each of his muscles tense and bunch as he crawled his way up the bed toward me, his stance that of a predator stalking prey...and holy fuck was it both fucking frightful and mouth-watering.

There was a nudge in the back of my mind that told me this was wrong. That I shouldn't want this. He had forced me into a marriage I didn't want, belted me, then brought me to the brink again and again before he tied me to his bed. This wasn't real want or need, I was conditioned to want this by his stark manipulation of my body, but I couldn't find it within myself to care. Those worries were for future Ava to worry about. All I wanted right now was to feel that sinfully utter bliss he had provided me with earlier.

He shifted his grasp to my ankles. Moving slowly, he slid his hands up the lengths of my calves, his touch firm and decisive, but still tender, almost teasing. That surprised me. Sliding over the bend of my knee, he shifted his hands to glide up my inner thighs, spreading me effortlessly. I couldn't help but blush as he slid into place between my legs, his hips tightly wedged between my trembling thighs.

Before he could continue his assault on my body and turn me into a moaning mess, I moved my hands in between us to glide the delicious planes of his abdominal muscles and feel each dip and ridge of his abs with my fingers. He was all hard lines and jagged edges. A true Adonis if there ever was one. I wanted to do nothing but worship at the altar of his body.

Matthias stayed perfectly still, letting me touch him, allowing me to explore. The tense pinch of his forehead and the tightness in his muscles had me wondering if he ever let any of the women he was with before me touch him like this. Explore him. His gaze was heated and impatient, and I knew I didn't have long before he took back control.

Splaying my palms flat, I enjoyed sliding my hands up and over his strong pectorals before exploring the vast expanse of his broad shoulders, feeling each rigidly tight muscle underneath. Taking the opportunity, I slid my right hand down his flank to trace the raised scar tissue that was intricately woven with the ink on his back. He tensed under my fingers, and for a moment I was worried he didn't like me touching this particular area, but the positively feral gaze he turned on me told me otherwise.

What had happened to him for his skin to become so scarred?

Before I could contemplate any ideas, he surged forward, claiming my mouth with his own. The kiss was vicious this time as he gripped hard on my torso, pulling me up and into his body. His lips left my mouth, wrapping around one petal-pink nipple, scraping his teeth against the tender nub. Holy shit! I groaned sharply in surprise, gripping tightly on to his shoulders as he tortured the sensitive peak with his teeth and tongue.

His other hand didn't stay idle long. Cupping my other breast firmly, he rolled my nipple between his fingers, pinching sharply. My hips had a mind of their own as they rolled and lifted against his unconsciously, making him growl into my breast as he moved away from the now aching peak to leave more of his love bites across the tender flesh of my breast.

Grinding my teeth together, I tried to control the wanton noises spilling from my throat, but it was no use. He was tactical in his assault, taking advantage of each weak point on my body. Ones I wasn't even aware a person could have.

I dug my nails into his shoulders, groaning harshly, ripping another growl from his mouth as his hips rolled with mine, creating delicious friction between our bodies as he finished making a trail of bruises across my chest. So, he liked the pain. Not allowing me to protest, his mouth left my skin as he moved to sit up on his knees, giving me another lovely eyeful of his impressive physique. He took both of my wrists in one of his hands, lifting them above my head until I was stretched out beneath him.

"Stay." He growled. I forced myself not to move, allowing only my head to turn and follow his movements as he stepped off the side of the bed. In one quick move, he rid himself of his briefs. I felt the blush heat up under my freckle-covered cheeks, spreading down toward my chest as I tried my best to keep my eyes on his and not follow the path of the fabric now pooled at his feet.

I kept my eyes on his as he started crawling up the bed toward me. Stopping just before my legs, he ran his hands up over my thighs, letting my skin sizzle back into hypersensitivity by the feeling of his palms ghosting across my skin, rough and warm.

I couldn't help but let my eyes drift down as he moved to situate himself between my legs again. Fuck. Matthias was hard and ready; his size was impressive, and it sent a jolt of anxious anticipation surging up my spine. How was that going to fit inside me? I'd be lucky if he didn't split me in half. I should have known he would be hung like a stud. The rest of him had been an indication of that. Everything about Matthias was imposing...from his large form to his abrasive, unyielding personality.

"Don't worry," he whispered huskily. "It'll fit." He must have noticed my panic as he settled over me, his hips fitting back between my thighs, but not as close as we were before. He used one forearm to prop himself up next to me, angling most of his body to my left. I wondered if I was allowed to move yet. He caught the subtle twitch of my hands, his eyebrows furrowing as he locked his eyes on mine.

"No," he commanded, easily guessing I wanted to move out of the position he'd placed me in.

Grinding my teeth, I huffed at him impatiently. I just wanted to touch him, and here he was, being overly domineering and controlling. Not letting me—

His free hand slid up my inner thigh, tickling the tender flesh with his calloused fingers, halting my thoughts. I was almost frozen in apprehension, my thighs shaking on either side of him as he trailed those fingers over my core, testing how wet I was for him already.

His chest rumbled in a pleased sort of growl, his eyes making me writhe under his gaze as my heart thundered erratically in my chest, tattooing its shape on my rib cage. His finger circled my entrance, once, then twice, before pushing all the way past my folds, leaving me gasping and my hands clenching by my head as I tried to remain still. Hazily, my mind clouded in pleasure, I watched as his eyes narrowed on my face, his own control pulling taught as he started an excruciatingly slow pace, preparing me for him.

The slow coil tightening deep in my belly had me shifting against him, my hips rotating without my consent as I whined in need. Any time my eyes trailed away from his, he'd slow even further, forcing me to look back at him and keep his hungry stare. After several long minutes of torture, his thumb brushed over my clit as he pulled his hand away, forcing my knees to clench around his hips as I fought the groan of protest by biting down on my lip.

He didn't leave me wanting for long. A second finger joined the first, thrusting inside me, pulling a sharp moan from my mouth as I was left shaking in his hold. The coil of my impending orgasm wound up tighter and tighter. His pace was quicker now, but still far too slow as he worked those fingers in and out of my moist heat, pulling strangled moans from my lips as I pleaded to him with my eyes to end this torture of his.

The veiled aggression behind his eyes didn't scare me at this moment. I knew it wasn't violence behind those stormy depths. It was full-on primal lust tangled with dark promises. And they were all for me...

"Please," I whispered, my mind cloudy with desire.

His eyes fell shut as he took a deep breath through his nose, shuddering against me. My begging apparently affecting him in ways I hadn't anticipated as he did his best to hold himself in check. I knew he was holding back because he knew I was a virgin, but at this moment, I didn't want him to hold back. Because he had been right about him belting me. It had released something in me that I didn't know I had been holding on to, and right now I wanted him to release it again. That primal hunger that gnawed at my insides to be free.

"Matthias." I whined again, lifting my hips to his hands.

Eyes snapping open, he met my gaze again, eyebrows furrowed and irritated. He obviously had figured out that I knew exactly what my begging seemed to do to him. With a rough grind of his teeth, he picked up his pace, curling his fingers inside me to hit that perfect spot of bliss over and over again, his thumb tortuous on my bundle of nerves. With a sharp cry, I arched my back into him, lifting my hips as my orgasm washed over me.

As soon as I came down from cloud nine, he was moving, shifting to settle over me, his larger, muscled form dwarfing my small frame as he positioned himself above me, his hips wedged tightly between my clenching thighs, keeping them spread even as they quaked on either side of him.

Ensnaring my eyes again as he balanced on one palm, he reached down between our bodies to line up his length against my pussy. His eyes, while still dark, now glinted with intent. His tightly leashed control snapped in one painfully pleasurable movement as his hips surged forward as he buried himself to the hilt inside me, snarling as our hips connected savagely, making me scream for him.

My thoughts felt like they had been ripped from my head as he shook above me, holding himself in check as he waited for me to adjust to his rather impressive size. There were no soothing words of comfort, and he didn't wipe the few stray tears that had managed to slip down my cheeks. He simply stared down at me and waited. I felt unbelievably full, and oh-so-fucking-good. Just a bit more than a sliver of pain tingled up my spine as pleasure coursed through my body. I shifted my hands next to my head, anxious to see if he would bark at me not to move them, but no such order came.

With an almost agonizing slowness, I raised my hands to grip his biceps, my fingers digging into his flesh as I shifted my hips against him, testing how it felt. The sensation made me hold and clench down around him as my nerves went wild. He growled against me as he dipped his head down, his back arcing slightly as he nipped at my collarbone. Smirking slightly, I repeated the motion, shifting and rolling my hips the best I could while trapped beneath him. My nerve endings felt like they were on fire. He was so fucking deep, and every time I shifted, my whole world tilted.

That was all the incentive he needed. With a rough intake, he pulled away from me, retreating almost all the way before slamming back inside me, ripping a shriek from my mouth as he wrenched the control away from me. I watched through half-lidded eyes as a full-blown and rather dangerous looking smile crossed over his mouth. His pace was vicious, his thrusts hard and quick, pulling moan after moan from my lips as he mercilessly claimed me in the most ancient and primal of dances. I could do nothing but hold on and do my best to meet each of his violent thrusts as the tension began building up in my abdomen again.

This continued for what felt like hours, the fucking stamina of this man, and I knew in the back of my mind that I was going to have a constant reminder of this tomorrow.

His teeth found purchase on every patch of skin he could reach. His right hand attentive and insistent as he mapped out my body, committing it to memory, learning every curve, attacking every erogenous zone he could find. My hands didn't stay idle, either, they just couldn't. I trailed my fingers across all the hard muscles of his torso, scratched when the sensations became overwhelming, and pulled hard on his hair when he bit too harshly into my skin, his own control having not returned. He fucked with reckless abandon, and yet he was still precise and assured. It was maddening. I was pretty sure that I would never be the same again. He had taken my mind and had warped and corrupted it. All in one single night.

My legs were quivering on either side of him when suddenly, quicker than I could follow, Matthias pulled from my grip, my hands gripping nothing but air as he sat up, still fully inside me. He repositioned me quickly, managing to get my legs over his arms so my calves dangled over his elbows as he pulled my legs apart lewdly. Blushing fiercely, I wanted to protest. My own insecurities surfacing, but then he moved, resuming his relentless pace, this time even deeper, hitting that one spot just right.

My mind was gone as he pistoned his hips, his force brutal enough to have me reaching up to twist one hand in the sheets next to my head and the other bracing flat against the headboard above me. I couldn't keep his stare anymore; my eyes were practically rolling in the back of my head as my toes curled tightly. Matthias's expression turned savage, his movements bordering on erratic, his pace no longer even and precise in its onslaught.

With a scream, I came undone in his hold, unraveling at the seams as I arched and tensed, screaming his name. My world shattered in fragments, but vaguely I heard his feral snarl as he came with me, tumbling over the edge just a few thrusts after I did, our hips practically glued together.

He was still, almost statue-like, as we both slowly descended from our violent orgasms. The sounds of our ragged breathing the only noise in the otherwise muted atmosphere. I felt bruised. Bruised and utterly satiated.

That was until he pulled from me. I felt bereft at the sudden loss of fullness inside me. He didn't say a word as I watched him slip from the bed and face me. My eyes traveled to his length that was now coated in my arousal and my blood. My eyes flicked up to his. The primal hunger that had been there just moments before was gone. Replaced by an icy storm.

I scooted back toward the headboard as he pulled the top sheet out from under me, the evidence of my deflowering nothing more than a few drops staining the sheet. For a second, I thought he was just disposing of them so we didn't sleep in the blood and cum, but then I noticed he had folded it so that the blood was obvious before he disappeared into the bathroom.

When he came back out, he was fully dressed in one of his crisp suits, all evidence of our entanglement washed away. Tears stung my eyes when he barely looked my way as he slid on his shoes. He grabbed up the soiled sheet and headed toward the door.

"Get some sleep, Ava."

Then he was gone, and I was left shattered into a thousand pieces that would never be put back together again.

CHAPTER NINETEEN

Matthias

I had to walk away.

There was nothing else to be done. I could still feel her touching me, smell her arousal, hear her dulcet moans as she came on my cock. I'd been tame, struggling the entire time to hold the beast within me back as I took her for the first time. Normally when I took a woman, it was hard, fast, and from behind. When I was in the mood to sate the urges of my darker desires, I would tie them up in some form or another. But none of them ever laid their hands on me. Just their mouths when they sucked my cock.

Ava had touched me. Had touched my scars.

It was intimate. More intimate than I had planned. She had sucked me effortlessly into her gravitational pull with her wide, innocent eyes and trembling lip, which is why I had walked away with barely a backward glance.

Ava had been a scared little rabbit before I took her. Wolves devoured rabbits.

I'd made a point to have Mia ensure Ava's aftercare. I wasn't practiced in it. Valerie's girls were trained to deal without immediate aftercare. Instead, they received it back at the apartments they all shared. Their safe haven. I also knew, however, that if I had been the one to provide Ava's care, I sure as fuck would not be able to do it without wanting to take her again and again.

There was no time for that now. I needed to hunt down that worthless heir of Elias's.

I also didn't need there to be complications between Ava and me. There would be no filling her mind with abstract fantasies of me being a caring and loving husband. That just wasn't in my DNA. I would ensure that all her needs were met, that she was kept protected, but I was no romantic. There would be no flowers or chocolates. No date nights that weren't required functions.

That was more Vas's area of expertise than mine.

Ava was stuck in my mind, though. No matter how hard I tried to shake the feeling of her skin beneath my lips, her breathy moans, her cries of pleasure, I just couldn't. It surprised me how easily she responded to my touch and command after her punishment. Gliding along the edge of pleasure and pain had subdued my Little Red, even if she was furious at the act of punishment itself. Soon she would come to crave the punishments I would dole out.

Ask for it. *No.* She would beg for it.

Now, however, I was sitting at Club Contour, one of my newest investments. Nicolai sat beside me, whiskey in hand, as he poured over inventory and accounts. We were waiting for the man of the hour to appear.

Contour was exclusive, members-only, but I'd managed to

get one of Valerie's girls to drag Christian here under the pretenses of a good time. I'd never let anything happen, however. Valerie would tie my balls in a knot if something happened to one of her girls. Part of the appeal of the club was the Red Rooms where members could indulge in private dances and experience what some of my more adventurous employees had to offer.

"Why did we decide to buy another club?" Nicolai sighed as he poured over the accounts, his glasses perched on the end of his nose.

"Because the more legit businesses we have, the easier it is to funnel money into our more colorful ones."

Nicolai snorted. "Colorful is one word for it."

I shrugged as I took a sip of the bourbon the bartender had offered me. She was a petite thing with long pigtails and a wide smile. I hadn't missed the way her eyes appraised me when I sat down or the not-so-subtle sway of her hips as she walked away.

Under normal circumstances, it might have been something I indulged in. Take her into a back room, fuck her, then leave her. Just a simple fulfillment of my baser needs, but I had someone to take care of that now. My marriage to Ava was built on convenience. My vows were not. I'd remain loyal to her, something my father had never done with my mother.

"I thought crimson would be a bit obvious, don't you?" I teased him. Nicolai rolled his eyes behind his glasses, not bothering to take his eyes off the computer in front of him.

"Found that information you wanted." Nicolai clicked off the accounts on his laptop, bringing up an entirely new feed of reports. "I'm not sure who that cell phone belongs to, but it isn't Elias. There are only a couple of places you can get that phone anymore, and it isn't in the States. I traced the SIM card in this one, it's Russian."

"What the hell is my wife doing with a Russian burner phone?" I reached for the laptop, but Nicolai batted my hand away. Fucker was protective of his state-of-the-art electronics. I'd spent a pretty penny on his setup over the years, and adding Mark to the fold just increased that budget. Not that I needed to worry about money, but still, it was a shit ton more than I'd spent on most things.

"You think she was lying about who it belonged to?"

I was starting to think she might have been, but Ava wasn't good at hiding her emotions. They were splayed across her face at any given time, readily open for anyone to read and take advantage of.

"It's possible," I admitted. "But she seemed to believe that it belonged to Elias. Who else would ask her to spy?" Nicolai shrugged.

"We know Elias is working with someone behind the scenes," he pointed out. "Maybe the phone was given to her by Elias, but someone else gave him that phone to use."

That was a scenario that made sense. Someone had been feeding Elias information behind our backs. Had been helping him steal shipments and arm his men to gun mine down in the streets.

"You may also want to consider that she is a Trojan Horse."

"Really?" I shot him an amused look as I took another sip of bourbon. Ava was a lot of things, but a Trojan Horse was not one of them. Naïve? Yes. Sheltered? Certainly. But a trained spy? I had to resist the urge to laugh in my *Obshchak's* face at the suggestion.

"I'm just saying." Nicolai held his scarred, tattooed hands up as a sign of peace. "Don't just dismiss the idea because she's hot, naïve, and you've been inside her cunt. She may have been sheltered, but from the sounds of things, she was also groomed."

I sighed, rubbing my eyes in frustration at the thought of my Little Red being a spy.

"That doesn't mean she is a willing spy, brother," Nicolai continued. "Elias used her best friend to get her back home, then had her raped in front of her just to prove a damn point. Do you honestly think he wouldn't hold something over her head to get her to spy on you?"

As much as I wished I could, I knew I couldn't dismiss Nicolai's theory. I'd learned a lot about Ava over the past year from my spies within the Ward household, and none of it was good. Beaten. Starved. Kept segregated from the rest of the household. Ava had been nothing more than a prisoner in her own home. Not that I was offering her much more.

"Boss," Roman's voice crackled over the earpiece I was wearing. "He's here."

A sadistic smile crossed my lips as I nodded to Nicolai, whose eyes scanned the entryway as Christian Ward drunkenly stumbled through the club with Valerie's girl Alyssa on his arm. Her eyes flicked my way, displaying her obvious disgust for the man she was escorting. She'd avidly volunteered when she found out just what Christian did to the women he brought to clubs like this.

"Showtime." I stood from my chair, buttoning my jacket, and made my way after them. Nicolai followed. We remained out of sight until the door to the private room closed. Now we waited.

It didn't take long for Alyssa to use the code phrase we gave her. Nicolai threw open the door to the room, stepping aside to let me enter first.

"What the fuck?" Christian, who'd had his back turned, swiveled around to face us. His glare immediately dropped when he saw me, face paling. I jerked my head at Alyssa, who gave me a two-fingered salute as she passed me. Nicolai threw her a wink that had her giggling as she disappeared into the hall and back to work.

"Hello, Christian." His eyes widened, fixated on me, then he looked at the door. "You're not going anywhere until I say so."

"What do you want?" His voice trembled with fear. Good, that meant he still remembered what I'd done to him a year ago when I nearly took his life. He was lucky I wouldn't be doing that tonight. It was, however, just a matter of time before he ended up with a bullet between his eyes.

"You are going to give your father a message for me," I told him as I removed my suit jacket and handed it back to Nicolai, who was standing guard by the now-closed door. I rolled my sleeves up as I surveyed him.

He stood a bit shorter than my six-two stature and was leaner. The man had divested himself of his shirt in preparation for whatever he was going to do with Alyssa. Christian had near perfect posture. His shoulders were rolled back with his chin held high despite his near cowering in my presence.

This kind of form was automatic for someone who had been bought up surrounded by wealth and power. Christian had no doubt grown up with his father telling him he would inherit the world. That he could do what he wanted when he wanted. This was likely further cemented with the fact that Elias Ward had spent thousands of countless dollars over the years suppressing his son's misdeeds.

Sexual assault complaints. Aggravated assault. DUIs. My contact at the Seattle PD had given me a file nearly an inch thick with complaints and charges against Christian since high school. All of which had been buried or bribed away.

"Well, you are going to send a few messages to your

father," I corrected. "But first, I'm going to show you what happens when you touch something that belongs to me."

I didn't give him enough time to rebut before I sank my fist into his gut. Christian wheezed, grabbing his stomach as he dropped to his knees. My next few landed on his face. The sound of breaking bone and his cry of pain were music to my ears. I watched with smug satisfaction as blood gushed from his nose.

Christian cursed, one hand holding his bleeding nose, the other braced on the floor as he struggled to right himself. I didn't give him the chance. My foot dug harshly into his side, sending him sprawling across the floor.

"Now." Reaching back, I grabbed the sheet soiled with my wife's virgin blood from Nicolai and dropped it at Christian's feet. "Let's get a couple of things straight, Christian. First, if you ever touch Ava again, you won't be coming out of it with a broken nose and being roughed up a bit. Two—" I dragged the folded virginity certificate from my pocket, holding it up for him to see before I tore it to pieces. "Tell your father that Ava belongs to me now, and I'm on to him and his dirty little secret.

"He thought he could pull the wool over my eyes, but he was wrong and now I am going to tear down everything I gave him. Tell him I'm going to choke him out of everything until he has no other choice but to hand over the company *I* saved. I warned him, and now it's time he paid up. Is that understood?"

When he didn't answer, I ground my foot into the hand resting on the floor until he was screaming.

"Yes. Yes. I get it. I'll tell him." He let out a sob of relief when I removed my foot.

"Fantastic." Nicolai opened the door to the room to reveal Sergei and Lev, two of my top enforcers. "As soon as you've learned your lesson about touching other people's toys, make sure you crawl on home with my messages like a good little boy."

"Wait," Christian exclaimed as I strode out of the room. "You can't—" His plea was cut off as the door slammed shut behind me, sealing him in. We'd had the rooms soundproofed for obvious reason.

The man was a coward. He hadn't even bothered to fight back, either out of fear or the fact that he'd been drunk, I wasn't sure. The man had simply taken it, and something about that bothered me. Sure, he'd blubbered, but nothing like the last time I'd beaten him. That was a problem. Christian's body language told me that although he was, indeed, afraid, there wasn't the same level of fear as there used to be.

The bastard knew I wasn't going to kill him when I came into that room. He also didn't question or fight the fact that I wanted him to deliver a message to his father.

He'd been expecting something like this to happen, and that bothered the shit out of me. You can't command the board in chess if your enemy is already two moves ahead.

CHAPTER TWENTY

Ava

I wanted to hide beneath the covers of the soft navy duvet and weep. Curl up in a ball on this massive bed and sob out my pain. He'd been, for the most part, gentle as he took me. Sure, it wasn't romantic with flowers and candles and shit, but I had a feeling that for Matthias, this was outside the norm.

My cheeks heated as I replayed the night in my mind. Once again, my body seemed confused as the pain of the whipping merged with pleasure until I was no longer able to tell the two sensations apart. My body had throbbed with heat and desire, the feeling mounting when he had left me tied to his bed, unable to ease the ache between my legs until it felt like I would burst at the seams.

Conflict warred within me. My body was ruled by lust, desire, and the overwhelming need to feel his hands roaming my body once again. The deliciously dirty knowledge that I had enjoyed every second of his not-so-gentle taking of my virginity left me somewhat uncertain. I was sitting on a knife's edge. Confused by my excited response to the man who had all but bought me and forced me to marry him. He'd made sure I'd come. Let me reap my pleasure just as much as he reaped his.

I'd honestly expected him to simply pound into me and be done with it.

Instead, there was a softness to his handling of me that was unexpected and left me breathless. He'd explored my body like he was worshiping at an altar, memorizing it like a map he could later explore. He'd devoured me like I was his last meal. Then he'd left like I was nothing more than a quick fuck, making me feel like nothing more than a used whore who had readily spread her legs for the man who'd bought her.

I wondered what my price was.

A short rap on the door stole my attention, and Mia walked through a moment later, trailed by two girls dressed in maid uniforms that I hadn't seen this morning. One of the girls, who was short and blonde, slid into the bathroom, while the other girl, a tall willowy brunette, ducked into the closet.

"How are you feeling, Mrs. Dashkov?" Mia's voice was grounding as she approached my side of the bed. "Silla is running you a bath to help ease any discomforts. Then they will change the sheets for you."

A flush crept up my neck and into my cheeks at the thought that they were privy to what Matthias and I had done. I wasn't sure why. It wasn't like sex was anything new, and if this morning was anything to go by, they were probably used to their boss parading women in and out throughout the day.

"I'm capable of running my own bath, thank you." I tried

to keep the snarl from my tone, but from the way the woman, Ciara, flinched as she exited the closet, I hadn't quite managed it. Mia, however, looked nonplussed.

Instead, she gave me a warm, calming smile as she took my black robe from Ciara and held it out to me.

"I am well aware of how capable you are, Mrs. Dashkov." Her smile didn't waver as she continued to hold out the robe for me. Eyeing it wearily, I slid off the bed, wincing at the soreness that had settled between my legs and the sting of the sheets on my still heated ass. "But Mr. Dashkov put me in charge of your aftercare, and I plan on following his orders. As should you."

And there it was. In one sentence, Mia had managed to cement the new reality, which Matthias had set for me. A fuck toy to be discarded and put back together by his staff so he could play with it again later. The fact that the fuck toy happened to be his wife didn't matter.

I squeezed my eyes shut as I slipped into the satiny robe, damming up the tears that pushed to overflow. What had I been expecting? Flowers? Chocolates? Had I honestly thought he would come back to bed at some point to hold me in his embrace? Of course not. I'd been hoping he would, however, check on me himself. At least once. He did leave me to sleep in his bed after all.

Now, I wanted nothing more than to escape it.

Mia led me to the oversized bathroom. I couldn't help but marvel at the white marbled floor that sparkled in the lights from the crevices of silver that intricately snaked through it. The same white marble ran up the walls as well, but instead of making the space feel cramped, it made it feel lighter and airier.

A long white wooden vanity ran along the wall to my right with two round matte black sinks that sat upon the plain white tiled counter. Gasping, my eyes widened as I took in the sight of the tub. It stood alone at the far end of the bathroom, directly in front of the large floor-to-ceiling windows of the penthouse. It was round and large enough to fit two or more people comfortably and accented with silver attachments.

The air smelled of vanilla and spice. The girl, Silla, must have added something to the water. I slid the robe off and slipped into the warm water, hissing as the heat stung at my sore ass. It didn't take long for the pain to ebb away, and soon I was leaning back against the side as Mia hummed and washed my hair.

A few stray tears escaped down my face as thoughts of my mother ran rampant in my mind. Memories that I had long kept buried resurfaced. That, combined with the day's stimulating events, had me all but sobbing as Mia's kindness washed over me.

"Why are you crying, dear?" Her fingers stopped rubbing at my scalp, and she came to sit beside me, stroking my back as she cooed at me.

"I'm sorry," I whispered as I struggled to grab a hold of the wall that had all but shattered inside of me. "It's been a while since anyone has been this kind to me." Mia let out a long sigh as she ran a motherly hand along my cheek before returning to washing my hair.

"Don't worry too much, Ava," she murmured kindly to me. "Everything will be fine. Just wait and see."

I closed my eyes, slowly building up the wall inside my mind brick by brick because the truth was, everything wouldn't be fine. And I sure as hell wasn't going to wait and see. Matthias Dashkov may have bought me, but he didn't own me.

Not one single piece of me.

CHAPTER TWENTY-ONE

Ava

The bed was cold on Matthias's side when I woke in the late morning. I knew he had slept there. The covers were thrown back and his pillow was in disarray. That, and I distinctly remembered crawling my angry ass back into the bed in the other room before falling asleep. I must have been sleeping like the dead for that brute of a man to carry me back to *his* bed without waking me.

Asshat. I didn't understand his need to bring me back to his bed in the middle of the night when he was the one who had walked away without a second glance after sex, taking that damn sheet with him like I was some kind of conquest and my virginity was something to parade around to his men.

Then again, maybe I was.

I grimaced as I stretched. My body felt stiff, but the ache between my legs had eased somewhat since the bath. It was embarrassing how easily my body had responded to him. How easily I knew it would *still* respond to him if he were to touch me. Caress me. Kiss me. If I wasn't careful, I'd let him consume me, and I couldn't let that happen.

I shouldn't. *I wouldn't.*

Matthias Dashkov had shown me exactly what he thought of me and where exactly I fell on the chessboard. The man was playing a twisted game with my father, that I was certain of, but I wasn't his queen. He'd made that very clear. I was simply a pawn to be used up and later thrown away at his earliest convenience. Of this, I had no doubt.

Quickly, I threw on a pair of maroon leggings and a long-sleeved black shirt. It was cold, and I'd have to be careful; I was almost out of clothes. Archer hadn't bothered to pack me anything substantial when he'd raided my closet the night Matthias had come for me, and the clothes Mia bought were less than practical for someone confined to a cage. I tossed my hair in a bun on top of my head, slipped into a pair of Uggs, and followed the smell of fresh coffee. It was that delicious, heavenly smell that was pulling me from his room this morning.

It was Sunday, and with any luck, Matthias wouldn't be here.

I'd spent most of yesterday hiding in the spare room like a coward after he had punished me the night before, and as much as I wanted to do the same today, I was hungry and jonesing for a coffee. The penthouse was quiet, almost peaceful, and I wondered why Matthias owned such a large and luxurious home if he was the only one who occupied it.

Well, him and now me.

There was a hominess to the penthouse that was in stark contrast to the man himself. Although his bedroom was rather utilitarian with its white marble and white walls, lacking any distinct personality outside of the color of his comforter, the rest of the penthouse was the polar opposite.

The walls were painted in a warm, weathered gray and decorated with rich abstract art, each one telling its own unique story before bleeding into the next and then the next until the story was complete. Most of the doors were closed and locked. Those that were open, like the small room Matthias had brought me to last night, had an array of earth-toned furniture that looked worn and well-loved, arranged in a pattern that looked meant for large groups instead of a single solitary man.

Floor-to-ceiling windows lined the outside walls, giving me a panoramic view of Lake Union. The recessed lights were off, allowing the soft glow of the sun to warm the room. The floors were natural wood, dark, decorated with thick rugs.

Hearing clanging from the kitchen, I abandoned my snooping for the moment to find Mia. I'd expected to see her or one of the other girls from last night cooking a breakfast feast like the one she had laid out yesterday. Instead, I found Matthias humming an unknown tune as he mixed a few things together in a large blender.

At least he had a shirt on this time. He was wearing a pair of dark low-slung jeans. His black Henley T-shirt stretched across his massive chest, the top two buttons undone, showing a touch of skin. On any other man, it might have looked like something they just casually threw on, but on Matthias, it was as if every stitch had been specifically tailored to his Adonis of a body.

I wanted nothing more than to run and escape back to our room—I shivered—*his* room. Not our room. It would never truly be our room. However, I knew that I would have to face him sooner or later, and I'd rather do it somewhere open, like the kitchen.

He was confident and controlled as he moved around the large space, making what looked to be a smoothie and some eggs. It wasn't anything fancy, but the smell of the cooking eggs and fresh coffee had my stomach rumbling and my mouth watering.

I stared at him for a few moments, unable to wrench my gaze away from him as I watched in rapt fascination as the smooth muscles of his arms flexed beneath his tight shirt. A thrill ran down my spine as I bit my lip, recalling just how powerful those muscles were as he took me last night. Heat pooled in my stomach as I watched his talented fingers pluck a handful of grapes from a bowl left in the fridge. Those fingers had brought me to the edge of ecstasy again and again. I might not have liked being left hanging, but I sure as hell loved the buildup.

"If you're going to ogle me, Red," Matthias's deep tenor broke through my lust filled haze. "Then sit down at the table and do it." My cheeks burned at having been caught staring at him, lusting after him. *Jesus, what the hell is wrong with me?*

How he had managed to add a command to that was beyond me. Did he ever not just order people around? Seeing as how he literally commanded people for a living, I doubted it.

"I was expecting Mia," I told him, as though that explained everything.

"Mia has Sundays off for her family," he explained as he plated the eggs, adding a small helping of the grapes before he poured a cup of coffee. His brown hair was combed back. It looked like the type of hair a metrosexual would die for, but he wasn't rocking it in a deliberate "I have gel and I'm not afraid to use it" way like my brother. No, sir. Matthias sported the "I just got done wrestling a bear because I'm a man" look.

Bottom line, he was hot, and I fucking hated it. It would be so much easier to hate him if he looked like a toad.

His gray eyes were warm this morning, the dark thunderclouds seemingly chased away for the start of a new day. I could almost forget how cold and empty they were last night when he'd left me alone to be tended to by Mia.

"I told you to sit, Ava."

Frowning, I sat down at the table, the memory of signing our marriage papers creeping into my mind as I nervously tapped my fingers on the wooden top. Matthias set down the plate and coffee in front of me, along with a fork. Then he leaned down and pressed his lips to my forehead.

"Good morning, wife."

A lump grew in my throat at the small act of affection. My mind was a whirl of thick fog as I tried and failed to figure out just what the hell he was playing at. I felt like he was playing ping pong with my emotions on purpose, but I couldn't be sure. That, or he seriously needed a therapist for his mood swings. He joined me a moment later, carrying nothing but a large orange smoothie.

"That's all you're having?" I scrunched my nose up at the drink in his hand as he took a long sip.

"It's nearly ten in the morning." He smiled at me from across the table. I mentally sneered at the butterflies that fluttered in my stomach at the action. My body was a goddamn traitor. "I've been up since six. This isn't breakfast, it's a post workout snack, if you will."

Oh. That certainly made more sense. I couldn't see the man in front of me eating nothing but a smoothie for breakfast when he was all jacked and shit. Like Chris Pratt from Jurassic World. Yum.

"Now," Matthias set down his smoothie and leaned back in his chair, his eyes still warm, but I could see the coldness creeping in. "I'm going to ask you a few questions, and how this day goes depends on your answers. Understand?"

Dropping my fork, I grabbed the coffee cup from the table, holding it to me like a shield or a weapon. Not that it had done me any good yesterday, but the warmth of the cup was grounding against the chill of the room.

"Okay." Matthias quirked an eyebrow at me. "Yes, sir." That one was nearly a grumble, but I managed to keep out the sneer. Barely. I hated calling him "sir." It felt degrading, like I was nothing more than a fuck toy. Then again, maybe *sir* was the right word because that was pretty much what I was going to be. Matthias Dashkov's fuck toy.

"Good girl." I hated the way those two words caused my skin to tingle and my pussy to clench. "Are you positive it was Elias who put the phone in your bag?"

Well, he didn't waste any time getting to the hard questions. The honest answer was that I didn't know for sure it was my father who placed the phone in my bag. It could have been Archer, since he was the one who had ultimately packed the bag, but Archer was also Anderson, who was playacting as one of my father's guards. So, he could have placed the phone in my bag on behalf of my father.

Fucking hell. When had my life become a soap opera?

"Who else would have done it?" I responded to his question with one of my own. Matthias's brows shot up. *Shit.* Maybe that was the wrong thing to say. Would he suspect that I was playing double agent? What would Matthias do if he found out the other man I was spying for was FBI?

I felt like a ship at sea, lost in a storm. I was so far out of my element. Only two things were keeping me together right now. One was knowing how well I would fare in prison as someone's bitch. Libby was the other reason. A swirl of doubt snaked through my mind at my father's threat to hurt her. Would he follow through with it when he had done nothing but shower her and Kenzi in love over the years? Or was it a scare tactic to keep me in line? I'd missed the scheduled call at midnight. If the phone did belong to my father, had he punished Libby because I missed the window to contact him, or would he figure I was somehow compromised?

"You tell me." Matthias drank down some of his smoothie as he studied me. "Can you think of anyone else who would hide that phone in your bag?"

I shook my head, my mind a jumbled mess of lies I was trying to concoct to tell him. "The only two people who had access to that bag were my cousin and one of my father's guards."

"What guard?" Matthias sat up in his seat a bit, leaning closer.

"I don't know." I shrugged. "He came up with Neil to grab me when you came for me. Packed my bag and everything."

I once read somewhere that when telling a lie, it was best to keep it as close to the truth as possible. That way, it was easier to recall the lie later. The only truth I was leaving out was the fact that I knew who the guard truly was and his purpose.

"Did you get his name? Had you seen him before?" Matthias was fully invested now, and I had to resist the urge to squirm in my seat. I might not know a lot about my new husband, but I knew that he could read people as easily as the *Sunday Times*. I'd never been the best liar in the first place, and now I was just digging myself a larger hole I'd never be able to climb out of.

"I'm not allowed to know their names." That was the truth. My father forbade any interaction with his guards who weren't family. They were there to keep me in line, not become my friends. It was another form of isolation.

"Had you seen him before?" Matthias repeated the question. I shook my head. Sighing, Matthias leaned back in his seat before he stood up and came around to my side. He crouched next to me, taking the coffee cup from my hands and placing it on the table before he turned my chair to face him.

"I need you to be very honest right now, Ava." His tone was sharp as his hard eyes held mine. Gone was the warmth I had seen not just minutes before. Replaced by those dark thunderstorms. "What did Elias want you to do for him?"

The lump was growing. I swallowed hard, trying to dislodge it, but nothing. Instead, I shook my head, lowering my gaze to my hands that were fiddling restlessly in my lap. There was no way I could tell him what my father had wanted me to do. What he still expected me to do.

A woman's best weapon is between her legs.

Those words made my skin crawl, causing goosebumps to break out like hives on my flesh, and fresh tears clung to the edges of my eyes. I blinked them back, refusing to allow them to fall. Fuck all this crying.

"*Krasnyy.*" His voice was a warning. Deep, slicing like a blade through my mind.

He—" Why was it so hard to admit? Because once I told him what my father had asked me to do, he would ask me how I planned on acquiring that information. I didn't want to tell him my father's plan for me. What would he do to me if he knew my father had expected me to sleep my way through his men like Mata Hari to gain information for him? Would he kill me? Punish me?

Although Matthias had shown no proclivity for physical

beatings like my father, he had still shown that he would punish me. Something I wasn't altogether sure I hated.

Yep. I needed therapy.

"He wanted me to spy."

"I know that." Matthias sighed. "What information did he want you to obtain?"

I managed to swallow back the lump in my throat. Barely. "Codes. Layouts. Passwords. Anything I could get my hands on."

"And how did you plan on getting this information, Red?" He growled. "Elias isn't stupid. He would have known that I wouldn't freely offer up anything like that." No, he wouldn't. Even if my pussy had managed to captivate him somehow. Matthias was more controlled than that. He had to be. My body lit up with shame, heat coursing through me like a rampant volcano as I struggled to keep calm.

"Tell me."

I shook my head, not wanting to answer him.

"Please don't make me," I murmured dejectedly. Matthias's thumb and index finger pinched my chin, forcing it up so I was staring directly into his eyes again.

"Tell me, Ava, or you won't like the consequences," he all but snarled. "I don't want to punish you, but I will. And this time, there won't be any orgasms afterward. I guarantee that. I will use your body for my pleasure and leave you panting, breathless, and wanting for more."

"He wanted me to open my legs to your men, okay?" I shouted at him, pushing his hand away from my face as I brought my knees to my chest as if that small barrier would protect me from his rage. "Is that what you want to hear? He told me that a woman's best weapon was between her thighs and that I needed to use that. Happy now? Does it make you feel better knowing that the woman you married is no better than the common whore you treat her like? Makes last night a whole lot easier on you, doesn't it?"

"Oh, Red." His eyes darkened, the storm clouds shifting in his gaze. "You think I treated you like nothing more than a cheap whore last night? You don't know the half of it."

CHAPTER TWENTY-TWO

Ava

"I will teach you, Ava," Gasping, I had little time to brace myself as he roughly pulled me out of my chair and pushed me to kneel on the floor in front of him. "I will teach you exactly how a whore gets treated."

My eyes widened as he unbuckled his belt and released himself from the confines of his pants. I hadn't gotten the best view last night. Now, it was on full view for me to see, and I couldn't believe that thing had fit inside me. Like Matthias himself, it was large, thick, and erect.

"Wait," I swallowed nervously. "I don't know...I can't do that."

Matthias's eyes darkened; his smile turned sinister as he tangled his fingers in my hair, pulling my head back. God, why did I love how that felt? My scalp tingled, and my heart was beginning to gallop like a pony at the track. Who knew hair pulling could be so erotic?

Fuck. Therapy was definitely needed.

"Open your mouth."

"I bite." I snarled.

Matthias sneered down at me. "You'll crawl and beg, too. Now, open your mouth."

There was a war going on inside my mind. The prospect of giving him head had me wet between the thighs, but at the same time I knew he wasn't meaning for this to be erotic. He wanted nothing more than to use me. To show me what it would truly be like to be a whore on her knees.

In the end, I did as he told me. There was no use in fighting what he had planned for me. I would take my punishment now and be free of him later.

His erect cock slid between my lips. Tentatively, I closed my mouth on him and sucked, curious about the feeling. Sure, I was sheltered, but I wasn't a nun. Sex may not have been an option due to my overly watchful father, but I had a Kindle, and porn was free and kept my hands busy.

Matthias groaned, and my stomach flipped traitorously. I expected him to stop once I began to gag, but he kept pushing forward. Panicking, I shoved my hands against his thighs, gagging as the head of his cock touched the back of my throat. His hand in my hair prevented my head from moving.

"Relax your throat, Red," he snarled, pulling tightly on my hair. The action caused me to gasp, forcing me to swallow more of him. I tried to breathe through my nose, to quell the fear rising in my chest. My nails dug into his jeans as he thrust deeply, yet slowly. Saliva was dripping from the corners of my mouth, the sound of me slurping his cock filled the room. Then he pulled back. Coughing, I sucked in a few ragged breaths. I attempted to pull away from him, but he still had a tight hold on my hair.

"Please," I whimpered as he fisted his cock, bringing the bulbous head back to my lips. "I don't want to do this."

Matthias tilted his head and stared down at me. His gray eyes were fog-filled, devoid and uncaring. Like he was shutting himself off to my pleas.

"Whores don't get a choice, Ava," he growled. "Remember that next time you decide to accuse me for treating you like one." I cried as his hand gripped my jaw, fingers digging into the soft flesh of my cheeks. My mouth opened wide for him, and without care, he shoved his cock in.

The hand in my hair held me steady as he thrust in and out of my mouth like it was nothing more than a hole for him to seek his pleasure. I tried to shut down. Tried to close my eyes against the press of his thick length gliding along my lips, the musky taste against my tongue. He filled me so fully, and despite the harshness of his thrusts and the slice of his words, I was growing wetter by the second.

I choked and gagged as his tempo increased and his thrusts became deeper and more erratic. My jaw ached. My lips were no doubt swollen. Tears rushed down my heated cheeks and drool slid down my chin. With a roar, he came. Warm, salty cum filled my mouth, sliding down my throat.

"Swallow it all, *Krasnyy*." I did as I was told, swallowing it all down. "Good girl."

My pussy clenched at his words.

"That is how whores are treated, Ava," he said, tucking himself back into his pants. "They are used as nothing more than a warm hole to fuck. They don't get to come. They don't get to touch me. Whores take what is given to them and leave with a handful of cash."

Eyes cast down to the floor, I nodded. I wasn't ashamed that he had used me, and I sure as hell wasn't quiet because I voiced my opinion. He wanted to know what I planned on doing and I told him. I'd do it again, even if it ended the same way.

I was, however, wet and horny as hell. If there was any shame to be had, it was at how my body reacted to his brutal taking of my mouth.

"Now—" He lifted me to my feet and spun me around until I was bent over the kitchen table. A delicious moan left my parted lips unbidden when he once again buried his fist in my crimson curls as he spread my legs wide with the tap of his booted foot.

I whimpered when he pressed my face into the table. Cool air suddenly hit the bare skin of my legs as he tore my leggings down until they were bundled at my ankles.

"I'm going to show you how good it can be, Red."

Shivers raced up my spine as he dragged his fingertips up and down my heated inner thighs. My body was still betraying, reacting to his featherlight touch like a goddam traitor. The dark chuckle he emitted behind me told me he knew just what he was doing to me. *Bastard*.

He let his fingers skate along my folds, dancing back and forth until I was writhing beneath him, attempting to push back on his hand.

"Please..." I didn't know what I was begging for. It certainly wasn't for him to stop. It should have been, but it wasn't. The thudding of my heart was so loud in the quiet space that I had no doubt he could hear it beating like the little drummer boy. My tongue darted out to wet my lips, dry from panting. From sucking his cock. "Please..."

"You want to be touched, Red?" His voice was almost mocking. I groaned in protest when his fingers left my folds, only to cry out as he slammed two fingers into my wet heat. "Like this?" My eyes rolled back in my head as he pressed his thumb to my clit. The bundle of nerves stole a moan from me. I could feel him growing hard again, his erection pressing up against my ass, hardening with the sounds he was forcing from my lips.

"Are you wet and needy from getting your mouth fucked?" He whispered in my ear, his hot breath cascading over the shell of my ear. My body shivered in his hold; the smell of his aftershave combined with the heady musk of my own arousal turning me on even more. "Did you like being treated like my little whore? Whores don't get this, baby. Only you."

This wasn't right. It couldn't be right. I promised myself I wouldn't let him affect me this way, but my body wasn't getting the same message as my brain. There was a disconnect in my neural pathways I wasn't sure how to fix. Or that I even wanted to.

"Relax, Ava," he warned with a light swat to my ass. "Let me show you what the whores are missing out on."

His hand released from my hair, lingering for a single moment as a silent warning before it snaked up my shirt to my right breast. My nipple hardened beneath his gentle touch, the coil in my stomach growing tighter as he gently pinched it. Fireworks burst beneath my eyelids as his thumb applied more pressure to my clit.

"You like this, Red?" I nodded, unsure that I could speak without moaning like the wanton whore I had accused him of treating me like. "Good girl." My pussy clenched around his fingers at those two words, and I didn't have to see him to know he was smiling.

"Someone likes to be praised." He chuckled as he pushed his fingers in deeper, curling them at the knuckle. I couldn't help but push back into him as he picked up his pace. Heat spread through me at how much my body was betraying me, but I didn't want him to stop. "So tight, baby. So fucking wet for me."

Another cry pierced the room as he bit down on my shoulder and pinched my nipple. The coil was winding tighter and tighter, my body bucking beneath him, unashamed of its reaction to the stimulus he was providing.

He bit me again as he pressed the heel of his hand hard against my clit, rubbing in circles. I should have been ashamed of the sound his fingers were making as they pumped in and out of my wet pussy almost viciously, but I couldn't be bothered because every muscle in my body was tensing, ready to burst. Before I knew it, I was screaming my release, his name reverberating off the walls of the kitchen as the coil within me snapped.

I was breathless by the time my pleasure faded into a murky haze. My heart was pounding erratically in my chest. Matthias's fingers were still buried in my tight passage, his hand hadn't left my breast. As I came down, he slowly pulled his hand from between my legs, leaving me with an empty feeling.

"Lick them clean." He brought his fingers to my mouth, nudging the entrance of my lips. I stuck my tongue out to taste myself on his fingers, but Matthias, ever the impatient one, shoved the digits in my mouth without thought. It was a weird, musky taste, but not altogether unpleasant like I thought it would be. I'd always turned my nose up when the hero of a book made the heroine taste herself.

Now I understood the appeal. It was the act, not the taste, that made it arousing.

Matthias bent down and drew my pants back up my shaky legs. He'd released me, but I was still coming down from my high, so I stayed leaning over the table. I heard the screeching of a chair on the tiled floor, then his arms wrapped around me, dragging me back onto his lap.

"I'm not going to apologize for the way I treated you last night," his deep voice rumbled. "Nor am I going to say that it won't happen again. It will. This is your reality, Ava, and you need to learn to accept that. I will keep you safe. I will provide for you. In return, I expect you to be obedient, and in time, you will give me an heir. That is what this is. You don't have to like it, but you will not fight it."

He kissed the top of my head, a gesture that was opposite of the words he had just spoken.

"I will never beat you or mistreat you," he continued. "But if you disobey, you will be punished. If you lie, you will be punished. I don't take betrayal lightly, Ava. You need to know that."

I nodded, looking up at him. The thunderclouds in his eyes had receded, and once again, they were filled with the same warmth I had seen earlier this morning.

"You won't—" Shaking my head, I sighed rather than finishing my sentence.

"Won't what, Ava?" He cocked his head to the side. "Finish your sentence."

"You won't..." I bit my lip. "Cheat on me?" It came out more like a question than the demand I was hoping it would be. Matthias smirked but shook his head gently.

"No, Ava," He told me with all seriousness. "I will honor my vows."

"But the woman yesterday..." I tried to push, but one look from him silenced me.

"That was business."

My face darkened as I glared at him, crossing my arms against my chest. "So, it's okay to cheat if it's business? Do you get to write it off as a business expense on your tax sheet?"

Matthias groaned, running a hand down his stubbled jaw. "Nothing happened, Ava. Not everything is as it appears, and I'm not having this conversation with you right now. I was planning on an outing, but if you're going to act like a brat..."

"No," I shook my head violently. Outside meant sunshine and freedom. And the possibility to escape. "I'll be good. Promise."

"We'll see about that," he chuckled. "Go get cleaned up. We leave in half an hour."

Nodding enthusiastically, I scrambled off his lap to make my way out of the kitchen.

"And Ava," I stopped when he said my name. "Don't think that this means you can try to escape. If you run, I will find you, and you won't like what happens when I do."

Giving him a short nod, I swept from the room, my chest lighter than it had been in days. He might have warned me about escaping, but that didn't mean I couldn't plan. That I couldn't wait for the most opportune moment. I'd just have to make sure that when it struck, he wouldn't be able to find me, because I knew that if I stayed here much longer, Matthias would devour me whole .

CHAPTER TWENTY-THREE

Matthias

That certainly wasn't how I thought the morning would go. Couldn't say it was bad. I certainly enjoyed shoving my cock down her throat and hearing the sweet sounds of her orgasm had made me hard all over again, even after blowing my load in that hot little mouth of hers.

It had taken every ounce of willpower I had not to sink my cock into her pussy when I had her bent over the kitchen table, knowing she was probably still sore from last night. Still, every inch of me vibrated with the need to devour her again, to mark her as mine.

Her accusation about me was spot on. I couldn't deny that. I had treated her much like I treated the whores I once used, but I had done it to draw a line. For her to understand that intimacy and romance were two things she would not get from me. If that made her feel used, then so be it.

Ava needed to properly understand her role. She was my

wife, not my friend, and being my wife came with responsibilities. The top one being obedience. I would treat her with kindness, and I would show her affection in the privacy of our home, but there were still boundaries that couldn't be crossed.

I would not allow her to become a weakness.

The elevator to the penthouse beeped and then opened. I shook off the last few moments, clearing thoughts of mine and Ava's deeds from my mind as I strode from the kitchen toward the entryway. Both Nicolai and Vas were waiting for me.

"Boss," Vas greeted me. "Car's ready."

"Good." I reached into the hall closet to grab my coat. Donning it before snatching up the new one Mia had bought Ava. It was a waist-length black peacoat similar to mine. "Jesus," I muttered under my breath. That woman was anything but subtle.

"I'm ready." Ava came waltzing down the hallway wearing dark jeans that were tucked into a pair of knee-high riding style boots and a soft olive-green sweater that hung loosely off one shoulder. Her mess of red curls was up in a bun at the top of her head, something I was learning was the norm for her when she didn't want to take the time to deal with it.

"Let's go then." I held out the jacket for her, and she put it on without complaint. Vas input the code to the elevator, holding the doors open as we all stepped in. He pressed the button for the lobby, being sure to keep his access code from Ava's eyes. Smart man. I wouldn't put it past her to spy on any of our codes. Not that she would get much of a chance to use it since they rotate every week.

The ride down to the parking garage was quiet. I held her hand in mine, both as a way to keep her from running off and to feel her small hand in mine. Nicolai opened the back door, and I let Ava slide in first before taking my place next to her.

Once Nico and Vas were settled in front, we headed out, flanked by another set of black SUVs, one to the front and one behind us.

"Where are we going?" Ava piped up from beside me as her eyes took in the sights through the tinted glass. Sometimes I forgot that she hadn't seen the city she was practically raised in, and I made a mental note to have Mia add some activities to her schedule in the coming months once she'd proven to be obedient. We might not be a traditional married couple and she might be my pawn, but I refused to keep her as heavily isolated as her father had.

"We have a special compound for recruits," I told her as I scrolled through emails on my phone. "A sort of training camp up near Tiger Mountain. It also functions as a school for younger members who are born or brought into the fold."

"A school?" She looked over at me, her eyes shining. "Like a boarding school?"

I nodded. "Yes," I said. "It houses children from middle school through high school. Then, they can either choose to train for a spot in the *Bratva* right away or attend the local college before joining."

Her forehead creased. "Do they have to join?"

It was a fair question. I could only assume that Dante Romano didn't give his family much choice when it came to joining the mafia, but I couldn't be sure.

"No." It was an honest answer. We didn't force children to join after they graduated, but I had never had one of them walk away. The *Bratva* was all they had known growing up. We taught them from the moment they walked in our doors what was expected. "But everyone, even the children, who comes through our doors knows what we expect. Some may leave for a few years to go to college, which we pay for, but it is for the benefit of the Brotherhood. No one has walked away yet."

"Okay." She went back to staring out the window. I'd expected more from her than a simple word of understanding, but that was all I got.

It took about twenty minutes to get to the school. The highway could often get busy during the week, which was why we also had a helicopter to take me out there when needed, but the weekend traffic was usually light enough.

Vas pulled off the main road. About a mile down was a large, heavy, black iron gate that circled the length of the compound. I owned somewhere around two hundred and twenty acres, which meant that I had fenced almost twenty square blocks to ensure the safety of my men and students.

Armed men guarded the perimeter at certain vantage points around the clock, but just like my building in the city, I relied heavily on state-of-the-art technology. Each student, teacher, and worker was awarded personal access codes that allowed them into the buildings. That ensured that no one could go where they weren't welcome. I didn't need any of the younger students getting curious and accessing the gun range before they were ready.

Although we taught our younger students about the brutality of working for the *Bratva*, we liked to first instill loyalty and make sure they were mentally prepared for further training. Once inside the gate, Vas pulled our brigade through the circle driveway, parking us directly in front of the main building.

"Wow." Ava's eyes widened as she took in the large campus. No one besides Tomas knew the location of the compound, though some had come close. We monitored the main road and local radio chatter to ensure it remained out of sight. I didn't need my enemies finding out where it was. It was my job to guarantee the safety of my students and those who worked here. "I'm not sure what I was expecting, but it wasn't this. How do you keep this fortified? Do people just apply to be part of the *Bratva* or are they recommended? Does everyone go through here? Including adults, or is it just children?"

Nicolai chuckled as he opened the door. When she wasn't afraid or angry, she was certainly a curious woman. I couldn't blame her for that, knowing the way her father had kept her locked up. She'd been isolated nearly her entire life; this was new for her.

"Not now, Ava," I told her. "Keep your questions for later when we are alone. Right now, you need to be my obedient wife. No speaking out of turn, and you will do as I instruct, or there won't be any more outings. Clear?"

Sighing, she nodded her head, eyes seeking the floor dejectedly. I knew I shouldn't have shut her down completely or threatened her with isolation, but it was important for the men and students here to know that my wife was obedient to me. If the *Pakhan* couldn't control his wife, how could he control the *Bratva*? That was what they would ask, and I couldn't have anyone questioning my position.

Taking her hand, I led her up the stairs of the large white building we used for administration and mail. It also housed my private suite on the top floor, separate from the barracks. My cousin Roman was waiting at the top for us, a boy around fourteen standing next to him, holding open the door. He was tall for his age, gangly, with a shaved head and a fearless look in his eyes. Roman had told me about him; his name was Ollie, and he was nearly killed by his father in a drunken rage. His father was now dead, and Ollie, who was technically a ward of the state, was brought here.

"Roman." Letting go of Ava's hand, I embraced my cousin

in a brief hug. "How is everything?" Roman shrugged a shoulder.

"Pretty quiet," he reported, knowing that I would want a full rundown of how operations were running. "We have two graduating this week, ready to take their places on the streets. They work well together, and I was thinking about placing them down in Highline under Maxim and Yelena."

I considered that for a moment. Maxim and Yelena were a married couple who both ran the role as Brigadier further south in a small section of King County. They were the first couple in *Bratva* history to run a territory together as co-brigadiers. The *Bratva* still held tightly to old traditions, but I had already blown most of those out of the water by allowing non-Russians to become made men or *Vor*, so I thought, why the hell not? Yelena would never be able to wear the stars of the *Vor*, but that didn't make her any less powerful in my Brotherhood.

"Go ahead." I gave him a short nod as we stepped inside the building. Ava stuck to my side, her head turning every which way as she took in her surroundings. "Roman, this is my wife, Ava. Ava, this is my cousin, Roman."

Ava turned her eyes to my cousin and gave him a shy smile. Roman reached out his hand and she took it. "It's nice to meet you, Ava." My wife simply nodded her head before dropping his hand. She went back to taking in the building, watching as a few students chatted in the halls while a few of the faculty came out to greet me.

"Why don't we take a walk over to the lecture hall so Ava can see where the children learn." At my words, Ava looked up at me, her mouth curved into a bright smile as she eagerly followed behind me while Roman led the way through the side door toward a large three-story building on the east side of the campus.

"There are ten buildings total, including housing," Roman rattled off as we walked. The sun was shining today, and the wind wasn't as biting as it normally was, so I wasn't worried about Ava being too cold. Not that she would notice anyway. She was too busy listening to Roman talk about the school to notice if it was cold or not.

"The adults are housed in a section on the other side of campus that is attached to the training building." Roman pointed farther south. "Student and teacher housing are down that way. There is a cafeteria, gym, pool, gun range, and a full medical center as well. And this..." He stopped as we approached building three. "Is where you will be working, Mrs. Dashkov."

CHAPTER TWENTY-FOUR

Matthias

Roman had left us to our own devices, giving me time to watch Ava as she wandered around the small classroom that would now be hers. Well, hers and Roman's. I wasn't ready to let my Lil Red fly on her own just yet. The compound might be more secure than Fort Knox, but I wasn't taking any chances.

Her bright eyes took in the whitewashed walls and large windows that overlooked the small courtyard below. The desks were slightly curved, able to fit two bodies comfortably, each row long enough for six students max. Two more sets of rows sat behind the first one, each with a small incline going up the dais.

"What do you think?" I asked her. I was honestly curious about her opinion on the space. Despite Ava having no practical experience in the classroom, I knew her mother had once been a music teacher. Would Ava have wanted to follow in her footsteps if she had been allowed?

"Honestly, I don't know what to think, Matthias." Her blunt response surprised me. "About any of this."

"Elaborate." One thing I noticed is that when she became frustrated, she tended to be vague. *About any of this* was an all-encompassing statement and she knew it.

Ava let out a frustrated sigh as she paced in front of the teacher's desk, *her* desk, fiddling with the sleeves of her sweater. A nervous habit, I'd learned. The woman wasn't hard to read, she wore her emotions like a shield. Fear and pain were the only things I had seen her attempt to hide. No doubt, a mechanism of defense her mind learned when it realized how much its tormenters fed on them. It was no different than her body learning to curl in on itself when it expected pain.

"I mean, why are you doing this?" The look on her face read disbelief, but her eyes glimmered with a small sliver of hope for at least some margin of freedom. Ava had been locked away for so long her taste of freedom while on the run was no different than a drug. She wanted more. "Do you really plan on letting me teach here? Whatever, *here*, is?"

Shrugging out of my coat, I laid it across one of the desks. Her beautiful eyes widened at my approach, and she scurried behind her desk in an attempt to put a barrier between us. My *Malen'kaya Krasnyy* had no idea how much that small move ignited the predator within me.

My blood was still pumping from this morning. My mind replaying the images of her mouth wrapped around my cock as I fucked it like she was a common whore. She'd gotten wet. My Little Red had been turned on by the thought of being used like one of Valerie's girls.

"I already explained to you what the compound is," I told her. "And you are here because you have a degree that I have

JO MCCALL

use for. The history teacher is on maternity leave for the foreseeable future, and Roman can't keep filling in. My cousin is many things, an accurate historian is not one of them."

Just the other day, I caught him telling students how Russia was the supreme influence in several of the key moments of World War Two and that the pyramids were built by aliens. The students, luckily enough, weren't that gullible.

I rounded the side of the desk, but she mirrored my movement in the opposite direction, keeping distance between us. My brow creased in confusion at her actions. She was like a scared little rabbit with the way she kept dodging away from my advances.

"What are you doing?" She hadn't been avoiding me before now. If anything, she had sought some minor comfort in my presence when we first arrived. Something I relished.

"I don't want to be punished," she mumbled somewhat petulantly. Her full bottom lip was pushed out in a pout, an action I had seen many women do in order to achieve an end goal, but on Ava, it was completely innocent.

"Did you do something wrong?" I asked her curiously, cocking my head to the side. Her top teeth came out to bite that delicious pouting lip as her eyes lowered to the ground.

"Well, no." She fidgeted with her sleeves again. I hated how adorable that small action was. It wasn't something I should find adorable.

"Then why would I punish you?" It was a question I wanted to know the answer to. As much as I wanted to punish her and see the pale skin of her ass steadily grow red under my hand, I didn't want Ava to constantly fear it. If done right, she would one day come to crave my punishments. Crave the feeling of the supple leather against her smooth, unblemished backside. Crave the control I had over her.

"You looked angry."

There it was. Three simple words that had my blood boiling beneath my skin. The beast clawed at my chest, wanting to be free, to avenge her. To kill for her. And one day he would. Soon. But for now, I had to play it smart.

"I'm not angry, Red," I assured her as I came around the desk. This time, she didn't move away but let me approach her. There was still a cautious look in her eye. The kind of look that told me she was still wary of my intentions. "And I won't punish you if you haven't broken any rules. I am not Elias or Christian. You don't have to be afraid to ask questions, especially when we are alone. As long as you aren't questioning my authority in front of my men."

She swallowed hard and nodded, still not looking directly at me. I took her chin in my hand and forced her to meet my gaze so she could see that I was serious. That I meant every word.

"Now, I have business here for the next few days." I let my thumb caress the side of her face. She leaned into my touch, almost like she was seeking comfort. "Roman will help you acclimate to the classroom, answer all of your questions. You'll teach three days a week for four hours. Do you think you can handle that?"

"Yes," she whispered, giving me a small smile, her eyes burning just a bit brighter than normal. "I can handle it."

"Good girl." Her breath caught on those two words, confirming my suspicions from this morning. My naughty Little Red liked being praised. A knock came at the door, interrupting our small moment.

"We'll continue this later." I planted a gentle kiss on her forehead before I stepped away, giving her some space. "Someone has been waiting patiently to see you."

Her head shifted to the closed door as I called out for Roman to enter. A small, choked sob left her parted lips as she took in her guest, her eyes filled with tears as she let her gaze roam over them. It wasn't the surprise I wanted to give her, but this would do for now until I could get the intel and help I required to pull off a stunt that big.

"Hello, Ava."

CHAPTER TWENTY-FIVE

Ava

"Mark?"

I could scarcely believe it. He was standing before me like a whole new person. His hair looked washed, eyes no longer drooping and bloodshot. He was also less haggard looking since I had last seen him a year ago. We'd attended the same school, but the age difference had us running in different circles. I'd seen him around, the loner kid, much like me, but I hadn't officially met him until Maleah introduced us.

He was the one who had forged my new identity. Birth certificate, social security number, everything. I hadn't thought about him since I'd been forced back to Seattle. We had no ties. But here he was, alive and...Mark didn't exactly look "well." His hygiene had improved, and he no longer looked like he was doing drugs, but his face was mottled with yellowing bruises. His bottom lip had stitches, and his nose was slightly askew.

"What are you doing here? What happened..." I stumbled over my words as my brain tried to process what my eyes were putting together. My mind had apparently been restarting, but the moment it booted up properly, it all came together. "It was you. You told them about Maleah."

Mark had the good sense to look ashamed. His narrow face tinted pink beneath the bruising, and his gaze cast down to the floor in outright shame. Good. He should be ashamed. Maleah was god knows where, probably being sold to some prick overseas, and he was standing here, alive and mostly unharmed. How was that fair? Maleah had never harmed anyone. Never stepped a toe out of line. Mark had grown up doing drugs and ran credit card schemes. He was a cheater of the system.

I put a stop to the toxic thoughts, halting that train of blame before it went careening off a cliff. It wasn't his fault.

"Ava—" My name was a soft murmur of regret on his cracked lips. Mark's gaze darted to Matthias, who was standing quietly to my right, before it settled back on me. Almost like he was asking for permission to continue.

I turned away from him, anger and frustration welling up inside my chest as I turned a cold glare on Matthias. This wasn't Mark's fault. It was his. The man who refused to simply let me go. To give up the chase. The man who forced me to be his wife. Everything was his fault. *And mine.*

The train of blame was starting up again, and this time I wasn't going to stop it. If I went hurtling off the deep end, I'd take him with me.

"Did you do that to him?" I snarled up at Matthias. Why'd he have to be so tall? "Is this what you did to find me? You beat him to gain information? Is that what you do? Beat those weaker than you until they cave? Does that make you feel like a man?"

"Ava." Matthias's face darkened, his tone low, warning me that if I continued on this path of destruction, I would regret it. And maybe I would, but at the moment all I wanted to do was give the man who had ruined the three of us a large *fuck you* and the middle finger.

"Ava," I mocked his surly growl. "What did I ever do to you? Huh? Tell me. What did Maleah ever do to deserve what my family did to her? Do you know what they did to her, Matthias? What they made me watch? All because you couldn't just leave it alone. Couldn't leave *me* alone."

The look on his face said it all. He knew. He damn well knew what Christian had done to my best friend, and it made me sick to my stomach. What kind of man had I been forced to marry? Sure, I thought him hard, unyielding, and somewhat cold in his demeanor, but I never thought he would turn out to be as bad as my father. He'd shown that he was different, but this? This served as a chilly reminder of just who Matthias Dashkov was.

A monster.

"Do you mind if have a moment with her, sir?"

I swung around to stare open mouthed at Mark. Sir? What the hell? Now he was calling Matthias sir? The man who had rearranged his face to look like a Picasso painting. I didn't need to be looking at Matthias to know that his gray eyes had become thunderous. The heat of his no doubt impressive glare could probably melt iron if given the chance. I could sure as hell feel it burning a hole in my back.

"You have five minutes." That was all the monster said as he stormed from the room with Roman, slamming the door behind him on his way out. That was a trait my father had. Whenever he was angry, he would slam something, break something, beat someone. Usually me. That was the cycle I had become accustomed to. The one I had been hoping to break.

Matthias had said he would never beat me, but how long would his anger stow itself away before it finally popped? If he could beat Mark for information, what was stopping him from turning those fists on me?

Nothing. That's what. Men who couldn't control their anger were dangerous. Men who beat lesser men were monsters. Matthias might look like a sheep in his sheep's clothing and charming smile, but beneath the surface prowled a predator. A wolf ready to bite into the weakest sheep of the herd.

"Ava," Mark murmured my name again, slightly stronger than the first time. His light eyes bored into mine, clouded with guilt and shame, but there was something else I hadn't seen before. Life.

When Maleah had taken me to Mark after I had managed to escape my father's property, he'd been nothing but a shell of a man. A dried-up husk consumed by alcohol and drugs. His eyes had been clouded, holding nothing more than turmoil and distress.

Now, they held a spark of something new. My mother would have called it hope. She used to say the eyes were windows into a person's soul. You could tell just how far gone someone was by looking into their eyes. When I had first met Mark, he was so far gone I doubted I would ever see him alive again. If the drugs and alcohol didn't kill him, something else would. Now, he looked like he had a purpose. A reason to live.

His clothes were no longer baggy and hanging off his too-skinny frame. He'd gained some weight. Not a large amount, but enough to make him look less like the walking dead and more like a human. The needle marks on his arms were nearly healed. Only small, pale scars remained.

He looked...healthy.

"I'm sorry, Ava," he whispered before letting out a long, deep sigh. One full of release. It was like he had been waiting to say those words, and now that he had, he was lighter. "Dashkov managed to somehow find out that I had forged your paperwork, and he came looking. I tried. Honestly. I tried so hard not to give up Maleah's name, but—"

He didn't have to say it. *But the pain was too much.* Mark had drowned himself in booze and pills for years to *escape* pain, not beg for more. How many times had I done the exact same thing over the years? Given in because I could no longer stand the pain being etched into my skin. Shit, I had pretty much drunk my nights away the last year just to keep the shadows at bay.

Mark had sold us out, but I couldn't bring myself to hate him. That was reserved for someone else entirely.

"My brother raped her." I hadn't meant to, but the words blurted themselves out before I could stop them. "In front of me. He made me watch. Told me it was my fault."

"I know."

He knew? Just like Matthias knew. Everyone knew, but the only four people who had been in that cell were Neil, Maleah, Christian and me. How could everyone know?

"I don't understand."

"There was a..." he hesitated before continuing. "...video of what happened put up on a black-market site that deals in human trafficking. Dashkov had me attempting to take it down to prevent any bids, but Elias had already sold her before I had a chance. Ever since then, he's had me searching. Even has Valerie, one of his working girls, keeping her ear to the ground in case something pops up."

Valerie? The blonde in his room yesterday? I'd heard Vas talking to Matthias about her. Bile rose in my throat at the thought of Matthias using whores to get off. Even if he was having them search for Maleah. Did Valerie want to be with him? Was she willing? Or was she just another victim like my father's women?

"How did you end up here?" I shifted away from the topic of Valerie before my stomach could tie itself up in knots. I'd let him touch me. Those hands that had forced women to meet his demands had touched me. Caressed me. Brought me to orgasm. The very thought had my skin crawling.

Mark smiled. A real smile, one that lit up his eyes, causing them to crinkle at the corner.

"Well, after Dashkov's men were done beating the shit out of me, he offered me a job. Three square meals a day, a place to sleep that was safe, and a hell of a good salary." He shrugged. "I mean, I'm not allowed to drink or do drugs anymore, but I've found I don't really miss it, ya know? I went cold turkey, and it was hell, but I came out the other side better."

"What does he have you do?"

"A little of this. A little of that." He leaned against one of the desks and crossed his arms. The more we talked, the more confident he seemed to become. It was like a weight had been lifted from him now that he knew I didn't blame him for what happened to Maleah. "Upgraded their entire security system, helped create new documents for some of the kids here who were rescued. Patrol the dark web. Those sorts of things."

"You look better."

His smile morphed into a stunning grin. "I feel better. More alive. Despite our rocky beginning, everyone here has treated me well. Given me a purpose. I didn't have that before. My father was a drunk and my mother wasn't around much when I was little. So..."

So, he was just as messed up as me. The one difference between us was that Mark had been given a purpose. A home. I had none of those things. What was my purpose? To be Matthias's pawn as his wife? Give him a child and then one day be forced out once he tired of me?

"Listen." He peered around me at the closed door. His expression became guarded. There wasn't a window, but I wasn't naïve enough to think that there weren't eyes in here, watching us. "Time is almost up. Do you think we could talk Wednesday before you go back to the city? There is a small cubby on the east side of the building, not far from here that isn't monitored. Meet me there between your third and fourth class."

I cocked my head. "Why?"

"I have something you need to take a look at," he pressed. "Just...just don't tell anyone."

"Fine," I acquiesced. "But just so you know, I've got stalkers who follow me everywhere." Mark chuckled.

"Let me take care of that."

"Why don't you just..." My words halted when the door to the classroom burst open. Our time was up. I was somewhat surprised Matthias even gave us time alone. I appreciated the gesture, but he was still a monster. Mark waved his goodbye as he followed Roman out of the room, once again leaving me alone with Matthias.

CHAPTER TWENTY-SIX

Matthias

"Let's go, Avaleigh."

I knew she would question the use of her full first name, but it got her attention. My tone left no room for her to argue, but I could see the conflict rising in her crystalline gaze as she warred with herself. An angry flush had crept up her neck and her small fists were clenched tightly at her side. Tears shimmered in her eyes, threatening to tip over the dam, but they weren't sad tears.

They were tears of fury and anger. My Little Red was trying not to show her claws.

Snatching up the coat she had discarded earlier, I held it out for her. She gave a cute little huff before pushing her arms through and wrapping it around her supple body. A body I'd been thinking about sinking my cock in for several hours. But that would have to wait. There were a few things that needed taking care of first. I donned my own coat before I led her out of the room.

Ava was oddly silent as we exited the building. My long strides chewed up the distance as I led us back to the administration building that housed my suite here at the compound. I needed to get her alone before my own fury erupted. She struggled to keep pace with me, but I ignored her, pulling slightly harder on her arm so that she was forced to keep up.

My body was rigid and coiled. The beast within struggling to rise to the surface and show her what a monster I could truly be. Her sharp words rattled around in my brain like a ball in a pin-machine ball. Back and forth, up and down. I'd expected her to be angry over Mark's appearance, but the outright hostility she had displayed caught me by surprise.

It was the only reason I didn't turn her over my knee right then and there for both of my men to see. I'd asked very little of her, obedience in front of my men was one of them. Something that wasn't all that hard, in my opinion.

The building was empty and silent as we entered. It was nearing lunchtime, and this building was hardly ever populated in the afternoon and evening hours. Our footsteps echoed loudly off the tiled floors, the sound harsh in the large space, jarring my senses. My little redhead stumbled over her feet a few times before I released a heavy, frustrated sigh. I didn't bother to slow my pace, instead, I turned, bent down, and hauled her over my shoulder.

This was easier. Simpler. And the view was certainly five stars. Ava's protest earned a sharp swat to her backside. One that was hard enough that she would feel it through the denim that covered her pert, delectable ass. I let my thumb caress her leg as I kept walking, completely undisturbed by the maddening girl on my shoulder.

Her huffs of anger really were cute.

Jesus. What the hell was this woman doing to me? I couldn't remember the last time I used the word *cute* in a sentence regarding anything. Not even those ridiculous cat Tik-Toks Vas kept showing me. I was more of a dog man anyway.

"Matthias." I loved the way she said my name in that pleading voice that was half filled with want and half with anger. Two sides fighting each other for dominance. I wondered if she realized just how hot fucking would be if she let those two emotions play together.

Despite her sexy little plea, there was no stopping me. The large wooden door of my suite loomed before us, and I opened it with my free hand, careful to duck low enough so that she wouldn't hit her head on the door frame. Then I kicked the door shut with my foot.

Ava had stopped wiggling in my hold, and I didn't have to see her face to know that she was taking in the room. If she was smart, she would be looking for signs of egress, but I knew my Little Red didn't think the same way I did. No, my little minx was most likely psychoanalyzing the space so she could get a deeper feel of me.

She was no doubt coming up with reasons in her head for why the space held very little sentimentality. No pictures. None of those little chachkas many Americans seemed to possess. The space was all clean lines and bare walls. Somewhat different than the shared space of my penthouse, which held a more homey feeling.

Her struggle renewed, but only mildly so, as I stepped into the bedroom. This one was considerably smaller than the master suite back in the city. The bed was a queen, rather than a king, and the walls were a soft cream instead of a stark white. The furniture was older, a dark oak that had small veins of gold running through it.

It was the showiest thing I owned in this space.

Ava let out a small squeak when I dumped her onto the firm mattress of my bed. Her panicked gaze darted around the room; her body frozen momentarily before it finally caught up with her brain. She took one look at my expression, her eyes widening, and scrambled for the edge of the bed.

"Ava." The dark tenor of my warning caused her to still. She shot me a baleful glare that I'm sure could collapse nations if given the right opportunity. Ava looked like a goddess sitting there, her red hair falling out of its bun, emerald eyes shining with defiance. I wanted nothing more than to get on my knees and worship her, but that would have to wait.

She had broken one of my rules.

I paced back and forth in front of the ornately carved dresser, trying my best to calm down my racing heart before I punished her. Punishment was never to be doled out in anger. I would need to be calm and controlled, and right now I was far from that state of mind. My body wanted nothing more than to claim her, mark her. Every inch of me vibrated with the need to devour her. To show her she was mine.

"Do you know how infuriating you are?" I wasn't expecting her to answer. Of course, she didn't know. How could she? The woman was brimming with innocence. I needed to punish her disobedience, but I couldn't deny how hard my cock had become when she had stood up to me. That was the kind of fire I wanted to see in her when we were alone.

"You can't seem to obey simple commands. All I asked of you were two simple things, Ava. Obedience and loyalty."

"Like a fucking dog," she snarled at me, but she still didn't move from the edge of the bed. Her body was poised to advance, but the hesitation in her eyes told me she knew better. Ava knew I had the mind of a predator, and she didn't want to become the prey. If she ran, I would give chase. She knew this.

"If the shoe fits," I growled, removing my coat. I threw it over one of the chairs in the corner of the room before turning my focus back to her. It was harsh, calling her that, but I wasn't in the mindset to care. "Don't think I haven't noticed how your pussy clenched around my fingers every time I called you a *good girl.*"

Her face turned a bright shade of crimson, and I didn't miss how her thighs subtly clenched together. Shit. Even just casually saying those two words seemed to affect her.

"Fuck you, Matthias Dashkov." She stood up, her voice dripping with venom as she faced me, the adrenaline of her anger making her brave. Good. I wanted her to be brave. I wanted her to challenge me.

Just not in front of my fucking men.

"You think you're all high and mighty. The big bad Russian leader, but you're nothing more than a bully and a beast. Just like my father."

And then she had to cross that fucking line.

I struck out like an angered snake, my fist snatching up the hair that had fallen from her bun and gripping it tight. Her face contorted in a grimace, and I could see tears swarming the surface of her eyes as she struggled to keep from crying out. She was caught somewhere between anger and fear as she took in my tight expression.

Ava was well aware she had just stepped over a line, but I knew that wasn't going to stop her. I may not have known her for very long, but one thing I learned was she had a hard time knowing when to stop. My jaw clenched and I pursed my lips, breathing heavily through my nose as I struggled to remain in control of my baser desires and the urge to rip her clothes from her body and fuck her until she learned who was in control.

"I am nothing like Elias, Red." I leaned forward, my grip tightening on her hair, using the soft strands to crane her head back farther so she could see directly into my eyes. The action caused her back to arch and her chest to push out. I would bet good money that beneath her coat, her nipples were hard and pressing against her soft sweater, begging to be pinched, to be sucked.

Fuck. My cock was lengthening in my pants at the thought of wrapping my lips around one of her pretty pink nipples. What was this woman doing to me?

"Let's get that straight right now." I didn't let my eyes stray from hers as I pushed back the primal savagery that threatened to overflow like a riverbank during a rainstorm. Our faces were barely a breath apart and I wanted nothing more than to lean in and kiss her, but there wasn't time for that now.

"You sure as hell act like him," she scoffed as she brought her hands up to my wrist that was attached to the hand wrapped in her bouncy curls. It was a weak attempt to get me ease the pressure on her scalp.

That wasn't going to happen.

"Beating up the lesser man to gain information. Handing Maleah over to my father knowing full well what he would do to her. Forcing me to marry you."

Her hands left my wrist with a frustrated sigh and pushed at my chest instead. It took everything I had to keep from laughing as she attempted and failed to move my bulky form. She was like a little wolf pup biting at its sire's ear to earn a howl when it had no teeth.

"How about the fact that you use sex workers? Huh? Do

JO MCCALL

you pay them like a good gentleman, or do you threaten to kill them to keep them in line?"

A frustrated growl erupted from my chest, but I didn't move to silence her. She needed this time to vent. To let it all out. Fucking Mark had to go and tell her that Valerie was a call girl. Didn't bother to elaborate, otherwise she would know I don't use Valerie for sex.

"Look in the mirror, Matthias. Those are some pretty scary similarities."

"You know nothing about me." The anger that had filtered my tone had calmed now, but I could tell that hers hadn't. She was frustrated and confused and no doubt tired of trying to figure out where to draw the line. She'd been docile compared to what my spy had informed me was her "firecracker attitude."

When I'd forced her to marry me, I had expected rage, fire. Anything but the tears and resignation she had given me. Then, I confronted her about the cell phone Elias had given her, and she had run in fear. The most fire I had seen from her was the first night I had taken her home and punished her. It looked like she was now done walking on eggshells around me. Good. Her fight was a lot hotter than her being a docile little lamb.

"Because you don't tell me anything!" she all but screamed in my face. Shit, now her lower lip was trembling. *Blyad'*. *Fuck*. I didn't want her to cry. These weren't tears that got my dick hard. "In the forty-eight hours I've been with you, you've told me zilch. Zero. Nada. The only thing I've learned is that you're a serious neat freak, you don't have anything sentimental, and you PMS more than a chick. You blow hot one second and cold the next. They have medication for that, you know. Try taking some."

My eyes closed tightly as I took a deep breath, fighting

back the irritation at her words. Her honest words. Maybe Vas was right. I wouldn't hurt her physically, but not including her, shutting her out, those things were already taking their toll on her, even if she didn't see it herself.

The PMS comment was a little harsh, though, if not creative at getting her point across.

"I'd stop while you're ahead, Red."

It was an outright warning. A giant stop sign in the middle of the road, but I could tell from the dark look on her face that she wasn't going to obey. Bring it on then.

"No. I'm done being told what to do and how to act." Her eyes found mine and held them. I had to give her credit, that took balls. There were grown men who couldn't stomach looking me in the eye, and here she was, blatantly glaring up at me. She kind of reminded me of Tinkerbell, that little fairy from an old children's movie. Robust and defiant.

"Why the hell couldn't you just leave me the fuck alone? I was happy in Texas. Finally getting to live my own life, and then you had to send it all crashing down."

"Living?" My hand left her hair, and I took a few steps back, my face twisting in utter disgust at what she considered to be "living." "Is that what you call that pitiful existence? You lived above the dive bar you worked at. Sampling the booze every night to chase away the shadows. That crappy apartment was one inspection away from being condemned. You had no friends. No lovers. No one who knew who you really were. That wasn't living, Ava. That was barely surviving."

"You made it that way," she screamed again. This time she launched herself at me, her small fists pummeling my muscled chest. The move caught me by surprise, and I simply stood there and let her cries of anger and pain rent the air. "You're the one who had to go and accept my father's deranged offer. This is all your fault."

Then the dam broke free. Small rivers of tears slipped down her face as she continued to take out her frustrations on me. I let her. She needed this, and when she was done, she would learn her lesson and we would move on.

"So, my life wasn't all that glamorous. Big deal. So, I drank to forget. Who hasn't?" Slap after slap. Punch after punch. None of it fazed me. I let her have this moment. "You know what the most important part of all that was? I had the choice to do it. I chose to work at that crappy bar. I chose to live in that shitty apartment. I chose to drink my days away. ME. Not my father. Not my brother. Sure as hell not you. ME."

The problem with having sudden control when it's never been given to you before is that you could end up spiraling. That was exactly what Ava had done in Texas. She may have been responsible and gotten a job, but she'd drunk most of her money away that wasn't on rent. Her clothes were old, mostly stained, and from a secondhand thrift shop. She barely ate, barely slept.

Ava had choices all right; she just hadn't made the right ones.

"Would you rather I left you to Elias?" My words halted her assault. They weren't bitter or angry. Hell, I even managed to keep the mocking out of my voice. It was an honest question. "Trust me, Red. What he had planned for you was far worse than anything I would ever consider doing."

"And what did he have planned?" There was no way in hell I was going to tell her that. Not right now. Not while she was still under his spell. "See, this is exactly it. You take me from my father, but you don't tell me why. You force me to marry you, but you won't say what's in it for you. You told me not to worry about the blonde chick, Valerie or whatever, in your room yesterday morning, but you won't tell me why I shouldn't."

Horror drew across her face as it dawned on her what she had let slip. So, my Little Red was jealous. Well, jealous and suspicious that I was using working girls like Elias did.

"I don't have to share anything with you."

If she was jealous before, she was murderous now. By refusing to share information with her, she felt like I was isolating her. Keeping her out of the loop in order to control her. Manipulate her. What she didn't know was that it was simply to keep her safe. If Elias thought she meant something to me, she would become a bigger target than she already was.

"It's my life! I should know what is happening in *my* life. I should get a say."

I let out a long sigh, my hand running down my no doubt exasperated face as I struggled to hold myself in check. I wasn't used to having to explain myself.

"You need to trust me," I murmured as I took another calming breath. "There are..."

"Trust you?" she asked incredulously, her voice thick with emotion. Ava didn't want to trust me because in her mind, I hadn't earned the right. "You haven't earned my trust. You haven't earned a damn thing from me, Matthias."

Now she was outright sobbing.

"I saved you from a fate worse than Maleah's," I admitted. "Trust that."

"So what?" She let out a short, humorless laugh, her lips curling up in a sneer as her body continued to tremble with her small broken sobs. "You're my knight in shining armor? Don't make me laugh. You are nothing more than a beast, Matthias. A Big Bad Wolf ready to take a bite out of me."

Well, she wasn't wrong. I wanted to do much more than bite right now, though. My hand came up to cup her cheek, and I let the pad of my thumb wipe at the wetness that coated her soft ivory skin. So fragile. So breakable and completely mine.

"Is that what you want, Little Red?" I asked her softly as I leaned into her. "A knight in shining armor? Because if that is what you have been waiting for all this time, you were never going to find it. There is no such thing as a knight in shining armor, Ava. No such thing as good or evil. Black or white. There is just gray and the different shades within it. I'm a killer, and there is no changing that. Just like there is no changing your fate or Maleah's. I do what I must to get ahead. To keep my men safe. I take what I want, and I won't apologize for it."

"You're a monster."

I contemplated her words as my hands went to the buttons of her coat. "I may be a monster, Ava. But I'm your monster." I slid her coat off her slim shoulders, letting it pool on the floor at her feet. She met my gaze again, hard and steady, her chin tilting up slightly as she spoke her next words.

"I don't want a monster."

A dark chuckle left my lips.

"Too bad." I leaned in toward her, my lips grazing her ear. "That is exactly what you got."

CHAPTER TWENTY-SEVEN

Ava

"Now." His teeth nipped at my earlobe, causing me to gasp as one hand dipped down to undo the button of my jeans. "Up on the bed, Red. Hands and knees and lower your pants."

What? Pulling back, I shot him a look of disbelief. I was met with his stupid smile that was drenched in sin. His eyes darkened as he went for his belt. My thighs clenched together without my consent, and I could feel my body already responding to the stimuli he had yet to provide.

"What? W...why?" I stumbled over the words like a scared little girl. His smile widened; his face once again stretched into that youthful appearance I had seen the morning he had forced me to marry him. That was a panty-dropping smile, all right. Fuck. A girl could orgasm just from seeing it.

Not that I would be doing that...

Someone please call Dr. Phil or maybe schedule a

lobotomy. I told him I didn't need a monster. But I couldn't help being attracted to him all the same.

"Don't make this worse than it already is." He stepped toward me, forcing me to walk backward until my knees hit the edge of the mattress and I was forced to sit.

"Wait." I held up my hands as if to ward him off, but my weak shield shattered in a matter of moments as his hand encircled my throat. "Please. I'm sorry for yelling at you in front of your men."

Yep. I had knocked right through that rule like a wrecking ball through a concrete wall. Miley Cyrus would be proud.

"I know you are," he assured me gently. "But I'm going to make sure you remember how sorry you are for days. Make sure it sinks in. So, you can take it like a good girl and get rewarded later or you can fight me and regret it. Your choice, *malyshka*."

I shot him a cold look of defiance and rolled my shoulders back before I turned around and settled on my knees. God, this was humiliating. The sudden excitement that jolted my body as I lowered my jeans to my knees and braced myself on my elbows would have a therapist psychoanalyzing me for years.

There shouldn't have been any level of thrill right then. Not when I knew I was about to be belted, but my body tingled, and goosebumps broke out over my skin in anticipation as his hand gently grazed my bare ass. That was what I got for wearing a thong.

"Brace yourself, Ava."

That was all the warning I got before the whistle of leather disturbed the air to land across both of my ass cheeks. I hissed at the sting, my body lurching forward to escape the pain. Matthias merely *tsked* at me before shifting me back in place.

"Don't move or I'll start over."

Then he did it again and again and again. I whimpered as heat spread across my backside, and I bit my bottom lip to keep from crying out. But it wasn't just in pain. Each white-hot lash of the belt suddenly began to morph into something—more. My pussy clenched with each strike, and I could feel the wetness beginning to drip down my thighs.

My cheeks burned at the thought of Matthias seeing the evidence of my arousal caused by his hand. I let out a sob as one of his strikes landed where the bottom of my ass met my thighs. Fuck, that spot really hurt.

"Matthias!" I cried out, heavy tears rolling down my cheeks as the pain-pleasure sensations began to overwhelm me. "Please! I'm sorry. Really, I am." My forehead hit the soft duvet when my arms were no longer able to support my weight.

He laid his belt across my ass a few more times before I heard the jangle of the buckle hit the wooden floor. I sighed through my sobs, letting the tension of my body ease. The bed shifted as he sat beside me, one hand gently caressing my back before he picked me up and cradled me in his embrace.

I buried my face in his soft shirt to avoid his gaze. There was a war going on inside my head. Two sides facing off in a battle of wills. On one side, I felt humiliated and degraded. This was nothing like the riding crop he had used. It wasn't erotic, it was chastising. Like I was a little girl who'd been caught with her hand in the cookie jar.

Then there was the other side. It craved the pain he offered, the control. My body eagerly responded to the crack of his belt and the sear of leather against my supple skin. One side was angry, while the other side wanted to snuggle into him like a soft kitten. Unable to choose, I simply did both.

Angry snuggles.

I should get that on a T-shirt.

"I don't require your obedience because I am some kind of tyrant, Ava." He sighed as he held me to his chest and stroked my hair. He hadn't done this the first time he spanked me. Or even after sex. Mia called it *aftercare*. "But you can't confront me like that again."

"So, what?" I scoffed. "You won't ever hear what I have to say? What matters to me?"

Yep, I was still snuggled into his chest so I wouldn't have to face him. Cowardly? Maybe. But I was afraid that if I looked up at him, I would see the same swirling emotions in my eyes reflected in his.

"You can confront me all you want, *Krasnyy*," he assured me. "When we are alone. It is the same for my men. But when you challenge me like that, in front of them, it gives them an opening to defy me. Not all my men are completely loyal. There are those who would take the opportunity to kill me and take my place. I cannot allow this."

Well, when he put it that way.

"Will you start answering my questions when we are alone?"

He contemplated this for a second, silence filling the room. Then he sighed, but it wasn't out of frustration or irritation. It was resignation.

"Not everything," he admitted, tilting my chin up with his knuckle so he could see me. "But some things, I will."

"Then why did you take me and force me to marry you?" Something flickered in Matthias's eyes when I asked him that question. Something I'd never seen before.

Sadness. Why was he sad? What had my father done to cause the stoic man to elicit such a strong emotion, even if it was still buried beneath the silver storm of his gaze.

"Because you are going to help me destroy him."

CHAPTER TWENTY-EIGHT

Ava

B*ecause you are going to help me destroy him.*

There was a weight on my chest as I contemplated his words while I sat in the back seat of a small black Subaru that was driving across the compound toward the treelined boundaries.

Matthias had shown a small amount of tenderness as he held me for a few more minutes after my punishment. He'd removed my boots and jeans completely before he tucked me into bed to rest while he called for lunch. He hadn't said anything more about my father, and I hadn't pressed the issue. As much as I wanted to know more, I was still too emotionally exhausted from my rant.

The sky was already beginning to darken, the sun hiding behind the thick foliage of trees. I wanted to ask where we were going. There weren't any buildings out this way that I could see, and the dirt path was beginning to fade away to rougher terrain. I wondered why we were heading away from the relative safety of the compound's center hub. If I didn't know that he needed me to help take down my father, I might have been worried he was bringing me out here to bury my body.

"Where are we?" I asked as the truck slowed, entering a small circular clearing. There were a few other small trucks already there, but nothing else. My question was met with silence. Great. We were back to that again. Roman parked the truck before both he and Matthias exited. I waited for Matthias to open the door for me before sliding out myself.

Only because I knew the child-locks were engaged.

The winter air was cold and brisk. I buried myself into my jacket, my hands going into my pockets as Matthias guided me out of the clearing, his large hand on the small of my back. There wasn't anything to see at first. But the farther we walked from the clearing, the more I could see a small cement structure rise up from beneath the foliage surrounding it.

The cement fortification was inset, converging on a large metal green hematic door with a circular red handle at its center. I couldn't believe what I was seeing. Even my father didn't have something as secure as this. The *stables* were secure, but with enough force, it wouldn't be hard to penetrate through to the cells below.

A bunker was something completely different. This was James Bond-level shit.

The heavy clunk of the locks filled the air as Roman opened the door, holding it open for us. I shied away from the dark entry, the darkness emanating from beyond the door smelled musty, and the shadows seemed to want to reach out and ensnare me.

I'd never coped well with the dark. Matthias didn't give me time to think about the inky blackness as he led me forward. I couldn't help but cling to his side as we stepped through the door. Matthias might be a monster, but he was king among them. He could keep the other monsters at bay.

It was silly for a grown woman to fear the dark. But I knew what lingered in the abyss. Monsters. Ones created over the years by my father. I was fourteen when he first locked me away in the small basement beneath the shed that stood in our backyard. It was where he conducted the more savage side of his business. Where he taught his lessons.

The small room had smelled of rust and mildew. The concrete floor was stained darker in some areas, and large cutting instruments hung along the walls. I'd been bored that day. Kendra and my father had taken the twins out for ice cream and Christian had disappeared. I'd invited one of my friends over from school. Jimmy Parsons. He was a year older than me, smart and funny. We'd been paired together for a social studies assignment, and since I was never allowed to go anywhere, I thought it would be fine.

God, how wrong I'd been.

The action had been innocent. A simple kiss on the cheek as he left, but one of the guards had seen and reported it back to my father. Jimmy Parsons disappeared that day, and Elias Ward had shown his true nature.

I still didn't understand his reaction. Or Christian's. My brother had been furious. He'd come home late, his clothes stained a crimson red. It had taken a few years for my mind to process what my younger self couldn't. Jimmy Parsons was dead, and I was the cause.

Three days. That was how long I had been kept in that dank cellar, locked in a cage like an animal with only bread and water for sustenance. I'd been weak when he let me out. Weak and scared. What fourteen-year-old wouldn't be? But I had also felt something deeper. Loneliness and betrayal. It rooted itself deep in my mind that day, and I'd promised myself that no matter how long it took or how much I had to suffer—I would escape.

From that day forward, I learned to play the game my father set before me. Just because he wouldn't teach me the rules didn't mean I couldn't learn them. I listened when he spoke to his associates. Stashed away cash and goods the twins gave me. My daily walks outside became time to assess the grounds for weaknesses. I memorized when the guards changed their stations and to whom.

My father kept a neat and orderly home. He was predictable, and so were his men. Two years later, I'd attempted to escape. I had made it to the bus station before they caught up with me. If the bus hadn't been delayed, I would have made it. I would have been free.

The scars he made that day were more than just skin deep. They had etched themselves in my soul, branding me, changing me. Gone was the little girl who believed in knights in shining armor and brave, handsome princes. No one was coming to rescue me from my tower, and no one could be trusted.

My world had darkened that day, and nothing going forward was ever the same.

The door groaned shut behind me, the heavy click of the lock jolting me from my thoughts. I'd been so caught up in my memories that I hadn't even noticed the dim yellow lights that now illuminated the darkened stairwell.

We descended what felt like several floors before landing at the bottom and proceeding through a dimly lit corridor.

It was cleaner than I expected it to be. The walls on either side were clean-cut stone with exposed piping up above and bundles of wires along the side. With the door shut and locked, Matthias removed his hand from my back, and I immediately missed the comfort and warmth the small gesture brought me, despite knowing it had only been there to keep me from running.

Not that I could. There was nowhere to run. A fact I was all too aware of. At this point, I didn't even think I would run. At some point, yes. But now? Now I was too invested in learning where he was leading me.

Matthias led the way through the spacious corridor. My gaze darted from side to side, taking in everything I could. Not that there was much to see. It was all the same. It wasn't until we reached another large iron door, not unlike the first, that anything changed. The stone around the door was smoother, less rigid. The door itself was bigger and lacked the worn, rusted look of the one outside. This area must have been newer.

It wouldn't surprise me if the outside of the shelter had been built during the cold war. Washington had several of them littered throughout the state, but most were now owned by the department of transportation because it was illegal to prepare for a nuclear attack after the state had passed a bill in 1984.

Why Matthias thought he needed a nuclear Cold War bunker was beyond me. *Eccentric much?*

I moved out of the way so Roman could open the door. Unlike the entryway, it required a series of numbers to release the heavy locking mechanism in place. That definitely wasn't Cold War issued. I took a deep breath when a wave of air rushed over me like a tidal wave the moment the door slid open.

The air was recycled, but fresher than the air inside the corridor. I could hear a murmur of voices coming from deeper within the room, and I curiously followed behind Matthias like a lost puppy. It had an old-world feel to it that mixed well with the rough military feel. The small entryway fed into a vaster room.

It was easy to tell that Matthias hadn't redesigned the bunker to withstand a nuclear attack, but if anyone like my father came knocking, there would be no way for them to penetrate it. Not without some serious power.

I'd read somewhere that as long as a building was built with five-foot-thick reinforced concrete it could withstand a one megaton ground burst bomb from a mile away without being underground. These walls looked just about that thick.

"What is this place?" I asked as we stepped into the large, open room. Matthias opened his mouth to answer, but someone else beat him to it.

"The Bat Cave, of course."

I turned my gaze to my left to see Vas sitting at a large wooden table shaped in a half circle, a glass of amber liquid in his hand and a giant grin on his face. The table had ten chairs, with the largest chair centered directly in the middle, facing an immense wall filled with flat screens stacked one on top of the next to make one giant screen.

No doubt that seat was Matthias's. It had *I'm the boss* vibes written all over it.

"How many times have I told you," Roman sighed as he removed his coat and went to join the small group of men at the table. "We are not calling it that." Vas's grin just grew as he slid a crystal glass toward him.

"And how many times have I told you" —He pointed a finger at Roman— "I outrank you, and what I say goes."

Roman shrugged.

"It's still stupid," he took a sip of his drink. "We aren't in a cave. This is more like the Justice League or even the Avengers."

"The Avengers had a tower." Vas sounded almost

appalled that their secret bunker was being compared to the Avenger's tower. "Not a bunker."

"Technically, they had a mansion."

All eyes in the room turned to me. I shrugged out of my jacket and handed it to Matthias, who was patiently waiting.

"No, they didn't," Vas argued. "They had a tower and then some sort of compound after that." I couldn't help the small laugh at how riled up the big bad Russian man was at this.

"In the movies," I told him, and he deflated mildly. "In the comics it was a mansion in Manhattan that was spread over several city blocks."

"Whatever," Vas mumbled petulantly, but he sent me a small wink. "Still calling it the Bat Cave."

"You can call it whatever you want, Vas," Matthias guided me toward the table. "As long as it's in your head."

"Yes, boss."

Several of the men chuckled as they took their seats. The boss was here now, and it was time to get to work, apparently.

"Ava, I'd like you to meet some of my men." Matthias's hand settled on the small of my back again. Not to keep me from running, but to make a statement of possessiveness. I was his. Or so I would let him believe. For now. "Vas you already know. The one next to him is Maksim, and the fucker next to him is Leon. I'm sure you've seen Nicolai around the penthouse.

Briefly, but he'd made an impression. The Russian was older than anyone else in the room. He looked like a mix between a tattooed college professor in his sleek navy trousers and black pullover knit sweater and a mountain logging man with his graying black mid-cut swept to the side. It gave him that messy, just-woke-up look. But it was the beard that pulled it all together. It was bushy, but still well-kept and no doubt had women throwing their damp panties at him.

While Nicolai's roughness held an edge of refinement, Maksim was all rough edges. He wore faded jeans with holes in them and muddied biker boots. His T-shirt was tight against his muscled chest, the black accenting the multitude of colored tattoos that ran down both of his arms and up his neck. His hair was long and secured in a bun at the back of his head. He held out his hand for me to shake; it was calloused and stained black.

Leon was the opposite. His accent when he said hello was mildly tainted, and I recognized the same cadence as my Uncle Jerry. He was Italian. That was surprising given the fact that Matthias was head of the Russian *Bratva*. Leon was clean cut and dressed in dark blue trousers and a black button-down. He was the only one dressed up. Even Vas was wearing jeans and a T-shirt, albeit cleaner than Maksim's.

Unsure of what to say, I simply told them it was nice to meet them. And it was. They were friendly, but I was still unsure of what the hell was going on.

"What am I doing here?" I turned to focus my attention on Matthias.

"You wanted to know why I took you, right?" he asked. "Why I married you?"

I snorted. "You want me to give you inside information on my father." That wasn't news to me. "I'm not dense, Matthias. But you didn't have to marry me to get that information. What I want to know is why. Why do you want to take the company down?"

"Not the company." Matthias motioned for me to take a seat in the chair next to his. Once I was seated, he took his own. He motioned with his head to Nicolai, who nodded before getting up and heading over to a large bar situated at the other end of the room. "Just Elias and Christian. The company will still be standing in the end. I need it, after all." It didn't escape my notice that he hadn't answered my question.

"You know I won't inherit anything, right?" I disclosed honestly. "I'm not in his will. None of the women are. If you murder him and Christian, it all goes to my Uncle Dante."

Matthias smirked. "Let me worry about that, Red."

Yeah, sure. Let him worry about that. He was holding back. The man had something up his sleeve, there was no way he didn't. What was the point in forcing me to marry him if he already knew he wouldn't gain anything by it? It couldn't be just to fuck me. He wouldn't need to marry me to make me submit to him. Matthias might not be one to take a woman by force, but he'd already proven to be manipulative enough through seduction to not need to force me.

My traitorous body responded to his advances despite my brain's abject protests.

"Fine." I leaned back in my chair and crossed my arms against my chest. "You want my help? Then you need to start answering my questions. No more keeping me in the dark. Otherwise, have fun on your own."

The room grew silent, and the air thickened with tension as I continued to hold Matthias's stare. I wasn't backing down on this. He wanted information? Wanted me to betray my family? Then I wanted answers and a few assurances. Matthias didn't understand what a war with my father would cost him, and if he didn't play his cards right, it wouldn't be my father dead in the end. It would be him.

"So?"

He continued to stare at me, his silver gaze searching mine as if he was looking into my soul. It made me want to squirm in my seat, and not in fear. His eyes were heated, silver flecks glistening in the light, looking as if he wanted to devour me. The hunger in his eyes had my chest heaving in small pants and my panties dampening as I did my best not to rub my thighs together.

I licked my bottom lip. The action drew his gaze to them. My breathing stilled. For a moment I thought he might lean in and kiss me. Up until now, his affection in front of his men had been a show of possessiveness, but I wanted more than that. I knew he felt it, too. The red-hot electricity surging between us.

The sound of crystal on crystal broke the moment, and I could hear Nicolai mumbling a mild apology as he strode back to the table with two drinks in his hand. Whiskey for Matthias and a soda water for me. I rolled my eyes, but I kept silent.

"All right, Ava." He smiled behind his glass. "But be careful what you wish for."

CHAPTER TWENTY-NINE

Ava

B*e careful what you wish for.*
Truer words had never been spoken, and as the screens on the wall came alive, I realized just how far Matthias was willing to go. The video was real time, the angle of the camera giving a top-down view that could have only meant it was attached to a drone. Row on row on row of colorfully painted shipping containers stretched out below the camera lens, stacked four to five high.

We were looking directly down at the Port of Seattle. More importantly, we were looking at my father's shipping containers.

"Feed is live, boss." A low voice drifted through the speakers, filling the room. "Ready on your say so."

"*Khoroshiv*, Dima." Matthias nodded his head a few times as he studied the screens. I knew what that word meant.

Khoroshiv. It meant *good.* "Any sign of security or the Port Master?"

"The Port Master looks like he's cleared out for the evening," the voice answered promptly. "There are a few of Elias's guards, but that is it. I was expecting more muscle after your run-in with his son the other night."

Run in? When had he met with Christian? The only night he could have gone to see him was—my cheeks flushed as I recalled how he had taken the soiled sheets from his bed with him. At the time, I hadn't thought much about it, but now, it all came together.

"I'm only counting ten at the most." Dima sounded somewhat worried that there weren't more guards. And he should be. They weren't the right containers. That specific lot were decoys, rarely used except when necessary. My father wasn't an idiot. He had enemies, and he knew how to strategize the long game. It was when immediate pressure was applied that he would flail around and sink.

I had no doubt that was why he had so suddenly offered me up to Matthias. The Russian boss coming in the middle of the night to take Christian's life hadn't been something he had planned for. Christian had always been the one to think on his feet. My brother did his best work under pressure. That was where he thrived. He knew how to read a situation and take advantage, but he lacked the foresight needed for future planning.

"Make it hurt," Matthias ordered.

"Those aren't the right containers." As much as I resented Matthias for forcing me to marry him, I couldn't let him walk into that. I hated my father more than I detested my new husband. Okay, detest was a strong word, but still. I wasn't exactly happy with him. "They're decoys."

All eyes were on me, the silence deafening.

"What do you mean they're decoys?" Matthias's jaw ticked, his eyes darkening as he took in my words. I doubted he was used to hearing that he was wrong. That things weren't going to go exactly as planned. My chest felt tight as my mind began to spiral. I knew I didn't owe my father any allegiance, but I couldn't help but feel like I was about to betray him. Betray my sisters.

"Those aren't the actual containers he uses for shipments," I told him as I sent up a silent *fuck you* to my father. He had never done anything for me. And I'd make sure Matthias kept my sisters safe. He would do what I asked if he wanted those shipping containers. "He has other containers he uses under another name so they can't be traced back to him if they are compromised."

"And how do you know this?" Maksim's thick Russian brogue spoke up from the other side of the table. "You are telling me that Elias Ward just spouted information off in front of someone that could potentially destroy him?"

"Who would I tell?" I asked him honestly. "The police? My father has most of them in his pocket, not to mention the little fact that I was never allowed to leave the property, and even when I was, I was guarded."

"Still doesn't explain how you would know any of this."

I gave a short, humorless laugh. "Because my father never noticed me until he was angry. Because what harm is it to speak freely in front of someone who is shackled with nowhere to go. Because as much as I hated the loneliness and solitude he inflicted on me, it had its uses. You are not the only one who has been trying to get out from under him. Go ahead with your little plan, but hitting those containers isn't going to do anything."

A hushed murmur settled over the table. I turned my attention back to Matthias, who was silently assessing me.

"Go on then." Matthias waited expectantly, his gray eyes holding mine captive as if he was trying to pull the truth from me. But I wasn't just going to roll over like a good little girl and give him what he wanted. Not when I wanted something, too.

"I want a few assurances first."

Vas chuckled in his seat next to me. Matthias raised an eyebrow as he continued to stare me down. He was still assessing me. Analyzing every word, every facial expression, wondering if I could be trusted or if I was simply stalling for time.

I wasn't. My father's one slipup was that he always talked freely around me, emboldened by the fact that he believed I would never escape him. Never be free of him.

"Assurances, hmm?" There was a slight tone of amusement to his voice. A more playful rise in his voice that I had only glimpsed a few times since meeting him. "And what would those be?"

"Tell me your plans."

Matthias huffed a laugh.

"You wanted assurances, *Malen'kaya Krasnyy*, not my battle plan."

"What does that mean?" I cocked my head to the side curiously. "You always call me that."

Matthias smiled wickedly, eyes shining mischievously.

"Wouldn't you like to—"

"It means, little red." Maksim groaned gruffly. "Can we get on with it now?" Matthias shot his soldier a dirty look. I was in awe of the comradery these men had, but also the balls. My father's men would never speak up like this to him. They were soldiers, not friends. But the men at this table were more than just a part of Matthias's army.

"Fucker," he grumbled, still glaring. I couldn't help the small smile that quirked up at the corner of my mouth.

"In order to know what assurances I need; I have to know what you are planning first."

Matthias glanced around at his men, taking their silent vote. When it seemed they had all come to some kind of mute agreement, he smirked.

"Okay, *malyshka*," he agreed, and I internally groaned at not knowing yet another Russian nickname. "My plan is to hit your father's containers with a small amount of military grade C-4. Enough to ensure that he wouldn't be making any runs in the near future. At the same moment, during the chaos, Dima is going to hit your father's house—"

"Libby," I gasped, interrupting him. God, what if she was caught in the crossfire? "Please, Matthias, you can't hurt her. She doesn't know anything."

"Is that the assurance you want, Ava?" he asked me seriously, any amusement had slithered away. "Your sisters' safety?"

I nodded my head furiously, my eyes pleading.

"Don't get her involved in this," I begged quietly, his powerful gaze on me had my hands growing clammy, sweat forming on my back as I stared him down. "Promise me you will take her somewhere safe."

"I never planned on involving your sister, Red." I breathed a sigh at relief at hearing him admit that. "But I will make sure Libby is taken somewhere safe. Your stepmother is out of town, and your sister is currently at a friend's house. I'll be sure we intercept her on her way home."

"And..."

Matthias chuckled lightly, and my heart lifted a little. It was such a carefree sound. One I'd only heard a few times in the two days I'd known him, but I decided I loved it. He seemed more at ease here with his men. Less like the harsh, controlling leader and more like a normal man.

I huffed. "Yes."

"Proceed, then."

Like I needed his permission. Even when I was the one making demands, he still managed to give the air that he was the one in control. This was *my* negotiation.

"Swear to me that you don't sell women and children like my father," I demanded. Matthias's eyes flashed with something unrecognizable. It almost looked like hurt. Almost. "Promise me you'll stop using prostitutes to make your money."

Roman, who was sitting to Matthias's left, snorted. "You think we run a prostitution ring?"

The men around me stifled their laughter behind their drinks, eyes dancing with amusement. Like I was some kind of act or show they were enjoying.

"I know you do," I pressed. "Mark told me that Valerie was one your working girls. Now I know why she was in your room the other morning sucking you off without being the least bit disturbed someone walked in on you."

Vas spat out his whiskey onto the pristine wood tabletop. The overly jovial Russian struggled to catch his breath as he coughed on the liquid that had obviously slid down the wrong pipe. It didn't help his situation that he was also laughing. Loudly.

"Jesus, Matt," he wheezed as he tried to get himself back under control. "What the hell? You didn't tell her about Valerie?"

Matthias groaned, pinching the bridge of his nose, utter exasperation overtaking his features. I was waiting for him to explode at his men for addressing him so informally. My father killed his men for less. But that was the thing, wasn't it?

He wasn't my father. Sure, some aspects were similar, but Matthias had proven that, although I still believed he was a monster for hurting people. Killing people. He did have lines he refused to cross.

Matthias led with a mix of comradery, building loyalty through respect. Did his men still fear him? I had no doubt. But there was a familial connection between him and the men in this room that no one could deny.

My father led with fear and an iron fist. There were no second chances. There was no mercy. He believed that it was better if his men feared him than if they respected him.

In this moment, I could see how wrong he was.

"I don't understand."

Fuck, was I lost. I hadn't expected there to be anything else to say about Valerie except that she was one of his working girls. My stomach churned at the thought of her being something more. Maybe she was his girlfriend.

Nope. Nope. *Do not go down that rabbit hole.*

"Valerie isn't a working girl, Ava." Matthias let out a sharp sigh, running a hand through his chocolate hair. "Well, she is a working girl, but she's not—"

"For fucks sake," Maksim growled, losing his patience. "She's a spy."

Matthias shot him a hard look, but the burly man simply ignored it. Now I was really lost.

"But I saw her—"

"You saw what I wanted you to see." Matthias's voice gentled slightly, his eyes softening as he looked down at me. "Valerie works for me as a spy. So do the girls she runs."

"You force them to spy for you?" My head was reeling and nothing he was saying made any sense.

"We don't force them," Leon, who'd been quiet until now, spoke up. "They are there of their own free will."

"Why would they do that?" It was glaringly obvious how naïve I was. How silly my questions were, but I didn't understand why anyone would want to trade sex for money willingly.

"Some of them have nowhere else to go, Ava." Matthias's voice was still gentle, but I could hear the mild reprimand beneath it. The warning. He thought I was judging them, and he didn't like that. Why did he care how I saw them?

"Most women are like the ones your father sells," Vas explained. "They've been sold two, three times over. This is all they know. We give them a chance to take back some of their power. Turn the tables on those who took advantage."

"None of them are ever harmed," Leon added. "We don't allow that. Those who have a family to go home to, we help them. Those who can't go home for one reason or another, but don't want to work with Valerie, we set them up in one of our legit businesses."

"I still don't understand what Valerie being a spy has to do with her blowing you in your room."

The room erupted in raucous laughter. Even Dima, who had been listening in from the other side of the coms, was chuckling. Matthias's smile returned.

"The men in this room are the only ones who know everything," he told me, his face sobering. "They are the only ones who know every facet, every detail, every kill. No one outside of this room, save Dima, has that kind of access."

"I don't understand."

Matthias took a calming breath as he struggled outwardly with finding the right words.

"You just have to trust me, Red," he told me with all seriousness.

Trust. There was that word again. I barely knew him, yet he expected me to offer up something that I held tight to my chest. It wasn't something I offered up freely to anyone. Trusting the wrong person could get me killed. What other choice did I have? If I didn't trust Matthias, then I would have no one. No one to protect Libby. No one to Find Maleah. I'd be living in a state of perpetual anxiety, waiting for the next attack. Wondering.

He was telling me to trust that the situation with Valerie wasn't what it appeared. That the words he spoke to me about our wedding vows, however fake, were real to him. I would have to trust that although facets of him were similar to my father, he wasn't him.

Matthias Dashkov was his own man, and I needed to start seeing him as such. It wasn't fair to him for me to keep seeing him as a shadow of my father. But there was still one thing I needed before I could lean into that trust.

"I want in."

CHAPTER THIRTY

Matthias

I couldn't believe I hadn't seen it.

It had been right under our goddamn noses this whole fucking time, and it took Ava for any of us to notice it. Elias had hidden his containers under her mother's name. Her fucking mother's name. We'd searched the entire port roster and hadn't even batted an eye at that name. It was enough to make me want to lash out at something.

This wasn't a coincidence. This wasn't Elias. He wasn't that smart. There was no way in hell he had come up with that plan on his own. Or maybe he had, and I was underestimating him. Still, something in my gut told me there were more moving parts to Elias's plan that I couldn't see, and I didn't like that.

Ava had been a mask of fury when she'd told us about the containers. She'd overheard Elias talking about them well over a year ago, before she left. He'd been talking with one of his seedy lawyers and she had done what she did best in a household that barely noticed her; she had spied.

Dead bitches don't go to prison.

That was what Elias had said about her mother as he discussed how to keep the containers out of his name. If they were ever found, nothing could be traced back to him. Nicolai had all the data regarding the port under Kathrine Moore's name within minutes of Ava's confession.

Pizdets. Dammit.

I looked over at Ava as we sped from the bunker back toward the compound. The night hadn't been a complete success, but it had certainly gone better than it would have if Ava hadn't been there. We completely cleared everything out and lit up the containers like the Fourth of fucking July.

The look on my Little Red's face when she'd seen the footage of the women being held there stirred something inside me. Her face had paled and her emerald eyes gleamed with unshed tears as my men had led them away. I could see her scanning each face that walked past the camera, looking for Maleah, no doubt. She wouldn't find her there, but I didn't have the heart to tell her that.

Maleah's fate wasn't among these women, it was much darker.

"Where will they go?" She asked. "The women on the video. Where will you take them?"

"To Valerie." My hand tightened on her thigh where it had been resting lazily. "She has a halfway house set up for women in this kind of situation. A doctor will look after them, and they'll be given their options."

I'd promised her transparency. That was the deal we'd struck, but I knew that she was still hiding something beneath her façade of absolute candor. It may not be an outright lie, but the omission still counted. However, I could not fault her for keeping something to herself when I was holding a dark secret myself.

Vas had lectured me several times about keeping her in the dark, but what I had to say to her was something that would no doubt shake the foundation of everything she knew, and I could not bring myself to do that. Not just yet.

"And my father?" she asked quietly. "What about him?"

I let out a long breath. That was the bust. We'd had to sacrifice a dual attack on the shipping containers and his house, choosing instead to hit both of his container spots at the same time to mitigate the risk of losing the secondary container site. It was a risk, I had known that when I made the call, but having the containers in our possession and choking him out of the port would be enough for now.

"We'll find him," I assured her.

"You don't know him like I do," she whispered sadly. "He has a million and one places to hide. He'll do everything from the shadows and make everyone else bear the grunt work."

Pursing my lips, I kept silent for a moment as I thought about what to say to her. How to comfort her. This wasn't something I was good at. Comfort. I rarely gave it, and growing up, I had rarely received it. There was only one thing I could do to make her feel secure, and I couldn't exactly do it in the middle of a crowded truck.

"Then we will draw him out," I told her. "Find something he wants and dangle it in front of him." Ava just nodded silently like she didn't quite believe my words. Roman pulled the truck up in front of the administration building and put it in park, letting it idle as he waited for Ava and me to exit.

"Have Vas grab Libby tomorrow before she reaches home." Roman nodded. "Set her up in one of the guest suites until we get back on Thursday." Without waiting for a response, I slid out of the car, Ava right behind me. I had promised to keep her sister safe, and I would do just that. Roman was the clear choice to arrange for her pickup since he was closer to her age, but I needed him here with Ava. Vas was the only other member of my inner circle who was easily approachable. More amiable than Maksim's surliness or Leon's constant need to charm a woman out of her panties.

Speaking of panties.

Ava opened the door to the suite, and the minute I was through it, I slammed it shut. My Little Red gasped at the sudden noise, her body jumping slightly as she turned to face me.

"What—?"

I didn't give her time to finish her sentence before I crashed my lips against hers. My mouth hungrily devoured hers, and she responded eagerly, as if she had been waiting for this moment all day, just like I had.

God, watching her take charge and stand up for what she wanted had my cock straining in my pants for the last few hours. I never wanted to temper the fire burning in her veins, but she would still be mine, still submit to me. In that room with men and in our bedroom, I would give her more freedom to speak her mind, but there were times when she would need to learn to curb her tongue.

I shifted one of my hands lower, gliding my fingers along her soft ivory skin to her breast, which I kneaded roughly. Her moan of pleasure ignited something inside me. Something I had never felt with any other woman before. Everything about Ava brought something alive in me. Like the Tin Man when he finally got his heart. I would never tell her, never admit it out loud, but Ava was slowly digging her way beneath my skin. Burrowing herself where she didn't belong.

Still, I would allow us these moments.

Ava sighed when I snuck my hand even lower, dipping

inside the warmth of the leggings she had put on after lunch. Her eyes met mine for a brief moment, a silent consent. There was no stopping me now.

Lifting her up in my arms, I brought my lips back down on hers. She wrapped her legs around me as I carried her to the bed. I quickly toed off my shoes before setting her down on the soft comforter. My hands went to her leggings, and hers went to her top, ripping it up and over her head before I even had her lower half bare. Her enthusiasm made my cock painfully hard. It was pushing against my zipper, begging to be let out.

I jerked my shirt over my head and climbed on top of her, my lips finding hers again. I buried a hand in her hair, the soft silky smoothness heaven against my calloused, blood-covered fingers. Every inch of me vibrated with the need to devour her. To make her mine.

My mouth shifted to her neck, and I nipped and kissed my way down to the sensitive skin of her collarbone. I shifted my free hand to her bra and wrenched, the material rendering easily beneath my strength, and tossed it away. Her protest was cut short by a loud moan when I closed my mouth around one of her pink, erect nipples.

I pinched her nipple as I let my teeth graze over the other, and I nearly came as her back arched off the bed, pushing her chest farther into my mouth. One of her hands gripped my hair while the other roamed my back, the delicious pricks of her nails inciting the beast within. I sucked, squeezed, and pinched her breasts, playing with her, torturing her until the need in her eyes grew thick and heavy, and the smell of her arousal permeated the air around us.

Her gaze met mine, the green of her eyes swallowed by the blackness of desire, as I mapped a trail down her stomach with my lips. Her panties tore just as easily as her bra, and now she was once again bare before me. My gaze roamed hungrily over her lithe, pale body as I pushed myself up to get a thorough look.

She was a goddess. A redheaded enchantress who had me under her spell, and I wasn't entirely sure I cared. Ava bit down on her lips, a flush creeping into her cheeks as she lifted her knees and spread her legs. My little minx was still shy, and I craved that. Craved her innocence. It was like a powerful drug I couldn't get enough of.

A smirk slid across my lips as I gripped her thighs, my fingers digging into her skin, before I buried myself between her legs without warning. My tongue slid over her pussy before I thrust it inside. She thrust her hips up at the sudden intrusion, a strangled moan leaving her lips, but I held her thighs tight enough to keep her in place.

Her breath came out in short little pants as I lapped at her, my tongue flicking over her engorged clit, sucking at her tender flesh. Ava's body was wracked with pleasure, and it only took a few more twists of my tongue before she let out a loud cry, her release pulsing through her unexpectedly.

I let go of her trembling legs and pushed myself up, watching as her chest heaved while my hands went to my pants. I unzipped them and yanked them down my legs, along with my briefs, letting my erect cock spring free. Ava's eyes widened slightly as she took in my size, and I had to resist the urge to chuckle.

Climbing back on the bed, I could see the fear slowly creeping into her eyes, but I simply ran my hand up and down her legs reassuringly. I positioned myself between them, still caressing her skin, my eyes trained on hers. It was natural for her to still be nervous, but soon I would be sure that fear melted into pleasure.

Ava tensed when I let the tip of my cock graze her

entrance. I rubbed myself against her, stimulating that little button between her legs until her eyes fluttered shut, and then I shoved myself inside. I groaned at the feeling of her tight, hot walls around my cock. *Blyad*, she felt like heaven.

A brief grimace crossed her pretty face before it faded back into the pleasure it had been filled with before. I pulled out and dove back in, stealing her moans with my mouth.

She was fucking perfect.

Ava Dashkov was fucking perfect. I leaned over her, stealing kiss after hungry kiss as I quickened my thrusts, fucking her deep and hard. She writhed and moaned beneath me, my name a prayer on her lips as she chanted it again and again.

Her hips rushed up to meet mine, her warm body molded to mine so perfectly it was like she belonged there. The bed beneath us shook hard, the lurid sound of our bodies connecting and her moans filled the air like a perfect symphony. *Blyad*. Why did she have to be so perfect?

I could feel my balls starting to tighten, my body tingling as I pumped harder, deeper, drawing moan after moan from her perfect lips. Ava's eyes fluttered shut, her breath growing ragged and eager. Her pussy clenched against my cock a moment later, her shrill cry echoing off the walls before her teeth latched on to the skin of my shoulder.

Fuck. The pain mingled with pleasure, and I came with a roar, my hot seed filling her.

My forehead rested against hers for a brief moment, our bodies tangled together, our breath mingling. Jesus, she was fucking perfect. I kissed her, long and slow, before I pushed my weight off her and glanced at my shoulder.

And here I thought I was the beast.

Her eyes met mine, and her lips twisted into a timid smile as she eyed her bite mark. I chuckled and rolled off her to lie on my back next to her. My chest heaved with the intensity of my orgasm. No woman had ever made me come that hard.

I looked over at Ava, who had snuggled up against my side, her messy crimson hair strewn about her pillow. Slowly, I pulled the duvet out from underneath her and tucked it around her. Her hand shot out, ensnaring my wrist as I went to stand.

"Please don't leave this time," she whispered sadly, her eyes still closed like she was afraid to open them. Afraid to see me walk away. I gulped back the lump forming in my throat at how desperate her small voice sounded. How vulnerable she was being with me right now.

"I'm just rearranging the covers, *malyshka*," I assured her before I did just that. Carefully, I climbed into bed next to her, tensing when she sidled up to me, burying her face in the crook of my neck while one hand caressed the birthmark along my right wrist. Everyone on my father's side of the family bore it. My one reminder of him.

I'd never slept with someone, not like this. Cuddling was never something neither I, nor the call girls that frequented my bed, cared for.

Her warmth surrounded me. The scent of vanilla and honeysuckle embedding itself permanently in my senses. I'd never be rid of her. Even if I pushed her away. Even if I made her hate me. I would never be rid of her. Ava was a weakness. I'd said it before and I would say it again, but maybe having a weakness wasn't a bad thing.

Maybe a weakness could turn into a strength, and Ava was certainly strong.

CHAPTER THIRTY-ONE

Ava

Matthias was relentless.

Maybe that wasn't the right word for it. Matthias had stamina. Yep, that sounded better. Thanks to him, I had gotten little sleep over the past few days. My insatiable Russian husband couldn't keep his hands off me whenever we were alone. He'd take me several times during the night. Moving me this way and that to fit his carnal needs.

Not that I minded. I loved how he manipulated my body with ease. The affection he showed while in the bedroom was the most I had ever received since my mother passed. I only wished he would show the same attitude when we were with his men.

Okay, maybe not exactly the same, but it would have been nice for him to show some kind of intimacy when we were out. Instead, I felt somewhat left out. Forgotten. Lonely. His men often engaged me in conversation, but there wasn't much

I had to share. Hobbies, free time, bucket lists... those things were for people with freedom. Something I sorely lacked.

It was Wednesday.

The sun had yet to peek over the lush tree line, leaving the early morning hours eerily quiet. It had snowed last night, several inches. I could see the faint whiteness of it clinging to the limbs of the pine tree that stood just outside the bedroom window.

Matthias was still sleeping. His soft snores, muffled by the pillow that obscured half of his face. I noticed he liked to sleep on his stomach. The blankets stopped just above his delicious, toned backside, hiding it from view. He was still very much tantalizingly naked...tempting me to reach out and stroke down the powerful muscles of his back.

I had rediscovered a bit of modesty in the early morning hour when I had gotten up to brew coffee. Matthias's large white button-down shirt fell to mid-thigh and hung off one of my slender shoulders, leaving the slightly cool air to nip at my skin as I leaned against the headboard next to him, watching him sleep. I felt like a bit of a creeper, but since I had often caught him doing the same thing, I rolled with it.

He was resting peacefully, so peacefully in fact, I was almost convinced he was sleeping.

Almost.

He was just relaxing, though. Waiting to pounce and ravish me all over again, just like the morning before this and the morning before that. Since our romp in the sack on Sunday, he made me scream his name over and over and over whenever he got the chance. I couldn't help the shudder that raced down my spine, tickling my senses and making heat pool in the apex of my thighs once more.

Fuck. Just the mere thought of it...the man had ruined me. Now I was sex-craved for him. Fantastic.

"Matthias?" My voice was soft, but still too loud in the muted atmosphere. I was almost afraid my words would violently break the peaceful silence, like shattering glass. I loved these moments when it was just us. No *Bratva*, no family, nothing. Just him and me and all the time in the world.

Matthias hummed in the back of his throat in response, I took it as an okay to continue, though. I was still slightly afraid to. I didn't want to mess up this moment, to ruin what we had going. Things were still tense between us on some levels. He knew I wanted to be included in his plan against my father, but I could tell he was still holding back from me. I wanted to say something, get him to confess, but I didn't want to go back to where we started.

"Do you think..." I swallowed thickly. No, that wasn't right...*ugh*...fuck. *Just blurt it out, Ava, it will be fine.* "Do you think I could take Libby out later this week?" The sentence was practically one very long word with how quickly I rushed the words out of my mouth.

I felt like I was waiting on bated breath as the silence once again stretched between us. Seconds feeling more like minutes. I'd never been allowed to do anything with my sister outside of the house, and even that was limited. I couldn't help but wonder if he was honestly mulling over his answer or trying to figure out what the fuck I had even said. Good job, Ava, A-freaking plus.

Finally, after what felt like years of waiting, his gorgeous gray eyes opened to look at my face as I sat there, half-tucked under the blankets next to him.

"As long as I have guards to spare, yes." His voice was nothing more than a gravelly relaxed rumble.

Holy shit, had all the fucking we'd done make the big bad Russian reasonable? This was one of those moments for the ages, I was sure. Honestly, I was kind of glad no one was around to document it. This would be a weird section in a *Bratva* history book.

Smiling, I shifted closer to him, watching closely for any signs of movement. He stayed perfectly still, his eyes following me to watch me close the gap between us. Swinging my leg over, I straddled his ridiculously amazing ass, my hands instantly finding purchase on his broad back. The muscles were tense, his flesh heated. I caught the curious look he sent me over his shoulder but ignored the silent question. This was the first time I had initiated contact. Up until now, Matthias had been the one to start any kind of intimacy between us.

I let my action do the talking, choosing to remain silent and let the bubble of contentment surrounding us expand. Since the first night I'd met him, I'd had the insatiable urge to touch him, and now that we had all but vaulted over the drawn line he had put up before and opened up, I was going to touch him all I wanted—within reason of course.

He was still a monster. A killer. My warden. I could never forget that. The way he acted around me with his men, not just Vas and the others, but with his soldiers, told me he was still drawing a line. Still putting up barriers. Outside of this room, he was back to the way he was before, and I didn't like that.

Pressing my fingers firmly into the curve of his lower back, I started to knead the taut muscles, easing the tension and strain slowly. I just barely caught the slight hitch in Matthias's breath as he realized what I was doing, and I couldn't help but grin broadly, pleased that I had obviously surprised him.

As much as I wanted to enjoy the moment, even gloat a bit and ask if he was enjoying himself, I didn't want my cheeky sass to make him stop me. It wasn't a secret that Matthias didn't have this kind of relationship with any of the women he had slept with before me. Vas had made it obvious that they were simply a fuck and dump.

His words. Not mine.

So, I was more than content to just massage his overworked muscle and enjoy the closeness of his body. This was an entirely different kind of intimacy, and I craved it as much as I craved him thrusting into me.

As I worked farther and farther up his back, I noticed a slight change in his posture and overall aura that he always seemed to give off. The Big Bad Wolf was relaxing under my hands, practically sinking into the mattress as his eyes fell shut once again. This was better than I could have hoped for, and my heart practically stuttered in my chest, the traitorous fucker. He was trusting me enough to relax with me.

It seemed today was a momentous occasion.

"What are we going to do about my father and Christian?" I asked softly, trying to keep the mood light.

Without any warning, Matthias suddenly rolled, sending me toppling off his back and onto the center of the plush bed. Before I could right myself and send him a well-deserved glare for startling me, he was moving. The man was off the bed in one swift, fluid movement, baring his gorgeous and very naked form to my eyes once more. When he moved like that, he reminded me more of a jungle cat than a burly Russian. Turning, he met my gaze, his hair tousled, and his stubble looking slightly more pronounced than it normally was.

He looked *wild.*

Matthias eyed me, his gaze crawling over my form, making me shift under his scrutiny and forget the fact that I was going to yell at him. What was he thinking? He was looking at me as if we hadn't just fucked like rabbits, but he really, really wanted to. I decided I liked that look. It made me feel beautiful and wanted. Like I was on top of the fucking world, and nothing could possibly tear me down.

At least while I was in this room.

Moving forward, he scooped me off the bed and into his toned arms easily, leaving me nothing to do but obediently wrap my arms around his neck.

"Where are we going?" The air was a bit too chilly for my tastes. It was biting at my bare legs and arms, making goosebumps appear across the pale expanse.

"Shower." Was his simply stated answer.

Wait. Hold the phone...

We were going to shower together? Like...together-together? Right now?

Fucking fudge cakes. My brain officially felt like it had been turned topsy-turvy. My stomach fluttered way more than it should have at the news. A shower with Matthias? Sign me the fuck up. I didn't know what I'd done to rack up so many good karma points in a row, but whatever I did, I'm glad I did it.

I tried not to let my overly eager feeling show on my face and instead opted to keep what I hoped was the cool, neutral expression he seemed to adorn all the time. In a matter of seconds, Matthias had the both of us in the bathroom, and I was once again standing on my own two feet. The expensive tile was icy beneath my feet, and I resisted the urge to shift from one foot to the other as Matthias gathered towels and turned the water to what I hoped was a very hot temperature.

The shower was big enough to fit both of us comfortably, considering Matthias's large bulk. I found myself suddenly hit with fresh nerves as he closed the space between us once again, his naked form both enticing and intimidating. It wasn't because I didn't want it or didn't want this moment with him. It was just the realization of how fast we were going and how much I had to lose if he one day decided he no longer needed me.

How far I would fall...

We'd barely been married a week, and yet at times, it felt like we had been married a lifetime. I put my trust in him far more easily than I had anyone else, including my sisters.

He was the man who'd bought me. Who had forced me to marry and hurt my friends to get to me. He was the man who was cold one minute and hot the next. Who spanked me and belted me because he thought I was disobedient.

But he was also the man who set my skin on fire. The man whose touch made me feel like I might combust. His presence was both calming and reassuring. I had no doubt he would protect me, but as much as I wanted to believe in that good part of him, he was still the boss of a criminal organization. He was still a killer.

Fate had a strange sense of humor.

I'd prayed for freedom, and instead I got a slightly bigger cage with fringe benefits. I prayed for normality, but I would never get that with this man. I wasn't blind to his ways. He wasn't a romantic. There would be no picnics in the park. No destination vacations. No flowers or chocolates.

Matthias's hand smoothing up my thigh sent every thought that wasn't him flying out of my head. Shifting, I met his intense, burning gaze with my own startled eyes. The subtle quirk of his mouth told me he knew I had been lost in my thoughts.

"As much as I like you in my shirt, *Krasnyy*..." His fingers played with the hem of said shirt lightly before he ripped it from my body, sending buttons flying, the ping of them hitting the tile floors sending a shiver of excitement through me. *Animal.* The playful tone of his voice sent my heart hammering against my ribs, threatening to split my chest open in front of him.

The cold bit into my skin from every direction, my nipples tightening from the air, and the hungry look on Matthias's face as he once again drank in my appearance almost languidly. His irises darkened as lust overtook his stormy eyes once more.

Oh boy.

With a subtle but sharp intake of breath, he took hold of my upper arm and guided me into the shower ahead of him. I couldn't help but smile at him, always manhandling, always pushing. That was something I doubted would ever change, and it was oddly comforting, helping to ease my nervousness at being naked in a very exposing light.

He certainly had nothing to be ashamed of. The man was built like a god, his chest and back covered in the colorful myriad of tattoos that had first stunned me in the kitchen the morning after our first night together. I was average. Too many freckles, my own constellation of scars, and—I stopped short as I glimpsed my hips.

Oh.

I had several new bruises to add to my fading collection.

Love bites littered my chest, and I imagined my neck and shoulders as well. Jeez, bite a guy one time...

Hand-shaped bruises decorated either side of my hips and thighs. Bruises that didn't make me cringe with self-loathing or fear. I, of course, had left a few love bites of my own down his chest and on his back.

I sent him a quick, playful glare, which he caught as I pointed to the particularly fun bruises along my hips. Smirking, he moved forward and pushed me under the surprisingly strong shower spray. The water was nirvana. Just hot enough to jar my senses and immediately start easing the tension in my back. Closing my eyes, I tipped my head back, letting myself unwind and forget my insecurities as well as my fears. I could do this.

This was Matthias, after all. The man had seen every inch of me already. Several times. In several different positions. His broad arms wrapped around my midsection as he slid up against me, joining me under the oversized shower head. I didn't think it was possible for two people so opposite to fit together so well, but we did. His body melded perfectly against my frame.

He didn't stay stationary for long, forcing me to open my eyes to figure out what he was doing. Grabbing the shampoo bottle, he poured the golden liquid into his large palm before he shifted his eyes to catch mine in a purposeful gesture.

"Step forward."

Too curious to argue, I did as I was told.

Matthias shifted around to stand behind me, his chest molding against my back as he nudged me completely out of the spray with his body. All the while tangling his hands in my hair, working the shampoo into the fiery strands with a precision that was honestly surprising. His fingers felt ridiculously good as he massaged my scalp and worked through the tangles he had created during the night. Letting myself relax, I leaned back against him, tipping my head back for easier access.

A girl could get used to this.

Biting my lip, I willed myself to remain still as he shifted me backward to rinse my hair. He was careful, and I found that this was another thing Matthias was just naturally good at. His fingers worked through my hair like it was second nature, he was methodical and worked with the utmost care. His actions settled hard into my chest, in the darkest part of my heart, finding a home with everything else he did that I shouldn't allow myself to get used to.

Turning, I shot him a look, trying my best to convey with my eyes what I wanted.

"My turn," I demanded, itching to run my fingers through his hair in a more casual setting. Sure, I had pulled said strands enough in the last several hours, but I wanted more. A lot more. I was greedy for him; I wasn't going to deny that. At least to myself.

"And how are you going to accomplish that?" He gestured between us with a finger, drawing attention to the blatant height difference as I stared up at him.

Shifting to the side, closer to the shower wall, I gestured at him to switch positions with me. Slinking forward, he did as I asked, moving forward while I moved back until the spray of the shower was once again beating against the tired muscles of my back. His eyes were locked on mine as he gazed down his nose at me, waiting for my next command like one of his soldiers.

"Bend." I tried to keep the bossy tone, but the unspoken *please* practically bled into my voice.

Sending me a rather mischievous look, Matthias slowly kneeled in front of me, a lot lower than I expected him to. His large hands caught my hips as his face leveled into my sternum, his warm breath fanning against my skin, causing my brain to short-circuit. I knew then with almost ridiculous certainty that Matthias was a fucking tease, and a good one when he set his mind to it.

He smugly caught my eyes once more as he lifted the shampoo bottle to hand to me, his stubble scraping against the seemingly oversensitive flesh of my stomach as he leaned to press a kiss to the bottom of my rib cage and in between my breasts, almost ghosting before suddenly taking a quick nip with his teeth, sending me hissing and shifting forward against him.

"Matt," I growled in warning.

He chuckled in response, not looking the least bit apologetic.

Narrowing my eyes, I stepped out of his reach and pointed at the water.

"Rinse," I demanded, trying to ignore the fact that I was wet and aching for him. Again.

He stood up, his movement smooth, and leaned forward just enough to invade my space.

"*Da, Krasnyy.*" The ghost of his Russian accent tickled the shell of my ear as he brushed past me, sending me shivering and struggling to contain my groan of want.

Hell, this man was literally going to kill me. Matthias Dashkov, *Bratva* leader and secret fucking lady killer.

I sent another glare his way as he tipped his head back under the water. I couldn't help but follow its trail as it slid down the strong chords of his neck, onto his firm, broad chest...over the sinful ridges of his abdominal muscles and—

Tearing my eyes away, I focused on the opposite wall, trying to will my mind from wandering back to the naked and wet god standing behind me. Large, heated hands gripped my shoulders, pulling me carefully backward until my back was resting against his chest. Adjusting slightly, he suddenly had my vanilla bodywash in his hands, idly waving it in front of my face so I could see his intentions.

"Don't move," he breathed, his voice thick and hot as his breath tickled the shell of my ear once more. Swallowing hard, I nodded.

Oh yeah, piece of cake. No problem.

Confident I wasn't going anywhere, he poured the soap into his hands, rubbing them together to create a rich, foamy lather. He moved slowly and teasingly. Starting at the slope of my neck, he followed the natural curve of my body. He glided down my shoulders, over my arms, and then back up my sides before slipping across my stomach and up to my breasts, cupping them firmly.

Tensing slightly, I willed myself to stay perfectly still as he toyed with my nipples, twisting and pulling until standing still became a chore. Groaning, I shifted slightly, trying to ease the growing ache between my thighs. It was barely a move, but he noticed. With a reprimanding twist, he harshly pulled on the hardened peaks, pulling a surprised cry from my mouth. Pleasure bled with pain, and my confused body just grew more heated.

I liked him rough. I liked him demanding.

"What did I say, Ava?" His voice was a low, amused rumble. His low tone vibrated through his chest into my spine, sending a new surge of arousal straight to my core.

"Don't move," I repeated breathlessly.

Humming in the back of his throat, he shifted us back just enough that we were both under the hot spray of the shower once more, rinsing the soap from our bodies. Once he was satisfied, he moved us both forward again. The shower had grown foggy with the steam, creating an almost other-worldly atmosphere. Everything was muted, so isolated in our own little world. It was almost like a dream.

One I never wanted to wake from.

His free hand nimbly traced down my sternum, over my stomach, and between my thighs, cupping me firmly, ripping a strangled moan from my lips.

"Are you going to behave?" he questioned mercilessly, no doubt feeling how embarrassingly slick for him I was already.

Not willing to risk my voice shaking, I simply nodded again, arching into his touch almost wantonly.

"I can't hear you," he teased, nipping at my ear.

"Yes," I rasped, my voice huskier than I thought it would be. I was practically shaking with the effort to remain still. Every nerve-ending felt too sensitive, my skin just a little too tender. I was attuned to his touch, and damn, I needed more of it.

Parting my folds, he slid a single digit deep into my pussy, stroking the sensitive walls almost lazily, sending my knees shaking and my lust soaring. A second finger joined the first as his teeth sank into the juncture of my neck and shoulder, causing me to wobble back against him. Sliding his other arm around me for support, he gripped on to my opposite shoulder, holding me steady and upright against him. His thumb swept idle little patterns against the skin of my arm, making my mind dizzy as his fingers worked a different tempo on my insides.

My hands shook at my sides, gripping at air as I resisted the urge to reach up and grip on to the muscular forearm across my chest. His onslaught of attention didn't stop there. His mouth, which was as dangerous as any other part of him, started peppering kisses across the length of my shoulder and onto my neck.

Humming thoughtfully, he bit down onto the slope of my neck, no doubt leaving a perfect impression of his teeth in bruise form. The action pulled a hiss from my already clenched teeth. He soothed it with his tongue, licking almost lewdly up my neck before adding a little nip to my earlobe as he sank his fingers particularly deep inside me, sending my head crashing back against his strong supportive shoulder.

He pulled away from me with an amused chuckle, leaving me frustrated and shaking in his absence. Oh hell no. Fuck that.

Growling, I whipped around, grabbing a hold of his firm

length before he could so much as take another step backward. He hissed through his teeth at my bold move. His intense, almost feral gaze found mine, his eyes a maelstrom of emotion. Pure, unadulterated lust burned like a city on fire behind his eyes, but there was a sense of desperation there, as well as a shine of surprise at how I'd managed to turn the tables. His jaw ticked as he clenched his teeth harder, the action accenting the firm line of his jaw and the more pronounced shadow of his facial hair.

My eyes narrowed slightly as I stepped closer, stroking the length of him as I did, allowing my thumb to firmly stroke over the head of his arousal in a slow, circular pattern, brushing the sensitive underside with every downward turn.

I watched his gray eyes darken like the sea during a storm as a flash of violent longing spiraled through his gaze. With another pump of my hand, I moved into action, letting my instincts guide me before I lost the courage to do what I wanted. Dropping to my knees in front of him, I glanced up to see his reaction, the slight widening of his eyes proved that I had once again surprised him. The slight hitch in his breath told me that he wasn't displeased with this new direction. However, the twitch of his hands told me he was getting impatient with me being in control.

Gathering my courage, I leaned forward and swiped my tongue on the underside of his cock, letting his thick length sink to the back of my throat.

I stamped down the last bit of my nerves as I pulled away slightly, swirling my tongue around the tip before barely scraping my teeth across the sensitive head. The grip he had on my hair was borderline painful as I relaxed my mouth and throat to take more of him, humming lightly to create what I hoped would be a nice vibration as I gripped the base of him harder, eager to see him unravel.

Matthias growled lowly, his control snapping.

With a rough yank, I was up and off my knees, facing down a very aroused Russian who had lost his patience with our foreplay. So much for that. His impatient and dominant nature just wouldn't allow me to be in control for long, even if it was all for him.

His hands found the sides of my face as he pulled me up onto the tips of my toes and crushed his mouth against mine, stealing the breath straight from my lungs as his tongue swept over my bottom lip before his teeth sank into the tender flesh, pulling a gasp from my mouth and offering him what he wanted. Without quarter, his tongue swept into my mouth, curling against my own, pulling mine into a dance of dominance I was sure to lose. He nipped and plundered, taking what he wanted. His fingers were bruising as he curled them around the back of my neck, keeping me in place.

He was all teeth and tongue, all desperation and hunger.

Flicking his tongue against mine one last time, he ended the kiss, turning instead to pepper kisses down my jaw. He bent low and took a nipple into his mouth, sucking sharply. I arched my back into him, gasping, my hands winding into his hair before I fully comprehended what I was doing. He scraped his teeth against my sensitive peak, pulling a moan from my lips as my knees weakened and wobbled.

He pulled back slightly to give the underside of my breast a quick nip before turning and letting his nose skim along my chest as he found his way back the side of my neck to my ear.

"Arms around my neck," he demanded huskily.

Reaching up, I wound my arms tightly around his neck as his hands came down to grasp the back of my thighs, fingers digging in harshly. In one swift motion, he had me off my feet and against the shower wall, holding me firmly in place. He met my gaze evenly, a certain edge of dark mischief present.

"Make love or fuck you, Ava?" his deep voice rumbled sinfully. "You decide." His tone had dropped extra low, turning into gravel as he studied my face with those stormy eyes.

Well, shit.

Swallowing hard, I clenched my eyes shut tightly as he rotated his hips against mine, creating delicious friction against my clit. I tried to soothe my racing heart before I once again looked up through my lashes to meet his eyes. He was giving me a choice, and I wouldn't disappoint.

"Fuck me, please."

I didn't care how wanton I sounded. Nor did I care how utterly debauched this entire situation was. I just needed Matthias inside me. My pussy was so fucking wet it was dripping down the inside of my thighs. I had an ache that I was sure was never going to leave, an ache that only he could fill and satisfy. Matthias Dashkov had ruined me for all men going forward. Even if he threw me to the curb and never wanted to see me again, he owned my body now.

Matthias growled in appreciation as he pulled my arms up and onto his shoulders, making sure I was gripping him tightly. Once he was sure, one of his hands wandered back down to my thigh, grasping to mirror its twin. With a sharp intake of breath, he moved impossibly quick, his hands left my thighs to bruise my hips as he pulled me down onto him while he surged upward, burying himself inside me in one smooth stroke that ripped a shriek from my mouth.

My senses were suddenly overloaded with nothing but him as he filled me so completely, I felt like my brain was going haywire.

With a long, drawn-out pull of his hips, he manhandled me like I was nothing more than a doll as he pulled out of me until only the head of his arousal was left inside me, leaving me aching and whimpering.

I didn't have to wait long.

He thrust back inside of me brutally, bruising my insides in a way that blended pleasure with pain and set my nerve endings on fire. Without thinking, I tipped my head back, exposing my throat to his ravenous mouth. He nipped and sucked, creating more of a warzone on my throat than I already had. All the while, he kept his pace. Each time, he pulled out slow and easy, leaving me both wanting and full of appreciation as I waited for the hard thrust of his hips as he buried himself back inside me again and again, until I was sure his intention was to make me forget every word except his name.

My toes curled as the coil deep in my core pulled tighter and tighter with each passing moment. I dug my nails in his shoulders, hanging on the best I could, even as my legs began to tremble and the aches from before amplified.

His name spilled from my mouth more times than I could count as he slowly stole away my sanity one thrust at a time. Matthias's thrusts turned erratic, he had lost the patience to be slow and teasing when he pulled out of me. Now, he was thrusting with reckless abandon as he neared his peak, pulling me right along with him.

I wasn't sure anymore where I ended and he began. With one last pull of his hands, he practically snarled as his release washed over him, pulling a sharp scream from my throat as my own followed quite suddenly.

My legs felt like Jell-O as he slowly pulled out of me, releasing me to stand on my own two feet, his hands helping to stabilize me. His gaze was softer than I had ever seen it, relaxed even as he stared down at me with a fondness I had never seen before. Sure, I could blame that momentary blip of tender emotion on the fact that we had quite literally fucked ourselves silly—but I wasn't going to. Unless Matthias's emotions were out of control, he never showed anything he didn't want to in those heart-shattering silver depths of his.

That look he gave me had been purposeful and for my eyes only. In this moment, I wasn't his captive, and he wasn't my warden. He was simply Matthias Dashkov, my husband. And me? I was just Ava Dashkov, his wife.

And for right now, that was enough.

CHAPTER THIRTY-TWO

Ava

Everything with teaching had fallen into place over the last two days, and today was no different. I had a feeling this wasn't like teaching at a normal school where the kids barely paid attention, offered up lewd jokes, or often didn't show up. The kids in my class were well trained, keeping their eyes and ears open as I tried to make the history of the criminal justice system sound at least somewhat appealing to them.

My third class of the day was a group of middle schoolers, no older than fourteen or fifteen. I could see the struggle in their eyes as they attempted to feign interest in a topic that held no appeal to them. Why would it? They were all destined to become criminals like their parents. Despite Matthias's reassurances that once graduated they would have the free will to choose their futures, it just didn't seem plausible.

Not because he wouldn't allow them to pursue a career outside of the *Bratva*, but because of the simple fact that this was how they were raised. Some of the kids had parents who lived here on the compound, others were soldiers or brigadiers, and those who were left had been rescued. They owed their life to the *Bratva*, why leave it?

When the bell signaled the end of the lesson, I was more than relieved to see them pile out, offering me wide smiles and enthusiastic goodbyes as they headed off to their final class of the day. Matthias didn't hold to the normal school day schedule of six-hour days, five days a week. Instead, he carefully plotted out smaller time periods that allowed for recreation in the afternoon. He also didn't allow large homework loads either and made sure that all topics covered were relevant.

History, math, and language were important, and he made sure the topics covered with them helped the children succeed later on down the road. He had teachers emphasize on balancing check books, the importance of credit scores, and how to take out loans and open a bank account. Students were required to take more than one language. And history, though important, was to be kept to relevant information.

As in, no one cared how many wives Henry VIII had or how they were killed.

They were all taught how to cook and clean, how to build and repair. Matthias said he wanted them to be prepared for the real world and not the world that schools create. When I thought he could do nothing else to surprise me, he did exactly the opposite. I wondered how many more layers he had beneath his gruff *Pakhan* façade and if I would be allowed a glimpse of them.

"I'm going to run to the restroom," I told Roman, who was busy fiddling with his cell phone in the back of the class. He got up from his chair, tucking his phone away to follow me, but I held up my hand to stop him. "Roman, I can go by myself."

He sighed, pinching the bridge of his nose as I once again pointed out that I was an adult and not a toddler needing an escort. We'd been having this argument since Monday, and it hadn't gotten me anywhere yet. The problem was, if he followed me to the restroom, I wouldn't be able to meet with Mark.

"And I've told you that Matthias—"

I huffed, crossing my arms against my chest with an irritated snarl. "I don't care what Matthias said." Roman raised his brow at me as if to say, "really?" "I just want to be able to do something on my own for once without you up my ass all the time."

"I am not up your..." He stopped mid-sentence when his phone beeped. "Shit." Roman looked between his phone and me, a pained look stretching across his youthful face. "Fine. I have to take this, but if something happens, I am selling you out to the boss."

I smiled up at him. "Deal." Without waiting for him to change his mind, I strode from the room, attempting to keep my steps calm and controlled when all I wanted to do was rush to the alcove.

The hallway was quiet and deserted. Most of the students had gone outside for the half hour break before their last class of the day. When I reached the alcove, Mark was leaning against the wall on one side, his fingers tapping nervously on a large manila envelope he held in his hand.

"Finally." He let out a long sigh of relief. "Took me forever to get the guards to call Roman for backup."

"What did you do?" I asked, concerned that he had done something that would get him caught. He simply shrugged.

"Nothing that can't be easily fixed." Mark pushed away from the wall, striding toward me with the envelope outstretched for me to take. It was thick and heavy in my grasp, and I wondered how important the contents were if he had asked me to meet him in secret. And why.

"What's in here?" I asked, not bothering to open it yet. That would be for later, when I was alone.

"Information about your past." Mark swallowed hard. "When Maleah came to me about forging your paperwork, she had me look into your mother. Said she had heard something that didn't make any sense."

"I don't understand." My brow creased in confusion. My mother was a high school teacher at an inner-city school who had gotten involved with the wrong man and then got pregnant with me. Nothing special. "What didn't make sense?"

"All of it."

"All of what?" I nearly screamed in frustration, but somehow managed to temper my voice to a harsh whisper. "I don't get what you are saying, Mark."

"Your entire history is gone, Ava," Mark growled. "Everything. There is no record of a Katherine Moore or an Avaleigh Moore. No record of her teaching in Portland or even living here in Seattle. Nothing. You were both ghosted."

I stared at the heavy envelope in my hand. "Then where did you get this?"

Mark sighed, running a hand down the lower half of his face. "When you left, I went digging. Forget the dark web, I had to go old school and hunt down everything by hand. Her birth records, your birth records, everything I could possibly get my hands on, I had to find it in paper form. Everything digital is gone. According to the world, you don't exist. Not even your social security number. That takes talent and money."

"That makes no sense, Mark." I shook my head in disbelief. "Who would do that? My mother taught high school. She wasn't a criminal or on the lamb. She was..."

"Born Katherine McDonough," Mark interrupted. "She grew up in a small Irish suburb in Boston before moving to Seattle for college along with her high school best friend. In the middle of her sophomore year, she disappeared. Her friend filed a report but there was nothing. No leads. No evidence. So, the case went cold."

My world was shattering around me, breaths coming out in small pants as I struggled to understand what he was saying. That couldn't be true. Whoever Katherine McDonough was, she wasn't my mother. My mother was Katherine Moore, music teacher, best baker in the Pacific Northwest, but she wasn't...she couldn't...

None of this was real. None of this was real.

It couldn't be. Had our entire life been a lie? The timeline didn't make sense. If Katherine McDonough disappeared at nineteen and she had me when she was twenty-two, where had she been for those missing years? With my father? That was his story. She was his mistress, and she ran away when she found out she was pregnant with me.

My father said she loved him, but I knew my mother. She would never love someone like him. She couldn't love someone like him because if she did, what did that make her?

The sound of the warning bell rung above us, jolting me from my thoughts. Tears had gathered at the corner of my eyes, but I sniffed them back. I couldn't walk back to class crying. Roman would get suspicious. If he wasn't already.

"Matthias is going to be tied up with business tonight," Mark assured me. "I found everything I could about your mother, and I put it in chronological order as much as I could, but I think you will have a better time doing that."

I didn't trust myself enough to speak. If I did, I was afraid I would scream and never stop, so I nodded instead.

"In that folder is also a phone," he whispered, his voice dark, like he hadn't wanted to put it in there. "Once you look through the paperwork, call the only programmed number."

"Who's on the other end, Mark?" I was tired of all this cloak and dagger bullshit. Tired of my life being yanked in too many directions and barely knowing which way was up.

"Agent Archer."

My blood ran cold. I'd been hoping he would leave me alone, but here was his proxy, another pawn, just like me.

"You're working with Archer?" I hissed at him. "Are you fucking kidding me?" Mark let out a resigned sigh, his face falling.

"He threatened my family, Ava." His eyes found mine, broken and scared. He didn't want to do this, that much was clear. Mark had found a family here with Matthias's men and betraying him probably hurt. "Said he would make every drug charge in my mother's past stick this time. I can't...I have a sister, and my mother has been sober for years."

"Dammit," I cursed, my blood boiling. What was Archer's plan? I hadn't thought about the FBI agent over the last couple of days. Matthias had proved that the phone belonged to my father, and Archer hadn't reached out.

"He's the one who tipped Matthias's men off about me forging your paperwork," Mark continued. "Said that if I did what he asked, when he asked, he would make sure my mother's unresolved drug history disappeared."

I waved him off, too angry to speak, but my anger wasn't directed at him.

"Whatever you do, Ava," Mark cautioned. "Don't trust him."

My forehead creased. "Trust who? Matthias?"

Mark shook his head. "Archer," he said. "No matter what he tells you, you can't trust that he is giving you the right information."

"No one has been giving me anything," I growled. "That's the problem. Why shouldn't I trust the one person who is on the right side of the law?" *Even though his tactics were a bit unscrupulous.*

"Because Agent Archer is too perfect," Mark told me. "He's clean. Too clean. I can't get any kind of read on him."

"Of course he's clean," I sighed. "He's an FBI agent." Mark snorted.

"There's clean and then there's bullshit clean," Mark pointed out. "And Archer, he's bullshit clean."

"I don't even know what that means."

"It means that most agents have something in their background. No one has a perfect life, Ava. Parking tickets. Speeding tickets. Some kind of black mark on their school record. No one is as clean as a whistle." His tone had darkened, eyebrows pulling together as he tried his best to explain his gut feelings. "Archer...his background is too perfect. Too clean. Like someone constructed the best possible childhood and stuck it on a sheet of paper."

"You're saying that he isn't FBI?" I asked in disbelief. Mark's jaw clenched.

"No," he sneered. "He's FBI, all right, but Jonathon Archer is either up for sainthood, or his name and past are a construct. Someone who is using tactics like blackmail and harassment, wouldn't have a shiny clean background like his."

"Why would someone fake a background, spend years training in the FBI, just to take down Matthias?"

"That's what I don't understand," Mark ran a frustrated hand through is hair as he paced the small area. "I can't suss out his motive. Anything to do with Archer is like peering through a blurry windshield splattered with bugs in the middle of a rainstorm, and it shouldn't be that way. There shouldn't be any blurred lined. He shouldn't be okay with using people the way the men he hunts do."

Mark was right. Collateral damage was a word I had heard often in my house growing up. Archer was waging a silent war against the Dashkov *Bratva*, and despite his promises, he didn't care who was caught in the middle. That wasn't something a normal FBI agent would be okay with.

"Ava." Roman's voice echoed through the hallway. Fuck. Our time was up.

"Go." Mark nodded his head. "Don't worry about me. I have everything covered." I shot him a skeptical look. Matthias would kill Mark if he found out he was giving me a phone that rang directly to the FBI.

Hell, he might kill me, but I doubted that. Matthias still needed me. That much I knew.

Without a second glance, he walked through the exit behind us. I snuck into the ladies' room just across the hall, hiding the manilla envelope in one of the paper towel holders where no one would find it. I'd come back for it in an hour when the last class ended.

With one final glance around the empty bathroom, just to be sure it was in place, I swung the door open, revealing an irate Russian bodyguard.

Fucking great.

CHAPTER THIRTY-THREE

Ava

It was all a lie. Everything I had ever been told had been nothing more than one giant falsity after another.

I wanted to reject the evidence Mark had given me. Chuck away the manilla envelope and pretend like nothing had ever happened. But now, there was no going back, and I'd be sure the people responsible would pay. That was my promise.

My stomach churned, the contents of my lunch threatening to make a reappearance as I stared down the cold stone truths set out before me on the kitchen table. I wished I could deny everything. They said the truth would set you free. Bullshit if you ask me. All the truth did was remind me how dark and cruel the world was.

There was no denying the woman in the photo was my mother. She was younger, bright brown eyes full of promise and hope as she stared up at the man holding her. There were very few photos of her in the packet, but the ones she was in, so was he.

Her name was Katherine McDonough, just like Mark had said. She was born to Sheila and Seamus McDonough in 1976 at Boston Memorial Hospital. A perfect ten, apparently. I knew the name Seamus McDonough from my father. He had been a shipping Tycoon out of Boston rumored to have ties to the Irish Mob.

Whenever my father spoke of him, it was with smug satisfaction about how he had all but blacklisted the man from the port years ago. It was the biggest coup. One he still gloated about at parties and board meetings.

With each turn of the page, the life I had been living seemed to melt away, and Ava Moore disappeared, leaving a ghost in her wake. The life my mother had built was nothing more than a fabricated web of deception. What made her leave her life behind to become Katherine Moore? Who was the man in all the pictures?

The next few pages were my mother's missing persons report filed by one Marianne McAlister. It was filed a week after her professors noted her absence. *That was interesting.* Most missing persons reports were filed within the first twenty-four to forty-eight hours. Mark must have thought the same thing because at the bottom of the page was a small sticky note with the words, *why did she wait so long?*

Why indeed? Surely her roommate, who had shared the exact same classes, would have noticed the first day or two that she hadn't come home. And if not, why? The report was barely filled out. No eyewitness accounts were made, barely any foot traffic. Hell, the police hadn't even bothered to check out her apartment.

Nothing. Nada. Zilch.

The only notes on the report were made at the front desk

by someone who had been making daily inquiries into the progress of the case. Liam Kavanaugh. That was a name I knew all too well. He wasn't just leader of the Irish Mob in Seattle; he *was* the Irish Mob.

My uncle Dante called them Irish rats. Vermin that scurried in the Underground, living off the scraps of the bigger families. An infestation that needed to be eradicated. Before Liam Kavanaugh took up the mantle of leadership, the Irish had been nothing more than a small gang.

Now, however, they were becoming a large force of power in the city. Their businesses were more low-key than the high-end companies my uncle owned, but they still took over a good chunk of the city. Mostly dive bars and strip clubs. At least that was what my father told Christian.

Was he the man in the photos? The one my mother clung to so happily it was like nothing else existed but the two of them? I'd never seen Liam in person, and the man's face in the photos was obscured. The red of his hair was obvious, and I could just make out the intricate Celtic knotwork that slithered up his neck on one side.

A strangled sob wrenched itself from my throat, muffled by the sound of my hand against my mouth as I flipped to the next page. Tears pricked at the corners of my eyes, and I had to blink them back to keep them from falling and ruining the paper. My chest was heaving, breath coming out in short bursts through my nose as I struggled to keep quiet. I didn't want the guards outside my door to come busting in.

All the pieces were starting to come together in a dark twisted puzzle that left me cold and shaking.

Her face was bruised and bloodied. Eyes full of pain as her blood red hair was pulled taut behind her by a large burly hand, forcing her to stare directly into the camera. She stood almost defiantly; her face twisted in a sneer. She was clothed in nothing but a pure-white sheath that was nearly see-through, even in the picture.

It was a symbol of her purity. Of her virginity.

It was a fucking bid sheet.

Everything from her age to her weight were listed. Hobbies. Interests. Whoever took her had been watching her. I recognized the doctor's signature at the bottom. It was same tubby-ass man who had performed my exam at my father's request. Fucking hell.

I scanned over the sheet, my eyes widening at the total that was scribbled at the bottom.

Twenty-million dollars.

That was how much her virginity was worth in the Underground. There were no names, simply numbers attached to the winner of the bid. The number thirty-two was stamped next to the amount owed.

Thirty-two.

Bile rose in my throat as I connected the dots from one to the next. How many times had I seen that paddle on the shelf in his study and never questioned why he had it? The wood was made of a smoky oak with the number thirty-two engraved in bold white letters on either side. He displayed it openly, like a trophy, and it was.

It was the trophy that represented his greatest coup.

Regret filled me as I thought back to every curse I had ever uttered about my mother since I had started living with my father. I'd never understood how she could choose to love a man who was obviously a monster. Every day I blamed her for my predicament. Blaming her for her obvious error in judgement.

Suddenly, my life growing up made more sense.

We hadn't owned a television or phone. I wasn't allowed to participate in after school activities she didn't supervise, and picture day was a no-go. Our home had more security than any other home in the neighborhood. She never took me to the hospital, and we had never traveled or taken vacations. My mother never went out and she never brought anyone home.

I never thought much of it before. Maybe that she was bit eccentric. A little too protective, but she had filled the house with so much warmth and love that I never once felt isolated or lonely. It was her and me, and that was all I needed.

Leaning back in my chair, I sighed, blinking back the tears, wishing I could take back every cruel thought I had ever had about her. She was only trying to protect me, and I had cursed her for it. Condemned her for her actions.

There were so many lies being uncovered, so many truths being revealed that I shouldn't have been surprised by the slightly faded paper that came last among the pile. My birth certificate. I'd never seen it before, not once, but here it was, laid out before me like some kind of weird offering.

I traced my fingers lightly over the small typeface font that was my name. *Avaleigh McDonough.* I'd been right. Avaleigh Moore didn't exist, and this was the proof. It caught me by surprise really that my mother would risk everything to run but put her legal last name on my certificate. Birth records were public, but then again, if my father hadn't known she was pregnant, there had been no reason for him to look.

March 26, 1997. At least my birthdate wasn't a lie.

My gaze wandered down the page to the bottom where my father's name would be staring at me, mocking me. I'd expected the letters across the line to spell out my fate and tie me to the man for the rest of my life.

But I was wrong. Out of everything I had learned today, everything Mark had uncovered, this shook me the most. I knew the name that was permanently etched in black ink across the green tinted page, but I'd never seen him outside of the pictures in this envelope.

Liam Kavanaugh was typed neatly on the line next to the bold statement of *father*.

It felt like as soon as questions were answered, there were at least a dozen more to take their place. If my mother had been bought by the man masquerading as my father, how had she become pregnant with me? Why hadn't she gone back to him? Or even back home to her family? The biggest question, though, was why had Elias Ward pretended to be my father? What did he have to gain?

Now is not the time.

I barely made it to the kitchen sink before I heaved the contents of my stomach in the silver basin. The words my father had told Christian a few days after my eighteenth birthday banged around in my head like a toddler playing with metal pots. *Now is not the time.*

There was no part of me that could guess his overall plan for me, but now that I could see through the thickening fog, I better understood what was going on around me. I'd let myself be blinded to everything around me. I didn't question or wonder.

Matthias was right. I was never really living. Just simply surviving.

The small silver phone had been nestled at the bottom of the envelope. It was slim, discreet, and didn't make a single sound as I powered it on. There was only one number programed into it, and it took everything I had to press the button.

It rang. Once. Twice. I almost hung up until I heard the telltale click of an answer.

"Hello, Ava."

"Archer." My voice was cold, emotionless. No matter

what side of the law he was on, he was just a deviant as my fath—as Elias.

"Glad you called."

I snorted. "You didn't really give me a choice," I pointed out. "Apparently you have a knack for threatening people into doing what you want."

"I do what I have to do, Ava," I could practically hear the smile through the phone. "Which is why you're going to start helping me like you promised."

"That old threat isn't going to work anymore, Archer," I spat at him, losing my calm. "If you think you can use that line now, you're wrong."

"It wasn't that line I was going to use, Little Lamb." His use of my brother's nickname had the blood in my veins turning ice cold. "That's what your brother calls you, right? A sacrificial Little Lamb?"

"Fuck you, asshole."

Archer chuckled. "That's not very nice."

"I'm done being nice," I snarled into the phone. "I'm done letting you threaten me, you arrogant fucking pr—"

"What if I told you I know where Maleah is?"

I stopped short. *Maleah.* "How do I know you're telling the truth?"

"Look at your phone."

Bringing the phone away from my ear, I looked at the small screen where a picture had appeared. It was of Maleah, her hunched form laying in the middle of a large bed, her body covered in blood and bruises. Fucking hell.

"Where is she?" I rasped, my throat had gone dry, tears now flowing freely as I brought the phone back to my ear. "What did you do to her?"

"I didn't do anything, Ava," he scoffed. "That is the

product of one very sick man, and I will tell you where she is, once you do what I want."

"Please..."

"No." His tone darkened, and I had to fight the urge to yell at him. To fight him. "There is a micro-SD card in the phone. I need it."

"How am I supposed to get it to you?" Didn't he know I was constantly watched? Constantly guarded?

"I'm sure you'll figure out a way," he said. "Just make sure I get it before the end of the week, or I'll make sure you never find your friend."

The line went dead, and I was left with nothing but a stack of lies and empty promises.

CHAPTER THIRTY-FOUR

Ava

The drive back into the city the next day was quiet. Matthias had a lot on his mind, and I couldn't blame him. Elias and Christian had taken to acts of guerilla warfare on the streets, attacking Matthias's people at random. So far, he'd lost two legit businesses and one of his Underground fight clubs.

Not that I was in much of a talking mood, either. I'd ditched the cell phone, making sure to keep the micro-SD card, before tucking away all the papers Mark had given me in with my school stuff. Matthias wasn't likely to look in those, and neither was Mia. As soon as we'd arrived at the penthouse, he left without so much as a goodbye. There was tension in his shoulders as he typed furiously away on his phone with Leon trailing on his heels.

It was sad, but I'd grown used to his abrupt way of leaving. I knew he didn't mean it as a snub, it was simply who he was.

Hell, he even did it with his own men, so I tried not to take it personally. Still, I knew he was growing distant again after the whole shower scene yesterday morning. He'd displayed more emotion in that moment than he had in the time leading up to it.

That was what stung. I didn't want to go back to the way it was. I liked him taking control of my body each night, twisting and turning me as he sought his pleasure and mine.

"Look, I don't need you to keep following me around inside the penthouse."

A silent chuckle left me as Libby's voice rose from the other side of the bedroom door.

"Maybe I just like following you around, princess."

Libby groaned. "You know who follows their owners around?" she asked. "Dogs. Are you a good dog, Vas?" I stifled my laughter behind my hand as I eavesdropped shamelessly on their conversation. They were outside *my* bedroom door. Libby let out a small shriek.

"Don't do that," she gasped.

"I'll do whatever I want, princess," Vas growled lowly. Jesus. Were all Russian men dominant asshats? I thought it was limited to mostly Matthias, maybe Maksim because, well —he just put off that vibe. But Vas was silly and relaxed. He didn't seem the spanking type.

"I'll tell my sister."

Now I was really laughing, and when the door opened to reveal the pair, I laughed harder. It had been a while since I'd had the chance to just smile and laugh at something as silly as those two. They both looked at me like I was nuts. I probably was at this point.

"Go ahead, tell her," Vas invited, his hand held out toward me, daring her to do just that.

JO MCCALL

"Be nice, Vas," I warned him. "Her bite is worse than her bark. Trust me, I know."

"I heard yours is, too."

Now it was Libby and Vas's turn to crack up as my cheeks heated in mortification. Fucking hell. Did he share everything with his inner circle? Bite a man one time...okay twice...maybe three times. Honestly, I'd lost count.

"And now you are leaving." I pointed my finger at the door, trying my best to keep my glare on him. It was hard. Vas was just so likable. Well, not to Libby, apparently. Vas waved off my dismissal with a huff as he left, closing the door behind him.

"Thank god," Libby let out a long breath. "That man was driving me crazy. Are all Russians like that? Just follow you around like a Pitbull?"

"Yup."

"Great." Libby flopped on the bed next to me. "Just fucking great."

"You get used to it," I offered as I took a sip of my coffee. "Trust me, Vas is the most tolerable of the group when it comes down to it." *I believed he was anyway.*

"I don't want to get used to it."

"I know."

There was nothing more to say after that. Not about them anyway. Instead, I let her dive headfirst into talking about her latest activities. Her time with her friends. It wasn't until sometime later that she finally broached the topic I had been sitting on pins and needles to bring up.

"What are we going to do about Dad?" Libby asked as she flipped through one of the magazine's Vas had bought for her a few days ago. She'd already read it cover to cover, but none of the books in Matthias's library interested her, so she'd settled.

"I don't know."

And I didn't. Elias had gone into hiding after the press had swarmed the port.

"You need to draw him out," Libby piped up. I cast my sister a sidelong glance. "Dad doesn't do well when he is pressured. He likes to plan, and he wasn't able to plan for Matthias taking the port. That was a smart idea, by the way."

It was a smart plan, really. The containers under my mother's fake surname were cleared out, the merchandise loaded by Matthias's men into Elias's backup containers. Then, they staged a fire, drawing police, the press, firefighters, port security. Everyone. Weapons, ammo, some of the women who had stayed behind, it was all caught on camera for the six o'clock news. My father's name was ruined.

No. Not my father.

I hadn't told anyone besides Libby, who apparently already knew. That wasn't surprising, she'd always been rather astute, but she'd sarcastically rolled her eyes and told me that anyone could see from a mile away that I wasn't in any way related to Elias Ward. *Yeah. Okay.* When I told her what Mark had given me, she'd given me *that* look.

The look that said I was an idiot for not telling Matthias.

"You aren't giving yourself an advantage," she had told me. "If anything, you're hindering yourself."

"How is that?" I asked. "Matthias has done nothing but keep secrets from me. Telling me it is in my best interest not to know, but I think that's just bullshit. He's just like everyone else. The less I know, the more he thinks he can control me."

"Maybe that's true," she admitted, taking my hand in hers as her bright eyes lit up with mischief. That was the look she got when she was planning or plotting. "If you tell him you already know the truth then it takes something away from him, though. Doesn't it? He can't lord it over you any longer. Can't control you with it."

Well, shit.

"When did you become such a little Yoda?"

Libby scrunched her nose up in distaste.

"Yeah." She shook her head lightly. "No. I'm more of a Joan of Arc."

"You know she most likely had schizophrenia, right?"

Libby shrugged. "But she still won battles."

"And then was burned alive for heresy."

"By men who were obviously frightened of the power she held." Libby smirked. "Plus, she was canonized as a saint in the Catholic Church."

"So, basically she is nothing like you."

Libby squealed, appalled at my words, and swung one of my pillows at my head. She hit the mark. Laughing, I picked up a pillow of my own and swung back. Minutes later we were laughing hysterically on the floor, having both rolled off it in our attempt to win our impromptu pillow fight.

This is what I needed to fight for. Libby was right. It didn't serve a purpose hiding what I knew about my heritage. It was a divider, but my gut still churned at the thought of trusting the man who I knew was still holding secrets. I wasn't under the illusion that Matthias knew who my family was. Maybe not right away, but the man had a year to dig around in my past to find exactly what Mark found.

The problem was, if I told him about Mark, I would need to tell him about Agent Archer, and I wasn't ready for that conversation. I looked over at Libby who was now fast asleep next to me. The girl loved her naps. No matter what, she would always be my sister. Blood or not. She was my light. Her and Kenzi.

Libby said she had tried to reach her, but nothing. It just

went to voicemail, but she said that wasn't uncommon since Kenzi was a few time zones ahead and often buried herself in the library where phones weren't allowed. She was the one who managed to get away. To escape. Even if it was with my father's blessing.

If you could call it that. Kenzi was the useless twin. That's what he had said. Even Kendra treated her differently than Libby, all because she couldn't have kids. Couldn't reproduce. In Elias's mind, that made her useless. No one wanted to make a deal for a wife who couldn't bear him sons. Kenzi held no value to him without a womb.

I'd be glad to rid the man from our lives. Matthias had assured me that Libby and Kenzi would be safe and taken care of, and that promise meant everything to me, because there was no one in the world that I treasured more than those two girls whose smiles lit up a room.

Carefully, I slipped from the bed, throwing on a pair of slip-on shoes before heading out the door to find Matthias. He had been in meetings all afternoon with Vas and Nicolai. Plotting. I didn't know what I would say, but Libby was right. It was time to come clean. I wanted Matthias to trust me. To make sure he kept his word that Libby and Kenzi would be safe.

The world would burn before I let anyone harm them.

CHAPTER THIRTY-FIVE

Matthias

Things were going exactly as planned.

For the most part. The press was eating up the story of Elias Ward's shame, spreading the news far and wide. Just what I wanted. Investors were pulling out. Clients were tearing up their contracts. It was utter perfection, and my name was tied to none of it. The mayor, the man who'd let Elias sell his own daughter, was now making a grand speech about how corruption would not be tolerated in this city. That Elias and Ward Enterprises would be prosecuted to the full extent of the law.

Blah. Blah. Blah.

Jesus, Ava was rubbing off on me.

Vas and Nicolai were both sitting across from me, watching the announcement as we waited for the grand finale. I may not have found Maleah yet, but that didn't mean I couldn't bring a little karma back around. For Ava. Not that I had told her I was doing this. I didn't think she would completely approve, but this was who I was, and I wouldn't be changing that.

We all grimaced as a shot rang out over the newscaster's video. Chaos ensued as the Mayor's head whipped back, body falling lifelessly to the ground, his blood staining the podium. Yep. Karma. Not to mention that I would now be able to put my own man in his seat. One by one I would eliminate Elias's support system. Mayor Ford could have crowed to the heavens all he wanted about Elias being dirty, but that wouldn't have stopped him from supporting him from the shadows.

Now that wouldn't be a problem.

"Well, that is one part of the plan down." Vas clicked off the television with a smug smile. "Now we just have to execute the others." Nicolai snickered at my *Sovietnik's* choice in words. They were children. Fucking children playing at being grown-ass adults and I was surrounded by them.

"Everything is falling into place," I agreed. "I would have rather had Elias by now, but the plan Ava came up with is definitely working." It had been her idea to take some of the stashed merchandise and set him up. Frame him. Although it wasn't technically a frame job since the merchandise was actually his, we simply made sure it was found. In a big way.

"Speaking of Ava..." Vas trailed off. I knew where he was going with this. "Are you still keeping to your original plan for her?"

I didn't know. Was I? Ava had turned out to be different than expected. There was a fight in her that I was drawn to. Her unwillingness to fully submit except in our bedroom where she let me devour her in every way possible.

"You know," Nicolai started. "If you simply told her who

her father was, you would probably get better results." I scoffed.

If I told her who her father was, she would no longer believe she would need to rely on me. I wouldn't have the same control over her as I do now. She wouldn't want to stay with me. Ava would want to get to know her birth father. The man who probably would have wanted her if he had known about her.

Ava hadn't tried to escape because we had a common enemy. Elias. Even if she believed he was her father, he had done nothing to deserve the title, and she knew that. Her rage grew into hatred, and her hatred morphed in needing vengeance when he had taken her best friend and sold her.

Would she want to stay if I told her the truth? If she didn't, I would be forced to keep her under lock and key. I wouldn't let her go. She'd come to hate me the same way she hated Elias. Then again, if she found out I knew and didn't tell her, she would probably still hate me.

There was no winning. Not really.

"I'm not sure."

Vas sighed, dragging a hand through his hair, eyeing me. That was a look his father used to give me when he was disappointed in what I'd done. I hated that fucking look.

"You know I'd follow you to the depths of hell, brother," Vas confided. "And no matter your decision, I'll stand by you. Even now. But—this part of the plan is shit."

"Do you think it's smart? Marrying Ava and impregnating her so you can use that blood tie with Irish Mafia in this war?" Nicolai chimed in. The fucker. "That is no better than what Elias had planned for her."

It was my turn to scoff. "That's not true. I didn't plan on murdering them all."

"Oh." Vas's eyebrows raised in mock surprise. "Yes, it is so much better that you weren't contemplating murdering your bride's family. Excellent. Five stars."

"Jesus," I groaned, taking a moment to collect myself and sip my whiskey. I turned my attention back to my men. "Look, she is a means to an end and—"

"She *was* a means to an end, brother," Nicolai pointed out. "Maybe you should start acting like it is past tense instead of continuing to leave her in the dark. I understand this is hard for you. You've never done this before. Never cared for a woman like you do her, but if you keep playing hot and cold, she is going to try to leave anyway. Whether she knows the truth or not."

I went to defend myself. To make him see *my* point of view, but nothing came out.

"Look..." My phone rang, vibrating against my desk, interrupting the little speech I was about to unload on those two assholes.

"Dashkov."

"Sir." It was Conlin, one of the security guards on duty today. "We have a security breach in the parking garage."

Ava. Shit.

"Lock it down." *Fuck.* Without waiting to see if my men were following, I stormed from the room, hopping into the open elevator, fuming.

"Looks like she used your code." Nicolai was scrolling through his phone.

"Why would she suddenly be leaving?" I wondered. Vas huffed as he held up his own. The video feed showed Ava about to knock on my office door just moments ago. Then she hesitated, her head tilting toward the door before her face morphed into solid fury. She looked like an angry goddess, her red curls flying out behind her as she dashed down the hallway and into the elevator.

"Fuck," I growled, snatching up Vas's phone and throwing it at the wall. The sound of breaking glass soothed some of the anger.

"Hey!" he protested. "That was brand-fucking-new."

"I'll buy you a new one," I snapped. Dammit. The only reason we had been alerted to her leaving was because she had attempted to start one of the cars without an access badge. Now, it looked like she was on foot. My feet hit the ground running the minute the doors to the elevator opened.

"Ava!" I roared her name as the metal gate came crashing down, locking me in the parking garage. Vas and Nicolai were busy shouting orders at the guards to get the gate back up, but it was too late. My Little Red shot me a venomous glare, her emerald eyes pooling with anger and betrayal before she turned on her heel and ran.

CHAPTER THIRTY-SIX

Vas

"I don't care what it fucking takes," Matthias yelled into the phone. "Fucking find her. She can't have gotten far on foot, and she doesn't have any money. Track her down but stay in the shadows. Alert me when you do."

"Men are already starting a search grid," I assured him as I went to dig my phone out of my pocket, only to remember that he had all but destroyed it. Damn, that thing was brand new. The latest version of iPhone that Mark had souped up for me. I could finally watch the good porn without getting a virus. Or so he'd told me. I didn't believe he'd actually put what I asked on it, but the ability to track in real time and start my car from it was still neat.

"Maybe you should have told her the truth." Great. That was all Matthias needed right now. A lecture from a fucking pixie.

"Unless you know where she is," he snarled at Libby.

"This is none of your business." His tone roused something in me. I didn't like the way he was speaking to her, but there was nothing I could do. He was my *Pakhan*. My leader. And she was not my woman. Not that she needed much help since she was currently laughing in Matthias's face. The nerve of this one.

"You keep telling yourself that," she chuckled.

"Where would she go, *Malen'kaya Feya*?" Matthias shot me a stunned look when I called her Little Fairy. In all the years we'd known each other, he'd never heard me give any woman I had ever been with a pet name.

The term of endearment had simply slipped from my lips the first time I met her.

"Even if I knew." She scrunched up her nose at me, like she was smelling foul. "I wouldn't fucking tell you."

"I could always make you," I threatened, my tone dark. Libby shrugged. "*Feya...*" It was a warning. One she wasn't heeding. Matthias had all but disappeared down the hallway back to his study. No doubt to brood until he was able to get news on Ava.

"What are you going to do?" She tilted her head to the side, her long blonde hair cascading down one shoulder as she quirked an eyebrow in challenge. "Shove me in a trunk again?"

I smirked at the memory of her small body against mine as I dragged her from the street and into the trunk. I'd offered her the chance to ride in the back seat with me, but she'd been stubborn. And feisty. Her small little fists had beat against my broad chest, and it had taken nearly all of my restraint not to take her then and there with the way her body melded against mine.

"I gave you a chance to ride with me," I reminded her. "You didn't take it."

"Yes." Libby rolled her eyes. The action caused my hand to twitch. If she were mine, I would have hauled her over my knee for that. "Because I was taught to take ride from strangers."

The fire. The sarcasm. I had never come across a woman willing to go toe to toe with me. Most feared me. Rightfully so, but this little pixie was all sparks. Like Tinkerbell.

"It isn't safe out there for her, Libby." I tried to reason with her. That maybe if she understood the risk to her sister, she would help. I was wrong.

"It isn't safe for her in here, either."

CHAPTER THIRTY-SEVEN

Ava

I ran until my legs were sore and I was out of breath. Literally. I couldn't breathe. My lungs were burning. How did people do this? Fuck. When did I get so out of shape? Oh, right. Texas and the beer bottles. That would do it.

Man, did I miss Texas right now. A lot. I'd go back there if I could, but I didn't have enough money. Actually, I didn't have any money. Great. I looked around at my surroundings, realizing that I'd run pretty far into downtown. I didn't recognize any of the buildings, but the name of one caught my eye.

McDonough's.

No fucking way. I gave myself a moment to catch my breath before crossing the street onto First Avenue. The buildings were older here, made of brick. The sidewalks were uneven, and some of the shops were in disrepair. So, this was the little spot of Irish heaven in Seattle. It wasn't bad. It had a homey feel to it that the bigger businesses lacked.

I stopped in front of the bar, watching from the shadows of one of the trees as the people inside laughed and drank their day away. I didn't necessarily believe in coincidences, but I doubted anyone other than my birth father would have named a bar after my dead mother. Something pulled at me to go inside, but I ignored it. What would I do? What would I say?

Hi, I'm your ex-girlfriend's daughter and you're my father.

That didn't seem like it would go down very well. Plus, I didn't even know if this place belonged to him. It really could just be a coincidence.

"Ava."

Fuck it all to hell. Just when my day couldn't get any worse. Fucking Daddy Kink was here.

"Archer," I repeated in the bored tone he'd approached me with.

"Do you have it?"

I snorted. "Nice to see you, too. How have you been? Me? Not so great. I've recently found out my entire life is a lie. My father isn't who he said he was. The real one doesn't know I exist. The man who bought me was planning on using me for some kind of alliance, pretending he actually cared about me, and everyone appears to be in on the joke, except me."

Archer sighed, pinching the bridge of his nose like he was deciding if I was worth it. Served him right. "It's nice to see you, too, Ava. I'm great. Where's the fucking SD card?"

"Here, you fucking senior citizen." I dug the chip out from the little pocket of my jacket, but I didn't hand it over. Not yet. Archer growled when I wrapped my fist around it, refusing him what he wanted most.

"Here's the thing." I grinned up at him, but my eyes were

hard. At least I hoped they were. "You want something I have, and I'm inclined to give it to you on one condition."

"You really think you have room to negotiate?" Red crept up his neck, his fists clenching and unclenching at his sides, the vein at his neck throbbing. Oh, someone was angry. I wondered what was on it that had him in such a tiff.

"I mean—" I let my arms stretch out so that my fist dangled right above a drain. A big one, too. There wouldn't be any salvaging it if it fell in there. "—Yeah. I do."

Well, if he wasn't homicidal before, he was now. His silver eyes were so wide I thought they might bulge from his head, and his face was beginning to turn an ugly shade of purple. And here I thought that only happened in movies.

"Don't test me, Avaleigh." He pointed a finger in my face. Kudos to me for not biting it. "I will destroy you and everything you hold dear until I am the only thing left, and you are all fucking alone."

"Your threats don't mean shit to me when I'm the one holding what you so desperately desire over a fucking sidewalk drain." Archer cursed.

"Fine." He stepped back and took a calming breath. It took him less than a minute to become the jovial FBI agent I had seen in Texas. Yep. Psychopathic. "What do you want?"

"Besides Maleah's location?" I asked. "Leave Mark and his family out of this."

"Fine." His lips drew back in a snarl. "Deal. Now give me the SD card."

And I did. Against my better judgement, I handed it over. I could feel my heart breaking knowing that whatever was on that SD card would likely be something he could use against Matthias, but then I remembered how he had planned to use me, and the feeling eased. Who was I kidding? No, it didn't.

No matter what Matthias's plan had been or was, I still couldn't help but love him.

Nope. Fuck that shit. It wasn't love. It was lust. Orgasms, I loved. Him, I tolerated because he was the one who gave them to me. But it definitely wasn't love. Maybe fondness. That's it. I was fond of him. Like an owner is fond of its cat.

"Nice doing business with you, Ava." Archer tipped his head at me as he strode away. My face paled.

"Wait," I called after him. "What about Maleah?"

Archer smirked before turning and striding away. "There is still work to be done."

Well, fuck. Not the brightest crayon in the box after all. Maybe I should have learned to play chess and strategize better. Sighing, I turned back to the bar, barely noticing that the afternoon sun was beginning to fade, and with it, its warmth.

"Going inside?"

A small yelp eased from my throat as the quiet solace of the street was broken. There was a shadow blocking the light, and when I looked up, I nearly cried.

That would be embarrassing.

"I'm sorry?" I asked, my voice wobbling a bit as I struggled to keep it together. He was here. This was him. I would recognize the tattoo along his neck anywhere. He smiled, his face lighting up, and I couldn't help but smile back.

"I asked if you were going to stand out here all afternoon or come inside."

"Oh."

Great vocabulary skill you've got going there. Couldn't come up with anything better?

"Oh?"

"Umm..." *Keep this up and he might think you're handicapped. Or stupid.* Jesus. "No. I was just taking a walk and

JO MCCALL

saw the sign. Interesting name." The man nodded his head like he was humoring me more than believing a word I said. God, why couldn't I be a better liar?

"Really?" His emerald eyes twinkled. So that's where I got them from. I'd always wondered since my mother had brown eyes and

so did Elias. "Fancy a rest and a pint, then?"

"Oh, I don't drink, but thank you for the offer."

"All right then, lass." He pursed his lips a bit, his eyes sizing me up. He wasn't leering but looked more like he was curious about something. Did he recognize my mother in me, or was he just giving me a once-over since I was creeping in front of his bar? "Come back anytime, all right?"

I nodded my head, not trusting myself to speak without spilling the beans. I doubted he would believe me anyway. With a nod of his head, he strode to the door, casting one more thoughtful look at me before opening it and disappearing inside.

That had been my chance, and I was too much of a fucking coward to take it.

IT HAD BEEN NEARLY an hour since I left McDonough's, and now I was lost. Like, really lost. I'd been attempting to find my way back to Matthias's building, but I had somehow managed to get turned around, and now I was in a part of the city I sure as hell didn't want to be.

"Lost?"

Fucking hell. What was it with people jumping out at me? I turned to see a young man, about my age, wearing a clean set of jeans and a Carhartt jacket. He must have been one of the workers from the construction site I passed.

Shrugging my shoulders, I gave him a small smile. "A bit. Went for a walk and got turned around."

He nodded his head at that, lips curling thoughtfully. "Where you heading?"

"The Dashkov Corporation on the hill."

"You really are lost." He chuckled. "Come on, I'll walk you back to the main road and point you in the right direction. It's not too far."

"I appreciate it." The man nodded as we walked back up the streets I had come down. Apparently, I had managed to walk in the complete opposite direction of home. *Home.* Is that what it even was? Did I even want to go back there?

Then again, where else did I have to go?

The cold was beginning to bite into my skin, but at least my companion was nice. He was married with two kids. Nice enough fellow for someone I'd randomly met. I was just glad he hadn't turned out to be a serial killer or anything. I laughed at one of his jokes as we crested over one of the hills back toward First Avenue where I had started.

When I looked up, Matthias and several men were waiting for us at the top. I couldn't mistake the look on his face, not when it was so obvious. He had a treacherous, vacant look in his eyes, his jaw firmly set and a perilous frown etched across his face. Shit. This wasn't good. His body was tense, poised for violence. If his face hadn't spoken volumes about his mood, his body language sure as hell did.

Matthias Dashkov was not pleased.

"Everything okay?" The man beside me asked as he gazed past me, his forehead puckered with worry as he looked back and forth between me and my so-called husband. I vaguely wondered how I looked to him at the moment. Frightened that Matthias had come for me? Happy, maybe? Plain-ass crazy?

Matthias's unforgiving, wickedly vacant eyes were on me, catching my gaze with purpose. I watched the slight flicker, that momentary disturbance in his unrelenting gaze. The exact moment he turned his calculating stare onto the poor, unsuspecting man next to me, and then he was moving.

He sauntered forward, his boots not making a single noise as he stalked toward me leisurely. As if he had all the time in the fucking world. I knew the threat in that walk, knew what it signified, and yet I couldn't bring myself to fucking move. It was like his gaze was pinning me down where I stood; promising a worse fate if I tried to flee. If there was one thing Matthias had down pat—it was one hell of an intimidating stare.

There was an agile grace to his movement, especially when he was angry. He looked like an enraged wolf going in for the kill. The man beside me, who hadn't even gotten a chance to properly introduce himself, lifted his gaze from me to meet Matthias's irate eyes. I had to give it to him, I didn't know the guy, but he was either incredibly stupid or just extremely nice. The only sign of his nerves was the slight bob of his Adam's apple before a sunny smile crept on his face.

"Someone you know?" he guessed, his tone still polite.

Matthias was close enough to interact now, his seemingly casual but swift strides had closed the distance easily, his men right behind him.

"Her *husband*." He didn't bother hiding the possessive undertone of his gruff voice, the one that promised bloodshed if distance wasn't created between the nice worker and myself.

"Ah, you're a lucky man." There was a slight falter to his otherwise casual and composed tone. It wasn't that he was disappointed, but that Matthias thought he had some kind of ill intentions.

"I'm well aware." Matthias's voice lacked the polite, socially acceptable edge. He was all growls and aggression as he reached his destination; my side. His glove-covered hand reached out and latched on to my smaller hand. It dwarfed mine, and I was surprised by the relatively gentle grasp, but I could still feel the tremor in it.

He was straining to control himself.

"Time to go, Red," he growled lowly, aiming his comment at me as he crossed in front of me, a move designed to twist me away from the helpful man without so much as a casual goodbye.

"It was nice meeting you," the man called to both of us. I winced as Matthias's grip on my hand tightened painfully, his control slipping.

"Take care of it." I heard Matthias whisper to one of his men. One I didn't recognize. Fuck. The poor innocent man was heading back the way he came with a few of Matthias's men trailing after him. He wouldn't hurt him for helping me, would he? It's not like he helped me escape. He was just being nice.

I walked alongside him silently for several agonizing minutes, Matthias's hand still gripping me tightly, before I addressed the issue.

"What did they do?" I kept my voice quiet as he led me wherever it was we were going.

"Don't worry about it." Was his simple and complete bullshit response.

"No," I was alternating between watching where we were going and looking at his face, observing his expressions. His jaw clenched slightly when I brought it up. His furious gray eyes caught my gaze. "What are your men going to do to him?" I pressed again, not backing down from the warning in those devastatingly handsome yet infuriating orbs.

His chest rumbled with a warning growl, low and feral. The sound sent my heart hammering away in my ribcage, and I almost tripped over my own two feet as he led us farther away from the busy street. This wasn't anywhere he would be able to park one of his cars, which meant we weren't heading for home.

"Why do you care?" His voice was the same low pitch as his growl. I threw caution to the wind, I needed to know what he'd done. He couldn't just go around killing people for talking to me. For helping me. Especially since he was the reason I ran off and got lost in the first place.

"Did you order them to kill him?" My voice was surprisingly even.

"No." His eyes were focused ahead of us now. His fingers, however, pressed into the slender flesh of my neck, making me wince. Suddenly, he was shoving me forward. My shoes slipped on the wet concrete as I practically skidded into the alleyway he had forced us into before backing me into a small alcove a few feet down.

Alone.

"How did you find me?" I asked. "That was kind of a random spot to know where I was."

"You aren't that good at hiding, Red." He smirked. "I have some of the best technically inclined men and women at my disposal. Hacking traffic cameras was not all that hard."

Well, fuck.

Running away and escaping just weren't my forte, apparently. I sucked at it. I blamed my shitty childhood and the fact that I was never allowed to play hide and seek with my sisters. That game was a life-building skill. Now, here I was, trapped in a tiny alcove with a beast. A monster.

"Why won't you just let me go?" My voice was nearly

shrill, the swirling mix of exhaustion and frustration swinging at me like a bat on a pinata.

I was the pinata.

"You're mine." He shrugged as if it was an everyday thing that he took a woman as collateral and then forced her to marry him. "You're my wife. Why would I let go of something that belongs to me?"

"You may have forced me to be your wife," I spat at him, my hands pushed at his chest. "But I am not yours! I'm just your fucking pawn. You admitted it. I heard you."

His chest rumbled with a warning growl, low and feral. The sound sent my heart hammering away in my ribcage. His large, calloused hand came up to encircle my delicate throat, and I gasped as my back collided with the chilled bricks of the wall behind me.

"You are mine." His lips curled into a devilish smirk, his stormy eyes dark and unrelenting as his gaze bored into mine. "Know this. You can run, Little Red, but I will always find you. No matter how far you go or how well you try to hide. You will always be mine."

If this were any other man, those words might have been a promise that made my knees weak and my heart melt. But this wasn't some fluffy romance or A *Walk to Remember*. He wasn't Mr. Darcy, and I wasn't Elizabeth Bennet. This man was the Devil, and those words weren't just a promise, but a threat.

"Now," he grumbled roughly. I could practically hear the impatience dripping from his voice. "I'm waiting."

"For what?" I wasn't quite sure what I'd missed, what he wanted from me. His jaw ticked as he took a forced, controlled breath of air in through his nose.

"I answered your question. You didn't answer mine," he rumbled. "Why did you want me to spare him?"

His voice had turned malicious, cutting through the frigid air rather sharply as his anger twisted around him. I'd never seen him like this. Sure, I'd seen him express a few emotions over my time with him. Anger, disappointment, more anger. This was different. It was more like he wasn't just angry, but dare I say—jealous. This new emotion was now twisted around him like a gnarled rosebush that had grown out of control, and I didn't understand it.

Well, if there was one thing I lacked, it would always be self-preservation.

"You didn't answer my question, though!" I argued. "What did your men do to do him? All you said was that they didn't kill him. That leaves a whole realm of possibilities with you." I tried to keep my voice quiet, but Matthias had a way about him that brought the worst of my temper to the surface. Maybe it was because he was always so damn calm and put together. Even when I was throwing shit at him and raging, he was still stoic and cold.

Maybe it was because I knew that even though he would punish me, he would never truly hurt me. Physically, at least. He would never stoop to beating me or starving me like my father and brother had when my temper couldn't be contained.

Matthias's face contorted into a half-snarl as I argued with him. His eyebrows furrowed, his lips curling momentarily to flash me his teeth as he sucked in a sharp breath of air. He was trying to keep control of himself. Quicker than I could keep up with, he was moving. His body shifting forward as he changed positions. The fabric of his dark coat slid angrily across the brick as he transferred his weight onto his forearm, slamming it right above my head, his fist clenching tightly. The arm around my neck slid up until it was grasping on to my jaw tightly, his large palm cradling my chin in his grip as he aggressively forced my neck back so that our eyes remained locked.

Momentarily stunned by his sudden proximity, I was brought back down to earth by the sudden realization that he didn't have his gloves on anymore. When had he taken them off?

He was closer now, too close. The position switch had him practically pressed against me, dwarfing me with his size. It was always moments like this that I was acutely aware of just how much bigger than me he really was. His body heat was searing me through my clothes, a ridiculously prominent contrast to the frozen bricks at my back.

"They didn't kill him," he repeated, growling in my face. "He's fine." His grip around my jaw tightened, the dangerous calloused digits pressing into my cheeks tightly, but not painfully. "Now, answer the goddamn question, Red."

"Because I didn't want him to die for simply helping me," I snapped back, my heart hammering painfully in my chest. "He was just trying to help me; he didn't mean any harm." I tried to jerk my chin out of his palm, but his fingers just dug in tighter, forcing me to keep his vexed stare.

Matthias clenched his teeth tightly, grinding them together harshly as he tried to ground himself. "Not—" He paused to suck in a deep breath through is nose, clenching his eyes shut tightly as he tried to force his rage back under control. "—good enough," he breathed, letting some of the tension roll off his shoulders. His grip, however, didn't slacken any. I wasn't going anywhere anytime soon.

Despite how calm he tried to make that sentence; all I could hear was how unreasonable he was being. I was telling him the fucking truth and he was ignoring it. There was no calming the storm of anger that was now raging in my mind.

What else should I have said? He was the one being ridiculous.

"What more do you fucking want from me?" I snarled into his face, losing the rest of my patience for the man in front of me. Reaching out with both of my hands, I shoved hard at his chest, trying to create some distance. He didn't move. Growling in rage while doing my damn hardest to ignore how good he felt under my palms, I twisted and tried a more tactical approach. Twisting my leg, I aimed for the side of his knee like Roman had taught me the other day.

He quickly swiveled his foot, letting go of my face and jerking his leg away from me, avoiding my attack. Faster than I could comprehend, he was back on me, anger radiating from him in intense, suffocating waves as he surged forward to stop my flailing limbs. His large hands grasped on to my hips tightly for a moment, his fingers digging harshly into the denim of my jeans. I tried to scramble sideways, out of his grip, but his hands slipped down quicker than I could follow and gripped on to the back of my thighs, yanking me up and off the ground.

I shrieked as he shoved himself forward between my parted thighs to pin my body back against the icy bricks, my legs on either side of his waist. Not even pausing for a moment, he released his hold on my legs, letting his lower body support me against the wall as he snatched up my still-moving arms with ease. His hands easily wrapped around both of my forearms, firmly shoving them next to my head.

This position put us face to face, and fuck, was he angry. I'd wanted to see him lose control, and here it was. His eyes were an overcast gray, almost molten, as his emotions corrupted the normally frigid stare. There was no way in hell I was going to let my hormones distract me. No, no, no. He was being irrational. I would know. I was queen of irrational.

Especially when I was supposed to be angry, and all I could now think about was how good he felt against me, his warmth taking over.

All he'd ever done since we'd been together was take. Even when I'd told him no, he'd simply played my body like the string of a guitar until I was wound so tight, I was begging him for release.

"You're mine," he thundered lowly. His voice was coarse and thick with emotion, like broken glass. For a single moment I wondered if we were being too loud while arguing. I mean, sure, we were in a pretty desolate alley, tucked into a small alcove, but still. Then I remembered that this was all his fucking fault, so if someone wandered over to us and saw him being an ass, that was his problem, and he could fucking deal with it.

"You've said that. I know!" I argued back, willing my mind to stay focused. "You say it all the time. Growl it. Demand it. But you never show it. You don't talk to me or spend time with me. All you do is demand, demand, demand. You demand my obedience and my loyalty, but you haven't once shown me that you deserve either. You fuck me, comfort me, then leave me. You can say I am yours all you want, but just like every orgasm you've given me, it's by force and not willingly. If you want willing, you're gonna have to work a lot harder."

I tried to lift my arms off the wall, but he was having none of it, his iron-tight grip didn't let me move an inch. I struggled against him, arching my back off the wall in a futile attempt to get some distance, to hopefully clear my head of my increasingly perverted thoughts. Despite my excellent proclamation that I was his, but he wasn't mine, my body had other ideas. Like always.

His fingers flexed against my skin in response as he

growled in warning, his chest rumbling and distracting me further. My breath hitched at the noise as my heart stuttered. Much to my annoyance. Fucking fuck, Avaleigh. *Are you incapable of focusing fully when he's touching you? Get it together. There could be no turning into a hormonal puddle of goo when you were trying to prove a point.*

Matthias's eyes slid slowly to meet mine, ensnaring my gaze instantly, practically shutting my brain down with one look. My chest tightened violently as I stared up at him, too dumbstruck to look away or continue yelling. Why was he staring at me like that? He looked—

"Fuck it," he breathed, finally responding to my last statement and successfully cutting off my thought process. His voice was eerily calm despite the aggression in his stance. His tone was nothing more than a gruff whisper.

Lunging forward, he closed the small distance between us, swallowing my anger as he crushed his mouth to mine fiercely.

His kiss was like a switch in my brain, my rational thoughts shutting off the moment his lips met mine. He gave me no quarter, no moment to adjust to the change of the situation before his teeth nipped roughly on my bottom lip. I gasped into his mouth as his tongue plundered and stole my breath away, swirling with my own. He tasted minty, and I couldn't help but groan into his mouth as his tongue battled mine into submission.

Pulling back slightly, he turned so that his breath was hot against my ear. "Wrap your legs around me," he demanded, his voice no more than a low, husky whisper. I didn't even think as I wrapped my legs tightly around his strong waist. He hummed his approval lightly before turning and once again catching my lips with his.

His grip left my arms, one of his hands sliding down to

grip on to the side of my neck, tilting my head where he wanted it as he continued to kiss me breathless. The other hand wandered to my waist, sliding past the material of my hoodie and shirt to get at the skin underneath. His heated touch practically branded me when his rough palm slid up my chilled side and I arched against him.

Fucking hell.

His mouth abruptly tore from mine again, but before I could protest, the hand on my neck tangled in my fiery hair, yanking it to the side to expose the tender column of my throat. Butterflies erupted in my abdomen and my legs shook on either side of him.

"Matthias—"

He didn't let me finish as he dipped his head and attached his mouth to my neck, nipping at my pulse-point roughly before soothing the tender skin with his tongue as I cried out against him. Reaching down, I tangled my own hands in his hair, pulling hard on the soft, dark strands. He growled in response as he sucked at the now-bruised flesh of my throat.

He continued his assault on my neck, easily skipping the black fabric choker, leaving a trail of bruised skin in his wake as he sent my hormones into overdrive. He didn't stop until he had sunk his teeth in the juncture where neck met shoulder, ripping a moan from my mouth as I gripped on to his hair tighter, pulling hard.

"Stop." I had to stop this madness. My blood was boiling with his touch, but I couldn't let him think I was giving in. That he could just keep taking everything from me by force. "Let me go."

"No."

His nails dug into the flesh of my side as he groaned, his body shifting forward, crushing me even tighter against the wall. My abdomen clenched tightly from the sound. Fucking hell. No matter how much I wanted to resist this man—I couldn't. He was like my perfect storm. My captor and my savior. I wanted to push him away but pull him close.

Everything was out of control. I felt like I was drowning, and he was the air I needed.

The rough stubble on his face scraped against the hypersensitive skin of my neck as he lifted his head, turning to capture my lips again. They moved roughly against mine as he unwound his hand from my hair, gliding it down my side until he reached the edge of my hoodie. Letting go of his hair, I wrapped my arms loosely around his neck as his chilled hand slipped underneath my shirt to slide up the delicate flesh of my stomach.

My abdomen tightened as his hand slid up and under my bra, cupping my breast firmly. I couldn't stop the flush that spread up my neck and covered my cheeks as I shuddered under his touch. He moved to roll my nipple between his thumb and forefinger, making me gasp into his mouth. The corner of his lips twitched upward as his tongue swept against mine once more before he pulled back, leaning his forehead against mine as he turned that purposeful, intense gaze on me.

His breath was a bit ragged as his hand slipped from my side, down my stomach, to the hem of my jeans, his dexterous fingers flicking the button open easily. His hand abandoned my breast, leaving me aching and wanting more as it moved back down my side to latch on to my hip firmly, his fingers digging in tightly as he pinned my hip in place against the bricks.

Shifting slightly, he wedged the other hand between us a bit better, his fingers pulling my zipper down with a flick of his wrist. Without taking his eyes off me, he shifted his hand and slid underneath the hem of my panties. His fingers dipped low until two of his cold digits pressed tightly against my clit, sending a spasm of pleasure through my body that had my eyes clenching shut.

The hand at my hip was bruising as it tightened quite suddenly. Fucking hell, this man was going to be the death of me.

"Look at me," he demanded. His low, coarse voice cutting through the silence sharply.

Swallowing thickly, I opened my eyes to meet his lustful, stormy gaze, immediately caught up in how intimidating his stare actually was. His fingers pressed and circled once, then twice against my clit, pulling a sharp moan from my mouth as little sparks of pleasure rolled up into my core. My cheeks stained a deeper pink as his eyes darkened at the sound.

"Eyes stay on me," he commanded. "Understand?"

Taking in a deep breath through my nose, I nodded my head slowly, not trusting my voice in the slightest.

"I need a verbal answer, Red."

I resisted the urge to growl at him. "Yes, sir."

Abruptly, he dipped his fingers lower until he was cupping my pussy, my breath hitched but I forced my gaze to remain on his. His middle finger slid between my folds, testing how wet I was before pushing up into me to his first knuckle. Biting down on my lip, I stifled a moan as I flushed harder under his gaze.

"Good girl," he breathed out, pleased with my compliance, his normally stoic voice tainted with need. The new and delicious tone caused a shudder to race down my spine. He was definitely going to be the death of me.

"Now," he growled suddenly, his voice taking on a darker edge. "Let me hear you."

His middle finger suddenly pushed the rest of the way into my pussy, forcing a cry from my throat as I threw my head back against the bricks. It was harder than I thought to keep my eyes locked on his as he overwhelmed me with his touch. He started at a maddening pace, it was slow, tortuously slow as he worked his finger in and out of me. Every time I tried to stifle my moans, he'd rub his thumb against my clit firmly, forcing a whimper from my throat.

A coil was beginning to tighten in my core as he manipulated my body with his touch. I felt heated and I was aching for more, but Matthias was punishing in his attentions. Every little bit, he'd suddenly slow dramatically until he was barely moving, forcing the coil to unwind slightly and leave me more and more frustrated each time. Just like the first time he had punished me this way, I wasn't going to last under this kind of torture. I was going to lose my fucking mind.

"Matt—" I whimpered, not caring that I was begging him to show mercy. "Please…"

He stared at me intently, taking in my words with a clench of his jaw. I knew how my begging affected him. After a moment's pause, he growled and pulled back. I couldn't help but whine in protest as his finger left me aching. I wasn't left waiting long, however, as he suddenly thrust two thick fingers back inside me, ripping a strangled moan from my mouth as my back arched off the bricks, one of my hands clenching onto his jacket. Digging my nails into the back of his neck, I heard the rumble of approval as he sucked in a sharp breath.

His fingers worked quickly now, his pace furious and unrelenting as I squirmed against him, the coil pulling tighter and tighter inside me. The intimacy of keeping our eyes locked wasn't lost on me, and if anything, it was just making me madder with desire. The flame of protest I'd originally had in the beginning had been extinguished. Replaced by a roaring fire that fed off need and wanton lust.

The hand at my hip was bruising as it kept me perfectly still, exactly where he wanted me. With a firm roll of his thumb against my bundle of nerves, he curled his fingers inside me, brushing up against a spot that had me coming undone. Surging forward, Matthias claimed my lips in a bruising kiss, muffling the scream that would have been his name as wave after wave of pure ecstasy washed over me when the coil finally broke.

Both of my legs were trembling as he ended the kiss. I was struggling to stay wrapped around him, feeling like Jell-O in his arms.

My mind was spinning with thoughts, but I couldn't manage to grasp on to a single one of them at the moment. Pleasurable little aftershocks were shooting up my spine and taking way all of my rational thoughts. Slowly, and a bit hesitantly, I moved my hand up the back of Matthias's neck to brush my fingers into his hair.

With the utmost care, he slowly detangled himself, and with a few quick motions, he had my jeans done up again and my shirt and hoodie back in place as if nothing naughty had transpired. This was the moment I was dreading. This was the moment he always walked away like nothing had happened. I braced myself, ready for him to turn on his heels and walk away, dragging me behind him without another word.

Instead, he shifted his arms, pulling me away from the bricks just enough to slip his arms up my back until he was grasping my shoulders firmly. Holding me tightly, he leaned forward, letting my weight rest against his strong arms as he dropped his head down until his forehead was resting against my shoulder, obscuring his face from view.

"I'm sorry." His voice was husky and low, laced with emotion.

I was incredibly confused. Matthias wasn't one for apologies.

"I know I'm not an easy man to deal with," he stated, his voice no more than a whisper against me. I swallowed hard. "I'm selfish with you. I can't help it, *Krasnyy*."

That Russian nickname again...Fuck.

"Matthias..."

I could sense he had more to say, so I forced myself to remain quiet.. "You're like a drug, Ava. One hit is never enough, and I keep coming back for more. When it comes to you, I can't keep my emotions in check. You draw them out of me to the point where all logic goes out the fucking window."

His fingers tensed, gripping my shoulders tighter as he buried his face in my neck, inhaling deeply. I realized he was trying to calm himself.

"You have no idea the torrent of emotions that ran through me when I found out you were gone." His voice was a bit darker again, as if the fact that he cared about my disappearance bothered him. "I thought someone had taken you. That you were in the hands of my enemies. That maybe your father had taken you back. You are a weakness, Ava. That was why I kept you at a distance. If I thought of you as nothing more than a pawn, it was easier to distance myself. But I don't want to. Not anymore."

He pulled back from my neck to gaze at my face, still flushed from his affections. His arms slipped down, settling on my waist to support me against him.

I searched his eyes carefully; they were confusing the fuck out of me. They were open and vulnerable, but they were also steely in their resolve. He was one hundred percent serious, and it was staggering to think that I caused this intimidating leader of one of the most powerful *Bratvas*, to lose his composure simply by running away. He had admitted I was his weakness, and my heart felt like it was soaring.

Clearing my throat, I tried to keep my voice steady. "Then

don't." My voice was barely above a whisper as I spoke. I knew things with Matthias wouldn't be easy, we had covered that already. All I wanted was him, even if he was unreasonable.

"We can make this work. Especially if this is your new form of punishment." Despite my purposeful flirting, I felt the heat rise in my cheeks as I thought about what had just transpired between us. Sure, we'd fucked plenty of times since our wedding day, but it was never this intimate.

Matthias blinked once at me; his face momentarily frozen. After a solid moment of contemplative silence, his lips twisted into a sad smile, and I knew that whatever he was about to say, I wasn't going to like.

"If only it was that easy." He took my hand in his and led me toward the mouth of the alley where his men waited dutifully. My chest constricted as I struggled to hold back my tears. He'd finally shown me a more vulnerable part of him. He had basically told me he wanted me. What was holding him back? It wasn't like we weren't married. How much closer could we get?

Unless he didn't plan on staying married to me once he got what he wanted. Was that it? Swallowing hard against the lump in my throat, I made a vow.

Matthias Dashkov may have been able to command my body, but he would never command my heart.

That was the lie I would continually tell myself in the weeks to come.

CHAPTER THIRTY-EIGHT

Matthias

"Where did you park?" Ava asked as I pulled her along beside me, out of the alley and down the street. It was quiet. Too quiet, and suddenly I had become weary of staying out in the open any longer. Even with my security.

I knew the consequences of what I had just done, but it no longer mattered to me. Admitting how I felt about her was almost freeing, but it wasn't going to be easy. I walked a dark, dangerous path, and even though I had tugged her along with me, kicking and screaming, I didn't want her to become a target. But I knew that after today, there would be no keeping that bullseye off her back.

"Just down here," I grunted as we turned the corner to where my small motorcade was parked. "Get in." I opened the SUV's back door for her and climbed in beside her once she was settled, before slamming it shut.

"Why are you in a rush all of the sudden?"

I shook my head and signaled for the driver to go. "I'm not."

"Sure as hell seems like you are," she muttered petulantly, crossing her arms against her chest, drawing my gaze down to her breasts. Damn. I was getting another hard-on just thinking about how her hard nipples had felt beneath my fingers. Ava liked the pain I gave her when I dominated her body. She craved it. That alone had me adjusting myself slightly.

Fuck. Would this need for her ever end? I hoped not.

"Don't start sulking, Ava," I warned heatedly. "I'm already keyed up to punish you for running away. Don't make it worse."

"You're a dick," she hissed. "You can't use punishment every time something doesn't go the way you want it to. Plus, I didn't run away. I was clearing my head, after *you,* admitted you knew that Elias wasn't my real father the entire time. Not to mention, you were planning on using my lineage to get ahead with the Irish."

My gaze met hers in a battle of wills. "That was a private conversation, Red," I pointed out. "You shouldn't eavesdrop on conversations you have no business listening in on."

Ava scoffed in disbelief.

"Fucking serious? If I hadn't eavesdropped, would you have even—"

The end of her statement was caught off by her scream. A sound so gut-wrenching I knew it would etch itself into my soul forever. I tore my seat belt off, covering her body with mine as glass rained down on us from above. Gunfire rippled the air around us, tearing through the car without any real precision. These were amateurs.

I grunted as the SUV surged to the side, the impact of another car hitting us sent me flying with Ava in my arms. She was scrunched beneath me, her body trembling, chest heaving as she covered her head.

The doors on her side sprang open at the same time as mine. Hands grabbed at me, pulling me away from her, and in my disoriented state, I was too slow to stop them. Ava screamed my name as they dragged her from the car kicking and clawing at the man, but she was no match for him. He might have been an amateur, but he had at least a hundred pounds on her.

There were two sets of hands on me, grabbing at my jacket. That was a mistake. I pushed against the SUV, rearing back and catching the two men off guard. They staggered back, taking my jacket with them. Free of their hold, I instinctively went for the gun I kept at the small of my back, and I popped off two shots into the intruders' chests.

Another man on my left shouted something in Italian, his eyes wide as he took in his fallen comrades. He held up his hands in a sign of surrender, but that wouldn't help him today. I fired another two shots. One at him and another at the man who'd been trying to hide behind the front of the damaged SUV.

More gunshots tore through the air, and I dove behind the back of the SUV, head down, hands gripping my gun like a lifeline. I needed to get to Ava before they could take off with her. I cursed as I fired a few extra shots, hitting one man in the head and another in the arm. They were all running.

I could hear my men cursing in Russian as they came up behind me, weapons drawn. No doubt they had their own ambush to deal with. Fuck. Should have brought Vas and Nicolai.

"Matthias!"

My name tore through the silence as the perpetrators fled.

All but one. Slowly, I strode around the side of the SUV, gun at the ready, my eyes taking in the scene before me.

The beast inside of me roared at the sight of her. My Little Red Riding Hood. One eye was nearly swollen shut, her lip bruised, and her right cheek was tinged red and beginning to swell. My eyes cut to the man holding her in his grasp. He had battle wounds of his own, and pride swelled within me knowing that she had fought back.

My Little Red was a firecracker.

The man's dark eyes widened in fear as he took in my narrowed gaze. Ava's body relaxed in his hold the moment, her frightened gaze caught mine, her emerald eyes shifting from fear to sheer determination.

I knew, at that moment, she didn't need the man, but the monster lurking just beneath the surface. The beast. And that was exactly what I was going to give her. Without a second thought, my finger inched on the trigger before I made the hardest snap decision of my life and fired.

Ava screamed as the bullet tore through the man's head. He'd used her body as shield, but Ava was far shorter than he was, and he hadn't even bothered to crouch. Something I would be eternally grateful for.

The minute his body hit the ground, she launched herself at me, burying her face in my neck as her body trembled with left over adrenaline. I could hear her sniffling, trying not to cry. We didn't have time for hysterics now. She could do that all she wanted back at the penthouse.

"Are you okay?" she asked, her voice small, muffled by my shirt. I shook my head before pulling her away from me to look her over. I touched her body, her chest, her hips. Everything within reach before deciding that the wounds on her face were the only ones she had received.

"Who were they?"

"Italians," I spat as I pulled her away from the scene and toward one of the SUVs that was still intact. "Probably Elias."

She nodded her head, hesitating for a moment at the open car door before taking a long, cleansing breath and hopping inside. I took one of my own, running a hand down my face as I thought about how this could have played out. I could have lost her. Lost everything.

In that moment nothing mattered more to me than getting to Ava. Making sure she was safe. Unharmed. There wasn't another thought in my mind. I had known from the moment I saw her in Elias's office that first night that she would be my weakness. A chink in my armor.

And I had been right.

CHAPTER THIRTY-NINE

Ava

"I'm sorry, you want to what?"

I must have heard wrong because the words coming out of my sister's mouth sounded absolutely fucking ridiculous. After Matthias had opened up in the alleyway, things had been progressing forward at a steady pace over the last few weeks.

Mildly.

Slothfully.

Although the man himself had started to show some minor signs of affection, and he had indeed confirmed that at one point he had planned to use me as a pawn for the Irish, we had taken a mild step back from where we were before I had overheard his conversation. On my part anyway.

I wasn't too proud to admit that hearing his original plans for me had stung. Or the fact that he had been willing to keep my rightful heritage a secret from me. But seeing as how I had

JO MCCALL

hidden the fact that Mark had given me a complete dossier on my mother, we'd called it even.

The attack on his motorcade had shaken him. I wasn't sure if it was because he could have lost me as a bargaining tool or if it was because he truly cared, but whatever had gone through his mind that day had changed him. Sort of.

"She has a point," Vas agreed. *Vas agreed?* What kind of parallel world had I woken up in? The two had been bickering all week like a married couple, and now, out of nowhere, he was agreeing with her? On this?

"Okay, first of all, who shoved aliens up your asses? Because the last time I checked, this was already a done deal."

That could have come out better. Matthias chuckled beneath me. I was currently sitting on his lap, struggling not to move too much since his erection was currently poking me in the ass. My eyes narrowed at him, the heat between my legs growing as the vibrations rumbled through me. I'd wanted to sit next to him like a normal person, but man had insisted I sit on his lap while we all discussed what to do next.

At first, I thought I was endearing. Sweet. Then I realized it was so I couldn't storm out of the office and refuse to listen to their insane plan.

"It isn't a bad idea, Red."

My jaw dropped. Matthias Dashkov, big fucking *Bratva* Leader, was siding with an eighteen-year-old girl? Yep. Aliens. Hell, Nicolai could waltz in here and start a striptease and I'd be less surprised.

"Seriously, you too?"

"We know Elias had planned to groom you to marry Christian," Matthias shrugged, and I scrunched my face up in disgust. He'd spilled everything he had learned about my so-called father's plan, and I couldn't say I was impressed. Disgusted was more the word. "That way he would have the bond of marriage to tie him to the mob. He kills Liam and his son, you inherit."

"I'm a girl." Matthias laughed.

"I am intimately aware of that, Red," he growled huskily. Libby and Vas were busy making gagging noises from their chairs. I shot my sister a dirty look, but that didn't deter her.

"The Irish don't have misogynistic tendencies toward leadership," Vas piped up. "If your mother were still alive, she would one day have inherited the McDonough Clan. Actually, Seamus and Sheila never had any more children, so you would technically inherit that as well as the Kavanaugh Clan branch."

"Just what I need," I muttered. "More reasons for people to try to use me." It didn't escape me that what Vas had said was a big deal. It was huge. The McDonough and Kavanaugh Clans were two of the largest sects of the Irish Mob in the states. I'd be inheriting a fortune, and if Elias had his way, it would have all been his.

"So let me get this straight," I repeated just so I understood. "You want me and Matthias to stage a fake 'wedding,' so my fake 'brother' and my fake 'father' try to crash it?" This reiteration came complete with air quotes.

Libby smiled. "Exactly. No one knows you're married except Matthias's inner circle. If Dad gets wind you're getting married, he'll come out of hiding and try to grab you."

"This is insane." I threw up my hands, exasperated that no one was taking my side. "It'll never work."

"I think it will, and so do Vas and Nicolai," My husband said. "We pick the time, the place, and the vantage point."

"How long have you guys been cooking this up?"

"All week." Libby smiled. "We knew you wouldn't want to do it, so we kind of...did it for you."

I had a feeling she wasn't just talking about not wanting to do the wedding.

"What did you do?"

Libby fidgeted with the end of her long blonde braid as she beamed at me.

"I always wanted the chance to play wedding with you as a kid," she giggled. "Now I get to." My mouth fell open, gaping like a fish out of water as I stared at her. She didn't. She couldn't possibly mean that she...

"Libby planned your wedding, Red, isn't that nice?"

"What do you mean you planned?" Was it possible to die of anxiety? Of stress overload? My palms were sweaty, my chest starting to rise and fall at a rapid rate as I processed just what in the hell was going on. "That is past tense."

"Congratulations, sis!" Libby exclaimed as she stood from her chair. "You're getting married on Saturday!"

"Saturday?" My head was darting back and forth between Matthias and Libby so fast I probably looked like a deranged bobble head. "That's two days from now!"

"Libby didn't want to give you time to run away, and since all you need to do is show up and look pretty, I agreed." This was too much; my bullshit meter was pegged to red at this point as I did my best not to combust.

"Did you order me a dress, too?" The snark in my voice did nothing to deter my little sister's enthusiasm.

"Designer will be here in one hour."

This was all happening too fast. It felt rushed. Like the ending of a book you want to last forever but you know something is coming. It always came out in the second book. Didn't it? All the secrets. All the lies. Those little tidbits you were waiting for throughout the entire story.

The first book never gave it away. Never. But that didn't mean the ending was rushed. It was just moving things along a bit faster. I wished my life was a book. Simple. Easy. A beginning, a middle, and an end.

"Oh," Libby clapped her delicate hands delightedly. "We can look at Pinterest for makeup and hair ideas."

Rolling my eyes, I removed myself from Matthias's lap. He was trying to hide a smirk. *Asshole.*

"Mani and pedi." Vas mocked her enthusiasm. Libby stuck her tongue out at the Russian before marching out of the room.

God help me, I was going to kill every single fucking one of them.

CHAPTER FORTY

Matthias

"What are you doing up, Red?"

It was the night before our so-called wedding. The sham wedding as she had come to call it, but I could see her slowly warming to the idea the more Libby dragged her into it.

"Couldn't sleep," she whispered as she wandered around the gym idly in her pajamas. I'd been down here trying to work out some of the extra tension. The last two days had been busy. Too busy. Even though we'd been planning for more than a week behind Ava's back, putting everything in place, I wanted to be sure. Things had needed to be checked and double checked, and before I knew it, it was well past midnight.

Not wanting to wake my sleeping angel, I had opted for a quick workout instead. Something to ease my mind and troubles. Looked like I wasn't the only one. She looked like she had more to say so I kept quiet. We were married, that was a fact, but that didn't mean Ava wasn't nervous about tomorrow. It may be fake, but this was something I hadn't given her when I forced her to marry me.

That was the crux of it all, really. I was the man who had forced her to marry me. I was her captor, her warden, and I knew that if we never got past that, if we never fixed that, I would constantly be chasing after her.

"What do you want after all this, Matt? When everything is said and done, and Elias is taken down. What do you want?"

She didn't have to add the "from me" at the end. It was hanging out there like fruit hanging from a low branch. Removing my boxing gloves, I tossed them aside and sat down on the practice mat, motioning for her to join me. She did, without complaint.

"I want you to be happy, Ava. With me." That was the god honest truth. Maybe I didn't love her. Not yet. But there was something about her I didn't want to let go. Something about her that pulled at the dead part of my soul that I had long thought was salted and buried. "I'll keep you here as long as I need to for you to realize that you want to be happy with me. That might be selfish, but I never said I was anything different."

Ava cleared her throat, swallowing hard as she blinked her bright ethereal green eyes at me before a heated blush crept up her cheeks and she looked away. Still so innocent. I couldn't take my eyes off her. Whenever she was in the room, they automatically found her, searched her out. I knew I wanted her. Her presence, her laugh, her tears.

That was why I couldn't let her go, but I knew that one day, when everything was said and done, I would have to give her the choice.

"What do you want, Ava?"

She shrugged her pretty little shoulder, a sad smile gracing her lips. "What I've always wanted. Freedom."

"And one day you will have exactly that." It was a promise I didn't know if I could keep, but I would certainly do everything I could to give it to her, even if it meant battling my own inner beast. She leaned in to kiss me, her mouth was soft against mine as she probed my lips. Fuck, she tasted so sweet. She pulled back and smiled softly.

"I want you."

She didn't have to say anything more. My body surged forward, hands ripping her top off as my tongue plundered her mouth. She moaned into my kiss, nipping gently at my lip as I pulled away. I pushed her to her back, slipping my fingers into the waistband of her pajama shorts. Her butt lifted a little to allow me to drag the flimsy fabric from her legs, so she lay before me naked.

"Spread your legs. Open yourself to me, baby." My voice was low and husky as I tugged off my own shirt and shorts. She did as I asked, opening herself wide for me, letting me see that full pink pussy. I opened her lips, bringing my mouth to her, licking the length of her pussy once, twice, before taking her clit in my mouth and suckling. I watched her, my eyes never leaving her face as she bucked her hips toward my mouth, her mouth slightly parted, her eyes closed.

"Matthias, fuck."

I sucked harder, pushing one finger inside her, waiting for her muscles to start tightening before I stopped sucking.

"Please—"

How I loved to hear her sweet voice beg.

"Please, Matthias, please."

I smiled as I shifted to my knees, stroking myself as my hungry eyes roamed her flushed body.

"What do you want, *Malen'kaya Krasnyy*? Use your words."

"I want your cock, Matthias."

"You want my cock?"

Ava nodded her head enthusiastically, and I hissed as she boldly gripped my steel length. Fuck, this woman would be the death of me.

"Please, I want it hard."

Yep, the death of me. I'd never been one for dirty talk. Sex was always something I had done to release tension, and the whores I'd fucked could care less how talkative I was. They wanted to fuck, get their money, and get out. It was very rare for one to actually want to stick around.

"Be careful what you wish for, baby," I murmured as I flipped her onto her stomach then yanked her hips back so that her ass was in the air in front of me. "I think it's time you try something new."

She looked back at me, her face a swirling mix of confusion and fear.

"What?"

"My cock is craving something else today, Red, and you are going to take it like a good girl."

I'd been holding back on this because I knew what Christian had done to her friend, but I wasn't him. I never would be. I fingered her pussy, brushing the tips along her clit, gathering her wetness before dragging it back to the little dark hole between her perfect cheeks. Her eyes went wide, and she opened her mouth to protest, but it was too late. I circled her puckered hole a few times before pressing inside.

A small whimper left her lips, and her body tensed. I rubbed my hand on her lower back, soothing her trepid nerves as I slowly pumped my finger in and out of her tight little ass at a languid pace. My finger kept this pace until her body began to relax and she was easing back against it. Then I added another.

"Do you like this, Ava?" I asked as I thrust a bit harder, circling inside to spread her wetness just a bit more along her tightened walls. "Do you like the feeling of my fingers in your ass?"

Her cheeks heated, and her top teeth bit into her plump bottom lip before she nodded her head. What a little deviant I had on my hands.

"Good girl." Her muscles tightened at the praise. Pulling my fingers out, I gathered more of her increasing wetness and spread it on my engorged cock. I pressed the tip of it against her dark hole, feeling her tense. "Touch yourself, good girl. Make yourself come with my cock inside your ass."

Doing as I asked, she began rubbing her herself slowly as I pressed the head of my cock into her ass, easing myself in, stopping when her hand stilled and her muscled tightened.

"You're too big," she whined, the need in her voice outweighing the pain. "Please.."

"Relax, Red. Open for me." I moved in and out of her, slowly rocking my hips, resisting the urge to slam into her as she furiously worked her little nub.

"Fuck, Matt!"

The orgasm violently ripped through her body, her walls clenching tightly before relaxing fully and allowing me to work myself in deeper. She was so fucking tight that I knew I wouldn't last long. She cried out when I began to move, her fingers still working her clit, another orgasm racing on the heels of her first until she was once again coming, my name screaming from her lips. It was that sound that pushed me over the edge, and I emptied myself inside her.

If this wasn't heaven, I didn't know what was. What I did know was that we weren't done. Not by a long shot, but I'd let her rest for now because neither of us knew what tomorrow would bring.

Something was coming. Years of instinct pricked at the back of my neck, warning me. Cautioning me. I needed to be ready for whatever came my way. There wasn't room for error. Not when so much was on the line.

Easing myself from inside her, Ava gave a small mewl. I couldn't help but smile at the sound. Just like a kitten.

My kitten.

My Lil Red.

The chink in my armor.

CHAPTER FORTY-ONE

Ava

My bridal suite overlooked the indoor courtyard where the wedding was soon to take place. Well, wedding wasn't exactly the right word since it was fake. After all, Matthias and I were technically already married. Elias and Christian didn't know that.

Ever since Matthias's strategic plan to push Elias out of the port and disparage his name, he'd kept to the shadows, no doubt using my Uncle's mafia ties to hide. No, not my uncle.

There was still so much to wrap my head around since I'd found out that Elias wasn't my actual father. He'd lied. Manipulated my life to suit his needs. I shivered at the thought of what he had planned for me. What Christian had planned for me. The wound still hurt, but it was no longer gaping. Knowing he wasn't my real father helped ease some of my past pain that had left me feeling disposable.

"You look beautiful, Red."

Of course, he would find a way to sneak up to my bridal suite while Libby was out hunting down coffee. Matthias wasn't one to hold to tradition.

I turned from the window to face him, my eyes taking in his large, muscular form that somehow managed to fit behind his tailored tux. Fuck. He looked like a Russian James Bond. Hell, he was hotter than James Bond. His growing brown hair was effortlessly swept to one side, the blue of his tie accenting the gray thunderclouds of his eyes. He'd even shaved for the occasion. I could smell the spices of his aftershave wafting through the air, the simple scent causing my nipples to harden beneath the ridiculous corset I was wearing.

Things were still tense between us since his confession in the alleyway. He wanted me, but the part of him that had grown up like me, the broken part, wouldn't let him love me. I was the weak link in his chain. His Achilles' heel. If he let himself love me, I would be his downfall. His Helen of Troy.

Internally, I snorted. Yeah, that was too much even for me. My bullshit meter was pegged to red the minute he tried to explain why he couldn't let himself fall for me. Matthias Dashkov wasn't worried about me being a chink in his armor, he was fucking scared, and he knew it. Not that he would ever admit it aloud. That was why he kept himself emotionally unavailable.

Physically, however...I licked my bottom lip, remembering last night's *cardio* session in the gym. Physically he was completely available. I'd take those baby steps if it meant more orgasms.

I did notice he was trying. It was small things that made me sit up and take notice. The way he held my hand in front of his men or the way he curved his large body around mine while we slept. It was in the way he listened when I talked about my day or the fact that he took me for a walk in the gardens near Soho when I was beginning to feel cooped up.

Or like now. His gaze made me feel wanted, and right now, that was as close to love as I was going to get from him. He was standing before me, pupils blown wide as his gaze roamed hungrily over my nearly naked form. Libby told me that I needed to wait until the last possible moment to put on my wedding dress so I wouldn't accidently ruin it before I walked down the aisle. Now I was glad I had listened.

Not that I cared. It wasn't real, and Libby knew that, but my sister couldn't care less. My eyes darted down to the bulge beneath his black trousers, and the feral grin that spread across his handsome face nearly had me coming right there.

Too bad there wasn't time for what I had planned.

"You do know it's bad luck to see the bride before the wedding, right?" I winked at him before stepping closer.

"Oh, I've seen plenty already, Mrs. Dashkov." A small giggle escaped me before I could contain it.

"Why, Mr. Dashkov, how improper of you." My southern accent left a lot to be desired, but the laugh that left his lips was enough to make my heart soar. I loved it when he laughed. His normally surly features brightened, and he looked years younger and less stressed. Like he didn't have the weight of the world on his shoulders any longer.

"I'm about to do something improper if you don't get your ass in your fucking robe before Vasily comes in," he growled playfully as he snatched up my red silk robe off the vanity chair. Smiling, I let him wrap me in it. "I don't want to have to kill my *Sovietnik* and my cousin because they saw you nearly naked. Good help is hard to find."

"Why are you killing me this time?" Vasily teased as he stepped into the room through the open door, carrying a small blue box with him with Roman on his heels.

"Because I can." My husband glared at my robe as he tried to close the gap at my chest more. Rolling my eyes, I swatted his hands away and turned my attention to his men, who were beaming at the two of us.

"They just grow up so fast." Vas dramatically wiped at his dry eyes. "I feel like it was just yesterday that I was giving you the birds and the bees talk, Matthias."

"I thought it was the eel in the cave talk you gave him?" Roman butted in cheerfully. Vas shrugged.

"Either way, he learned where to stick it."

"At least we hope so." Roman smiled as he watched his cousin's face begin to turn a rough shade of red. I couldn't tell if he was angry or embarrassed. Maybe a bit of both. Whatever it was, inner me was rolling with laughter while outer me tried to keep a straight face. "Could still be a virgin for all we know."

"That's true." Vasily tried not to laugh. "Now that we know what he was really doing with Valerie in his room all this time, it's possible he's never wet his cucumber until poor Ava here."

"Cucumber?" Roman questioned, ducking a solid punch that came flying his way from Matthias's meaty fist. "I heard it was more like a pickle." The two men laughed as Matthias gave them a good-natured shove that was still just a tad bit aggressive. I was honestly surprised he wasn't trying to hurl them out the windows.

"Okay." I held up my hands, trying to keep composed at their antics. This was the side of Matthias I loved. It was the side I only saw when he was around those he trusted the most. He might be their *Pakhan*, but he was also their brother, their confidant, and their friend.

Otherwise, those two hooligans wouldn't have gotten away with nearly half the shit they did.

"Are you three going to tell me why you have invaded my bridal suite?" I asked curiously, trying to ignore the heat pooling between my legs as Matthias idly played with an errant curl. Libby had spent nearly two hours trying to turn my mess of curls into beautifully mastered ones that were more uniform and less wild.

"This." Vas sobered a bit as he set a small black box on the vanity to my left. I opened it with trembling fingers, peeling back the ribbon before lifting the hinged lid. Inside was a small silver revolver and a red leather thigh holster.

"What's this for?"

Matthias reached around me to grab the deadly bundle, signaling to his men with a sharp nod of his head. Neither of them spoke as they left us alone again. He sat down on the low stool of the vanity and motioned for my leg. I gave it to him without question and watched with rapt attention as he slid his hands up my right thigh, the skin tingling with electricity, the ache between my legs growing even more heated.

"I don't know how today is going to go, Red," he whispered, his voice low and gravelly as he attached the holster to my thigh. "If anything happens, I want you to have a way to protect yourself."

This was big. There was no denying the trust he was putting in me with this. Not that I would run now even if I had the chance. He had captured me, body and soul. He was capable of so many things that scared me. The monster inside him would never be tamed, and I found that I no longer wanted to. He was right. I hadn't thought I needed a monster, but here he was anyway. That was something I had come to accept.

Sort of. Kinda. Okay, I was still working on it.

"Nothing is going to happen." I was saying it more for my benefit than his. Matthias was someone who saw three moves ahead on the chess board. He attacked and counterattacked. Strategized and plundered. He was built to see danger around every corner and to expect the worst possible outcomes. Matthias was a leader. A general among his men. It was his job to give them the best chance he could.

"I've been meaning to give you this." He stood up, gently moving my leg from his lap, and reached into the pocket of his tux to pull out a small, red velvet box. *Is that a fucking ring box?*

"Is that—" My mouth hung open, gaping like a fish as he opened it. *Holy shit, that was a ring.* It was the most gorgeous ring I had ever seen. The band was black, thorn like, with a red ruby nestled inside the center of what looked to be a lotus flower.

"Matt—" The big burly Russian was down on one knee before me, holding the ring out, waiting. He was waiting. That alone made the tears gathered in my eyes release from their prison. Matthias never waited for anything. He took. I almost laughed when I saw his hand trembling with impatience at how slow I was moving. I let out a small sob as I held my left hand out to him.

"No, baby girl," he whispered, reaching out to grab my right hand. "In Russia, the wedding ring goes on the right hand."

"It's perfect," I sniffled as I gazed down at it. The black band against my pale skin stirred something inside me. It was a picture of opposites melding together, and I loved it.

"I should have given this to you when we first married but —" he shrugged and didn't say any more. He didn't have to. But things were different then. It felt like we had gone through a lifetime of storms in the little time we'd been married. Things had been put into motion so quickly that neither of us had time to fully appreciate any of it.

"It's okay," I assured him, wiping gently at my eyes, trying to avoid smearing my mascara. "The important thing is we are here now. Together. At our fake wedding." Matthias rumbled in amusement.

"I want you to listen to me, Ava," he whispered, still bent on his knee in subjugation, still holding my hand. "You are everything to me, *moya lyubov'*." *My love.* If this were a period era romance, I'd be swooning right now.

"Ditto."

Matthias's expression dulled as he took in my words before his nostrils flared and his face twisted.

"Ditto?" he repeated, his Russian accent thickening slightly. "Fucking ditto?"

I pursed my lips to keep from grinning at his expression of amused outrage. Another contradiction. We were full of them, and I loved it.

"Yeah, ditto." My eyes batted at him playfully. "You know, like same here." Matthias huffed.

"I'll fucking show you ditto." He released my hand and brought his up to grip the back of my neck while the other one snuck up the skimpy negligée. His fingers nimbly moved my silky white thong aside, then stroked the length of my pussy. *Jesus.* Would I ever get used to how he could play my body so easily? I fucking hoped not.

"Matthias," I breathed his name as a wanton moan left my lips. He chuckled before slamming two fingers inside my tight heat without warning. I shrieked, my hands going to his shoulders for support. "Shit."

"How is this for fucking ditto, Red?" His fingers ruthlessly pumped into me while his thumb found my clit and made slow teasing circles. I moaned loudly, shamelessly riding his hand as the coil in my stomach tightened away. "Come on. Come for me." Shit. The dirty talk was really doing it for me.

Matthias was normally silent when we fucked, but this, this was something I could get used to.

"Matt," I gasped as he nipped at the top of my exposed breast before soothing it with his tongue. His hungry gaze eyed my corset-covered nipples, and I could tell he was close to ripping the thing to shreds. "Don't even think about it."

Matthias chuckled as he added a third finger, his thumb picking up its pace on my little pleasure button. My orgasm was building fast, and soon I was falling headfirst over the cliff and into the waves below. It hit me hard, and I let out a small scream that was his name while my pussy clenched around his fingers.

"God, I love it when you scream my name, Red." He chuckled as he removed his fingers and tugged the robe back in place. I sighed contently, giving him a languid smile, watching as he brought his fingers to his mouth and sucked them clean of my juices. *Why is that so hot?*

"Are you guys done in there?" Libby's voice shattered the euphoria around us from outside the suite doors. "Because things are starting to get moving out here and we need to get her in her dress."

"Yes. Yes." Matthias grinned at me as he stood and straightened his tux. "You may come in." The door opened to reveal a bashful yet mildly pissed Libby holding two cups of coffee.

"I swear to god, Matthias Dashkov," she nearly fumed. "If you ruined her hair or her makeup...O.M.G...is that a ring?"

I couldn't help the broad grin that stretched across my face as I held out my hand to my sister. Matthias chuckled, planting a small kiss on my forehead before he quietly left the room. The man still couldn't give a simple goodbye.

Libby cooed over the ring for another minute or two before she helped me into my simple wedding dress. We hadn't even had a chance to shop for one. Not after the attack. Matthias rarely let me leave the penthouse after that, so he had one of the designers bring a few up for me to choose from.

He'd set this one aside without telling me, and when I'd chosen it, the designer had all but clapped in glee, telling me that was the exact same one my husband had chosen. The man knew me too well. It was, what the designer considered, a minimalist white wedding dress. It had long sleeves and a low back. A small trail of buttons led into a pleated A-line skirt with a slit up one side.

If shit were to go down, I'd be able to move.

Libby fussed over me for a few more minutes before declaring me *absolutely perfect*. I was stunned to see the woman in the mirror. It didn't look like me. A small silver tiara was snuggled in my finely curled hair. Libby had managed to cover the yellowing bruises on my face with mild coverup, choosing to go with a lighter shade of lipstick and eyeshadow to balance it out. Something I was thankful for.

I never imagined this moment growing up. Libby and Kenzi had spent most of their childhood dreaming of marrying their prince charming and having a fanciful wedding. They'd play dress up on the lawn. I was just trying to survive each day.

Now, here I was, in a pretty gown playing dress up for a fake wedding. Except, I wasn't marrying prince charming. I was marrying a wolf.

"You did an amazing job, Bug," I rasped, trying to keep the tears from falling. Libby shucked off the compliment with a grin.

"Nah. Just made the palette a little more colorful, is all."

The two of us giggled as she helped me into my shoes. Flats, thank god. It was a specific request that the dress be just short enough to accommodate the low shoes. Nikolai was waiting just outside the door for us. He'd be the one walking me down the aisle while Libby went ahead with Vas.

Dark thoughts invaded my mind as I thought about my father. My real father. The one I'd glimpsed in the bar, happy with his family, and I wished he was here. The thought made me want to laugh. I didn't even know him, yet there was something inside me that yearned for him to be the one to walk me down the aisle.

It was, after all, every little girl's dream. But then again, my life wasn't filled with dreams, just steady nightmares.

CHAPTER FORTY-TWO

Ava

My hands trembled as the processional music began. I clenched and unclenched my fists, palms clammy with unfettered nerves as I watched Libby and Vas slowly make their way down the aisle. The pair had grown on each other in the last few weeks, their barbs toward one another had become slightly playful. Almost flirting.

Yeah, that was something I did not need to think about.

Libby may not be my sister by blood, but she was still my sister. My little sister. The thought of her flirting with Vas was not something I wanted in my head. Shouldn't be in anyone's head. Including hers. My gaze followed them, my breath catching at the slightest of noise, wondering if that was the start of the attack.

"She's safe with him," Nicolai murmured under his breath. "We planned for this, remember? No one gets to her."

No one gets to her. That was my assurance when this all started. When this all began in the bunker that night Matthias's men took the port. I knew Matthias wanted to protect me, but I needed to protect her. That little light in my life that had always been there. My little ray of sunshine in the darkest of times.

I nodded curtly, afraid that if I opened my mouth, I would sob. Or scream. Nicolai patted my hand in his arm reassuringly as he stepped forward, taking me with him. The moment I stepped out on the petal-covered floor of the aisle; I was a goner.

This is what our wedding day should have been. Instrumentals and rose petals. The look on Matthias's face as I walked down the aisle nearly stopped my heart beating in my chest. His gray eyes were wide, mouth slightly parted as he took me in. All of me. I'd been married in leggings and sweater, tears sliding down my face as he forced me to sign the marriage certificate.

Now I felt like a queen, whose tears represented nothing but joy and a wee bit of uncertainty. A lot of emotion for a fake wedding, but there was a small piece of me that wanted this to be real and not a trap.

The faces in the crowd were nothing but a blur. Most of them were Matthias's men, but there were a few of his business associates as well, a constant reminder that I had no one of my own to invite. Archer still hadn't given up Maleah's location. I didn't think he ever would, but that was fine, because what the lying snake didn't know was that he'd made a powerful enemy out of me, and I would be sure to take my pound of flesh.

Something twisted in my stomach, the hairs on the back of my neck standing up as we reached the halfway point to the altar. Libby smiled down the aisle at me, her eyes lighting up, a giant grin stretching across her pixie-like face. She'd taken everything with her father in such good stride, but that was just who she was. Libby didn't hold on to fantasies or cling to the past. If you presented evidence, she was on your side, and my Little Bug had found enough of her own evidence that she didn't need mine.

I was paces away from the altar when the disturbance rented the air, shattering the tranquility surrounding me. A single piercing scream, one that tore at the very fabric of my soul, wrenching it from my body.

Blood decorated the altar. I hadn't even heard a shot ring out. Nothing. It took me a moment to realize that the scream had been me. Now, I stood frozen as pandemonium raged around me. I was thrown to the ground, the cobblestone floor biting into my hands and knees, dirt and blood staining my dress. Nicolai's body covered mine. Gunshots rang out. Footsteps sounded. Someone was issuing orders, but I could barely hear anything over the sound of my blood rushing through my ears.

"Sniper!" That was Vas. Vas was alive, but she wasn't.

Blood. There had been so much blood. Her blood. My sister's blood. *Libby.* Oh, god. *Libby.* A sob escaped me, tears smearing the makeup she had just applied less than an hour ago. *Fuck.*

There was a tumult of voices and odd sounds, and then I was dragged to my feet. Matthias was beside me, his eyes were wild, his expression furious as he took me in his arms. "Are you all right, Red?" Then he was kneeling in front of me, holding me to him while his hands roamed my body, searching for injuries.

Any other time, and his touch would have set my skin on

fire. Now, there was nothing. I let my gaze wander over his shoulder, back to the altar. The white tulle that decorated the archway was covered in blood. *Her blood.* My sister's blood. I could see her small form lying beneath a white cloth just a few feet from where she was supposed to watch me take my vows. How had they covered her so fast?

There was no holding in the tumultuous waves of sorrow that came crashing down on me all at once. I didn't care that we were in front of all of his men or that he rarely showed any kind of affection, especially in public. I threw my arms around his neck, burying my face in the crook of it, and sobbed.

He didn't push me away but held me closer to his warm body, his familiar pine scent washing over me. I couldn't breathe, my chest felt tight, and my lungs burned as I tried to get oxygen into my body. When he stood, my legs trembled, unable to support me. He simply picked me up in his arms and carried me away from the bloodshed.

Through the blur of tears, I could see that several of his men were dead, and a few of Elias's were, too. I recognized a few, but luckily none of them were the ones I considered close. Neil wasn't among them, and neither was Giano. That was something to be grateful for, but it did nothing to deter the raging loss that echoed within me.

What would I tell Kenzi?

"Why?" I hiccuped the word between sobs. "Why would he kill her?" It didn't make any sense. The sniper had free reign to shoot me or Matthias, but the only hit it looked like he took was to my sister. I didn't understand.

"Because Elias doesn't suffer betrayal," Matthias whispered in my ear. "She was his blood. That is the biggest betrayal of all."

We didn't speak any more after that as he carried me out

to the waiting SUV. He was right. Libby was his blood daughter, and her betrayal would be something he hated even more than my own. Loyalty was everything to Elias, though he showed none of his own. Still, it didn't make sense to me that he had gone after her and no one else.

Men had raided the wedding with guns, but Matthias had been ready for that. We hadn't expected a sniper because all his men had been patrolling the surrounding rooftops. Which meant he had either been betrayed or someone had taken the shot from farther away, and I didn't know anyone in Elias's employ who could do that.

"Aren't you coming with?" My voice was meek, timid almost, as he settled me in one of the SUVs but hadn't made a single move to get in himself. Matthias shook his head.

"I have to take care of things here," he said, his gray eyes somewhat sad. I wasn't the only one who lost someone today. He had, too. His men. The people who were like his family. No, not like, they were his family. His chosen family. "I'll be home as soon as I can, I promise."

He kissed my forehead gently as I murmured my understanding. That would have to be enough. The door closed and he stepped away as the SUV pulled from the curb. It wasn't a long drive back to the penthouse, but traffic was heavier than normal. Over the past few weeks, I had taken to memorizing the streets I'd always wanted to explore, which was how I realized that the driver had missed the turn.

"Where are you—"

An explosion rocked the vehicle, sending glass flying. I brought my arms up to cover my face, my screams echoing in the enclosed space. I felt my head collide with the door, the sounds of car alarms blaring and rising voices muted by the blast. My vision blurred, eyes fluttering as I struggled to keep them open.

It was no use.

My body was exhausted, and soon I was sinking into unconsciousness. Matthias was the last thought to cross my mind before the heavy blanket of darkness descended around me.

CHAPTER FORTY-THREE

Matthias

I watched as the SUV pulled away from the curb and into traffic.

It killed me to let her go, but she wouldn't be of any use here, and I couldn't leave. Not while my men laid dead on the cobblestone. I wanted to roar my anger, my sadness, my hatred. To beat my chest and make a call to arms. The beast inside me was clawing at my insides, wanting to be free. To shed blood. To make our enemies pay for what they had done.

Blyad. Fuck. My eyes met Vas's as he kneeled over Libby's dead body. He'd grown close to the girl in the last few weeks. They complemented each other in a way that surprised me. The small pixie-like girl had a fiery temper. Vas had liked to call her Tinkerbell whenever she stomped her foot and pouted at him. It was an apt name for her.

The sadness and rage in my *Sovietnik's* eyes killed me. This was the man I called my brother. My friend, and to see him hurt like this—never had I wanted to take someone's pain away before. I approached him slowly, wary of what he might do. Did he blame me? This was my plan, after all. The one he had tried to get me to reconsider. Would he hate me now?

"Vas—" His name was a whisper of regret on my lips. Vas just shook his head as he silently cried. I hadn't realized the depth of his feelings for her, and I wished I had. But I'd been so caught up in my revenge, in my plan, in Ava, that I hadn't noticed.

"Tell me we are going to make those motherfuckers pay, boss," he snarled. "Promise me."

This I could do. "I promise this won't go unpunished."

Vas nodded his head before he shook it. "It doesn't make any sense. Why would he target her?"

That was something I had been wondering myself. I'd told Ava it was because Libby had betrayed Elias, her own blood, but I didn't think that was it. This didn't scream Elias at all. This was someone else. Someone who was trying to create the most amount of chaos possible. Someone who had known my plan.

Shooting at me or Ava was something we had expected. Planned for. But Libby was a bystander who had now become collateral damage. *Fuck.*

"FBI! Everyone put your hands where we can see them and stay where you are!"

Double fuck.

"Well, isn't this a surprise," I drawled as I lifted my hands in the air. "I'm sure you've come to take statements and hunt down the people responsible for ruining my wedding."

"Not so much, comrade." The blood pumping in my veins froze like rain in the arctic. I knew that voice. It was the voice Nicolai managed to grab from the security cameras outside Liam Kavanaugh's bar. "You are under arrest for murder.

Conspiracy to commit murder and anything else I can think to throw at you on the way."

"And who do you think I murdered?" I asked the agent.

"I've got a whole list of names. One of them being Elias Ward, who was found stuffed in his trunk two nights ago with his throat slit." The man smirked. That was news to me. If Elias was dead, then who had orchestrated this massacre? Christian? It didn't seem in his taste to gun down his own sister, but the man was a budding psychopath, so who was I to know.

"Boss," Nicolai growled from behind me, but I shook my head at him. I'd let them take me. There was no way in hell this man had any evidence against me. The agent smiled as he approached me. It was the smile of a cat who had gotten the canary. But I was no fucking bird.

"Mathias Dashkov." My name was a snarl on his lips. "You are under arrest for murder of Elias Ward. Anything you say can and will—" I tuned the rest of his bullshit out. It wasn't until he had tightened the cuff behind my back and leaned in that I stopped calculating and started listening again.

"You may think you are getting out of this, Dashkov," he hissed in my ear so no one else could hear. "But there is one name I will make sure you pay for."

My eyes widened as he whispered the name in my ear. A name I never thought I'd hear again. It was in that moment that I knew who had betrayed me, who had given me up. Whatever warmth I had in my heart froze like the Siberian tundra, my expression sobering as I processed the betrayal.

My own fucking wife.

CONTINUE MATTHIAS AND AVA'S STORY IN...

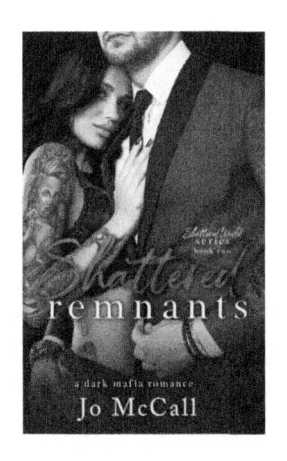

Get it Here

SHATTERED REMNANTS BLURB

AVA

They thought I was weak.
Nothing more than a pawn in their chess game.
Insignificant and easy to sacrifice.
I was blind before, but not anymore.
The curtain has been pulled back and now I'm ready to watch them fall at my feet.
Matthias stole me from my gilded cage
Stuck a ring on my finger and claimed me in his bed.
The hard exterior of the Bratva boss had begun to melt.
Now, he believes I betrayed him.
He thinks he can control me. Lock me up and throw away the key.
But this bird has had a taste of freedom and she isn't going back to her cage.
I may have been a pawn before.
Now, however, I am the Queen.

SNEAK PEEK SHATTERED REMNANTS

Prologue

AVA

A sharp sting of pain radiated through my chest as I came to.

My eyes fluttered furiously, like butterflies trapped in a glass cage, fighting against an invisible weight. I coughed and sputtered, the pain increasing as I struggled to take a breath. My chest felt like it was caught in the grasp of a boa constrictor. The cracks in my lips split even wider, blood pooling in my mouth as a hoarse cry rose in my throat.

Fuck.

It was like someone had pressed the mute button on the controller. The only sound I could hear was the ear-piercing ringing that tore through my head, sounding like one of those ungodly mosquito tones. Slowly, I managed to open my eyes, the invisible weight pressing against them slightly dampened by my fierce determination to live.

Dust and debris had settled over my unprotected face. I lifted my equally dusty hand to wipe at it, being mindful of my injuries, but it was like trying to wipe away mud with more mud. It just became worse.

A low keening whine spilled from my lips unbidden as I struggled to move the weight of my own body. My chest heaved in ragged sobs, tears spilling down my dirt-marred face as I crawled through several feet of debris toward the still body of Kristian, my guard. He was half-buried in the building's wreckage, his dark face covered in a heavy layer of white dust.

I reached out with a shaky hand to check his pulse.

Nothing.

He was dead. Just like the rest of them—and now I was truly alone.

The old me would have become numb. Would have curled up in a ball and let fate take over.

The old me was tired of war. Matthias was gone. The King. The Ruler. What else was there to do but give in to fate?

Except, this wasn't a game of chess where the fall of the king meant the end of the game.

No. This was war. And the war wasn't over until the queen was dead.

And I was the fucking Queen.

ALSO BY JO MCCALL

SHATTERED WORLD

Shattered Pieces

Shattered Remnants

Shattered Empire

Shattered Revelations

SHATTERED WORLD STANDALONES

Shattered Revenge

KAVANAUGH CRIME FAMILY

Stolen Obsession - Now on Vella

Twisted Crown

Crooked Fate

SAVAGE KINGS DUET

Savage

Kings

STANDALONES

Hunted By Them

NOTE FROM JO

Part of me still can't be believe that this is really happening. I've been dreaming about writing a book since I was a young girl clinging to the fantasy of Lord of the Rings and Harry Potter. I grew up reading books by Tamora Pierce and Judy Blume, imagining in my head what it would be like to be just like them.

A writer.

An author.

My life consisted of people telling me I would never become an author. To *try for something realistic* because I would never make it. Even now, on the cusp of publishing my first book, there are whispers of doubt and hisses of inadequacy that stalk my footsteps everywhere I go. There are so many stigmas that surround romance authors and indie authors. I'm both. But I won't let that deter me. I've fought for harder things than this, and I've learned that when you set your mind to something, there is nothing you can't do.

This book came to fruition from a picture and a quote. I can't show you the picture, but I can share the quote.

NOTE FROM JO

"Have you ever been in love? Horrible, isn't it? It makes you so vulnerable. It opens your chest and it opens up your heart and it means that someone can get inside you and mess you up."
— **Neil Gaiman, The Kindly Ones**

Zoe Blake's "*Savage Vow*" was the first dark romance I read, and suddenly I was obsessed. Like…really obsessed. I fell head over heels with the dark valleys and sinister twists. Stars grew in my eyes at the possessiveness of the man who had hunted her down for years to claim what was his. There is something so dirty and taboo about it that had my heart thumping and my skin tingling.

What can I say? Therapy is probably needed, but book buying is surprisingly cheaper.

I loved the fact that, just as in real life, love is messy and deranged and never follows a particular path. It makes you vulnerable in a way you may never understand. That is what drew me to this story. To Matthias and Ava. Two people with similar backgrounds but two different views of the world around them. Neither can trust. Neither has ever loved.

That doesn't make for fluffy romance.

Nope.

It makes for a dark, dirty mess. Mix in some actions, a little gore, a few well-times lines and you have a dark romance novel that only gets darker in the next go around.

At the risk of making this super long, let me get to the good stuff…

I'd like to take the time to thank my Girl Friday. My bestie, despite the fact that we have never met in person. The one who inspired me to keep going. Her own success on her debut novel showed me that anything is possible. Who needs fairy dust? Not me.

NOTE FROM JO

So, thank you, Kay Riley, for showing me that it's possible to achieve your dream and keep on going.

Jenna, my hype woman. Always there to encourage and push and make sure Vas gets his own book. Thank you for agreeing to be my Alpha Reader. You are amazing!

I'd, of course, also like to thank the marvelous Zoe Blake, who inspired me to sit down and write a dark romance in the first place and for answering my myriad of questions time and time again and putting up with my stalkerish tendencies. I really appreciate all of the help and support!

Sarah Bailey, who has also put up with my stalkerish tendencies and was the first member of my Forced Besties club. She is always there to answer a question or talk something out with me or distract me with her books. You have been such a big help and inspiration.

My amazing editor, Beth from VB Edits. Literally, this book would not be what it is without her going through it with a fine-tooth comb! I'm not kidding. I can write...grammar is a whole other issue. So, thank you, girl, for being so patient and having my back. I enjoyed every minute of working with you!

Then there are my amazing beta readers! You guys are all troopers, and I enjoyed every single piece of your feedback. Even if I wasn't able to use it! Your input and thoughts were amazing and helped shape the story. Even if some of you were angry at the end!

I'd also like to send a big shoutout to my mum, who will never read this book, but automatically wanted the first signed copy. We may have two different views of the world around us, but she is always there to support me, even if she doesn't understand.

And finally, to my sister, who has constantly shared her love and enthusiasm for my writing. Who always encourages me and listens to my plans and ideas without complaint. She

NOTE FROM JO

never pushes but is always there to guide, and I am so happy to have the relationship I have with her today!

And that is all! I can't wait to see you all in the next book. And please, if you would be so kind as to review, whether you liked the book or not, this always helps us authors out!

Stay Savvy,
   Jo McCall

Printed in Great Britain
by Amazon